A Girl Like You

A Girl Like You

A Novel

Maureen Lindley

BLOOMSBURY

New York • London • New Delhi • Sydney

Published by Bloomsbury USA, New York

All papers used by Bloomsbury USA are natural, recyclable products made
from wood grown in well-managed forests. The manufacturing processes
conform to the environmental regulations of the country of origin.

LIBRARY OF CONGRESS CATALOGING-IN-PUBLICATION DATA

Lindley, Maureen.
A girl like you : a novel / Maureen Lindley.—1st U.S. ed.
p. cm.
ISBN 978-1-60819-265-6 (alk. paper)
1. Japanese American families—California—Fiction. 2. Japanese
Americans—Evacuation and relocation, 1942–1945—Fiction.
3. World War, 1939–1945—Japanese Americans—Fiction.
4. World War, 1939–1945—California—Fiction. I. Title.
PR6112.I49G57 2013
823'.92—dc23

2012035081

First U.S. edition 2013

1 3 5 7 9 10 8 6 4 2

Typeset by Westchester Book Group
Printed and bound in the U.S.A. by Thomson-Shore Inc., Dexter, Michigan

To Clive, with my love

There will be no armed uprising of Japanese . . .
For the most part local Japanese are loyal to the United
  States . . .
Their family life is disciplined and honourable.
The children are obedient and the girls virtuous . . .
[The Nisei] show a pathetic eagerness to be Americans.
There is a remarkable even extraordinary degree of loyalty
  among this suspect group.

—SPECIAL AGENT CURTIS MUNSON—SENT TO THE WEST
COAST TO INVESTIGATE THE LOYALTY OF THE JAPANESE-
AMERICANS—REPORTING TO PRESIDENT ROOSEVELT
IN NOVEMBER 1941; HIS REPORT WAS IGNORED
AND KEPT SECRET BY THE GOVERNMENT

I'm for catching every Japanese in America, Alaska, and
Hawaii now and putting them in concentration camps . . .
Damn them! Let's get rid of them now!

—CONGRESSMAN JOHN RANKIN, CONGRESSIONAL
RECORD, DECEMBER 15, 1941

I am for the immediate removal of every Japanese on the West
Coast to a point deep in the interior. I don't mean a nice part
of the interior either. Herd 'em up. Pack 'em off and give 'em
the inside room in the badlands. Let 'em be pinched, hurt,
hungry and up against it.

—HENRY MCLEMORE, SYNDICATED COLUMNIST
OF HEARST NEWSPAPERS

CONTENTS

THIRD BASE

S CHOOL LETS OUT at three o'clock in Angelina. Its pupils
pour through the narrow portal of its door, milk from a jug,
water from the tap. Their freedom shouts can be heard at the bus
station half a mile away.

The white kids regularly hang around, the boys to throw ball
to basket and, while they're at it, obscenities to the girls. And the
girls, feigning indifference, to flick their hair and play jacks and
jump rope. Only the Japanese pupils take off for home as though
they are in a race.

All innocent from the smutty talk of the play yard, Satomi
Baker, blooming toward beauty in her fourteenth year, and her
friend Lily Morton are in the habit of parading themselves, pulling up their cute white socks, undoing the top button of their
cotton dresses. They think they know all there is to know about
sex and the "dirty thing" the boys want to get up to with them.
The threat of it makes the flirting irresistible.

Satomi's the best at jumping rope, she's higher and faster than
any of the other girls.

Californian oranges, fifty cents a pack.
Californian oranges, tap me on the back.

"Quick, Lily, jump in." The rope whistles, whipping up the air. It scares Lily a bit.

"No, let's play jacks, it's cooler."

It's early summer in Angelina, a sweltering, burning-up summer, so hot that even breathing comes hard. The heat haze hasn't let up for a month. It hangs in the sky, rocking gently like the spectral sails of a big old ship, allowing only occasional flashes of blue a look in.

"It's closing in," Satomi says to Lily. "Ghosts all around us."

"More like damp sheets on washing day," Lily says flatly. Satomi's fancies disturb her. It's all that reading that does it, she guesses.

"You should put your hair up in a band, in a real high ponytail, like mine," she advises, tossing her own dull brown tassel. "It'll make you feel cooler."

"It'll make my eyes slant, Lily, you know that."

"Oh, yeah, I forgot." Lily smirks, pleased to have hit the aimed-for spot.

"Oh, sure, Lily, you forgot."

It seems to Satomi that things are never going to cool down. The humidity clouds the shine on her black oxfords, takes the starch out of her dresses so that they never feel clean or crisp enough. At night the swampy air seeps through her window, scenting her room with a curious blend of sweet and rotten. That and the mosquitoes' whine make it hard to sleep. Her father says the earth is so parched he swears he can hear it cracking.

All the crops in her father's fields are tinted brown—"rusting up," is how her mother puts it. And even though the tomatoes are ripening, they need so much water that it's unlikely to be a profitable year.

What with the heat and the thought of small returns, it doesn't take much to get Aaron Baker riled. Satomi has been treading on eggshells around him for weeks.

"Never known a girl who needed to wash so much," he protests.

"Your mother and I need water too, you know. Guess you never give a thought to that."

Satomi rolls her eyes to heaven, she doesn't want to hear. She considers her father's moans beyond reason. It takes only small things that go wrong to set him at odds with the world. And things are always going wrong in farming: not enough rain, too many bugs, bad seed, the catalogue of his complaints is endless. Now, on top of everything, he has to bring water in by the tank-load and the tiniest bit of spillage makes him sick to his stomach.

"Hey, turn the spigot off, boy, it's overflowing," he complains to the tank driver.

"Getting to it, Mr. Baker, it's no more than half a cup, though, can't judge it any nearer."

"Half a cup to you, twenty cents to me."

"It's only a little puddle, Aaron, just a little puddle," his wife Tamura soothes.

Why can't he listen to Satomi's mother? He ought to listen to Tamura, she talks sense, but he just can't seem to manage it. Satomi suspects that his nature is as much a trial to himself as to everybody else. She thinks it nags at him like a sore tooth reacting to any kind of sweetness so that he is never at ease.

Lily says, with that arch look of hers, that Aaron is good-looking—"cute," is how she puts it.

"Can't see it myself," Satomi says, screwing up her face.

She finds no softness either in her father's looks or his character. He has the sort of face that on the movie screen would suit both villain and hero—strong, she guesses. He is big and muscular, with something driven about him, something that takes charge. His thick flaxen hair, cropped short so that he needn't bother with it, sprouts from his head like wheat stubble. His eyes, a shade between gray and blue, look at the world through dusty lashes, and are closed to all but his wife. He doesn't court friendship, thinks his neighbors untrustworthy and his daughter a burden.

"I'm not going to tell you again. Get up earlier and get your chores done before school. The world wasn't made to wait around for you."

"I had homework, Father, and anyway, I—"

"No excuses girl. I've had it with your answering back. Do your chores or . . ."

Her mother pleads her case with little success.

"Please, Aaron, ease up on her a little. She's young yet and she doesn't get an easy ride anywhere."

"You had to work when you were young, Tamura. We've all got to pull our weight. Nobody gets an easy ride. If it's the Japanese part of her you're referring to, well, it's the best part, if you ask me."

"He sure is disappointed that I'm not a boy," Satomi says, sighing, to her mother.

"All men want a son to walk tall at their side," Tamura says. "He loves you, though."

Despite the fact that the farm is modestly successful, that he is known to grow the best tomatoes in the area, something is eating him up. It's said locally that he is a hard man to like, not that you'd want to, him married to a Jap, and cocky, to boot.

Tamura is a different sort altogether, kind and charming, filled to the brim with the desire to please. Aaron is her world and she obeys him in most things, but she doesn't have the heart to chastise Satomi.

"Farming is hard on us all," she excuses him.

Tamura would like to have given Aaron a son, it's hard to disappoint, but such a child as Satomi was surely meant to be.

She had wanted to call her daughter Elena, after her neighbor Elena Kaplan, a good woman, her constant and only true friend in Angelina. Elena nurtures their friendship, despite the fact that her husband Hal is always shouting at her about it. He doesn't care for foreigners, especially those who make out that they are Americans, as if you can't see those slant eyes, that yellow skin.

"I'm putting my foot down, Elena, you hear? Keep your distance from the Baker woman, she's not our sort."

Aaron, a little jealous of Tamura's affection for Elena, doesn't encourage the friendship either. He had objected to naming the child after their neighbor.

"Just because a neighbor helps with the birth, Tamura, it doesn't mean you have to name your children for her." He had laughed to emphasize the point.

"No, but it's a beautiful name, Aaron, a beautiful American name. It will help her fit in around here."

"Can't see what's so good about fitting in. In any case, Satomi's a better name, honey. I looked it up, it means wise and beautiful. Don't see how anyone can complain at that."

It doesn't please him, though, that as his daughter grows, the wise bit, if it is there at all, loses out to her stubbornness. She is willful, too ready to stand her ground against him.

"She'll get there, you can't expect the young to be wise," Tamura says.

"Well, she's sure taking her time."

Unlike his wife's character, his daughter's is without humility. As far as he is concerned her beauty is flawed. He lives in a permanent low hum of irritation with her that sets him on edge in her presence. So he doesn't much mind that she does her best to stay out of his.

"I can't see us having more," he had repeated often in the weeks after Satomi's birth.

"Oh, but one child hardly makes a family, Aaron. And with luck the next one could be a boy."

But, wounded by her husband's disappointment, by his lack of interest in their daughter, Tamura didn't push it. She feared another daughter herself, Aaron's renewed displeasure.

"Only fools trust in luck, Tamura. Best not to risk it."

"Satomi is perfect, though. Isn't she just perfect?"

"No one's perfect, honey. I'll give you she's pretty, as babies go. Look, the truth is we can't afford to feed mouths that will never do fieldwork. It's just plain stupid not to learn from experience. It's not a good world to bring kids into anyway." He hadn't believed it himself, knew that he was irked by the demands on Tamura from Satomi that took precedence over his own.

From the moment of the child's first piercing bawl, he had been aware of losing a part of Tamura. The years haven't lessened his jealousy, it's a constant, tacking his stomach like a rat in a cage, it won't let him settle. He has never been good at sharing.

Resentment as much as prudence drove him into Angelina to stock up with a good supply of what, since he was twelve years old, he has daintily referred to as "French letters." Let others leave it up to nature, to what they liked to call "God's will." God meddles in too much, if you asked him. It wasn't up for debate, nothing he could do about Satomi, but he'd have no others at Tamura's breast.

"Well, I have a beautiful daughter and a good husband. What more should a wife ask for?" Tamura said dutifully.

"Nothing, I guess, honey. That's a good way to look at it."

In her early motherhood Tamura had radiated a maternal glow that Aaron found disturbing. He didn't want her spreading like those wives in Angelina, getting all round and shapeless like half-filled cotton sacks, getting satisfied.

A second-generation Japanese-American, Tamura is pretty in a picture-perfect sort of way, fine skin, eyes like little drops of molasses, lips like the crimson bows that you sometimes see on Christmas trees. There's something of a girl about her, a fragile narrowness that brings out a fierceness in him, the need to protect her. He would kill for her if he had to.

He thinks his wife the most beautiful thing he has ever seen, but Satomi as she grows is a girl whose reality is not clouded by love. She thinks her mother's face a little too round to grant her true beauty, her style too old-fashioned. She feels mean for thinking it, for, after all, isn't love supposed to be blind? Shouldn't every daughter think her mother beautiful?

Guilt sneaks into her dreams, messing her up, so that she questions whether she is normal, whether she loves her mother at all. But she can't help agreeing with Lily that beauty is blond.

"Can't get away from it," Lily declares. "Who would you rather be, Jean Harlow or Joan Crawford? See, no contest."

Satomi, smoothing her own dark hair, thinks that Lily is right as usual, nothing beats gold hair, nothing in the world.

In the steaming nights, marooned on the island of her sweat-drenched sheets, she has plenty of time to muse on such things. She longs to read the storybooks that her teacher Mr. Beck loans her, *Little Women*, *Huckleberry Finn*, *Tom Sawyer*.

"Good American literature," he says. "Can't go wrong with that."

Mr. Beck doesn't lend his books to just anybody, you have to be special, someone who is going places.

But reading in the dim glow of her bulb attracts the moths, the big brown kind that her mother says chew up cotton by the pound, so that the linen has to be rinsed in camphor, a hand-blistering chore that her father has made hers.

She hates the thick-bodied things fluttering around her room, the sickening sound of their powdery wings blistering on the bulb.

"Mama, come," she had called as a child, "come get them." And Tamura had come flying, catching them in her cupped hands, launching them through the open window, laughing her sweet laugh.

Tamura had been her world then, her beauty never in question. When had it changed? When had she begun to flush with shame at her mother's black eyes, her own shrinking heart?

She isn't a child anymore, though, can't call on her mother for every little thing. In the heat, as darkness falls, a longing for those few minutes before dawn when the light precedes the sun, precious minutes that have a little coolness in them, brings on a miserable sense of waiting.

"Stop fussing about the heat girl," Aaron says. "What difference does it make to you? It's me that's got to find the money for water. In any case, it stands to reason the rain can't hold off for much longer. I can smell it coming, any day now. Yeah, I can smell it."

Aaron is pretty much on the ball when it comes to the weather. He says his nose as much as his eyes tells him what's around the corner; it's the farmer's gift. And it's true that there is the faintest smell of brimstone on the air, but it has been coming and going for days now, signifying nothing, it seems to her. Her father's just wishful-thinking, the mean streak in him anticipating free water.

She doesn't feel like waiting until he is proved right. She has a longing to hold her head under the water tap in their yard, to soak her hair through to the scalp, let it drip-dry over her body. She imagines her tangled thoughts rolling away with the water, imagines a silvery stream seeping through the litter of fallen pine needles at the road's edge, leaving her cool at last. But Aaron has forbidden her to use the tap. It's out of bounds to her until the rain comes and tops up the well.

"You can't be trusted to be careful with it. Your mother will bring the water in, she never spills a drop."

"Too scared to, I guess," she had risked.

She had moved fast so that his slap caught her at the side of her head—fingers, no palm, hardly a slap at all. Still, she resented it, thought him a bully.

"If he forbids it, it's a surefire thing you're gonna do it," Lily challenged.

"If he catches me I'll get more than a slap. Don't know if it's worth the risk."

"Oh, sure, the risk. Never stopped you before."

It's hotter than ever the night before the longed-for storm finally rides in. So hot that the drenched air muffles the fox's bark and forces the moths to fly low. Satomi can hear them flapping against the wall by the quince bush. All the windows in the house are open, which hardly makes a difference, but Aaron, hoping to catch what little through-breeze might come, has left their bedroom door ajar.

Barefoot and halfway down the dark corridor, she catches sight of Aaron and Tamura in their bedroom. Aaron, in his work shirt and coveralls, is sitting on the edge of the bed unlacing his boots. Tamura is undressing, with her back to the door. In the shadowy passageway Satomi stands silent, staring. It seems to her that it isn't her mother she sees in the candlelight but the girl Tamura, who until this moment has been hidden from her.

Her mother's body, so delicate that she looks as if she might still be in her girlhood, is covered in little granules of sweat as though she has been sifted with sugar. With the red bow of her lips hidden, she looks all black and white, the cadence of her hair a dark cloud on the skin of her back, which in the candle's yielding light appears surprisingly pale.

Satomi sees her mother's beauty again, sees in her movements a sureness she had never noticed before. It occurs to her that the Bakers in reality are two, not three at all.

"Ah, Tamura." Aaron's voice is hoarse, surely too tender to be his. "Blow out the candles, would you?"

Tamura answers in Japanese, soft, all-giving words that Satomi automatically translates to, *Yes, my love.*

Her mother blows out the candles and in the dark her parents are entirely lost to her. She feels like crying, but doesn't know why. Her father, it seems, can claim the girl in Tamura at his will, peel away the layer of mother, of wife, even, and under his hands make her as burdenless as a bird. As though to confirm this, in the moment before she turns from their door she hears her father murmur, "Oh, my girl, my girl."

Back in her room, she picks up her hairbrush and starts to count, tugging the bristles through her hair, creating knots where there had been none, until her scalp burns with the force of it. She is aiming for a hundred but knows by the time she reaches twelve that she isn't going to make it. It hurts that there are things in life that she doesn't have a hold on, that she is out of the loop, way out.

Damn them all, she would go to the tap, do what she wants. Passing a moth that has fluttered to the floor seeking out the cooler air, she stamps on it with her bare foot. The sticky feel of its innards on her skin is revolting. She lets out an "Aargh" of disgust. Something close to remorse stirs in her.

The run of rusty water comes warm at first, then deliciously cool. It feels good being out in the dark yard, angry enough not to care if Aaron hears and comes after her. It hurts, though, that she is nobody's girl, that she is alone in the world.

Unable to keep from her mind the picture of her parents together in theirs, she scrubs at her skin, the skin that Lily says shines like gasoline. Lily has a cruel streak, but she never bucks the truth, you have to give her that. She kicks the tap and hears it creak.

Her parents' room, like her own, has always seemed ordinary to her, but this night it has become another place entirely, a shining mystical place, exclusive to them. Vivid in every detail, it's a picture she can't shake from her mind, her mother's silk robe carelessly spilled around the bed, their shadows moving on the wall, the little cloud of cluster flies bombing the candle, and the dark starless sky soft beyond the open window. It's their heated night, their hooting owl, their everything. She is overcome with childish jealousy.

Next morning, as she passes their room, she sees that the curtains are drawn against the light, the bed made, everything neat and tidy as usual, but somehow not as usual. Her mother's silk robe, the one with pink butterflies embroidered on it, is folded now across the chair. For the first time she notices that there are dark little moths scattered here and there among the butterflies. She doesn't like them.

With newly critical eyes, she sees the patched bedspread, the peeling paintwork, and the motes of dust like fireflies in the air. Nothing feels familiar anymore. Her world has shifted somehow, as though some small link from her senses to her brain has been broken.

"Damn—damn—damn," she curses. "It's too damned hot."

At breakfast she is sullen, out of sorts. Her father has already left for the fields; she must have slept later than usual.

"Guess I'm in trouble with him again, huh?" she says sulkily.

For once Tamura doesn't rush to Aaron's defense. "You slept well, Satomi, that's good. You've been sleeping so badly lately."

She tries to ignore her mother's sweet smile, but it has already caused a small fracture in her heart. Still, she isn't ready to be placated.

"Can't say I slept that well. Nobody's gonna get much sleep around here until this damned weather breaks."

"Please, Satomi, don't curse, you know your father won't have cursing in the house."

Hurt by her daughter's mood, Tamura turns from her, busying herself with making her *ocha*, the green tea that reminds her of home. She is fragile when it comes to love, has never resigned herself to the ups and downs of family life. As a child she had taken every little slight to heart, and nothing much has changed in the years since. Aaron knows it, so he is careful around her, gathering her up in her injured moments, telling her boastfully that she is safe with him.

"You take too much to heart," he says. "Don't let people get to you so easily."

He can't bear to see her hurt, wants to protect her from everything that the rotten world throws at her. She is the flower on the dung heap, the only pure thing he knows. And she has given up everything to be with him, a man she might never have met had he not one day by mistake taken her brother's bicycle from outside her family's grocery store in the suburbs of Honolulu.

When he returned it with the briefest of apologies, he saw Tamura in all her acquiescent beauty, lowered eyes, soft voice, and knew that he must have her.

She saw a big blue-eyed American, golden-haired and smelling sweetly of milk, and knew that he would. In an instant, Hawaii and the life she lived with her family became secondary to her need to respond to Aaron's call.

Putting down a larger than usual portion of the morning breakfast rice in front of Satomi, Tamura smiles forgivingly.

"The storm is sure to break soon." She touches her daughter's shining hair, notices the dark beneath her eyes, the way she won't look at her.

"I don't want *asagohan*. I want an American breakfast."

"I will make you eggs. It will only take a minute. Sometimes I feel like an American breakfast too."

"I'm bringing Lily back after school, Mother. We're paired up on a nature assignment," Satomi lies, hoping to annoy.

"Oh, Satomi, that's not a good idea. You know your father doesn't like Lily."

"He doesn't like anyone."

"Well—that's not— Anyway, you know what I mean."

And she did, they both knew that Aaron didn't care to know folks. When Tamura had taken him home to meet her parents, she had despaired at his offhand manner, his lack of desire to impress. They had known that their families would disapprove, had known since childhood the divide, where they were expected to draw the line between their races. But Aaron could have tried, might have made an effort.

For Tamura's parents, though, it hadn't so much been a dislike of Aaron that had angered them, but of the idea of their daughter marrying out of her race, her culture. Her mother couldn't believe that she would do such a thing, and had beaten her for even considering it.

"White boys are fine as friends, but not to marry. You are Japanese, be proud of it. If you do this we will all be lost to you. You will not be welcome in your own home. Your father will never speak to you again. Just think of it, a daughter not able to be in her father's presence, the disgrace of it might kill you."

Tamura did think of it. But she couldn't believe that her papa wouldn't come to love Aaron as she did. It hurt her beyond measure when, in the days before she left home to join Aaron, her father neither spoke to nor looked at her.

Aaron's mother, an unforgiving woman of harsh judgments, had snarled that the shame of him marrying a Jap was something she would never be able to live down.

"They're our cane-cutters, we don't marry them."

"Well, she's sweeter than our sugar, Ma. So get used to it, we're getting married."

"Can't say our family is perfect, Aaron, but none of them have ever sunk so low as to marry a Jap. Good God, boy, you'll be speaking pidgin next."

He saw the disgust on her face, suppressed the urge to slap her. "I reckon I'm getting the better of the deal, Ma."

"You've just been taken in by a pretty face, that's all. I'm telling you now, Aaron, that I don't care to know any half-and-half grandchildren. The truth is I just couldn't bring myself to touch them."

The idea to leave Hawaii had been Aaron's. Tamura, with her family's back turned to her, had agreed to it; if their people wouldn't accept them, they would give them up and set out in life as though newborn. They would let go both family and religion, his Christian, hers Buddhist, and be enough in everything for each other.

"We'll make the same sacrifices," he said. "That way we won't be able to blame each other in the future. We don't need anyone but ourselves to get along."

But equal as it seemed, it was not the same sacrifice. For Tamura it fought against her obedient nature and was all pain. The letting go of her family inflicted a wound that would never heal. Yet without knowing why, Aaron was pleased to do it. He walked away as though he had from the first been a cuckoo in the alien nest of his parents' home. He walked away a free man.

They had married in a civil ceremony, with strangers for witnesses, and had instantly left Hawaii for California, where Aaron used his savings to buy ten acres of Depression-cheap land on the outskirts of the small town of Angelina.

"Your father never looked back, but sometimes I still cry for my mother," Tamura told Satomi. "Love makes you do things that you never thought you were capable of."

But Satomi thought their desertion of their families heartless. If they needed only each other, where did that leave her?

The eggs are cooked just as she likes them, but as usual Tamura has made too many and she can't finish them. In any case it is too hot to eat, too hot to think, even.

"Don't bring Lily home," Tamura pleads. "No point in stirring up trouble."

Aaron thinks Lily sly, says that he doesn't like the way she looks down her nose at people.

"Don't know what she thinks she's got that makes her better than us. A scrawny scrap of a thing like her."

Satomi had rushed to the protection of her friendship with Lily.

"She's my best friend, Father. She's the only one who doesn't mind being friends with a Jap."

"I've warned you about that word before. I don't want to hear it from you ever again."

Jap, Jap, Jap, she had repeated in her mind, feeling heartsick.

Neither the eggs nor Tamura's pandering satisfy. She can't shake the feeling that her mother has betrayed her in some way, that she has shown herself to be an unreliable ally. Yet once out of the house, try as she might to hold on to it, her bad mood drifts away on the little breeze that fetches up a half a mile or so from the schoolhouse.

She senses it first on the nape of her neck, a delicious lick on the run of red where the sun has found her out. Walking backward, so that it's fresh on her face, she doesn't hear the distant thunder, but the faint smell of metal in the air tells her that at last the storm is coming. Aaron as usual has gotten it right.

She lingers at the roadside waiting for it, not caring that it will make her late. The light is eerie now, a hoary gray, the sun hunkered behind the clouds. And then the first drops fall big as pebbles, soaking her through so that her nipples and the line of her panties can be seen through the thin cotton of her dress.

In the cool air that follows the downpour her body seems to reconnect with her mind, and, being her father's daughter, her own immediate concerns take over. She tells herself that she doesn't care about anything, doesn't care about being on the outside, about being a Jap, about not being blond. But suddenly she is restless, can't wait to grow up, to pursue whatever that intimate thing is that is between her parents. She wants a magical room of her own, territory to feel included in.

School is out of the question. She can't be bothered to spar with kids who are little more than babies compared to her. Her teacher, Mr. Beck will raise his eyes at yet another absence. He won't mark it in the truant book, though, she knows that; knows it like she pretends not to know that he stares at her in lessons, lolling back in his chair, wetting his lips with his long pale tongue.

She'll go skinny-dipping in the river, feel the weeds between her toes. There will be nobody to spy on her at this time of day. She'll wade out to where there's still a bit of deep and submerge herself. After, she will lie on the sandy bank, light up, and practice blowing smoke rings.

In the years that followed the burning summer, Satomi glimpsed no other life on the horizon for herself.

"It's the same boring old road," she complained to Lily. "No bends or corners to turn, no surprises ahead, just straight on."

"Same old, same old," Lily agreed.

Satomi read and read, and laughed and argued with Lily, and fought her enemies, and attempted through her behavior not to be Mr. Beck's favorite. She swam alone in the river, slipping under the deep water, holding her breath until she felt like bursting. She hid from her father's demands in the pine woods with her book and her roll-up cigarettes.

Life was marked only by the smallest of things. A surprising flurry of snow one January, followed by a summer of glut that didn't please Aaron; too many tomatoes on the market meant the price went low and set his mood to match. And once, as she slept, an earth tremor came in the night and cracked their windows, putting Tamura's hens in a panic. But small concerns aside, the road went on, straight for as far as the eye could see.

Toward her fourteenth birthday she started her monthly bleeds and was told by Tamura that she was a woman now. It didn't feel like it to her. She still had to go to school, still had to dance to Aaron's tune.

Her first bra came around the same time as the bleeding and, seeing it hanging on the line, Aaron teased that it looked like a catapult for peanuts. She never hung it where he could see it again.

Her first kiss came too. Tom Broadbent, a boy with lizard eyes and an uninhibited nature, pushed her up against the school wall and pressed his dry lips to hers for a second or two. She had thought kissing would be better than that, something soft and tingly, something delicious, something like nothing else.

"He kisses everyone," Lily said contemptuously, jealous that on both counts, bra and kiss, Satomi had gotten there first.

Among Angelina's large white community, its small Japanese one, there is no one like her, no other half-and-half in the area. She'd ditch the Japanese half if she could. It takes the shine off how great it is to be an American somehow. The thought that she might be the only one in the world is too scary to think about. Lily says that there must be others the same, though.

"Don't get to thinking you're an original, Sati. Sure to be some like you in the city."

"Guess you're right, Lily. Guess nobody's a one-off."

What would she do without Lily telling it as it is? Lily's the reason she doesn't play truant more often, Lily and the fact that school's not so bad. At least it's an escape from her rule-bound home, a place to be disobedient in without feeling she's hurting her mother.

While slavishly following Satomi's bad habits, Lily thinks herself an original, a cut above the rest. Satomi thinks her fine too, and together they revel in being the risky girls, the ones who took up smoking first—took to cursing like the boys. The schoolyard rings with cursing. "Fuck" is the boys' favorite; "damn," the girls'.

If Mr. Beck catches them at it, the punishment is ten strokes with a brass-edged ruler on the palm of the hand. The devilish thing inflicts sooty blood blisters where the corner of it whips at the skin. Satomi wears hers like a badge of honor.

"Hey, Satomi, who gave you those love bites?" the boys taunt her.

"Come over here and get some more, I've never tasted a Jap."

"With a face like yours you never will." She's sewn up tight against their calls, too tight to let a bunch of no-hopers unstitch her.

There's one, though, whom she isn't immune to, so that on a truant afternoon lazing by the river, when the heat had seeped into her brain, turning her thoughts to mush, when even the birds seemed to be sleeping, she let Artie Goodwin, the best-looking boy in the school, get to second base with her.

In a torment of jealousy over Artie and not knowing her advice was already too late, Lily set down the rules for Satomi in a voice of doom.

"Don't let him get past first base," she ordered, staring Satomi feverishly in the eye. "That's just kissing. I guess that can't do much harm. Second base is kissing and touching over clothes, that's okay if you are going steady, which you aren't, are you?"

"Could if I wanted, Lily."

"Well, whatever, third base is out of bounds. They want to kiss and touch you under your clothes, ugh! Anyway, if you let them do it, it means you're a tramp."

"I can guess what a home run is."

"Home run is sex. Never allow a boy a home run, it could ruin you for life."

Lily's cousin Dorothy had allowed Davey Cromer a home run, and he had bolted when she got pregnant.

"Everyone knew that Dorothy wasn't good enough for him," Lily said. "His family being the biggest pea growers in the area an all. And that's no more than the truth."

Dorothy is the bogeyman in Lily's family, held up to the girls to show them what will happen if they let their morals lapse.

"Anyway, Sati, I don't know what you see in Artie, he's always strutting around like the 'big I am,' and you're not the only one he flirts with."

"Yeah, maybe so, but he sure is good-looking, you have to agree."

"I guess. If you like the pretty-boy type."

Lily tries not to let her jealousy show on her face. Satomi Baker is supposed to be her best friend, after all. She doesn't want people thinking that Sati has won the prize that she's desperate for herself.

"Guess you two ain't such good friends as you thought, eh, Lily?" smirk the girls whose friendship she has shunned. She hates that they know, in that way that girls know, that she's keen on Artie herself.

It's her own fault, she guesses. She chose Satomi as her best friend with the idea of showing everyone that she was something pretty special herself. Lily Morton isn't one to follow the herd.

You can't tell her what to do. Truth is, though, she wishes she had never set eyes on Satomi. Satomi is hard work, and now the worst has happened and Satomi has Artie. If only Artie hadn't been so cute, so curly-haired and fondant-lipped, she wouldn't ache so.

"Guess he likes Japs," the girls jeer. "Why else would he favor her over you, Lily?"

"Sex, for sure." She hadn't been able to stop herself from saying it. Well, it was no more than the truth, boys were always out for sex, and Artie knew he wouldn't get a sniff at it with a respectable girl like her. Never mind that she pouts her lips and crosses her legs in that come-and-get-it way whenever he glances at her.

In her daydreams Lily has Satomi running away from home, or dying quickly from some rare disease. She pictures disfiguring scabs, bad breath, sees herself comforting Artie, him falling for her.

In those daydreams Lily stars as the beauty; in reality she worries that her lips might be a bit too thin, her legs too up-and-down. She likes the dainty little maps of freckles across her cheeks, though, comforts herself that, better late than never, her breasts have started to grow. And one day she swears to God she is going to dye her mousy hair bright blond; then let Satomi watch out.

And I am white, after all, just like Artie, she reminds God in her prayers. *It would be better all around.*

Jealous she may be, but Lily knows that however much the boys might puppydog after Satomi, she will never be the one for keeps. You can't take a half-caste home to your mother and say this is the one. All she has to do is play the waiting game. Artie's bound to come to his senses.

"I don't think we can be friends if you go to third base with Artie," Lily threatens. "They'll tar me with the same brush as you, and I don't want people thinking I'm like my cousin. They'll say it runs in the family."

"Fine, Lily, I'll let you know when the time comes. You can drop me then."

But Lily will never drop her. They'll be best friends forever, she's sure of it. And Lily's advice is meant well, she's only trying to help, to save her from herself. It seems to Satomi that Lily knows the rules for everything. She marvels at how she lists them with such confidence:

"Red shoes are common."

"Eating in the street is cheap."

"Never, ever wear white after Labor Day."

Lily likes to think that one day she will have the kind of life where the rules matter. She gathers in the little nuggets of what she thinks of as wisdom, from advertisements, and the radio, and from the hand-me-down magazines her mother is given by the undertaker's wife she cleans for. She plans never to break the rules herself, they are as true for her as though she has read them in the Bible. She holds dear to the belief of the inexperienced, that there is such a thing as natural justice. Follow the rules and reap the rewards, is her motto.

Despite Lily's misgivings, Satomi longs for red shoes, finds seductive the idea that a home run might change things forever. Change is good, isn't it? Why wait for things to happen? Left to their own devices, they might never.

Those thrilling embraces, the weight of Artie as they lay together in the woods, the smell of leaf mold and fern in the air, keep from her mind Lily's warnings and the tale of Dorothy's downfall. She may not be ready to allow a home run, but everything else is up for grabs.

"Oh, God, you smell so good," Artie croons as he lights two cigarettes with one match shielded in his hand against the breeze. "You've got to give me some sugar."

"Oh, you get plenty of sugar, Artie."

"You know what I mean, Sati. Sure you do."

He takes a long drag on his cigarette, letting the smoke escape through his nose, and hands hers to her in the way he has seen it done in the movies.

"I want us to go all the way. You know I'm going to marry you, no matter what anyone says."

"Oh, that's big of you, Artie. But don't count on me saying yes."

"Come on, course you will. Guys like me don't come by the dozen."

"Hmm."

She isn't even sure that she likes Artie that much, but his embraces excite her, they induce the sweetest tingling of her skin, and strange little leaps of longing that keep her blood singing. Lured by the meaty bulk of his body, the urgency in him, it's hard sometimes not to go all the way. But it's her own fears, not Lily's, that stop her. She may not like it, but there's something of her father in her that won't bend. Artie can go his own sweet way if he wants. It's her rules or no game.

"What's so great about Artie Goodwin?" one boy after another asks. "He's soft as shit. You want more than that, don't you?"

"I don't want any of you, that's for sure."

"Who says we're asking?"

"Oh, you're asking."

She and Artie figure big in the schoolyard gossip. Her reputation is taking a hit, while his remains intact. She may have Jap in her, but she's a looker, and he's just doing what guys do.

"They think they know what's going on," she tells Lily. "Boy, do they have vivid imaginations."

"Can't blame 'em for getting ideas," Lily says caustically. "You and Artie gotta be getting up to something in those woods."

"Yeah, swimming and smoking." She grins. "Real wicked, eh?"

These days, though, when Artie puts his hand up her skirt, she lets it wander until it reaches the soft skin at the top of her thigh, lets him pull a little on the leg elastic of her panties. The sense she has that she might be carried away and let it happen feels dangerous and exciting.

"Don't be a tease, Sati, nobody likes a tease," Artie pants.

"I'm not teasing, I'm serious."

"I'm serious too, pretty damn serious."

"Pretty damn serious, pretty damn serious," she mimics, until, red in the face, Artie rolls sulkily away from her.

"I don't know what makes you think you're so fine. I could have any girl I want, you know?"

She guesses it's the truth. He's a charmer for sure. A charmer with a rolling swagger, and the sort of hard body that stirs up girls' insides, gives them that dull ache.

"Think yourself lucky, Sati," he says. "You've got your drawback, that's for sure. I'm out on a limb, with you for a sweetheart."

Despite Artie's misgivings, he is relieved and a little alarmed when on her fifteenth birthday she accepts his class ring. You can never be sure how Sati will react to things. That day, though, as if she is rewarding him, she lets him unbutton her blouse and pull her brassiere straps down from her shoulders. She lets him cup her breasts with his farm-boy hands.

He closes his eyes, feeling as though he is sinking into himself, into a sweet safe place. It feels so good he could cry, but all he says is, "They're great, really great."

Letting Artie touch her bare breasts feels to her like giving a child one sweet too many. You feel generous and it keeps them quiet for a bit, but sugar gets them excited and you know you'll pay for it later. For sure the more Artie gets, the more he wants.

She won't tell Lily, no point in getting her in a stew. She'll show her the ring and say it's nothing serious. It's going steady but just for now.

Artie, though, can't keep his mouth shut. "You ain't seen nothing like them," he tells the boys. "Not a girl here to match them. Round and firm, and the scent of her like those big red apples. It's enough to drive you nuts."

"Hand her over when you've finished," they joke crudely.

"She's out of your league," he boasts.

"Yeah, from another fuckin' continent."

Much as Artie thinks himself a catch, the big mover and shaker, his school reports confirm that he is lazy, middling at pretty much everything he takes on.

Artie's trouble, Mr. Beck writes in his neat handwriting, *is that he is ambitious without being dedicated. He expects things to be handed to him on a plate. He must learn that effort brings success, or he will continue to fail.*

Artie laughs at the reports. What does a dried-up old guy like Mr. Beck know, anyway?

Mr. Beck, though, is a fine judge of boys, he knows what he's talking about. Satomi too senses Artie's weakness. He's full of want, but too lazy to work at things.

"Life doesn't owe you," she says when Artie annoys her with his boasts, when he tells her what a big success he's going to be once he gets to the city.

Artie's all for getting out of Angelina. He wants the big city, the hustle and bustle, lights and music. He wants the chance of a life that doesn't include dirt under his fingernails. And he wants the prize of Satomi Baker, wants her to give in, to go all the way. He feels lucky, he's good looking with that "it" thing going on, life owes him, he's just waiting for it to pay up.

Artie might not be Mr. Beck's favorite, but he's popular among

his classmates. In his sixteenth year, he's the best-looking, the tall-
est, the funniest, the most popular. If his friends want him along,
it means that Satomi comes too.

"See, Sati, whatever you say, you're just as popular as me."

"Oh, sure, Artie, course I am."

But as cool as she likes to think herself about Artie, life is better
with him than without. Him wanting her, when the girls who
excluded her want him, makes a sort of balance. Even Lily's jealousy, her little digs, can't spoil the fun she has with Artie.

"Let's not go to school today. I'll write your note, you write
mine."

"Artie, it'll be the third time this month. We won't get away
with it for much longer."

"Who cares, we'll be leaving soon anyway. You have to do what
you want in life, enjoy it while you can."

On their way to the woods they steal soft-shell peas from
Cromer's fields near the water hole, fruit from the orchards, sinking their teeth into ripe peaches, and the sweet red strawberries
that set themselves at the woods' edge. There is something of the
waning summer in those fruits, something lush and fertile and
close to decay.

"A smoke before or after?" Artie asks.

"After what, for heaven's sake?"

"A swim, I suppose, after a swim."

It's Artie, not her, who squeals at their submersion into the cold
river; Artie who won't swim out to the deep because he might get
caught up in the weeds that grow there. She can't help but sneer as
she grins and swims out past him.

"Chicken."

"Fool."

They smoke Lucky Strikes when they can get them, roll-ups
when they can't. She likes the roll-ups better. The ritual of opening

the little tin of tobacco, the crisp feel of the white tissue, the earthy smell as they light up, unclenches some tautness in her.

She knows what he means by "after," of course. It's what Lily with her mouth all twisted up calls "making out."

"You'll get yourself a reputation," Lily warns. "You don't want that, do you?"

"Thought I already had one." Satomi winks at her outraged friend.

Much as Artie wants to be with her, he doesn't care for the woods, they are too feral for his liking. He has a deep fear of snakes, of all wild things. The slightest rustle in the undergrowth has him jumping.

"No animals in the city," he says. "Just jazz clubs and bars and the streets all lit up. And coffee shops on every corner and the latest movies, no measuring out the water, no having to eat the bruised crop that you can't sell."

"Yeah, I know, all the men are handsome and all the girls pretty and dressed up smart all the time," she can't help teasing him, even though the pictures Artie conjures up are exciting.

But Artie's dreams are not hers. She hasn't worked hers out yet. Unlike him, she loves the woods, the sweet green stillness of them, the strange shadows that play there, and the mossy scent that stays in the air for days after a storm. They are lovely to her in every season.

In her childhood years she had played in them, never afraid to be by herself under the lacy canopy of the tall ghost pines. She loves the way the light filters through their needles, the clean scent of them. And in winter, when the wind sweeps through their boughs, their creaking moans keep her from being lonely. Angelina's woods hold only magic for her.

Once, at dusk, she had seen a fox in them. It had stood big as a dog, alert but motionless by the porcelainberry bush that was hung with poisonous drupes. Its thick musky smell had come to her on the breeze before she saw it staring, working out whether she posed a threat or not. She had held the creature's gaze with a pounding heart, the hairs on her arms standing on end, amazed and scared at its closeness. It had turned its head from her, sniffing the air, and then, looking back, had given her a wild stare before trotting away.

"Don't mention it to your father," Tamura advised. "He will want to shoot it, you will only get upset. He has to protect the chickens, of course, but . . ."

In the woods' cool clearings she picks armfuls of the rough apple mint that grows around the base of the big sitting rocks and that must be strewn on the packing-shed floor to keep the rats out.

"Better mice than rats any day," Aaron says.

And in the early morning when the light is new and the scent of the juniper like incense on the air, her mother sends her to pick mushrooms in their season. Tamura calls the little flesh-colored cups "*kinoko*," the children of the trees.

Torn between love and embarrassment, Satomi secretly delights in her mother's little sayings. In later years she will know that her heart lived in her mother, she will regret not having hugged to her childhood self the unique charm of Tamura.

All her life she will be drawn to woods, but none of them will ever quite match up to the fragrant forest of Angelina, where she and Artie practiced how to be grown-up together.

"You're exotic, that's what you are," Artie says, as though complimenting her, as though isn't he just the clever one to give that description to her.

Without knowing why, she doesn't like the sound of "exotic." The word has too much heat in it, a low sort of intimacy. It isn't the first time she has been called that, and it doesn't feel like flattery to her.

Mr. Beck, a man torn between duty and impropriety when it comes to Satomi, told her once that he found her exotic.

"Know what 'exotic' means, Satomi?"

"Different, I guess."

"It means someone not native to a country. Someone poles apart from yourself."

"I'm as American as you, Mr. Beck."

"I meant it as a compliment, girl. Learn how to take a compliment."

But she can't take Mr. Beck's advice seriously. It isn't impartial, that's for sure. For one thing, he is unreliable, one minute singling her out for his favors, the next picking on her for punishment. He trembles more than she does when giving her ten strokes on the palm of each hand, his odd smile disturbing her more than the pain he inflicts. He is always including himself in her world, flattering her, intervening in her fights, touching her. She wishes he would get off her case.

"You know, Satomi, you have a kinda disturbing beauty, the kind that could get you into trouble. It sure can open things up for you, but it can cut you out of them too. My advice to you would be to study hard, so that you aren't tempted to rely on it."

"Thanks, Mr. Beck, that's good advice, I guess."

But without effort she is always somewhere near the top of the class. English comes easy, but she wings her way in math, copying Lily's neatly worked-out sums. Lily sure knows how to count.

"Why waste your time on schoolwork?" Artie says. "Your looks are as good as currency."

She can't see it herself. Some crooked thing inside won't let her see it.

If mirrors could talk, hers would say, *This is who you are. You have your mother's long eyes, only wider and a little lighter, more the color of the bark of the Bryony that grows wild by the sheds; your hair is long and thick, and looks black unless you are standing next to your mother, where in the comparison it is dark, dark brown. You have your father's lips, cushion-full and faintly tinted as though with salmonberry. And your skin, the color of white tea, is smooth and finely pored. Your flaws are the stubborn set to your mouth, that look of refusal that stalks your eyes.*

If offered the choice, instead of her dark eyes, her mother's smile, she would have chosen to look fuller, lush, and plumped up like those freckled Californian girls. A regular American.

"There are many different kinds of Americans," Tamura says, catching sight of Satomi posing in front of the mirror, a yellow scarf draped as hair on her head. "Ask your Japanese friends at school. They are as American as your father, as Lily. We are all good Americans."

She doesn't have the heart to tell Tamura that she rarely speaks to the Japanese pupils. She doesn't care to, and they don't mix that much, don't seek her out. Apart from Saturdays when she and Lily see them on their way to their Japanese-language lessons, they are rarely met outside of school. Even when the carnival came to town, when the Ferris wheel beckoned and the sweet smell of cotton candy got all jumbled up in your head with the fairground music and the strutting boys, they were nowhere to be seen.

In any case, Tamura herself hardly talks to the Japanese. She may give a greeting when she sees them in town, but she never stops to talk. It would be pointless making friends; Aaron wouldn't like it, no matter if they are Japanese or not. Even on the rare occasions when Elena comes he is put in a bad mood for hours.

At school with Lily, Satomi talks the latest talk, chews gum, and thinks American thoughts. At home, in the vine-covered wooden house that sits back from the single-track road, a mile or so from town, there is no escaping the Japanese half of her. She knows the rules of both her worlds, moves between them with what seems like ease. Yet something in her struggles to find out which life she is playacting. It never occurs to her that it might be both.

In their small community, the Bakers stand out. Feeling neither fish nor fowl, it's hard to know where to place themselves. The Japanese feel uneasy with them, advise their children to keep their distance. They've heard the gossip, judge Satomi's behavior as *haji*. She brings shame on her family, a thing not to be borne. They're schooled in family loyalty over the individual, in ritualistic good manners, so obedience is second nature to them. What kind of girl goes alone to the river with a boy after all?

The whites made their judgments on the Bakers the moment they hit town. If anything, they have grown more suspicious of them, of Aaron in particular.

"I hear they eat raw fish. Snake too when they can get it."

"It don't seem natural somehow, marrying an Oriental. God only knows what goes on in that house, what kinda life an American has to live under that roof."

"It makes me sick just thinking about it."

Scoffing at the idea of Japanese-Americans, *has the world gone mad?*, the townsfolk pump each other up, spew their dislike of anything Oriental into Angelina's ether.

"One look and you can tell they ain't trustworthy."

"You ain't never gonna find a Jap doctor, no matter how much you try to educate them. Don't tell me that's not the truth."

Lately the irritant of having the Japanese around is grating nearer the bone. Japan is playing up, making itself felt, and not in a friendly way either. The townspeople have been holding their breath, waiting for trouble for months. Now they hear that the bastards are after their oil. Roosevelt is right. Why should America sell them oil? Why should America do anything to help them out?

The handful of liberals in town warn against sanctions.

"Only months to go before they run out of oil," they say. "They'll sure enough get aggressive then."

"Let them. They'll soon find out who's boss."

Immersed in his own world, the hostility of his neighbors hardly impinges on Aaron. He shrugs it off with an indifference that ruffles their feathers. He would have chosen to be Japanese if he could. Not the modern Japanese-American man that he feels is losing status, but the old-century kind, undisputed head of the family, obeyed in all things. He is entirely seduced by the idea of a strong man complemented by a subservient woman, a female who needs to rely on him. In Tamura he has found her, the girl who kneels before him smelling sweetly of rose oil, and eager to please.

"Do it this way, honey," he says, just to see the admiration in her eyes. "It's easy when you know how." Or, "I'll have coffee now," so that he might hear her answer, "Yes, Aaron, I will get it right away."

You can't put a price on being master in your own home. He doesn't need anyone or anything else to complete his world.

Tamura, though, is more sociable. She works at being liked, attempting to defuse rudeness with her sweet smile, her obliging nature. It hurts Satomi to see her trying so childishly to please.

"Your father reminds me of my own," Tamura tells her in a whisper, fearful of bringing her family into the conversation, into their home, where it is an unspoken rule that they are not to be mentioned.

"I know that he is stern, but he is fair. And he is full of pride, and that is how a man should be. How else should a woman know who to be herself? I hope that one day you'll find a husband as splendid as your father."

Tamura knows how to be a wife, she learned it from her mother, learned how to meet a husband's needs before he knew he had them. At night when his work is done, his dinner eaten, she massages Aaron's shoulders, easing those muscles that he has asked too much of during the day. Dressed in her silky wrap, she sits at his feet, the dark fringe of her eyelashes shadowing her downy cheeks. She keeps the coffee coming and his Camel cigarettes lit, while he reads, a day late, his mail-sent copy of the *Los Angeles Times*.

Satomi thinks of those long night hours, the ones her mother calls *the moon hours*, as being endless and boring, full of her father's demands, of which it seems to her there are far too many.

Aaron makes his regulations on the hoof. One day they are to pack the tomatoes this way, the next another—he decides randomly, and nothing is up for debate. Only he can make or break them.

"Dinner at the same time every day, honey, we know where we stand that way."

He means exactly the same time each day. If Satomi is a minute late to the table, her meal goes in the trash. The girl has to learn who is important in the house, who waits for whom, who comes first.

"That's the last *wagashi* cake," Tamura warns nervously. "Best keep it for your father, you know how much he loves them."

Inside the house Satomi has to wear the rough dust jackets that Tamura makes for her from twice-soaked flour sacks. The twine spurs in the weave scratch at her skin, leaving pinpricks of red on her arms.

"Yuck, they smell. I hate them," she moans to Tamura. "It's humiliating, like we're peasants or something."

"I will give them an extra rinse. Just wear them to please your father. He doesn't ask much of you, and they save your dresses."

"It doesn't matter how many times you rinse them, they still smell like throw-up. Nobody I know has to wear such stupid things."

It's sandals only in the house. Aaron likes the sound of wood on wood. Satomi likes the sound too, but would never admit to it.

"Please, Satomi, put your hair up before your father comes home," Tamura pleads, weary with having to appease them both.

In the times when she hates her father more than she cares to soothe her mother, she fights him on every rule, standing her ground, until Aaron, tired of the argument, picks her up as though she weighs nothing, as though she is nothing. He throws her on her bed, locking her in as he leaves.

It's easy to escape her locked bedroom, hardly a jump at all from the crumbling window ledge. Outside with her book and her roll-ups, she sits with her back to the wall of the house, reading and smoking, one ear listening for Aaron's heavy footfall along the hall. He is stubborn and it can be hours before he relents, before she hears him and she has to scramble back through the window and wait for the key to turn in the lock of her door.

"Can't abide all his rules," she tells Lily, shaking her hair loose, letting it spill around her shoulders in the way that Aaron has forbidden and her teacher Mr. Beck thinks unladylike. It's the latest fashion and all the white girls are trying out the style.

"It makes us look older. Like movie stars," Lily says hopefully.

Tamura too finds her own ways to skirt around Aaron's rules, especially his ban on religion.

"Stories for simpletons," he says. "That's all the Bible is, that's all any creed is. We don't need religion in this house to tell us what's right."

As though in compensation for the loss of hers, Tamura concocts little ceremonies out of the offerings she makes to the birds that come to her kitchen door. She kneels to set the crumbs down, her body bowed in remembered prayer, her eyes closed as she loses herself in the ritual. The small thrill of disobedience that accompanies the act never fails to please.

It would have pained Aaron to see her kneeling so, to know that she is thinking of her family in Hawaii, remembering the life she lived there. As far as he is concerned Tamura and he might as well be one person, sharing the same desires, needing only each other to be whole. She came with him willingly, after all, gave herself over as women must. Men take wives, wives give allegiance, and new families are made, it isn't something to be questioned.

If truth were known, he is glad that Tamura's people are not part of their lives. He couldn't have borne the intrusion of them. Propelled by his trusted inner compass, he keeps to the unquestioned path, defending himself against the idea that his wife might desire anything more than he provides for her.

Town is one of the few places where Tamura is able to express her choices without Aaron's eye on her. He doesn't care for the place: the bank four times a year, the odd visit for tractor parts, are enough for him. The year that he opened his bank account, his first season in profit, he had received a lukewarm invitation to join the local farmers' cooperative and had declined.

"Just an excuse to gabble and guzzle beer," he told Tamura.

With Satomi in tow, Tamura goes to Angelina once every couple weeks, driving the old farm truck as smoothly as the worn gears allow, just as Aaron has taught her. She picks up the farm's supplies and her regular order of *asahi* rice to make the *donburi* with tuna that he says calms his digestion.

To Satomi's relief her mother always dresses in Western clothes on their outings, smart nipped-in jackets and skirts cut on the bias that skim her slim calves. She is a fine dressmaker and doctors her old patterns to keep up with the latest styles.

"Too short for decency," is Aaron's habitual comment.

She wears the neatest little hats, feathered and netted creations that give her an air of sophistication. Satomi's favorite, yet the one she suffers most embarrassment from, is a downy affair that sits on Tamura's head at a rakish angle, bringing to mind a tiny bird preparing for flight.

Some women have a thing for shoes, for others it's ribbons or lipstick, but hats are Tamura's weakness. The moment one sits on her head her spirits are lifted, the color rises in her cheeks.

The townsfolk think she is putting on airs, while Aaron frets that she is making herself look ridiculous. He doesn't care much for the clothes, but he hates the hats. Something about them makes him think of the world outside that he doesn't want to know. Tamura wastes no time in changing as soon as she returns home.

"You look uncomfortable," he says pointedly before she is even through the door. "All done up like a parcel." It irks him that where her hats are concerned she won't bend to his will. It's a woman's thing, he guesses.

Tamura orders the little creations from the dress shop's catalogue when the annual sale makes them a bargain. She buys her dressmaking fabrics there too. With its pretensions to French fashion, the shop is always their first port of call in Angelina.

"How fine that striped cotton is, Satomi. You need a new dress. I have a lovely pattern at home, puff sleeves and a bow at the waist. You've never seen anything so pretty."

"I'm not a child. Puffs and bows are for the elementary kids."

"But bows are so pretty. You never like anything pretty."

Tamura is right. Satomi has a horror of pretty, of puff sleeves and bows and complicated stitching. She likes plain cotton, simple shapes.

"Might as well be a boy," Lily tells her. "There's nothing as flattering as a frill."

Artie agrees with Lily, he would like a frill or two, a ribbon, perhaps, in Satomi's dark hair. It's the way girls are meant to be, after all.

In Mr. Taylor's drugstore they drink bubblegum sodas at the wooden counter and buy bags of mixed candies, strings of licorice, fruit sours, and mallow twists that they eat in the truck on their way home.

"You sure do like your candies," Mr. Taylor says, opening the pack and adding one or two for goodwill. There's something about Tamura that he likes, and it's only good business, after all.

In the town's general store Tamura is reminded of the one she grew up in. The smell of rice and ripe apples, of candied fruits and peppercorns, returns her momentarily to her happy childhood. She likes to linger there breathing it all in, stretching out the time in buying sealing wax and rubber bands, things that she has no real need of.

Her English is perfect, her manners so fine that she often gets a smile from the shopkeepers despite themselves. It is one thing to disapprove of her, *the Jap wife*, when she isn't there, hard not to like her when she is.

So that Satomi might be fluent in both languages, she has spoken Japanese to her since her baby years. It pleases her that her daughter speaks the language of her own people so well, even though the rhythm of her American phrasing grates a little.

"It's a mother's duty to pass on such things," she says. "Perhaps you will do it for your own daughter one day."

"I'm not planning on having children. Lily says kids are nothing but trouble. I agree with her."

"Oh, never mind Lily. You'll want them when you meet the right man. We all do."

Her eyes track Satomi's long stride, she listens to her daughter's words, and notes her restlessness with trepidation. Teaching Satomi Japanese has been a rare success; all else has failed. It isn't in the girl's nature to fade gracefully into the background, or to move modestly. She is always in a hurry, eating her food quickly, racing through her tasks.

"Can't see why that girl's so gingered up all the time. More boy than girl in her, if you ask me," is Aaron's take on it.

But although she never quite achieves the graceful body language of her mother, or the sweet tempo of Tamura's voice, although a stranger might not have recognized the two as mother and daughter, there are things that are inherent. Sometimes she will turn her head just like Tamura, her hand brushing away the hair from her face in the same arresting movement. And often, if Aaron isn't looking, he can hardly tell which one of them it is that he can hear laughing.

Like her mother, she can put her hair up without pins in one flowing movement and make a gleaming knot of it that sits nestlike on the nape of her neck. She has watched Tamura do it since infancy and guesses that it is one of those skills that, like skipping, once learned is never forgotten.

Mother and daughter are not obviously alike, but for all Tamura's shyness, her gentle nature, there is a core of stubbornness in her makeup that is reflected in Satomi's. It shows itself in her refusal to see that Satomi will never become the daughter her father expects her to be. It's only a question of time, she thinks obstinately, it will sort itself in time.

"Slow down, take smaller steps," she begs.

If what Aaron wanted wasn't so important to her, she might see the spring of yearning in Satomi, the character that is already made. She might recognize in her daughter the bit of her husband's nature that she admires so much.

Lately on their drives home, sneaking glances at Satomi's full breasts, her tiny waist, and her long shapely legs, she muses on the fact that her daughter is hardly a child anymore. In no time at all she will be a young woman, lost to her. No doubt she will want to escape from under Aaron the first chance she gets.

Tamura's longing for more children has never left her. Over the years since Satomi's birth, she has ached for them. The thought now of losing her only one is made more painful for her by the absence of those others that never came.

"You don't call me Mama anymore," she says wistfully. "It's always Mother these days."

"I'm not a child anymore."

"No, but you are not a woman yet either."

THE DRAFT

IN THE FALL of 1940, Aaron receives his draft registration card. He has been expecting it, and even in the face of Tamura's apprehension he can't get vexed about it.

"It ain't gonna come to much, honey," he assures her. "They're just ratcheting up the numbers."

Talk of a spat with Japan has been around for months, but Aaron thinks it's all hot air. He reads the warmongering articles in the *Los Angeles Times* as though they are works of fiction, written to stir up the readers, to keep them buying the paper for the next thrilling installment.

"We'll have to show them who's boss pretty soon" is a regular brag in Angelina, but somehow Aaron's imagination won't stretch to the possibility of what might be heading his way. It's hard for him to accept that something he hasn't ordered himself might influence his life.

In Angelina, though, the moment those draft cards sat on mantelpieces, the Baker family took on the stink of the enemy. Try as they might to ignore it, the family couldn't fail to notice the now-open hostility shown toward them.

"Something's changed, that's for sure," Aaron says. "I notice they're not turning our business away, though. They're just a bunch of hypocrites, always got to have someone to blame when things ain't going their way."

For Satomi the teasing at school has developed an uglier edge. Her fellow pupils strut around, mouthing off to her the things they have heard being said at home.

"Think we don't know you're a yella spy?" they taunt. "We don't want your kind here."

She fights her way through it. "As if I give a damn," she says to Artie. "Sure, it's tough, but not as tough as it is for the Japanese kids. They're getting it bad."

"We're gonna whip you good," the boys threaten them. "Don't you Japs know you can't beat Americans?"

"We are Americans." But their words are drowned in waves of jeering laughter.

"Looking like the enemy doesn't make them the enemy," Satomi insists to Lily. "Don't let me see you joining in the baiting."

To her own surprise, coming across the school bully Mike Loder, who is twisting the arm of a Japanese girl who hasn't made way for him in the hall, she finds herself ready, wanting to act.

Mike's voice is high, pumped up with a venomous hatred. He is so full of himself that he might as well be thumping his chest with his fists. *Look at how important I am compared to you.*

"Stand aside next time, Jap. Get it?" He is leering into the girl's face, his own fat one shining with sweat and excitement.

"Why should she, Mike? You stand aside." Satomi grabs at his shirt, pulling him away from the girl. "What's so special about you?"

"Keep out of this. Keep your half-caste nose out of it." He shoves her hard so that she stumbles, hitting the side of a locker, grazing her arm, and banging her cheekbone on its metal edge.

After, she can't remember how it happened, what had propelled her fist into Mike's face, or the pain she felt when he returned the blow. She remembers, though, feeling good, not caring that she is in for it with Mr. Beck. Something about her action, her getting involved, has made her feel that she is safe in her own hands.

Aaron, checking the bruises on her cheek, the raw graze on her arm, says it's no big deal.

"You've had worse," he says. "Still, that kid needs a lesson."

Next day she is embarrassed to see him at the school gates.

"Start walking home, girl. I'll catch you up in the truck."

Outside the gate she waits and sees him buttonhole Mike Loder, hears his voice steady and menacing.

"See this fist, boy?"

"Yes, Mr. Baker." Mike's pigeon eyes look wary, his voice little more than a squeak.

"You touch my girl again, any girl, you're gonna see it close up."

Mike hangs his head, studying the ground, shucking his foot against a broken bit of asphalt. He thinks he might just kick out, get a good hit at Old Man Baker's shin before running off. He's not sure he can pull that off, though, and he has had enough of mixing it with the Bakers.

"Tell your father to come and see me if he's got a problem with that," Aaron calls to Mike's retreating back.

Hanging a left at the gate, Mike glares at her but he doesn't say anything. He doesn't say anything at home either. His brothers would only sneer at him for letting a girl get a punch in.

Even Mr. Beck has caught the fear. "I'm pretty sure there's going to be a war," he tells the class. "But you don't need to worry none. It won't take long to see them off. We've got right on our side and no Japs are going to set foot on American soil."

He attempts to keep his voice from shaking and fails. He is a patriot, after all, and loves his country. "We all love America," he says, not looking at Satomi's bruised face, or at the Japanese students who sit in his class with blank expressions and lowered eyes.

"Guess Mr. Beck doesn't like you so much anymore," Lily whispers, hoping that soon it will be the same with Artie.

After his little speech, Mr. Beck keeps Satomi in with the pretense of talking to her about her grades.

"You have to understand," he says, warily looking around before offering her a cigarette, staring at her in that squirm-making way. "You're gonna have to choose where you stand. I'd cut any ties you have with the Japanese if I were you."

She takes the cigarette and he lights it for her with a proprietary air. He'd like to be the one to always light her cigarettes.

"You want me to cut ties with my mother, Mr. Beck?"

"Well, no, of course I didn't mean that. I just meant you should choose your friends carefully."

"Are you my friend, Mr. Beck?" Her heartbeat amps up a notch, it seems too bold a thing to ask.

"I'd like to be." He touches her cheek lightly, leaning in so that she can smell his sweat, see the moisture beading above his top lip.

"Well, if you are, then I reckon you shouldn't make out like we're the enemy."

"We?"

"Us Japs."

She's judging him, ticking him off. He's a little amused, stirred by her. It's been a long time since a woman got pert with him. But he can't favor her anymore, the time is coming when he will have to kill his desire for the girl, stop keeping her in his sights. She isn't the only one who must choose who to play with.

As things worsen between the United States and Japan, Angelina closes ranks. What few friendships some of the locals have enjoyed with their Japanese neighbors go stone cold, as though they had never been.

Tamura, painfully sensitive to people's attitudes, refuses to go into town. She misses her outings with Satomi but she feels safer at home.

"I'll go when things simmer down," she promises. "No point in asking for trouble."

While they wait for things to *simmer down*, Satomi picks up the provisions after school, not pausing for the grocery clerk to say thank you, which he rarely does, and then only when from habit it slips out. She stares down those who are rude to her, never the first to look away. She holds her head up at the overt name-calling, wanting to smash them all, to put her fists into their smug faces as she had into Mike Loder's. She minds for herself, but cares more for her mother.

"Who in their right mind could think of my mother as the enemy?" she asks Lily. "I mean, Tamura Baker, Japanese spy, can you see it?"

"Well, I guess some might, not me, of course, but some," Lily answers halfheartedly. "I guess it'll pass soon enough," she adds without conviction.

"Can't say it surprises me," Aaron says. "It comes on the back of a century of hate for Orientals. They're just plain scared, and now that Japan is playing up, they're telling themselves that they were right all along."

The Stars and Stripes begin to flutter on every porch. The talk is all of patriotism and keeping America *safe for Americans.*

"They can wrap themselves in the flag as much as they like," Aaron says. "It don't make them more American than us."

For Tamura, the thought that Aaron might be taken from her fills her with fear. She can't imagine her life without him. She has forgotten what it is to be herself in the world. So it comes as a shock when at breakfast one morning he appears in a clean shirt and his kept-for best pants, and, as though it has just occurred to him out of the blue, tells them casually that he is going to volunteer that very day.

"I'm not waiting on some guy I've never met to crook his finger and tell me to up sticks."

"But Aaron, it may never happen. Even if there is a war, they are going to need farmers to keep the land going. Please don't go, wait a bit. Wait for a couple of months at least."

"Look, Tamura, it will be best for us all if I'm one of the first to volunteer. They can hardly feel bad about you and Satomi if I'm out there doing my duty, now, can they? Wherever they send me, it will likely only be for a few months."

It's the only time that Satomi has heard her parents arguing, although it is more like pleading on Tamura's part. Aaron, though, is not to be swayed, not even by her mother's tears. For herself she can't help feeling a run of excitement at the idea of life without Aaron on her case.

It upsets Aaron seeing Tamura so anxious, but he just can't bear the idea of being summoned by a higher authority to do their bidding. The way things are moving they are going to get him one way or the other anyway. He might as well make sure that it's his way.

He volunteers for the Navy, a strange choice, Satomi thinks, for a farmer, but then you can never second-guess Aaron.

Tamura isn't surprised. "Your father has always loved boats, loved being near the water," she says. "Hawaii does that to you."

In the week before he leaves, he stacks the woodshed to the roof with logs, cleans out the well, and adds Tamura's name to the bank account.

"You two will manage fine," he says. "The best part of the harvest is in, after all. And Satomi, I expect you to pull your weight, help your mother."

Tamura watches Aaron walk down the path, not slowing, not looking back, as he swings onto the road. While he's still in her sights she feels lonely. She stays at the window long after the dust from his heels has settled back to earth, as though he might think better of it and turn for home.

Satomi watches him too, thinking how Aaron being one of the first to volunteer will shut the kids up at school.

"See your father's still at home," she will say. "Guess he's not ready to fight for America, huh?"

"Don't cry, Mama," she soothes, putting her arm around Tamura. He'll be back before you know it. And I'm still here."

Aaron had talked himself into the idea that he was doing something grand, something that would involve muscle and guns, but before he knows it, he finds himself back in Hawaii as a battleship cook. He can't work out how that happened. He had written Hawaii as his birthplace on the Navy forms, adding beneath it that for personal reasons it was the only posting he didn't want.

Tamura laughs through her tears. As far as she is aware, Aaron has never cooked a thing in his life.

"How can he be a cook? Your father has never made himself a meal, never even brewed his own coffee."

"Guess the crew will find that out soon enough," Satomi says, doubled up with laughter. The thought of her father peeling vegetables and making omelets is just ridiculous.

In his first letter home, although it wasn't to be read on the page, both wife and daughter sensed Aaron's regret at his decision to enlist.

Life in the ship's galley is a sight easier than that of a farmer. The food's not bad although the tomatoes that have to be chopped by the sack full aren't a patch on ours. They have no

scent, nothing of the earth about them. The ship has the same
problem with rats as we do, only they're bigger here, less scared
of humans. Two days in and we were all taken off board while
they fumigated the holds and cabins with poisonous gas. They
say two whiffs of the stuff can fell a man, so I'm not breathing
deep for a while.

He writes that Hawaii seems different to him, not the least bit
like home anymore.

I don't intend looking up family. No point in dredging up
dirt, so you needn't worry on that score. In any case guys get
moved on all the time, I'm hoping not to be stationed here for
long.

Tamura had harbored a faint hope that Aaron, back in their old
territory, might relent, try to make amends with their families.

"I should have known," she says to Satomi. "Your father wasn't
built for bending."

His letters begin to arrive two, sometimes three a week, his big
scrawl filling page after page with what seems to them to be ram-
blings about nothing much, the weather, the ship's menus, how
it's never quiet on board. Tamura wants to hear that he is missing
her, missing home, wants him to tell her that she is doing well
keeping things going on the farm. But Aaron's feelings are nowhere to be read in his letters; something stops him from saying
what he feels, from pouring his heart out to her. He can't admit
that he has made a mistake. He feels himself a fool for having vol-
unteered in the first place. Good Lord, what had he been thinking? Life is harder for him in the Navy than he makes out to
Tamura. He hates being in such close contact with other men,
hearing them snore and sleep-talk at night, smelling the sweaty

animal scent of them. He thinks he sees in them the look of the
migrant worker, the look of men who are rootless. But really what
he sees, what he can't make any sense of, are men who haven't
chosen the land, men so unlike himself that he will never feel at
ease with them. He mimics their language, laughs at their jokes,
attempts to be a regular kind of guy, it's easier that way.

"Hey, Aaron, you got a pass for tonight? Real pretty girls at the
Pearl Bar."

"Another time, maybe. Things to do."

He has no use for the white-trash girls with their caked-on
makeup and sprayed-stiff hair that you can buy for a buck or two
at the Pearl.

"Yeah, we know, another letter to write, eh? You'll have to
show us a photo sometime soon. She must be some looker, to keep
you on the hop like that."

It's only when the bunks around him lay empty that he can let
go. He thinks then of Tamura, of the soft planes of her face, the
pools of her eyes, and the feather-weight of her body on his. He
takes his small comfort in the privacy of his narrow bunk, a moment's relief, and only a faint echo of what he so badly craves.

He has thought better about showing a photograph of Tamura
around. Perhaps it's not such a good idea to tell his so-called shipmates that his wife is Japanese. They wouldn't understand, and
he can't bear the thought of exposing Tamura to their crude
comments.

Some of the guys stick pictures of their wives on their lockers,
and then have to take the jokes, the wolf whistles and the mockery
that the good-looking ones will soon be sending "Dear John"
letters. Let them think him secretive, he'll sail through his time,
let the wind take him, keep his family to himself.

In the moments before sleep he closes his eyes and imagines
himself working his fields. He summons up the cool fragrance of

green tomatoes as they ripen in the sun. It's a source of pride for him that he can tell what stage his crop is at simply by the smell. First comes the sharp trace of green in the flower, the scent of cologne, then as the fruit buds a smell as close to pickle as you'll get, and then the ready-for-picking, full-blown peachy perfume that fills the packing shed for days.

Finding it hard to take orders, to have his days dictated by time sheets, he begins sending his own orders home, long lists of instructions for Tamura and Satomi, lists that comfort him and irritate them.

Make sure you clean out the rain barrels right down to the bottom. The water will turn brackish if you don't. And Tamura, I know you don't like it but the traps must be set in the packing sheds. We'll be overrun if you don't. Get Satomi to do it and tell her to be sure to get rid of the dead ones. And don't forget to order the fertilizer in good time, and . . .

Once a letter is stamped and posted, his mind empties for a bit, and he feels at ease. But a day or so later he has thought up a whole new list of things for them to do. He dreads the idea of returning to the farm and finding it neglected. You can't blame them, but women aren't up to the job, they won't see what's needed, and Tamura has never been strong.

Encouraged by the tone of the headlines in the *Los Angeles Times*, the folks in Angelina figure that war with Japan is a surefire thing. The men are already being called up, and those who haven't received their papers are rushing to volunteer before they are summoned. No one wants to be thought unwilling, unpatriotic.

The town seems half empty without them. Old men see their sons off with fear in their eyes, young fathers leave their families with trepidation. The land is left to the ministrations of grandfathers, schoolboys, and the women.

The old men gather together in the farmers' cooperative, feeling themselves in charge, half alive again. War is the main topic of conversation. The threat from Japan is changing things, taking away the routine of their lives, their ease of mind. Angelina's Japanese take the brunt of their anger.

"The whole damn lot of them got a secret allegiance to Japan."

"When push comes to shove they can't be trusted."

Lily, on the lookout for an excuse to ditch Satomi, is half sick with having to make-believe that Satomi is her best friend. She doesn't share her home-packed lunches with her anymore, refusing Tamura's fish and rice balls that she is usually greedy for.

"Can't stomach fish anymore. Guess I'm allergic or something."

Lily's mother has warned that Japs can't be trusted not to put something in the food. It's better to be safe than sorry.

"That's a shame, you loved them so much," Satomi says without sympathy. She knows what's going on with Lily, all right.

"Yeah, well, things change, I guess."

"I'm the same person, Lily."

"I know that, Sati." Lily stares her down. "I'm only talking about fish balls."

Despite that Lily is being weird, despite that she's getting a rougher ride at school, Satomi is enjoying life without Aaron around. It's easy now to get her own way, tempting to take advantage of her mother's gentle nature. She likes home better without her father in it, that's for sure. She can hardly remember his rules now, smoking as she does without a thought to being caught, leaving her hair down, getting behind with her chores. Every now and then, though, she hears Tamura sigh in her bed, and she suffers the loss of Aaron herself, the fear that life is shifting too quickly.

Things with Artie are still on, although she never knows where she stands with him these days. He is offhand with her at school, making out that things have changed between them, but full-on with her when it is just the two of them.

"No point in us riling people up, they're doing enough of that themselves."

"They are morons, Artie, all of them."

"Yeah, well, fuck 'em, eh?"

Artie likes it better with Aaron away too. He calls at the farm with the excuse that he has come to help Satomi and Tamura with the chores.

"Now that you don't have a man around," he preens.

He sits around the place, watching Satomi pile the wood up in the lean-to, clean out the sheds, and stack the tomato boxes, talking to her all the while. He doesn't mind releasing the dead rats from the traps, though.

"Girls shouldn't have to," he says as he practices flinging them across the fields, seeing how far he can make them fly.

In the seed store that stinks of the rats, a thicker sort of mousy, he kisses her, long, passionate kisses, the way he thinks girls like to be kissed. He gets a kick from the risk that Mrs. Baker might come looking for them, see his hands all over Satomi. He likes to think he might be a man with the power to shock. He pushes Satomi up against the wall, his hands wandering under her dress, wanting it so bad that he thinks sometimes of forcing her.

"Come on, Sati, don't hold out. Let's do it now." She is driving him crazy, getting him hot, and doing it on purpose, most like. "When are you gonna say yes, plenty of girls would have by now."

"I guess that I'm not one of them, then. Take your ring back, if you want, give it to someone else." She is tiring of Artie, if she's honest. She doesn't like the way he ignores her at school, thinks it cowardly.

"Who knows, maybe I will."

"Fine with me, Artie, just say the word."

Christ, he could have any girl he wants, why does it have to be Satomi Baker? If only she would say yes, they could do it and maybe he could forget about her, move on. Lily, for one, is panting for it.

Tamura makes them lemonade, laughs at Artie's jokes, and is kinder to him than Satomi is. She likes having him around the place, he livens things up, makes her feel that they are still part of the world, part of Angelina. She watches Satomi and Artie dance on the scrub of earth outside the kitchen door, to the records that Artie brings over, "In the Mood," and his favorite, "Down Argentina Way." Artie has rhythm, she thinks, that free vulgar sort of American rhythm. He spins Satomi into him, pushing her away, pulling her near, showing off his fancy footwork. He can boogie with the best of them.

"Come on, Mrs. Baker, give it a try," he offers.

She longs to but always refuses. She is too shy, contained in the way that Japanese females are. Modest, her mother would say. And what would Aaron have thought? He wouldn't approve of her entertaining Artie, that's for sure. She doesn't have the heart or the energy to forbid his visits, though. Artie is fun, and Satomi needs someone of her own age around. Lily, it seems, has deserted. She hopes, though, that Artie isn't the one for Satomi. There is nothing of Aaron's steel in the boy.

While her mother sleeps, Satomi stays up in the moon hours, driving the old truck over the farm, parking up behind the sheds, smoking and gazing at the skating stars. She imagines that if she concentrates on them long enough, their energy, which seems to her to be in some mysterious way linked to her own destiny, will somehow enter her bloodstream and a different kind of life will begin.

The waiting for that different life would be fine if only the thought of war didn't prey on her mind so much, if only she didn't fear Japan. The schoolyard talk is full of lurid descriptions of the cruelties that the Japanese *bastards* will inflict if they get the upper hand. Panic rises in her chest when she thinks about *the yellow peril*.

The occasional blink of a plane's taillight heading off into the night sets her to imagining foreign lands, lives lived more excitingly than her own. One day maybe something wonderful will happen and she will be on that plane. She will see deserts, and beaches with pink sand, and all the places Mr. Beck has told them about in geography.

"You're not the only one who wants to get out," she tells Artie. "I'm not going to get stuck in Angelina for the rest of my life. I want to see the world too."

"We could go to Los Angeles," Artie offers. "It's got to be the best place on earth."

"Who told you that?"

"Oh, people talk, things get around. No place on earth like Los Angeles, they say."

"You don't want to travel far, then, Artie?"

"No need."

In the space when she is not thinking about letting Artie go, or of the Japs coming to get them, she takes the time to notice that the house is unpleasantly quiet without Aaron, that the fields are weedy at the edges, that her mother is filled with sadness.

Tamura has become listless, as though while waiting for Aaron's return she has gone into slow motion. She works the land every day, exhausting labor even with Satomi's help. Yet without shirts to wash and boots to clean, she feels at a loss. Being a creature of habit, she cooks the same meals, serves them on the same day of the week that Aaron had insisted on. But she can't be bothered with the finer details and the meals seem flavorless to Satomi.

"No more soba noodles, please, Mama. You don't like them much, I hate them, what's the point?"

But as though bad luck will follow if she doesn't, as though some link between her and Aaron will be severed, Tamura goes on making the noodles that only Aaron likes. The velvety dough sticks to her hands, little flecks of it settle in her hair like snowflakes. It's a messy business, familiar and somehow comforting.

"Fat white worms, horrible soft gloopy things," Satomi complains to Artie. "I just can't bring myself to swallow them. Can't think why Father likes them so much."

She longs for hamburger, for steak, but never asks for them.

Used to having Aaron to guide her, Tamura turns to Satomi for confirmation of every decision she makes. It seems to Satomi that overnight mother and daughter roles have been reversed. Tamura is letting go, happy for her to be in charge.

When she notices that her mother has started squinting, she has to force Tamura to town for the sight test with the visiting optician. The steel-rimmed prescription glasses that Tamura receives a month later make her look older than her forty years.

"I won't wear them in front of your father." She grimaces into the mirror. "They make me look like my mother."

"Well, your mother sure must have been pretty," Satomi soothes. "Was she?"

Tamura doesn't answer. Since Aaron left it seems more important than ever to her to stick to his rules, to the pact they had made all those years ago. *The old families*, as Aaron has labeled them, as though they are some long-lost ancient dynasty, must remain in the past.

With twenty-twenty vision restored, Tamura sets about polishing.

"Why didn't you tell me things were getting so dusty?"

"I didn't notice, Mother."

"Oh, Satomi, what kind of wife will you make?" she despairs.

Lily hasn't been herself of late. She's been moody and more than a bit offhand with Satomi. Satomi's not taking her moods seriously. Lily will come around soon enough. Angelina being on alert must be as upsetting for Lily as it is for her. They'll ride the troubles out, still be friends when everything settles down.

Since they had smiled at each other on day one of first grade, their friendship has been steady, unbreakable, she thinks. So everything that happens on a Sunday morning in Miss Ray's after-service needlework class, as she blanket-stitches around her piece of patchwork for the wall hanging of GOD SEES ALL, comes as a shock.

Lily had talked her into joining the class in the first place, so that Miss Ray, who likes to save souls, would see that she was doing her best to bring Satomi into the fold.

"Everyone should do their bit for the church," Lily had coaxed. "And you get grape juice and a pretzel twist, two if you're lucky. You should really be a churchgoer, but I guess Miss Ray will let you off on account of your mother being, well, you know."

Satomi did know, but as usual with Lily she didn't push it. Lily didn't mean anything by it, it was just her way. The class wasn't so bad, it got her out of chores for a bit, and she never saw Artie on a Sunday anyway, what with his family being holy-rolling-religious.

"God and duty first," was Mr. Goodwin's fatherly advice to Artie. "Good Christians go to church with their people on Sundays."

"Yeah, good boring Christians," Artie complained. "Nothing but Bible reading and silence, it drives me nuts."

Just before it's time to return their needles and cottons to the pine chest marked PATCHWORK, Mr. Beck, dressed in his black Sunday-best suit, reels through the big pine door.

"Miss Ray, Miss Ray," he repeats at full volume on his way up the aisle, letting the door bang loudly behind him.

"Careful, Mr. Beck." Miss Ray extends her arm uselessly as he rushes toward her, knocking over the pattern stand, sending her book of patchwork pictures flying.

The class erupts in laughter as Mr. Beck cups his palm against Miss Ray's cheek and whispers something in her ear.

A note lands on Satomi's lap. "Pass it on," a voice whispers.

He loves her. Pass it on, it says.

They can tell the news is big by the way Miss Ray's eyes widen and go dark. Mr. Beck sure has the jitters about something. His body is shaking, his mouth twitching nervously, and he doesn't know what to do with his hands, which flutter about like the big white butterflies that come every year at pea-cropping time. He places one of them on Miss Ray's shoulder as though to steady her, to steady himself.

Satomi catches Lily's eye and smiles. Lily shrugs her shoulders, looks hostile.

"Time to go home now, girls," Miss Ray says in a high shaky voice, raising her arms in the air as though she is about to conduct an orchestra. "Be quick, now, your parents will be expecting you."

Outside the church hall Satomi catches up with Lily.

"What do you think it's all about, Lily?" she asks. "Mr. Beck and Miss Ray all fired up like that."

"Well, they ain't getting married, so I reckon we must be at war with the Japs."

Forgetting for once that "ain't" is common, Lily turns from her, her voice hard, dismissive.

Of course Lily is right. It can't be anything else. Satomi swallows hard, her mouth dry, she doesn't have enough spit and it hurts a bit. She looks down the street as though hoards of the enemy might already be on the march there.

A bunch of girls pass her, silent in their wondering, staring at her with narrowing eyes. They purse their lips, stiffen their shoulders, and start for home in huddled clusters keeping close for comfort. Mr. Beck has unnerved them. The Japs could already be nearby, in the bushes, perhaps, waiting for them on the road home.

"No need to make it a war between us," Satomi calls to Lily's retreating back. "Guess I'll see you tomorrow."

She starts for home. Perhaps her mother would know what it is all about.

Lily, running to catch up with the girls who are walking her way, links arms with one of them, keeping her back straight, her head tilted as though she is sniffing the air. If the news turns out to be war, then she has the best excuse ever to dump Satomi. Artie would have to do the same.

From the day that the Japanese bombed Pearl Harbor, she never spoke to Satomi again.

PEARL HARBOR

THEY HEAR THE president's speech on the radio, his voice
steady above the background sounds of flashbulbs flaring:

> Yesterday, December the seventh, 1941, a date which will
> live in infamy—the United States of America was suddenly
> and deliberately attacked by naval and air forces of Japan.
>
> The attack yesterday on the Hawaiian Islands has caused
> severe damage to American naval and military forces. I regret
> to tell you that many American lives have been lost.

As though standing at attention, Satomi and Tamura have positioned themselves a little apart from each other. Tamura is trembling, sheet-white, her head bowed. Satomi, returned to the
childhood habit she had when trying to figure things out, chews
at her lower lip. She's attempting to understand the president, to
make sense of his words, but her thoughts keep returning to Aaron.
She can't stop picturing him all burned up, hurting.

Reaching out, she takes Tamura's hand and squeezes it. Tamura
dares not look at her, dares not have her own fears mirrored in her
daughter's eyes. She has stopped listening to the radio and is form-
ing her own story in her mind. Of course Aaron is alive, wounded

maybe, in a hospital perhaps, but alive. They will hear from him soon, be able to count themselves among the lucky.

The day is tepid, warm enough for the time of year, but a chill has seeped through Satomi so that she has hunched her shoulders, as though bracing herself against a bitter wind. She lets go Tamura's hand and turns the volume up to full.

> Last night Japanese forces attacked Hong Kong.
> Last night Japanese forces attacked Guam.
> Last night Japanese forces attacked the Philippine Islands.
> Last night the Japanese attacked Midway Islands.
> I ask that the Congress declare that since the unprovoked and dastardly attack by Japan, a state of war has existed between the United States and the Japanese Empire.

In the moment that Aaron catches fire, Tamura is hauling bags of fertilizer onto the trailer, priding herself on how neatly she is stacking them. She has been working the fields for a couple of hours already, thinking that Aaron on Hawaiian time will still be sleeping. With luck he will be home for Christmas. He has written saying as much, although he advises against counting on it.

> Once the government's got you, you can't count on anything. I guess even if I make it home it won't be much of a break. I''ll need to catch up on things. Guess there's plenty that needs catching up on. You can't neglect the land for long before it starts paying you back.

She allows herself a moment of satisfaction. He is going to be surprised for sure when he sees how good the land is looking, despite the fact that she hasn't gotten around to the weeds that margin the fields, some of them so pretty in their flower that she hardly thinks of them as weeds at all. He should have more faith in her.

She pictures him walking up the road to their farm, smart now in his uniform, a rare smile on his face. The image sets an alarm off in her, so that she loses the rhythm of her task for a bit. In working the land she has neglected the house. Things are not as Aaron likes them, as he will expect them to be. She determines that she will clear her head and get on with the chores she has let go.

She will wash the floors, clear the bindweed from around the kitchen door, make jams and jellies, and pickles from the bruised cucumbers. She will pound the rice for Aaron's favorite soup. She will make sure that everything is just as he likes it. With Aaron home, life will return to normal, the awful uncertainty in her will lift. She will be her old self again.

An hour or so later, standing to stretch her back, she sees Elena Kaplan running down the field toward her as though her life depends on it.

Tamura's spectacles aren't so great with distances, things tend to blur, but who else can it be but Elena. Something is wrong, though, that's for sure. Only a child hurtles at that speed for the fun of it. It's a while before her friend's red hair, her wide shoulders, come into focus.

"Oh, Tamura!" Elena exclaims. "It's just so awful."

"Awful?" Tamura scans Elena's face, looking for the familiar signs of Hal's brutality, but can see only fading bruises from his last beating. One must be due, she guesses, he likes to keep them regular just so she knows she can rely on them.

You don't know, do you?" Elena says, pained at the sight of Tamura's innocent smile. "Oh, God, you don't know," she moves to Tamura's side and puts an arm around her shoulders.

Hal had relayed the news of the bombing to her, shouting it

through the window as she was hoeing the soil in her vegetable plot.

"Bad news, and worse to come," he called, beckoning her into the house. "If it wasn't for this damn leg of mine, I'd make those sorry bastards pay."

Elena is sick of hearing Hal go on about his polio-damaged leg. He blames his slight limp for everything that goes wrong in his life, for the bad luck that follows him, even as some sort of sick excuse for knocking the stuffing out of her whenever he feels like it.

"This is just about the last straw," he raged. "Don't let me catch you mixing with them down the hill anymore, you hear? From now on, you remember where your loyalties lie."

She was scared witless of him but already planning to disobey. Disobeying him is the only thing that keeps her sane. Just the thought of the meanness in him, his big ham hands itching to lash out, makes her stomach sink, but no way is Hal Kaplan going to choose her friends for her.

Hal's first beating had been on their wedding night, when, stinking of beer and rough with drink, he had shoved her face-down on the bed and attempted to mount her. She had pushed him away, desiring something more romantic, something more loving. She had learned her lesson that night. In Hal Kaplan's bed he called the shots.

"I'm going to town," he said. "Need to talk it over with the men. Don't know when I'll be back."

Before the growl of his pickup had faded she was running down the field to Tamura. How could she not go to her sweet neighbor at such a time? Over the years, Tamura had shown herself to be a true friend. She remembered the comfort Tamura had given when Hal, third day into a drinking binge, had blamed her for their not conceiving a child and beaten her until her face had swollen to the size of a pumpkin. Tamura had bathed her wounds, stitching with cotton and a small-eyed needle the deep split that had exposed her jawbone. The scar is still there, neat as anything, Tamura's tiny stitches a thin white tattoo on Elena's brown face. Tamura Baker doesn't judge, she just sets about making things better.

"It's a terrible shock, Tamura. You had better sit down. Let's go in, I will make you some tea."

There's a ringing in Tamura's head as she tries to make sense of Elena's news, a heaviness working its way from her feet, which seem too leaden to move, up to her stomach. Something painfully hot is tiding around her heart, churning things up.

"That Japan should do such a thing," she muses, feeling oddly betrayed. "It can't be true."

"I'll wait with you until Satomi comes home. She will look after you. The news has been too much for you. You need your girl."

"There's no need, Elena. It's terrible news, the worst I've ever heard, but Aaron can't be dead. I would know if he was. I promise you, I would know if he was."

"Your father is not dead," she repeats often and too brightly in the hours after the president's broadcast. "It's a good sign that we have heard nothing, bad news never keeps you waiting."

Satomi thinks of Mr. Beck arriving at Miss Ray's class with the bad news. It had certainly reached Angelina without much of a pause. And here only a day later they are at war. Perhaps her mother is right. Perhaps good news is a sluggish traveler.

She stays close to Tamura, brewing endless cups of tea, wandering aimlessly around the land with her, shaken at her mother's seeming lack of emotion. Her own emotions run the gambit through fear for her father's life to the sickening hurt at Lily's betrayal. They don't compare, she knows—the loss of a friend, after all, being nothing to the loss of a father—but still it eats away at her. The sight of Lily's retreating back yesterday had something of triumph in it, some pleasure in her cruelty. How could she ever have thought Lily Morton a true friend?

She tries to fight off the hurt, but no matter how she attempts to dismiss it, the nasty feel of it won't budge. She holds herself together, not crying, keeping her tears stored for Aaron in case it should come to that.

"She is a foolish girl," Tamura says. "Not made for true friendship."

As always, Satomi takes the initiative with Artie. She waits for him at the school gate, ignoring the catcalls of her fellow pupils, and gives him back his class ring before he can summon the courage to ask for it.

"You might as well have this, Artie. I'm never coming back to school, that's for sure. And we were never going to make it anyway. Chalk and cheese."

Artie makes a pretense of not wanting to take the ring. Not much of one, but a try, at least.

"It's just for now," he says sheepishly, dropping it into his shirt pocket. "You can have it back when things die down a bit." He pats the pocket to let her know he is keeping it safe for her.

"Don't sweat it, Artie. You and me, it was just a kid's thing. I'm not a kid anymore."

"Maybe." He shifts his weight from one foot to the other.

She can tell that he is relieved that she has made it easy for him. Well, she had known all along that he didn't have what it takes. Still, his obvious relief hurts, sets up something steely in her.

"See you around, then," he says, turning from her. His brother has been called to the Army, and he wants to get on with the business of hating the Japs without having to pussyfoot around her. She was never going to put out anyway.

———————

With an odd mixture of dread and relief Satomi sees the telegraph boy—not a boy at all, but Mr. Stedall, who is forty if he is a day—appear in the small plot of garden at the back of the house.

She taps Tamura lightly on the shoulder to draw her attention to his arrival. Tamura stands to face him, leaving the weeding they have been doing to keep busy, to keep the waiting at bay. Since Tamura won't allow the possibility of Aaron's death to be spoken of, despite that it is the text of their nightmares, the constant thought in their minds, they have run out of things to say to each other.

"Sorry to give you this, Mrs. Baker," Mr. Stedall says, offering the telegram. "Bad news, I'm afraid. Guess you know what it is."

Tamura looks toward the horizon as though something there, something far, far away, has caught her attention. She keeps her hands at her side, her body still. She has always liked Mr. Stedall, but the desire to please has left her, she can't bring herself to smile.

"Mrs. Baker . . ."

She shakes her head, as though saying no, as though she can dismiss Mr. Stedall, he is an illusion, he isn't really there, standing in her garden waving the telegram at her. She doesn't want to touch the ugly thing, see the stupid words written, so that she has to believe them. She isn't ready to give up on hope.

Satomi, feeling a run of shame and pity at Tamura's cowardice, takes the telegram from Mr. Stedall's trembling hand. He moves away from her, looking at her inquisitively, as though she might be about to faint away, fall perhaps into his arms.

"You can go now, Mr. Stedall," she says quietly. "I'm guessing that you don't need an answer."

A week or so after the telegram a letter from the Navy arrives. Satomi opens it, begins to read it out loud, but Tamura will have none of it.

"Stop, I don't want to hear it. Throw it away, Satomi. I know what I know."

"It's the truth, Mama. You know it is."

But Tamura doesn't want the truth. She wants sweet lies, the comfort of fantasy. The sight of the telegram had been bad enough, but somehow the letter, the leaf-thinness of it, the official Navy stamp, is worse. Taking to her bed, she buries herself under the sweaty shade of her sheets and attempts to fool herself into believing that Aaron is alive, that the *knowing* she talks about is real.

With her mother out of it, Satomi rereads the letter with absolute attention to every word. It speaks of the Navy's regret, says that Aaron had been a brave seaman who had lost his life in the defense of his country. Because so many had died that day, the Navy had to bury them quickly, laying them in death alongside the shipmates they had stood beside in life. The services had been dignified and each man had been named in them. Plot numbers and details would be sent to the families as soon as possible.

She thinks of all the relatives of those who died alongside Aaron in the attack on the harbor, receiving the same letter. A thousand paper missiles with only the deceased's names to distinguish one from another.

She thinks of her father's parents, whom she is not allowed to speak of. Do they know their son is dead, buried close to them in Hawaii? Probably not. Her mother must write to them when she feels better, it's only fair.

Bringing her father's face to mind, the sound of his voice, she attempts tears for him, but there's just a burning in her eyes, a lasso tightening in her chest. Her eyes water, not with the generous streams she owes him, but with bitter little salt courses that dry before they reach her cheeks.

With Tamura lost in denial, she takes to running the place on her own. She feeds the hens, collects their eggs, cleans out the sheds, and makes a tasteless version of Tamura's onion soup. She boils rice, beans, eggs, but Tamura refuses to eat. There is something dangerous in her mother's rebuttal of food, something that threatens them both.

Each morning she sits on the edge of Tamura's bed, the letter in her hand, freshly made tea on the bedside table.

"I don't want to hear it," Tamura whines, putting her hands over her ears.

"You must, Mama. You know you must."

"Why must I?"

"Because it is right that you should. Because it's childish not to." She can't help being irritated with Tamura. She is the mother, after all.

Eventually the morning comes when Tamura, emerging from under the covers, is ready. Hunger has finally won out. She sips her tea, nibbles at a thin slice of toast, and watches Satomi take the letter from its envelope. Her eyes are shadowed and bloodshot, strands of her black hair are stuck to her forehead, she hasn't washed for a week, and she smells musty. She looks a little mad.

"Tell me again, why I must hear it?" she asks.

"Because Father would want you to, because you are his wife, because it will comfort you. It says that Father was brave."

"I don't need them to tell me that. I have always known it."

Remembering back to the day that Aaron had accidentally driven the prong of a pitchfork clean through his foot, leaving as he withdrew it a hole the size of a fifty-cent piece, Satomi knows that it is true too. He had been brave then as the blood pumped hot from his foot, concerned more for his wife, who couldn't stop weeping as she had delicately cleaned and dressed the deep wound.

"It's a bit of blood, that's all, nothing to fret about," he had said, stroking Tamura's hair, looking skeptical as she had applied a thick poultice of yarrow to the gaping gash. Catching her father's eye,

Satomi had cut her smile before Tamura saw it. Neither of them had much faith in her mother's homemade remedies.

The memory of that day, the three of them together in the warm kitchen, the way her father had given her a comforting wink, both healed and hurt. The wound had closed, but forever after Aaron had sported a red starburst of broken veins just above the joint of his smallest toe. And suddenly at last, with the thought of that scar being burned away, of Aaron being burned away, her tears come, taking her by surprise, falls of them that she can't hold back.

"I wish that I could have been a son for him," she sobs to Tamura, who nods her head in what Satomi takes for agreement.

Silently promising Aaron, wherever he might be, that she will always look after Tamura, she hopes with all her heart that in his last moments he hadn't looked up and seen the red sun of Japan on the wings of the attacking planes. That he hadn't at the end lost his love of things Japanese.

In the days that follow Tamura's revival, Satomi listens to the radio, attempting to engage with the world. It's hard to know what to think about America being at war with Japan. She's on America's side, of course, but still that the enemy should be Japan, that her father's murderers should be Japanese, is strange to think of.

Despite the loss of Aaron, the reports of troops massing, the talk of *our boys in uniform*, it's hard in her isolation to actually feel at war. It might be easier to accept if she could hear the sound of distant gunfire, if she had Lily and Artie to talk it over with, to be scared with.

In the books she has read, war usually takes place on some distant plain, men's stuff, the women left to wait and worry. Heroes rally in the thick of it, some come back to figure in their women's lives, some like her father are lost from the plot. Now there's no one left for her and Tamura to wait for. Impossible as it seems, their lives must go on without Aaron.

They haven't the energy for making new agendas. She refuses to go to school, but still the crops must be tended, the sheds kept in order, the hens fed. Birds still sing in the trees, there is no need to run for cover.

Tamura now speaks of Japan as though it is a wicked relation that she is ashamed of. Japan has abandoned her, just as she now abandons it. Her loyalty to Aaron requires no less of her. Japan killed Aaron, it is beyond forgiveness.

"Thank God I'm an American," she says, as though to convince herself. "Thank God that we are an American family."

Satomi senses the conflict in her mother. Tamura is a child of both America and Japan. She is a democrat in the grasp of tradition, a Westerner with the blood of Japan in her veins.

The fact that Aaron isn't ever coming home, not even in a coffin, fights against the reality of his death. Still desperate for it not to be true, Tamura annoyingly continues to suggest unlikely possibilities.

"He could have been wounded, not killed. He might have lost his memory, forgotten his name."

"No, that can't be so, Mama. They buried Father, they had a service."

Tamura's stubbornness is both pitiable and exasperating. Her mother's insistence on hope when they both know that there is none seems unnervingly infantile to her. But Tamura's stubbornness is not about accepting Aaron's death any longer, it's about putting life on hold for a while, about learning to accept a different future than the one she had planned with Aaron. It's about the necessity she feels to stay loyal to who she was when Aaron was alive, to remain the American wife that he made her.

Now that Aaron has gone she must launch herself into widowhood, something she has no idea how to do, something that holds only revulsion for her. She thinks of her mother, her papa, her brother, and knows now that she will never see them again. No matter how much it hurts, she will be true to Aaron. For as long as she lives she will never break their agreement. It will just be her and Satomi. They must be enough for each other now. But everything is a struggle, so that there are times when she feels as though she is suffocating.

"I can't breathe," she wails. "It's as though I'm drowning."

Satomi puts her arms around Tamura, holds her close until her mother calms and pulls away.

"It will get better, Mama. It has to get better."

"It would help if someone would tell us how he died. I'm still waiting for someone to tell us whether he suffered or not."

They had heard about the burnings, the ships on fire, men and metal littering the water. How could he not have suffered?

Satomi can hardly bear Tamura's pain. Her smiling girlish mother has disappeared, perhaps for good. And it's not so different for her. She has never been so sad or so scared herself. They are alone, haven't spoken to anyone for days. Even Elena has stayed away, her absence serving to heighten their fears about going to town.

"It will be Hal, not Elena," Satomi consoles Tamura. "He'll be on her case more than ever now."

Nothing and everything has changed. They work their way through the days, the same chores, the same fieldwork, an infestation of roaches that draws little emotion from them. They feel strangely empty, ghosts going about the business of the living.

Tamura's nightmares are so bad that she has begun to fear sleep. She screams out in them as though she is being burned up herself, so that Satomi runs to her, shaking her awake, bringing her back to a reality that is as hateful to her as her dreams.

And then Mr. Stedall calls again with a letter from a man who had served alongside Aaron. Some of their questions are answered. Others, though, are posed that will never find an answer.

Dear Mrs. Baker,

I hope that it is okay me writing you. My name is Milton Howley, Milt for short. I don't want to stir things up but I thought that you would want to know how Aaron was at the end. I worked alongside him in the ship's kitchen and I guess that you could say we were friends. He was a pretty good cook and had a good sense of humor.

I was on shore about to return to the ship when the attack happened, so I was saved. Guess I was luckier than most that day. Anyway, I met the nurse who treated him on the dock, and she was of the opinion that I should write and tell you that he didn't suffer.

Aaron was blasted into the drink in the first wave of the attack. One of those Jap bombs set fire to our magazine and sunk our ship like a stone. I reckon he must have been unconscious before he was fished out of the water. The nurse I spoke of treated his burns with tannic jelly, but I think that he had already gone by then. So you see he couldn't have known much about it.

Only the officers were sent home to their families for burial, so Aaron was buried in Oahu Cemetery along with his shipmates in a very fine service. There's a cross with his name marking the plot, so it won't be hard to find when you come. Some of the locals put flowers from their gardens on the graves, red poinsettias and hibiscus I'm told. I'm not much of a plant man myself but I thought that you might want to know that. Aaron was a good buddy and I will miss him, not more than you and your daughter Elena of course, but I sure will miss him. I'm clear in my mind that we'll make those lousy Japs pay for what they did, have no fears on that score.

I pray for you both.

Respectfully yours
Milton Howley

"Elena! His daughter Elena! Why would Father have said that?"

"'Lousy Japs'?" Tamura shakes her head in disbelief. "Didn't Aaron tell him I am Japanese?" She gave a soft little mewl at the thought of being denied by Aaron.

"I guess not." Satomi kisses Tamura's cheek, her forehead. "Perhaps it was easier for him that way, Mama. What with all the talk and bad feeling around."

"I thought that he was proud of us."

"He wasn't ashamed of us. You know he wasn't ashamed of us. It was probably just less hassle for him that way."

"I wanted to call you Elena, you know, but he wouldn't have it." Tamura is wailing now. "He was firm that it had to be a Japanese name. He wanted it to be a Japanese name."

"There you are, then, Mama. It must have been just a way for him to get through. You know how mean people can be."

But in explaining it away to Tamura, she can't understand it herself. Aaron's denial of her name, of her, makes her question if she ever really knew him. For her father, of all people, to hide his Japanese family from his white shipmates went against everything she had always believed him to be.

No matter that she and Tamura agree that Milt Howley hadn't really known Aaron, that he couldn't have been a close friend, the hurt of it won't go away. The thought of it wakes her in the night, wounds her throughout the day.

"For one thing," Tamura says, outraged, "your father never

mentioned this Milt person in his letters, and I think that this 'good cook, good sense of humor' proves that they were never really close. I loved your father, but no one who knew him could say that he had a good sense of humor."

"No, you're right. Father never saw the funny side of things."

Neither of them wants to go on questioning who it is that they have lost, who it is that they are grieving for. They dredge up every memory of Aaron that they can and improve on it. While they are holding in mind the good husband that he had been, he is becoming in legend the good father that he had not been.

"Saint Aaron," Satomi says under her breath, without malice.

She has begun to care for her mother in the knowledge that she is the stronger of the two, but not strong enough, she thinks. It's no fun being in charge, she wants her old mother back. Under Tamura's steel-rimmed spectacles her eyes have lost their light, they are like dull little buttons. She looks but doesn't see. She hardly smiles at all these days, and she won't talk about the future.

"Let's be still for a while, Satomi. Live quietly in the day."

But since the day that those of her mother's blood had killed her father, the future looms as never before. She is full of fear for what might be ahead of them. Despite what happened to Aaron, no doubt they are outcasts now. Both are nervous about testing the water in town.

"It may not be so bad, Mama. And we can't hide out here forever."

Satomi doesn't feel as brave as she sounds. She doesn't believe Angelina will allow her to be the daughter of a hero, and they won't accept Tamura as the wife of one, that's for sure. Aaron's death, she thinks, will weigh light on the scales against the guilt of Tamura's race.

Rising at first light, going to bed with the dark, they are eager after the day to be out of each other's company, to stop for a few hours the pretense that they can continue as they are. They never discuss whether they can run the farm profitably without Aaron, whether they should sell up and find a new way to live.

"I've finished with school, thank God," Satomi insists, hoping that Tamura might find the parent in herself and encourage her to return.

"That's fine, Satomi. You're grown-up now, I guess."

After years of wanting it she longs now not to be grown-up, to be instead a helpless child, to have decisions made for her. But even in the face of their need Tamura seems incapable of action. They are running out of everything, living on hen eggs and their dwindling supply of rice.

"At least we still have eggs," Tamura says disinterestedly.

The hens, though, as if they know Tamura has given up on them, have taken to laying sporadically, and some days not at all.

"Even your cockerel can hardly be bothered to crow," Satomi says.

"They're not used to you, that's all," Tamura says. "It's no good just throwing the feed at them, you have to talk to them, encourage them."

"They want you back, Mama. They'll start laying again as soon as they hear your voice."

She herself misses the sweet bell of Tamura's voice singing the nursery songs of her childhood to her farmyard audience.

Neither of them can bear the idea of wringing a neck or two for the pot.

"Your father always said he couldn't understand it. Two squeamish farm girls. But I just can't do it. Those surprised little eyes, their warm feathers. I just can't."

"We're too soft," Satomi says in despair.

If they needed an excuse not to go to town, it comes in the form of Elena summoning them on the horn of Hal's truck, calling to them from the passenger seat, the bulk of Hal restless at the wheel.

"Give it a week or two, Tamura. People ain't making much sense at the moment. You're better off at home."

Satomi moves toward the truck. "Can you buy us some rice, some flour, Elena?"

Hal's face reddens with anger; he puts his foot down on the gas and the pickup starts rolling forward.

"Damn it, Elena, I said you could wave," he growls. "No way are you gonna do their marketing for them." He leans across her and begins winding up the window.

"Best you keep to yourselves," he shouts. "Elena's got enough on her plate with her own work."

If it was up to him he'd send them all back to Japan, or better still cull the lot of them. His wife is too soft, her judgment when it comes to their Jap neighbor way off.

As the truck hauls away, Satomi runs to the coop, picks up the nearest hen, and wrings its neck.

In the aftermath of December seventh, the town speaks with one voice. All Japanese are spies or saboteurs. No exceptions. Over the weeks leading up to Christmas, Angelina's Japanese do their best to hide themselves away. No Japanese child attends school, their parents rely for their meals on their stored supplies and what they can grow. Best to steer clear of Main Street for a while.

Those of the second and third generations begin to question their routines. Perhaps they don't need to go to their Japanese-language classes with Mr. Sakatani. Japanese is the language of the enemy, after all. Perhaps their mothers should choose fried chicken over sushi more often.

Mr. Beck, lacking drama in his own life and with an audience of white faces before him, is free to fire up his class with his own outrage. His lurid description of what happened at Pearl Harbor, the details he goes into of explosions and of good Christian

Americans innocently saying their prayers that Sunday morning before the attack, thrills his pupils in much the same way that his reading of Longfellow's "Paul Revere's Ride" had the year before. *Listen my children and you shall hear . . .*

Their teacher's righteous fury, his gory descriptions of shrapnel slicing through skin, of human balls of fire, heats their blood, invites them to accept that only Americans can be trusted to act honorably.

With shaking voice he raises his hand and quotes Franklin Delano Roosevelt.

December seventh, 1941, is a date that will live in infamy.

Artie, listening to Mr. Beck's ravings, suffers a twinge when he thinks that now he has to think of Satomi as the enemy. Mr. Beck has advised him to stay away from her, Japanese blood is Japanese blood, and that's that.

"If ever there was a time to choose sides, Artie, it's now," he counsels, as much to himself as to Artie.

Artie doesn't want to stay away, though. He wants to tell her that he is sorry for taking the ring back, that he'd just gotten caught up in the action, that she's not to blame for the attack. He thinks about her all the time, daydreams about running away with her after the war. They could pretend that she is Italian or something, she could get away with that easy. And now that Mr. Baker is dead she needs a guy around, a guy like him.

But he's in a fix with Lily. According to her they are going steady now, which is odd because he isn't sure how that came about, how suddenly his class ring is on her finger.

"This is for you, Artie," she had said, fixing a REMEMBER PEARL HARBOR pin on his shirt. I guess you should let me wear your class ring for the time being. Just so people know you're not hankering after Satomi. We've all got to pull together now."

"I guess that's the way to go, at least till things quieten down," he had said, handing over the ring, thinking that a week or two should get the message over. But Lily's showing no signs of handing the ring back, even though he's given enough hints.

From the moment she trapped him, he's had to put up with the feel of her pushing up against him, following him around as though they are meant to be together. It's not doing his reputation any good. She's no Satomi, and although he'd go there, no way would it be more than once. He's in a different league than Lily Morton, after all.

Artie rolls his eyes, crosses his fingers, and hopes for the best. But, propelled into war, the town isn't about to quiet down anytime soon. Along with the rest of America it's obsessed with Japan, with the nature of the beast that had attacked them. The radio comes at it from every angle, so that no other news gets a look in. Angelina, though, scarcely needs the rest of America's righteous anger to lend oxygen to the flame of its own fury.

Satomi listens in too, as fascinated as anyone. She doesn't know how things are going to change for her and Tamura, but she knows enough now to be afraid.

"I don't want to hear it anymore," Tamura says, sick at heart. "Keep that crackling thing in your room if you want."

She does want, needs to be in touch. Her world has narrowed down to the quiet house, the lonely fields. She has the sensation that Tamura is shrinking too. She seems shorter, thinner, the frown lines between her eyebrows deepening by the day.

She feels older herself, an equal to Tamura. If it wasn't for the sound of the Kaplans' pickup coming and going, they could believe themselves to be the last people in California.

Without school, without Lily, without town, where is she meant to place herself? Who is she now that Aaron is dead other than a girl with one parent, one Japanese parent?

Aaron's newspaper still comes in the mail, its pages filled with eyewitness accounts of the raid, photographs of the destroyed port, of felled sailors. She examines every picture in detail, as though she might find her father somewhere in them among the debris. *I know, I know,* she thinks with her stomach muscles clenching, *something must be done, we must have movement.* Tamura must be pulled back from the edge, they must face town, attempt to live normally.

On a day when long white clouds string the sky and the sun sits hazy in its field of blue so that everything looks new, she gathers up the books Mr. Beck has lent her, and on the pretext of going for a walk heads to the outskirts of town, where he lodges with the pharmacist's widow in a double-fronted weatherboard.

The old house is less imposing than she remembers it. Yellowing nets droop at the windows, the gate hangs crooked on its broken latch. Weeds crowd the grass so that the once-smooth turf is now more meadow than lawn. Despite its former style, its pretensions, now in its fading there is something of the shack about it. The wavering she had felt at calling on Mr. Beck unannounced slips from her.

Skirting an old incense cedar that leans toward the house at an unsettling angle, she takes the creaking steps two by two, and is assailed by the faint whiff of mold coming off an ancient cane rocker. Just the place for Mr. Beck, she thinks, substantial, but peeling.

Long before her ring is answered, she hears a slow shuffle along the hall, a heavy sighing.

"You wait here, girl," the widow says. "Sit on the porch if you like."

She doesn't sit, she wants to be standing when Mr. Beck comes.

"I'm returning your books," she says when he does. "I've finished with school, no time for it anymore; my mother can't manage the land on her own."

"Did you read them all?" he asks, taking the string-tied bundle from her, careful not to let his hand touch hers.

"All but *Little Women*. I never got around to that one."

"Ah. So what now, Satomi?"

"You tell me, Mr. Beck. Any suggestions?"

"Well, a girl like you wasn't made for farming, that's for sure. I'd head east if I were you, before things get worse 'round here."

"And leave our land, leave my mother?"

"It's a problem, I can see that."

Mr. Beck tries not to think about Satomi Baker these days. He'd like his mind to let her go, but you can't order those things, visceral things, he thinks. At the sight of her the old familiar rhythm in his heart has kicked in, a dull sort of pulling. He doesn't want to feel it, it's unsettling, will take him down a dead end, he knows that for sure. He can't fool himself, though, the cut has been made, and she has somehow been wired into his emotions. He smells the clean scent of her, notes her hands shaking a little. It has taken courage for her to come, but she has overcome her fear. She makes him feel old beyond his years, already on the downward slope.

"Can I ask you something, Mr. Beck?" She hadn't known that she was going to, or that she cared about his answer.

He pauses, putting his head to one side as though considering.

"I guess," he says hesitantly.

"I've always wanted to know where you placed me in your class."

"Placed you?"

"Yes, was I white or Japanese to you?"

"Oh, I don't know. Know that I favored you, though."

"Wrong answer, Mr. Beck."

"What's the right one?"

"Wish I knew."

Some way along the road home she hears him calling and turns, squinting into the sun, waiting for him to catch up with her.

"You should read *Little Women*," he says breathlessly when he does. "My present to you, no need to return it." He hands over the book. "If you do read it, though, the answer to your question might be that I think of you as half Jo, half Meg."

She takes the book and laughs. "Half and half, of course, that's just perfect. Thanks, Mr. Beck."

Much as it goes against its citizens' idea that the United States is the most powerful nation on earth, there is no disguising the fact that the Japanese have come out on top. The attack, lit by the rising sun, planned down to the last detail, had been exquisitely efficient. People can't sleep easy in their beds anymore. To be American, it seems, doesn't mean you can't get your ass whipped.

"They won't catch us sleeping again," they brag in Angelina.

"Yeah, chose their time, all right, the sneaky bastards."

"Can't call what they did a fair fight."

But however much they puff themselves up, the realists among them know that it is going to take more than bravado to send those *cocky bastards* to hell. Angelina along with the rest of America is already paying in blood, Aaron's included.

"Not one condolence letter from anyone in town," Tamura says. "Not one word of regret for our loss."

The harsh realization that Aaron's death is to count for nothing in the judging of them brings with it an anger that Satomi nurtures. Anger feels better than the grief that comes when she is off guard.

At first Tamura refuses to write to Aaron's parents.

"They didn't love your father. They chose to lose him years ago."

"Maybe, Mother, but it's your duty to let them know. It's only fair."

Unable to resist the idea of duty, Tamura writes a single page telling them of Aaron's death. She says that she feels for them in their loss, but that she will never return to Hawaii herself. Perhaps one day Aaron's daughter Satomi might.

A few lines come in return. Aaron, they say, has been dead to them from the moment he chose to marry her and disgrace them. They are old now and have no wish to know his Japanese family. They ask Tamura to leave them in peace.

"That's the end of it," Tamura says. "It's what I expected."

"It doesn't matter, Mother. You did your duty, that's what counts."

They greet Christmas without enthusiasm. Tamura catches a bad case of flu and stops eating again.

"I've seen blood on the moon," she says. "It means that there is worse to come."

"Well, if there is, we'll face it together. We still have each other, Mother."

"Satomi, you do not understand that without a husband a woman has no purpose. There is no dignity in being a widow."

"There's dignity in being a mother, surely?"

When Tamura takes a turn for the worse, complaining that she is freezing one minute, burning up the next, Satomi runs to town in a panic and asks for Dr. Wood to call.

"He's not here," his wife says. "Babies still get born, Christmas or not. They call him out at all hours."

"Be sure to tell him when he gets back," Satomi insists. "My mother is very ill. Tell him it's urgent."

"Sure thing," the woman says, and closes the door on her.

It comes to her later as darkness falls, as her mother's temperature rises so high that she imagines insects crawling on her blanket, that Dr. Wood isn't coming.

"Don't worry, I'll make you better, Mama. I promise I'll make you better."

It's a week before Tamura rallies and takes a cup of soup, and the last of the sweet dark beans that she likes.

"Sleep and food is what you need," Satomi says. "Everything will be fine, you'll see."

While Tamura sleeps, she walks the mile into town stoking her anger to keep her courage up and raps twice on Dr. Wood's door.

"You didn't come. You knew my mother was ill and you didn't come." She faces him with a racing heart.

"Listen, girl, 'bout time you knew your place," he snarls. "Strutting around our town as if you own it. If you want a doctor, get a Japanese one."

"There isn't a Japanese doctor in Angelina, you should know that, Dr. Wood."

"Nothing much I can do about that."

"No, but you took an oath, didn't you, a promise to care for the sick?"

"I don't have to answer to you, girl. Best thing you can do is to get yourself home, learn some manners."

"You broke your word, Dr. Wood. My mother has never broken a promise in her life. Doesn't make you much of a doctor, does it?"

She walks home, hardly noticing the slanting drizzle that soaks through her jacket, and slicks her hair to the color of her mother's. Stopping at the roadside to wretch up a thin colorless bile, she thinks that it is one fight after another, will she ever get used to it? Maybe Mr. Beck had been right, maybe she and Tamura should leave Angelina. It feels to her as though it has already let them go anyway.

Next morning at dawn she takes the feed to the chickens and finds a bag of groceries propped against the wire of their run. Two bags of rice, a small sack of flour, two lemons, and a paper twist of tea.

I'll fetch more when I can, is faintly written in pencil on the bag.

Elena had come in the night as Hal slept. Satomi sits on the ground and howls.

"I'm sorry to have missed Christmas," Tamura says. "I know that you like it."

"I don't care about it, Mama. I never have, you know that."

It isn't true; despite Aaron's scoffing, Christmas has always seemed to her a magical time. Lily used to give her a little gift of candy and a homemade card, and Mr. Beck buys the class a big bag of peanuts in their shells to share. The general store dresses its window with cotton wool snow, and sets a SEASON'S GREETINGS sign fringed with tinsel above its door. She thinks it enchanting.

"When I was a girl," Tamura says, "even though we weren't Christians, I always loved the lights they put up along Nuuana Avenue. Do you think they have put them up this year, despite everything?"

"We could go and see. We could visit Father's grave and maybe even see your mother too. We have money in the bank. Let's use it, Mother. Let's go."

"No, that would not be right. I will never return to Hawaii. Your father would not like me to break our agreement. I don't need a grave to find him. He is in the fields, in the candlelight, and in you. In any case I couldn't bear to see his name there among the dead."

"I know, I know. I understand," Satomi says, although she doesn't. Why would her mother not wish to visit her husband's grave? Why would she not wish to break the cycle of their confinement?

"Should I get the Buddhist priest to visit you, Mother? I'm sure that he will come if we ask, and it might help you."

Tamura shakes her head. "I do not know him, Satomi. In any case, I have no religion left in me, it would be pointless."

THE ROUNDUP

THREE MONTHS AFTER Aaron's death, the order to vacate their home is delivered to them by Mr. Stedall, the man they now can't help but associate with bad news.

"It's not my doing," he says, his forehead creased in concern. "Don't shoot the messenger."

"What is it now, Mr. Stedall?" Satomi asks.

"It's not good, not good at all, I'm afraid."

"When was it ever?"

"November '41, I guess."

The notice of *Instructions to all persons of Japanese ancestry, both alien and non-alien*, is issued by something called the Civil Control Administration.

"Never heard of it, myself," Mr. Stedall says.

He has brought the leaflet on his own initiative, knowing that the Baker women don't go to town these days, where the notices are tacked on poles and shop fronts and are hard to miss. Better they should know and have time to prepare. Mrs. Baker has suffered enough shock for one small woman, surely.

They have four days to quit their home, four days to leave their farm and their lives. No wonder Mr. Stedall feels bad at being the bearer of such news. No wonder he rocks on his bicycle as he peddles away from them.

Along with their Japanese neighbors, they are to be sent to a detention camp and must present themselves on the due day at the Angelina assembly area, which turns out to be the hastily re-named bus station, out by the peach-canning factory on the road heading west.

By Executive Order 9066, Franklin Roosevelt demands that all those of Japanese ancestry, those with any Japanese blood at all, are to be excluded from the entire Pacific coast. That means all of California and most of Oregon and Washington too. It means the Japanese residents of Angelina, and it means Tamura and Satomi.

Satomi reads the notice to Tamura, the paper trembling in her hand so that the writing blurs and she has to keep starting over. Tamura sits upright and very still in her chair, the formality of the phrasing confusing her. Surely it can't be true; Satomi has put the emphasis in the wrong place, or she herself has misheard. What is a *non-alien* other than an American citizen?

"Are you sure it says that? Can it be possible that it says that?"

"It does say that, but I'll read it again slowly, to be certain."

When she has finished, Tamura rises from her chair and says quietly, "Yes, that is what it says, then."

"How can this man remove us from our home, Mother? Surely he doesn't have the right, it's un-American."

"He is the president of the United States. We are nothing to him."

"Father voted for him didn't he? He must have trusted him."

The shocking news seems too much to be absorbed in one go, but the awful certainty that there is no way out brings them to the edge of hysteria. Something hideous is about to happen to them, something without reason, a horrible thing that they are power-less to stop.

The questions come, each one prompting another that has no answer.

"Where will they send us?"

"What will they do with us?"

"How will we live?"

"What will happen to the farm?"

"We must stay together, whatever happens," Satomi says. "We mustn't let them separate us."

"No, we must not be separated," Tamura repeats, while harboring an unspoken terror that even their lives might be in danger.

In the raw panic that overtakes them, tending the crop seems pointless; even cooking is beyond them. They walk about in circles, the shock the news has brought dragging at their insides. Satomi, as though watching through others' eyes, sees their pacing as spinning, it's the nearest thing to spinning, she thinks. By dusk they are tired out. Sliding into static mode, they wait as though on alert for the ice to crack, the sea to swallow them up.

Sleep is out of the question. Satomi takes herself to her mother's bed, where they talk and hold each other until dawn breaks and they feel the need for coffee.

"How will we make coffee at this 'detention center'?" Tamura asks.

"I don't know, Mama, I don't know the answer to anything. Maybe they will make coffee for us."

She watches Tamura walk the tidy house, watches her touch every bit of furniture as though taking leave of old friends. She watches her stroke the curtains, and lock the linen box, and take down the china from the big pine dresser that Aaron had made for her.

Seeing her mother's pain, she determines never to love too much the place she lives in, never to allow any building to hold part of her in its fabric. Yet under the eviction threat she can't help feeling a new love for the place herself.

After a couple of days the fog in her head clears and memories come flooding as she paces around their property. Memories of Artie kissing her at the side of the log shack, putting his tongue in her mouth so that she could taste the lemonade he had been drinking, sweet and sour at the same time. She recalls his voice as clearly, as though he is standing next to her saying it over again: "Don't be a tease. Nobody likes a tease."

In the packing shed she stands in a shaft of light remembering a day when through her fingers she had watched, with dread in her heart, her father tenderly, one by one, drown five perfect little kittens that had been born in the dark behind the box stack.

"Two cats are all the farm needs," he had said, as though speaking of spades or pitchforks. Her father's certainty seems like something wonderful now, something safe and protecting.

And how old had she been that long hot summer when she had spied on her parents? Thirteen, she'd been thirteen, and all grown up, she had thought then. The memory of the girlish arc of her mother's back, her father's rough work hands, the glowing room, is still crystal clear. Tamura had been happy then. Would she ever be again?

It comes to her that wherever life is to take her, the Baker place is the only home she has ever known, and that all her memories of her childhood on the farm will come now with a serving of pain. Order 9066 will in her future mark her past, and make it hard for her to call herself an American.

They shakily go over the list of orders that came with the notice. They are to take with them only those possessions that they can carry themselves. They should include enamel plates, eating utensils, and some bedding. They are not to pack food or cameras. Radios are forbidden, as is alcohol. They must report at ten A.M. They must be on time.

Tamura begins packing the one small suitcase they own, while Satomi uses the old duffel bag that usually hangs behind the kitchen door, housing potatoes.

Apart from a few clothes and the Indian blanket from her bed, there is nothing much Satomi wants to take, so Tamura fills the rest of the duffel with things that remind her of Aaron. Mania possesses her as she packs his clothes and shoes, a bar of his shaving soap, an old tobacco pouch. She is not to be dissuaded.

"I need to breathe him in, I want to breathe him in," she says, weeping. "And what will happen to them if I don't?"

"What will happen to everything here? Just take your own things, Mama, just the stuff you will need."

Sick at heart, she watches as Tamura fills the bag, hiding their last small sack of rice in the bottom. The sight of it fills her with shame. They are refugees now, to be herded to God knows where in their own country.

Elena comes sneaking across the field, hugging the woods' perimeter so as not to be seen by her husband.

"I've heard they may search your place," she says. "You should burn anything incriminating. Things will be bad enough for you, no need to bring extra trouble to your door."

"We have nothing incriminating, Elena. What could we have?"

"Oh, I don't know, Tamura. Anything that could tie you to Japan, I suppose. Photographs, that sort of thing."

"Photographs? Oh, yes, photographs," Tamura says, confused.

She takes Elena's hand, her eyes stinging with tears. "You are a good friend," she says. "We will not forget you."

"Life's hard enough on the land." Elena is weeping too. "You'd think they could leave us in peace to get on with it. You don't deserve this, Tamura. Look after your mother, Sati."

They watch her until she is halfway up the field, watch her dart in and out of the trees, skimming the margin between field and wood. They watch her go, willing her on. If Hal catches her, this time they won't be around to see bruises.

Tamura goes to the yard and starts a little fire with sticks and grass. She takes the book of Japanese fairy tales that Satomi had loved as a child, the photograph of her mother standing outside her father's shop that she had kept hidden from Aaron, and lets the flames eat them.

"They would prefer us to burn ourselves, I suppose," she says.

The day before they are due to leave, they summon up the courage to go to the bank to withdraw the money from the farm account, only to find that it has been frozen. The clerk, polite but juiced up with the power to say no, says that it is the same for all the Japanese.

"Rules are rules, Mrs. Baker, but you needn't worry none. I guess it will only be a temporary measure."

"Ha! And whose rules are they?" Satomi sneers.

"Government rules, Mrs. Baker," he says, ignoring Satomi. "We all have to obey the government."

When they are back in the truck, numb with shock, a weary resignation overtakes them. It is becoming a habit to accept. Even so, Tamura is too upset to drive safely. She tries, but her steering is erratic, so that she veers toward the middle of the road, alarming the oncoming traffic.

"We need gas, Satomi." Her voice is thin, shaky, she's on the verge of tears. "Just enough to get us home, no point in getting too much. I'll pull in and you can drive back. Who cares if we break the rules now?"

At the gas station, the JAP TRADE NOT WANTED sign brings Satomi back to herself with a jolt.

"We have always bought our gas here," Tamura says, shaking her head in disbelief. "I remember when they started up and were glad of our business. How can they do this to us now?"

"Because they are idiots, Mother. Small-brained idiots, that's why."

"Let's go, Satomi, it doesn't matter. We're the same people; it's them who have changed."

"It does matter, and they should know it."

Tamura parks up by the pump with a sinking heart. Satomi holds her hand on the horn, rousing the chained dog to barking.

"We ain't serving gas to Japs no more," the red-faced youth she knows from school tells her. "You'd best try elsewhere."

"Who are you to tell me that, Kenny Buchan?" she shouts, getting out of the truck, walking around it to face him. She's so fired up it's an effort not to hit him. Tamura slides over to the passenger side, calling to her to let it go.

"My father died defending this country, defending you." Satomi pokes him in the chest so that he staggers a bit. "You weren't worth it."

The boy shrugs, takes a step backward. He knows Satomi Baker isn't above landing a punch, but you can't hit girls, not even Jap ones, not even the ones who hit you.

"Don't make no difference what you say, we don't serve gas to Japs." He is on his guard, just waiting for her to make a move.

Something about the set of his stupid face, the lank hair cut straight above his ears, the hillbilly overalls, makes her want to laugh.

"Relax, Kenny," she says. "You're not worth bothering with."

Getting behind the wheel, she winds down the window and calls to his retreating back, "Just a kid doing his mama's bidding."

Five hundred yards or so from the farm, they run out of gas and leave the truck on the single-track road, walking home in silence.

That afternoon Tom Myers, a greasy sort of man with small eyes and a brain to match, calls at the farm in the bigger of his two trucks.

"Saw your vehicle a way back," he says. "We had to shove it into the bank to get past."

"We ran out of gas, Mr. Myers," Tamura explains. "I'm sorry to have held you up."

"Sure, no problem. I've come to help you out, Mrs. Baker. I'll give you twenty dollars for everything in the house, and thirty for the truck. You won't do better anywhere."

"I don't think so, Mr. Myers, we are not about to sell anything."

"It's cash, Mrs. Baker, and I'm betting you could do with cash. In any case, none of it's any use to you now. Who knows if you'll ever get back?"

"I can't tell you that, Mr. Myers, I don't even know where we are going. I do know, though, that I'm not selling."

"Well, that's your choice, of course—not a good one, but yours. At least let me take that old truck off your hands. Left there, it'll just rust up, and you ain't getting gas around here anytime soon."

"As I said, Mr. Myers, we aren't selling anything."

"More fool you, then, Mrs. Baker. Let me know if you change your mind." He cracks a mean, broken-toothed smile and swaggers back to his truck. "It'll all get stolen, you know. You can bet on it."

"Only by thieves, Mr. Myers, only by no-good thieves." A small muscle tightens in Tamura's forehead; she keeps her shoulders straight. It seems important not to cry in front of Tom Myers.

Satomi puts her arm around Tamura's thin shoulders and hugs her. She has never loved her mother more.

"Your father always said that Tom Myers was so greedy that he would eat the world if he could."

It occurs to Satomi that it is a wonderful truth that, no matter who has the upper hand, people like Tom Myers will always make a poor showing against people like her mother.

The day arrives relentlessly as any other. A while before dawn there's a spattering of rain, then in the rising sun a rainbow arcs over the house.

"I used to think that was a blessing, a time for spells," Tamura says. "What a foolish woman I am."

It seems that hardly any time has elapsed in the space between Mr. Stedall bringing the leaflet and this morning. The four days have merged into one so that Satomi hardly knows what they have done with the time in between. Shouldn't they have already closed the shutters, locked the sheds, checked the rattraps? They need more time, much more time.

In an act more of possession than of habit, Tamura makes her bed, tucking in the sheets tightly, smoothing the cover.

"Check that you have left your room tidy," she calls along the hall in a thin, breaking-up voice.

"What's the point? Who is there to care?"

"Only us, I suppose. Still, we have our pride."

To please Tamura Satomi plumps her pillow, straightens the sheets, and leaves it at that. The bed looks bare now without the lively colors of her Indian blanket, which is rolled around Aaron's tools in the duffel bag. She has put her seashell mirror, along with her schoolbooks, Mr. Beck's gift of *Little Women*, and the necklace that Lily made her from melon seeds, in an apple box under the bed, and shoved it tight to the wall. It has made her feel better, as though she will be coming back.

"These are going for sure," she insists, bunching up the flour-sack smocks into a ball and throwing them into the trash. A chalky powder rises up and catches at the back of her throat. The smell is worse than mothballs, worse than anything. There are some things she won't miss.

Tamura doesn't like the waste of it. "Don't get rid of too much," she advises. "Once they discover you are only half Japanese, you may be allowed to come home."

"Remember what they said, Mama?"

"No, there's too much going on to remember everything."

"They said one drop of Japanese blood justifies profiling—one drop, Mama!"

"My drop," Tamura says quietly.

"Father would have said the best drop, and I agree with him. In any case, it doesn't matter what they say, I don't care if it's one drop or a hundred, I'll never leave you."

To save Tamura from seeing it, she had thrown out the last copy of the *Los Angeles Times*. It had been jubilant at the announcement of the detention order, referring to the Japanese community as the enemy within and stating that "*a viper is nonetheless a viper wherever the egg is hatched.*"

They attempt to make the most of their last breakfast in the house. Who knows when they will eat again? An omelet for Tamura, and two eggs sunny-side up for Satomi. Neither of them have much of an appetite, though.

"Can you believe it, Mama, five eggs this morning?"

"A farewell gift." Tamura manages a smile.

She had gone that morning barefoot on the damp earth to the chicken coop and collected the warm eggs from under her sitting hens.

"How lovely," she told them. "Your eggs are beautiful."

She would have lain down with her cackling chickens if she could. Buried herself in their warm straw, let the world go its brutal way.

Taking a quarter sack of grain that the rats had been at, she made a trail of it halfway up to the Kaplans' place.

"Shush, go." She set them on it. "I won't be stealing your eggs anymore."

"They'll follow it soon enough," she tells Satomi. "Elena might as well have the benefit of them. The cats will have to see to themselves. It is unkind, but what can we do?"

"Cats are survivors, Mama. They will adopt a new family, I'm sure."

"Are we survivors, do you think, Satomi?"

Mindful that her answer might collapse what is left of Tamura's optimism, she answers, "You bet we are."

Knowing it is a drink Tamura always turns to in difficult times, she makes a pot of her mother's green tea and pours them both a cup. As they are sipping it, two dark-suited men walk into the house without knocking. They leave the front door swinging open so that the breeze bangs the back one shut.

"Federal investigators, Mrs. Baker," the bald one says.

"Aren't you supposed to knock, or show a badge or something?" Satomi asks, shaken.

"It's just an inspection, nothing to worry about. Everything legal and aboveboard."

The men set about a search, emptying drawers onto the floor, rifling through the closets, pulling the linen off the made beds to look under the mattresses.

"What's this?" the unsympathetic one says, holding out the pathetic little box Satomi had thought to squirrel away.

"It's trash, have it if you want it," she says, hot with shame.

"If you tell us what you are looking for, perhaps we can find it for you," Tamura says from the floor, where she is picking up the debris from the drawers.

"Any guns in the place, ma'am?"

"One." She nods toward where Aaron's rifle is propped in the corner.

"Hunting man, was he, your husband?"

"Just to keep the crows off the crops, the fox from the hens."

"It's confiscated for the duration."

Tamura watches him pick up the gun, run his hand slowly along the gleaming barrel of it admiringly. It's Aaron's gun and it hurts her to see the man handle it.

"We need to see the farm accounts and the will," he says, laying the gun on the table. Guess your husband left a will?"

"He didn't, he wasn't expecting to die so young, you see," Tamura says in the same voice she had used to refuse Tom Myers the truck.

"Where do you keep your knives, Mrs. Baker?"

She points to a drawer set in the kitchen table, and the bald one, who has been staring at Satomi, opens it and takes out a long carving knife.

"Show me where you keep seed, sacks of feed, and the like, honey." He guides Satomi toward the door.

"Don't push." Satomi shakes him off.

In the barn, with the knife he splits open every sack in the place. Fertilizer and chicken feed spill across the floor.

"Nope, nothing in them. I didn't think there would be, but you never know, girlie, you never know."

"I guess you're gonna sweep up all this mess." Satomi raises her eyebrows and tucks a strand of hair behind her ear.

"Not me, honey, not my job. You got a pitchfork in here?"

He takes Aaron's long-handled pitchfork from the rack, beckoning her to follow him outside.

"Best to be thorough," he says, raking through the compost heap, disturbing the worms.

Back in the house, she stands by the chair that Tamura has slumped in.

"It's okay, Mama," she says in an effort to comfort. "Everything will be fine."

"Sorry, Mrs. Baker, but we'll have to confiscate the radio and these binoculars. You'll get them back after the war, though. Everything done within the law eh?"

"So you keep saying," Satomi says.

"She's pretty, the girl, real pretty, ain't she?" the bald one announces to the room in general. "Don't you worry none, honey. Nothing to worry about, you're in America."

"Yeah, we're in America, all right," Satomi agrees.

"No need to be snappy, girlie. It wasn't us who bombed Japan, now, was it?"

"Can we go now?" she asks. "You don't need us here for this, do you?"

The fear has brought on a need to pee, but nothing would induce her to ask the men if she might use her own bathroom.

At the road's edge they turn to look back at the house and see the one who didn't smile pinning a FOR RENT sign on their door. A last check of the mailbox reveals an unsigned note written in pencil on the back of a feed label. *Good Luck.*

For a brief moment Satomi imagines it came from Lily and instantly feels foolish. Of course it isn't from Lily. How could she have thought it even for a second? Lily has let her go for good. Most likely Lily has a new rule to add to her list by now. No such thing as an American Jap.

"It's from Elena," Tamura says. "I guess she didn't want to sign it in case of trouble. They only tenant the berry farm. It's not a good time to take sides, is it?"

As though she is going somewhere nice, Tamura has dressed in her finest. She has chosen her blue-flowered dress to impress, a little felt pillbox of a hat to comfort. She slips the feed label into her mock-leather handbag, snapping the clasp shut with a sigh.

"There are still good people in the world, Satomi," she says. "Good people like Elena."

Every so often along the road Tamura has to stop and put the heavy suitcase down. Each time she does, something holds Satomi there long after Tamura has caught her breath. It is as though she has never seen the road before, never noticed the sweet scent of the pine trees, the little pockets of cattails, or the wild allium shoots springing up everywhere. She wonders briefly if there will be pine trees where they are going. She squats to pee behind some brambles and it occurs to her that like a dog she is marking her territory.

"Give me your case, Mother. I can carry both."

Like Tamura, she is wearing her best too. Her white for-Sundays-only dress, and over it a wool plaid jacket that had been Tamura's. Her shoes, a present for her fifteenth birthday, have inch-high heels that slim her calves and lend her the stance of a young woman. Tamura looks short beside her. She picks up Tamura's case, anxious not to show her mother how scared she is. Along with the farm, along with Lily and Artie, along with everything, she is leaving her childhood behind her.

Tamura is not yet recovered from her Christmas flu, which seems to have permanently stolen her appetite. She is pale still, and too thin. Her once-black hair has strands of gray showing through; her lips, too, have lost color. Despite her mother's rallying moments, Satomi knows that Tamura is crushed, and she fears for her sanity. She has read of such things, of women going mad with grief.

They hadn't been expecting anything good—how could it have been anything good?—but they aren't prepared for what meets them at the relocation point.

"Why are there soldiers with guns?" Tamura says nervously, not really expecting an answer, but needing to give voice to her fear.

The bus station is heaving with Japanese families, dressed, like them, in their best. Old men sit on their suitcases, looking bewildered. A huddle of elderly women surround the Buddhist priest, who is clutching his beads to his chest. He looks ancient and tired, too confused himself to be of any help to them. Children are playing in the dust at their mother's feet; they are subdued, silent in their play, as if they know instinctively that it's not a time to be troublesome. A lost child pulls at the hem of Satomi's dress. The little girl has a label big as her hand pinned to her coat, with a number scrawled in black ink across it.

"Where's your mother?" Satomi asks her in Japanese, smiling so that the girl won't be afraid.

The child starts to wail, twisting the fabric of Satomi's dress in her tiny hand, stamping her feet in the dust.

Dropping the case and bag to the ground, Satomi picks her up, cradling her in the crook of her arm. With her free hand she clasps Tamura's trembling one.

"It's all right, Mama, we're together, it's going to be all right."

The desire to take to her heels has never been stronger in her. She wants to run as fast as she has ever run—run to the deep woods, where the sweet whispering of the ghost pines will comfort her, lead her back to what she knows.

A frantic mother comes to claim the lost child, relief and fury mixed in equal measure on her face. Tamura thinks she recognizes her but can't remember from where. She says a polite hello. The woman hurries off without a word.

"I am glad that you are not a baby anymore," Tamura says softly, looking around her with horror. "How are these mothers to care for their babies without homes?"

Neither of them mentions it to the other, but they realize at about the same time that fear has a scent, a faint odor that conjures up sweat and piss and stagnant water.

"Join that line over there," a civilian with an armband directs them.

"No talking," orders a soldier young enough to be Tamura's son.

"Why do they have guns?" Tamura repeats, wanting an answer now.

"In case we try to escape, I guess."

A man in a civilian suit pulls them from the line and tells them to stand by the back of an open Army truck.

"Who are you? What is your family name?" he barks.

"Our family name is Baker," Satomi barks back.

"Point out your family."

"It is just the two of us, we are mother and daughter," Tamura says.

"You don't look Japanese." He looks at Satomi, his tone a touch less harsh than before.

"Maybe not, but I am Japanese. Japanese enough for this place, anyway."

"Where is your father?"

"He's dead." She stares him down. "He died in the attack at Pearl Harbor."

He pauses for a bit as though trying to work it out, but doesn't comment.

"Put your luggage up here on the tailgate. Open it up."

There is an air of refined brutality about him, something chilling in his pale eyes. Without knowing him, they can tell he is enjoying himself.

"What's all this stuff?" he protests, pulling out one of Aaron's tools from the Indian blanket, scattering his shirts around. "If it is just the two of you, why have you brought a man's things?"

He doesn't seem like the sort of person who would understand that Tamura needed to "breathe my husband in," so Satomi doesn't attempt an explanation.

He finds the rice, and a mean grin spreads across his face as he throws it into the back of the truck. The sack splits open and a shower of grains patter onto the metal floor of the tailgate. Tamura's eyes fill with tears; her hand flutters to her neck.

"I'm sorry," she says. "We didn't know, you see—"

"You were told what to bring, it was clear enough." He sighs and rolls his eyes. "It's all confiscated. You people never learn. Go and join that line over there, you need to be fingerprinted and tagged."

By the time their bit of the line has reached the bus station's washrooms, the men have been separated off. While the woman watch, they are strip-searched for contraband, for razors, for knives, and for the liquor it is held would drive them to mutiny.

The once-familiar bus station, a place where Satomi and Lily had often sneaked cups of ice from the cooler by the soda machine, has become a place she hardly recognizes. There is no one behind the kiosk bar, no Coke or candy on sale, no familiar drivers to joke with them about being truant from school. A mile or so from home, and they have become *non-aliens* on American soil. They are beginning to understand what the previously inexplicable words mean. They are politicians' words, sneaky, self-serving, hiding-from-the-truth words.

Quite a little crowd of townsfolk have come to see them off, a few name-calling, but most looking sympathetic. Mr. Beck is there, his face clown-white, his eyes seeking out Satomi in the crowd. When he sees her, his lips tighten and his eyes narrow as though he is in pain. She half expects him to do something dramatic, pull her away from the others, perhaps, and declaim that he must have his pupil back. But he doesn't move a limb, not even to wipe his watering eyes, which he can't blame on an absent wind.

Satomi looks for Artie and finds instead his father, Mr. Goodwin, holding up a hand-painted sign that reads REMEMBER PEARL HARBOR. The slogan has become ubiquitous. It is on stamps, on luggage tags, on belt buckles and lapel pins, it's hard-baked into ice-cream cones. How could the Japanese-Americans, of all people, ever forget Pearl Harbor?

It is past four o'clock by the time they are given numbers and their internees' records, which, to add insult to injury, have printed on them the advice that they should *Keep Freedom in Your Future with U.S. Savings Bonds.*

Satomi scrunches hers and gives it to Tamura to put in her bag.

"Stupid people," she says, too loudly for Tamura's comfort. "How can we buy saving bonds when they have stolen our money?"

Hand in hand, they join the line for the buses. Tamura's hand is warm despite the fact that she is shivering. Everyone is speaking Japanese, too quickly for Satomi to make much sense of. She is used to the plainsong of Tamura's slower intonations. With a burning rage that she has no idea what to do with, she bites her lip and moves forward in the line.

Inside the crowded bus the women and children are packed together without their men. They set to wailing when they are told to pull the window blinds down.

"They are going to kill our husbands," one woman shouts. "They don't want us to see."

"Oh, my son," another wails pitifully.

The children, terrified at their mothers' fear, join in, so that the driver has to shout over the racket to be heard.

"Settle down. The men will join you at the other end. The blinds are to keep the sun off you. You don't want to fry, do you?"

Some are still weeping a half hour later when the convoy of buses pulls slowly out of the station to start on the three-hundred-mile journey to a place that everyone fears reaching.

In the gloom of the shuttered bus, Tamura occupies herself with helping an elderly blind lady to settle on the narrow seat in front of her. She places the woman's tiny suitcase under her feet to make her more comfortable.

"I am Mrs. Inada," the old woman says. "I am sorry if my cough disturbs you. My chest is bad, but I will do my best to be quiet."

"I am pleased to know you, Mrs. Inada. My name is Tamura Baker."

"Ah, Tamura is a good name. Do you have a husband, a son, left out there?"

"My daughter Satomi is here with me. My husband is dead."

"Ah, then we are both widows. But at least you have a child. Mine, like his father, is dead also."

"There's no shame, only sadness in it," Tamura says, propping the old woman's jacket behind her shoulders in place of a pillow, touching her hand lightly.

It is the first time Satomi has heard her mother confess Aaron's death out loud. That she said there's no shame in it is reassuring.

"You should try and sleep, Mrs. Inada. You will feel better after a sleep," Tamura says.

The old woman grabs her arm. "You won't forget I'm here?"

"No, I will look out for you."

Satomi releases her window blind and the hazy afternoon sun pools into her lap. She watches the familiar landscape slip slowly away, the pea and strawberry fields, and the sign that reads CROMER'S UNBEATABLE PEAS.

Pressed up against the dusty window, she says a silent goodbye to the cemetery and to the rusty water tower where she had often sought shade. She says goodbye to the clump of self-set blueberries at the edge of the swimming hole, where she and Artie had dipped into the cool water on long careless summer days; days that were full of heat and desire and ignorance. She says goodbye to everything that feels familiar and suddenly unbearably loved.

TEMPORARY ACCOMMODATION

J UMPING THE STEPS of the bus in one go, Satomi turns at the bottom to help Mrs. Inada down.

"My case," the old woman cries. "I've left my case."

"I have it," Tamura assures her. "I am right behind you."

There is joy at being reunited with the men; husbands console wives, and mothers hug sons. Everyone, though, is dismayed at the sight of the long-abandoned racetrack, at the reek of decay, and at the cold officialdom that meets them at their destination. How are they expected to live in such a desolate place?

"It's horrible, nothing but a freezing half stable. How can this place be meant for humans?" Satomi gazes around in disbelief.

A single bulb hangs from the ceiling of their allotted stall, casting a dismal low-watt glimmer. Two Army cots stand against the wall, a thin blanket folded neatly at the end of each, nothing else. No furniture, no means of cooking.

They are told to line up to be issued canvas bags and a measure of straw to make their mattresses.

"I will collect ours, Mother, and Mrs. Inada's."

As the daylight fades to dark, Tamura guides Mrs. Inada into the stall with her.

"You must stay with us," she says. "We will look after you."

She is full of pity for the old blind woman, and everyone has to share. Better her than a total stranger.

An hour or so later, Satomi returns with the make-do mattresses. She has seen unimaginable things in the lines to collect the narrow sacks, grown men crying, women staring as though in a trance, adults obeying orders like children.

Mrs. Inada perches uncomfortably on the iron rim of her cot while Satomi arranges the mattress for her. Through the thin walls an old man's complaints come to them in Japanese, his voice shaking with rage. They guess it is his daughter they can hear attempting to quiet him in English.

"America makes much of freedom," he shouts scornfully. "But it has never truly understood what freedom means. They will not have it that it includes the right to be different."

"It's best not to be political, Doctor," a male voice calls from a neighboring stall. "We are in enough trouble as it is."

"Let him speak, it's only the truth," Satomi shouts, and Tamura *tsks* and puts a finger to her lips.

Satomi wonders if the old man is a medical doctor. It would be a relief to her if he was; Tamura does not look well, her eyes are dark-rimmed and sunken, and there is something febrile in her color. She hasn't taken even the smallest bite of the bread they were given as they left the bus.

"Take just a little, just a taste, Mama," she coaxes, attempting to keep her eyes from the walls that have been so hastily painted that bits of straw and spiders on their run to freedom have been caught up in the wash. What looks to be a mouse tail coils in a ball of fluff in the corner of the room; the floor is beaded with mouse droppings and splatters of whitewash.

With her back to Tamura, Satomi makes a fist of her hand and pushes it hard into her mouth to stop herself from moaning. Her knuckles bruise under the pressure of her teeth, a smear of blood salts her tongue.

It smells as though something has died in the hovel, something bigger than a mouse—a rat, perhaps. She must hold on to herself, try not to be afraid; she has Tamura to think of, after all. But for the moment, at least, Tamura seems to be doing better than her. She is talking softly to Mrs. Inada, covering her tenderly with the Army blanket.

"You will be fine, Mrs. Inada," she says kindly. "You can sit in the sun tomorrow. Everything feels better in the sun."

Satomi thinks that Mrs. Inada is lucky to be blind. She can't see the grim hovel, be disgusted by its filth.

"We should lay head to foot, Mama." She eyes the narrow cot. "It will work better that way."

They take off their shoes and lay down in their clothes. Satomi covers them with her Indian blanket that still has the scent of home on it. She watches Tamura drift into sleep. How has this horrible thing happened to them? This is America, they are Americans.

Unable in her exhaustion to sleep, she lies listening to the noises of the camp, to Mrs. Inada's crusty cough, to the calls of strangers, and to the crying of babies. Misery moves in her, solid and heavy as a brick.

That night, as in the nights that follow, they wake cold from their troubled dreams to a mottled light sieving through the perforated wood of their stable. Tamura's dreams return her to the burning ones she suffered in the month after Aaron's death. They find her falling, pitching into a murky sea, black flames consuming her. Satomi's are of running on hard ground while being pursued by some dark predator.

Tired and defeated, they stand around during the days trying to find a way to be, which seems impossible without even the simplest of utensils, not even a stove to make coffee, a chair to sit on. There is no housework to do, no land to work, only lines to join: lines for meals, for latrines, for showers.

"You could spend your whole day just lining up for things," Tamura says. "Thank God your father is not here. He was a stranger to patience."

"I'm going to move you up to the front, Mother," Satomi says on their third day waiting in line for their turn in the bad-smelling latrines. "It's only fair. You are too ill to stand for hours on end."

But Tamura won't hear of it. She says there are those who are worse off than her, and claims that she is feeling a little better every day.

Their neighbor in the next stall, Dr. Chiba—not a medical doc-tor after all, but a geologist with a political turn of mind—has taken to spending time with Satomi. He likes that she is as angry as him.

"We must learn a new language now, it seems," he snorts. "'mess hall,' 'barrack,' 'issue,' 'latrine.'"

"Don't forget 'halt,' Doctor," Satomi adds.

They are told that they will be moving on. This place that even the guards seem ashamed of is only temporary.

"Where you are going will be better," they say. "Of a much higher standard."

In a welcome turn of events, Tamura, in caring for Mrs. Inada, has recovered the mother in herself. She fusses around the old woman, collecting her food from the mess hall so that she won't have to stand in line, washing her gently, brushing her hair, and spoon-feeding her the unpleasant soup that tastes of stale potatoes.

"How can we complain at our situation, Satomi? This old mother is blind, her husband and her only child are dead. She is ill—tuberculosis, I think. We at least have our health."

"Mrs. Inada is lucky to have you," Satomi says, feeling sorry for herself. "You are like a mother to her."

"I am sorry to have neglected you, Satomi," Tamura apolo-gizes. "But I have found myself again, so you are not to worry about me. I will take care of you now."

"We will take care of each other, Mama."

Four weeks in, and things are going downhill fast for Mrs. Inada.

"It's worse than bad," Tamura tells Satomi on their walk to the mess hall. "She needs more than I can give her in this dirty place."

Her efforts, she knows, are merely a plaster on the deep wound of the old woman's disease. Mrs. Inada needs stronger medicine than kindness and thin soup.

"The old lady is very ill," she reports to the most sympathetic of the guards. "She coughs blood and cannot get up from her mattress. You must get her to a hospital or she will die."

And they do, taking Mrs. Inada off on a stretcher, telling Tamura not to worry. "She'll be taken good care of, nursed in an Ameri-can hospital," they say, as though there were another, less desir-able, kind.

"Her home is lost to her forever now," Tamura says, thinking Mrs. Inada close to death. "I wish that I could have done more for her."

"You did your best. It was more than anyone else did for her, Mama."

The few days that they had expected to be here roll through the weeks into the summer months. New inmates arrive daily, bewildered, unbelieving. People begin to get ill, diarrhea, vomit-ing, and a strange, never-before-seen rash.

"It's most likely the germs from the animal feces we smell about the place," Dr. Chiba hazards. "Couldn't be bothered to disinfect, I suppose. We are only Japanese, after all."

Tamura thinks it might be scabies. She saw an outbreak of it once among the sugarcane cutters in Hawaii.

"It's a disease of poor sanitation," she says. "We must keep our-selves clean, no matter how long we have to stand in line for the showers."

Among those without the rash, Satomi hardly has the space to feel sympathy. Her emotions are personal, her distress reserved for her own and Tamura's condition. Ashamed of their situation as she is, she feels herself an alien among the Japanese. Her mother may be Japanese, but these people are not her people. There are moments when she is all infant again, all gooseflesh fear, so that if she could find a place to be alone she would howl to the moon. There are other times, though, when her anger consumes her so that she shouts her feelings to whoever will listen, usually Dr. Chiba.

A couple of the men, brought low by their wives' longing for home, had challenged the guards, insisting on being set free. It comes as a shock to everyone when they are instantly put into solitary confinement until their cases can come to court.

Some consider making a break for it, but there is no way to get past the armed guards or over the barbed-wire fences. No way to make a run for home without risking life.

"They can call it what they like. They can call it impoundment, or enclosure, they can call it relocation as if it was our choice, but it is what it is," Satomi rages. "However they try to clean it up with crafty words, we are prisoners."

"Shush, Satomi," Tamura advises. "It's your rages that put peo-ple off you, not your white blood, as you would have it. We have hope, at least. The next place will be better, I'm sure."

"I'm not so sure. I wouldn't put it past them to herd us in even tighter, to build the fences even higher."

"I wasn't talking of fences. I was thinking that perhaps it will be warmer and maybe we will have more space. I would like it to have trees."

Dr. Chiba tells them that he has heard of some Japanese who refused to attend what is now being called with black humor "the roundup."

"They left the coast as soon as the notices to quit their homes arrived," he says. "They headed to the interior towns to seek work."

"Good for them," Satomi says.

"Yes, but it didn't work out. They were turned back by local peace officers, or herded out of town by armed posses."

"We might as well live in the Wild West, Doctor."

"I agree. It makes you feel for the Indians, doesn't it?"

"You spend too much time with that old man," Tamura says. "He is fixed in the past, you can't expect him to be optimistic."

"I like the doctor's company. No matter what they do to us, his spirit will never be broken. He is old, but he is not weak."

When the evacuation notices are finally posted around the camp, Satomi reads them with mixed feelings. She wants to go but resents being told where she must live. And then there is the unspoken fear shared by all the inmates since the shooting-dead of the old man who in his dotage walked beyond the barbed wire and failed to halt at the guards' command. Perhaps they are simply being rounded up to be shot.

"We are being sent to Manzanar, Mama. Wherever that is."

"I like the name, Satomi. It has a pleasant sound to it."

"It's Spanish for orchard," Dr. Chiba tells them. "It's mountain country, the Sierra Nevada."

"How lovely," Tamura says with a sigh, flashing Satomi a smile.

Having discovered in herself the ability not to think too much of home and all she has lost, Tamura departs the temporary camp with her heart lifted. Surely nothing could be worse than the terrible place they are leaving. Perhaps in this Manzanar they will have finer lodgings, a place to make tea, a table to sit around.

They might be free of the disgusting black beetles that thrive in their present quarters. "Stinky bugs," the children call them, making a game of stamping on them, their faces gleeful at the gratifying crunch, at the prize of the occasional ooze of eggs that squirm from the broken bodies like toothpaste from the tube.

Dr. Chiba and his stoic daughter are being sent to the Tule Lake camp, which he thinks might be of more geological interest than their present confinement.

"Your daughter is a girl with backbone, Mrs. Baker," he tells Tamura as they part. "You should be proud of her. She is of this century, not cast in the old mold."

"She came wrapped in her father's caul, Dr. Chiba. I cannot claim credit."

"Half her blood is yours, Mrs. Baker."

"Yes, more than one drop."

The old man spits on the ground. "Ah, yes, the one-drop profile. How they love that old southern standby."

"Don't tell me to make the best of it," Satomi says when Tamura advises as much. "If we make the best of it, we accept it. I will never accept it."

"Oh, Satomi, you are under the same sky as at home wherever you go. It is the same sun that sets and rises wherever you are."

MANZANAR

THE MAN-MADE GEOGRAPHY of Manzanar seems at first to place it firmly among the more ugly sights on earth. Tamura, reaching for optimism, points out to Satomi the beauty of the mountains in the distance, the sound of the water from the stream that margins the perimeter of the camp.

"Keep looking to the east," she says. "It is beautiful in the distance."

But even as she encourages Satomi, her own heart drops at the sight of the dusty acreage, at the ranks of squalid quarters, narrow and dark as coffins. Her disappointment is almost unbearable.

"We've been sent to hell!" Satomi exclaims. "Some orchard, huh?"

As they stand getting their bearings, the children of the camp are already at their favorite play.

"Kill the Nazis."

"Kill the Japs."

Their tinny shrieks shred what's left of Satomi's courage. How can they play in this desperate place, how can they be happy? All she wants to do is sleep a dreamless sleep until the devil has had his day, until he has grown tired of tormenting them.

"Damn it, we can't live here." she drops Tamura's case to the ground and covers her face with her hands. They are both shivering with the cold, their thin jackets little protection against the glacial mountain air.

"We have no choice," Tamura says. She picks up her case and heads toward the lines to be allocated a barrack number.

Situated between Independence and Lone Pine in Inyo County, Manzanar's ground had been a fruit orchard once, pretty then, perhaps, but rutty now, dirty-looking, with clumps of sagebrush hogging the land. A few gnarled half-dead pear trees are dotted about, black as witches' hats, their branches twisted as though in torture.

"Not the sort of trees you dreamed of, Mama."

It's almost autumn in Angelina, but winter comes early and hard in mountain country. The day is colder than any they have ever experienced, the sky dark, almost black. Satomi looks around for a splash of color in the camp but finds none.

"I'm sorry, my girl," Tamura says softly, as though she is to blame for their troubles. "You don't deserve this."

"You less than me, Mama."

Retreating to the horizon, the airless rows of barracks stretch beyond their vision. They have been constructed from planks harvested from old stables in such haste that no pride could be taken in the work. Wasted with age, the wood has splintered where it has been nailed unevenly to the studs that are already working themselves free. All sixteen of the barracks in the Bakers' allotted row are green with mold and warped where the tarpaper has rotted and peeled away.

"At least we have a stove," Tamura falters, almost in tears.

"But I don't see any wood, Mama."

"The beds are better here." Tamura pokes the hard Army cotton mattress. "They won't be so prickly."

At the end of each barracks block, three low buildings hunker down. The first, a laundry room, echoes with the dismal sound of dripping water. There are four deep sinks and some worn scrub boards. Cockroaches cling to the damp walls in the twilight gloom. The second building houses the foul-smelling latrines, where, with only an inch or two of space between the cracked pans, Manzanar's inmates must squat cheek by jowl with their neighbors, looking straight ahead so as not to offend. Only the last stall has a partition, a partition but no door, giving rise to the view that the intention was there but foiled, they suppose, by a dearth of wood.

"That will be the worst one to have, I should think," Tamura says as they inspect the facilities.

"Why, Mother? It looks like the best to me."

"Well, I imagine that people will check it first to see if it is empty. Whoever sits on that throne will be facing a receiving line."

The smell from the latrines makes Satomi wretch. She doesn't believe Tamura when she says they will get used to it. She never wants to get used to it.

Completing the squalid triad, a bleak shower house with a rough cement floor, its walls gloopy with soap scum, seems to Satomi to have been designed more for animals than for humans.

It isn't only the old who look at those buildings with horror. The young too feel the shame of having to share with the opposite sex, of being thought so little of. Of all that is hateful at Manzanar, the latrines are the things that seem to Satomi to diminish humanity the most. Never mind that fate has chosen them to be unlucky, or that they have lost their names and become government numbers: those terrible latrines speak more potently of their lost future as Americans than any of the other humiliations that are heaped on them.

Tamura and Satomi's barrack, indistinguishable from their

neighbors,' is placed two from the end of their row. The door doesn't fit, so that it has to be kicked shut, and there is a crack in the back wall as wide as a man's arm.

"Look, I can put my fist through this. Your chicken coop was a palace compared to this place, Mama."

"Oh, my sweet chickens," Tamura says in a shaky voice.

With her head up, glaring at the guards, Satomi goes about the camp collecting cardboard from the empty food boxes behind the mess halls. She ducks under the barracks, gathering up splinters of wood and rusting nails from the rubbish-strewn ground.

A guard passing her turns as she goes by and gives a low appreciative whistle. She stifles the urge to catch up with him, to spit in his face. She wants him to challenge her, to tell her collecting wood is against the rules. She wants a reason to kick his shins, to scream at him. She wants to scream herself hoarse, have a showdown.

"You will always have that problem," Tamura says pragmatically when Satomi tells her about the guard. "It's about men, nothing to do with being in Manzanar."

Stuffing the hole as tight as she can, Satomi spends hours compressing the cardboard, fixing the wood in a rough patchwork to the thin wall with bent and rusty nails, a rock for a hammer.

Tamura can't help thinking how useful Aaron's tools would be here. It had hurt to leave them with the pale-eyed man at the bus station. Perhaps he is using them himself; Aaron's big pliers, his pack of assorted screwdrivers, the little tool that she has forgotten the name of that he said he wouldn't want to be without, it was so useful.

"You have made a good job of it," she says, admiring Satomi's work. "Nothing will get through that."

But when their first dust storm comes, dirt and grit explode

through the wall, sending the cardboard flying, crumpling the
wood as though it is no more than paper. The force of the storm
shocks them. It's like nothing Angelina had ever thrown at them.

"Like the winds of Neptune," Tamura says in amazement.
They gasp and draw in their breath, laughing with relief when it's
over.

"Oh, Mama." Satomi hugs Tamura. "You are the bravest person I know," and suddenly she is crying along with the laughter.

America is punishing them, the weather is punishing them.
There is no forgiveness here, nothing gentle, only Tamura to hold
on to.

She comes to know that flattened-out tin cans would have
worked better on the hole. They are patched on most of the barracks, tacked around with nails that have bent in the gales but
somehow managed to hold on.

"I expect your father would have known that," Tamura says.

The same unspoken rules of the inmates that had applied in the
relocation center apply in Manzanar. Manners are all, and everyone must feign deafness, learn to look the other way, attempt
politeness.

"Best not to comment on our neighbors' conversations,"
Tamura advises. "Not to be too loud in our own."

The partition walls are so thin that it is impossible to have a
private conversation without being overheard. The sounds and
smells that the human body is subject to come rudely through
their walls, sighs and groans, spitting and farting.

But whatever the difficulties, the semblance of privacy must be
maintained or neighbor could not look neighbor in the face. The
children of the camp are beaten if they are caught spying through
the knotholes of the barrack walls. They can't stop, though, as all the
barracks look the same to them. It's easy to get lost, to think that
they will never find their way home.

"I was looking for my mother," they wail when caught out.

"It would have been better to have arrived in summer," Tamura says, stating the obvious as she attempts to light a few sticks of wood in their stove. "It takes time to become accustomed to the mountain weather."

They are not prepared for the icy air, for the ground set hard as a hammer. The cold thickens the blood, makes movement sluggish. Even the birds hardly sing in Manzanar. They perch rather than fly, in case their wings should freeze and they should fall frozen to the ground.

"We don't have the clothes for it," Satomi despairs. "You must use my blanket as a shawl, Mama. Stay inside, your cough is getting worse."

As the relentless storms rock them, a leftover hoard of Navy World War I peacoats arrive and are issued to every household.

"One for everyone," they are told. "You see, America cares for you, we have your interest at heart."

The coats are large, all one size. They are too big for the children, and on the women they trail to the floor and hang over their hands. Made of felt, they sop up the rain, making them too heavy to wear on wet days. It takes a week to dry them out, and the scent of mold never leaves them.

"They're better used as blankets, I suppose," Tamura says. "They're so heavy in the wearing they make my shoulders ache anyway."

If they didn't know it already, Manzanar during their first winter confirms to them that nature is boss. The wind howls at them, sucking its breath in, shrieking it out furiously, a mad creature intent on blowing them to kingdom come. It slams at the electricity poles so that the light goes and they have to take to their beds as soon as darkness falls.

It's bad enough faced straight-on, but they prefer it that way, even when it blows hard enough to move stones as if they are nothing but bits of cinder. When it charges them from behind, the barracks shake and tilt alarmingly.

"It's about to go," is the shout, setting neighbors to help knock in the loose nails, hammer the wood back together. On such occasions something of the atmosphere of a barn-build overtakes the detainees, a barn-build where your fingers freeze and your eyes burn in the whipping wind. A barn-build with no picnic to look forward to.

Satomi, bundled up in her peacoat, which flaps unpleasantly against her calves, wanders the camp, not knowing what to do with herself. People hardly acknowledge her, they are shy to speak to the tall, angry-looking white girl. They have heard that her father died at Pearl Harbor, an American hero, it's said. So why is she incarcerated here with them? Surely she must hate the very look of them, her father's murderers. But if that's the case, then what of her mother, the pretty Mrs. Baker, as Japanese as any of them?

"There's bound to be trouble when you marry out of your race," they say. "Bound to be complications."

On her walks around the camp she lingers by the groups of old Issei men, those born in Japan, who cluster together rubbing their hands and stamping their feet against the cold. They hardly know how to be either, or what to do with their days. They would like to huddle inside but, unable to tolerate the beaten look of their wives, the sense of loss in their families, they prefer to face the deathly cold. Their breath freezes on the air as they crowd around the fires they light in discarded tin cans. They speak of the war in hushed tones, wonder how it's going, how Japan is faring. Perhaps they never should have left the old country, never should have sired American children. Old loyalties stir in them, they are children of the Emperor, after all. They play *go*, an ancient game with mysterious rules involving black and white stones. The game attracts a rapt audience of their peers, who squat on the ground watching the stones intently. One old man sketches them as they play, with a piece of charcoal on cardboard, making swift flowing strokes, stopping every so often to blow some heat into his bony fingers. Satomi likes his work, thinks him a genius of the understated.

The veins on the back of the old men's hands rise thick, dark as bark, to join the burn marks they suffer from getting too close to the red-hot cans.

At first she had watched the matches and, like the old men, she had stood too close to the braziers and burned her hands. But after a while she lost interest. The game moves too slowly to hold her attention for long, and something about the players' patience seems too accepting to her. The fight has gone out of the old men. It's worrying.

"Playing games as though everything is normal," she says to Tamura. "And they hardly seem to notice the cold even though their lips are blue."

"They notice it, all right, Satomi, but what else can they do to forget their shame? It will be better for them in summer. The air will be sweet, they won't need their fires. Just think of it, we will be able to leave our door open, to breathe outside without burning our lungs."

"Some of them might die of the cold before then."

"Perhaps that is what they hope for."

DOG DAYS

Summer, when it comes, is not without its own trials. Rains flood the latrines, so that excrement runs down the alley and bubbles up beneath the barracks, where it settles in thick slimy pools. Drawn to the toxic smell, flies swarm, causing the residents in the Bakers' row of barracks to name their road "Sewer Alley."

The children make a game of the infestations, seeing how many flies they can collect. They stack them up in old gallon jugs and empty bottles, any container they can lay their hands on. One boy proudly claims to have collected two thousand of the dirty, dark-bodied things.

With the winter behind them, Sewer Alley is always crowded now with inmates who prefer to live their summer lives outside. Used now to Satomi's aloof manner, and charmed by Tamura, their neighbors greet them with bows and good-mornings.

Satomi talks sometimes with the girls of her own age in the alley, but she hasn't made a special friend of any of them, doesn't want to. Lily's fickleness has made her cautious. There's a boy named Ralph a couple of barracks away, whom she often talks with. Ralph's a freethinker with an irrepressible desire to right wrongs. She likes to listen to him, likes his knockout smile. She's more interested in his friend, though, her neighbor's son Haru, whom she can hardly look at, he's so dazzling, so bright.

Unlike her, Ralph and Haru have chosen to attend the new high school, which is being held in the open on the ground by the mess hall. Books have to be shared, pencils too, and sometimes it's just too hot to sit on the earth with the sun scalding your head till you feel as though it will split open like an overcooked squash.

"It's worth it just to learn, though," Ralph says.

Volunteers are hurrying to finish building the wood and tar-paper block intended to house the students, to keep them from the extremes of the Owens Valley seasons.

"It will be better once we are inside," Ralph says. "You should come, Satomi. Don't let them steal your education too."

"I'll think about it." She knows, though, that she won't. School holds no attraction for her. It would be like returning to childhood, and in the vein of her father she doesn't care to be told what to do.

She had thought Ralph to be like her at first, half and half, but he turned out to be a different sort of half-and-half altogether.

"I am like you," he told her. "Only I'm half Mexican, half Irish."

He doesn't even have the one required drop of Japanese blood to explain his presence in the camp. It had been his strong feelings of kinship and outrage that had brought him to, and keeps him, in Manzanar.

"I grew up in the Temple-Beaudry neighborhood in Los Angeles," he tells her. "We were a mixed bunch, Basques, Jews, Koreans, Negroes. It didn't matter to us, we liked who we liked."

When Ralph talks it's like being in the light, Satomi thinks. He's a special person, sixteen but a man already, not afraid to say what he thinks. He had been a high school student when the order for the Japanese to vacate their homes had come.

"They were my friends," he says. "They'd done nothing to deserve it. It was unfair and cruel. We were taught the Constitution at school and we were proud of it. Now it seems like it was all just words."

Ralph's mother is dead, and his father, thinking him to be at summer school, didn't miss him at first. It came as a shock to learn that he had joined the Japanese students, his fellows from Belmont High, as they had boarded the buses to Manzanar.

His sister wrote often after they discovered where he was, pleading with him to come home. Ralph, though, insisted that he wanted to stay with his buddies. Eventually his father gave him permission to remain in Manzanar.

"They must be proud of you, Ralph," Satomi had said when he'd first told her his story. He had given one of his smiles and shrugged.

Word of his act was hot news for a while in the camp. It's no wonder, Satomi thinks, that he is so popular, or that he has become a Manzanar celebrity.

"How wonderful that he should do this for us," it's said.

"Ralph Lazo will be spoken of long after we are all dead."

Despite that it's summer, the dust storms are as promiscuous as ever. There are mornings when they wake in a shroud of grime covering them from head to toe.

"We will make this place ours," Tamura determines, doing her daily sweep. "If we care for it, we need not feel shame."

Satomi raises her eyes to heaven, wonders if her mother has gone quite mad.

Their neighbor to the left of them, Eriko Okihiro, Haru's mother, is of the same frame of mind as Tamura.

"My mother lives with us," she told Tamura with a wry smile at their first meeting. "I don't want her to feel ashamed of my housekeeping."

The Okihiros, all four of them, jostle for space in their barrack, which they have divided in two with a piece of sacking.

"We are two widows, a boy, and a girl," Eriko explained with pride. "We are used to better, of course."

Eriko, along with her old mother Naomi and her sulky daughter Yumi, sleep on one side of the sacking divide, her only son Haru, head of the household since his father's death, on the other.

Haru strides about the camp and the girls sneak sideways glances at him, blushing when he looks at them. Satomi is no exception, although she affects disinterest. He has to duck his head when going through doors, which embarrasses him and delights the girls. He is dark-skinned, dark-haired, too serious for his age.

"There's a bloom about him," Tamura says. "A pleasing sort of energy."

At seventeen years and one week old, Haru likes to remind people that he is in his eighteenth year.

"He's at that halfway stage," Eriko muses. "More man than boy, and proud, you know?"

It seems to Satomi that when she stands near Haru all she can hear is the sound of her blood rushing to her head, swishing around in her brain like weir water churning. It's mortifying. The first time he spoke to her it was as if he had stood on her heart, stopped its beating. She loses herself when she's close to him, finds it impossible to think straight. She can't stop the heat that rises in her face, the dreadful feeling that she is on the boil. The side effects of being near Haru feel at once horrible and delightful. She admires his reserve, which has nothing of humility in it. If she has a criticism at all, it is that there is little give in him.

She looks for failings in him like those she had seen in Artie but can find none. He is nothing like Artie. He isn't a show-off, for one thing, and somehow his bossiness is reassuring.

"You should listen to Ralph," he says to her. "School would do you good."

She puzzles over the fact that there is something familiar about him, as though in some unexplained way she already knows him. He is interested in her, that's for sure, but she senses his disapproval too, his irritation with her. He is always quick to criticize.

"You should work on those manners," he says. "It costs nothing to be polite."

It feels preachy to her, but it could be his way of flirting. He's hard to read.

The Okihiros came direct to Manzanar from Los Angeles. In their previous lives they had run a fabric shop in Little Tokyo, and there is something of the city in the way they talk, in their quick step. They seem to shine brighter than those that came from California's farmlands.

"You would have loved our cottons," Eriko tells Tamura. "We had striped and gingham—and silk too—well, special orders of silk—so beautiful—so . . ." Her voice trembles with the memory of it.

After a while she stops speaking of her old life. It is too painful to go on boasting about what you have lost, what you may never get back. And just thinking of the fabrics, their vibrant colors, the clean glazed crispness of them, tops up the hurt in her.

The Okihiros spend a lot of time sitting on the steps of their barrack, beside which they have made a miniature rock garden. Its elegant simplicity has inspired others to do the same, and now in Sewer Alley stone gardens are quite the thing. Such refinements, though, are not for the Sanos, who live on the other side of the Bakers—they think the effort a pointless exercise.

"Might as well put a dress on a monkey," Mr. Sano says.

Mr. Sano, a wizened little man, is in the habit of touching his wife in public, pulling her caveman-style into their barrack in the afternoons so that everyone knows what they are up to. Never mind their daughter-in-law, or their grandchildren, who are billeted with them.

Mrs. Sano finds it hard to look people in the eye in case she should meet with a disapproving stare. She feels too old to be the object of her husband's copious passion; besides, his behavior is not the Japanese way. But then, her husband has always taken his own path, lived in ignorance of others' sensitivities. There is nothing to be done about it.

"A monkey in a dress could be cute," Satomi says to Tamura, causing them a fit of the giggles, which turns for Tamura into a bout of coughing.

Despite that Tamura and Satomi are treated by their fellow inmates with a measure of reserve, Eriko is pleased to have them as neighbors. She has befriended them enthusiastically, thinking Tamura delightful, a kind and modest woman in need of a friend.

"She is shy, I know, but charming, don't you think, Mother? I liked her from the first."

"She's too thin," old Naomi says pragmatically. "Ill, I think."

All the Okihiros glow with health, notwithstanding the unappetizing diet at Manzanar: canned wieners and beans and watery corn that tastes only of sugar. The women agree, though, that it is getting better. Sometimes now there is miso, and even on occasions pickled vegetables.

Eriko's hair grows thick, her teeth are long and white, and her face has a rosy flush even when she isn't exerting herself. Her five-foot-three frame is built so squarely that she appears to have no waist at all. She is energetic for a woman of her weight, and strong too. She can pick Tamura up without effort.

"You're hardly an armful," she tells her.

In comparison to Eriko's bulk, Tamura's slight frame appears sweetly girlish.

"She's so pretty," Eriko remarks to her mother.

"Hmm," Naomi grunts, thinking that unless things improve with Tamura, her pallor will soon be a match for the mold that is inching its way up their walls.

"We are lucky to have Eriko and her family as neighbors," Tamura says. Some would have turned their back on us."

"Plenty did, Mama, some still do."

Those who came to Manzanar without family, the old and the bereaved, the paralyzed, even, have to bear the indignity of sharing with strangers. One poor woman, for reasons no one can understand, was separated from her husband and billeted with strangers. Now her husband shares with six men, and she is told that nothing can be done about it.

All of them, though, had resisted being housed with the Japanese woman and her half-caste daughter. Things are bad enough without the shame of that. Just by looking at the girl you could tell she'd be trouble.

Every time it seemed likely that one or the other of them were about to be paired with the Bakers, they had stepped aside and joined another line, leaving Tamura and Satomi standing on their own. The guards got the message eventually and didn't push it. You had to choose your battles.

"I'd share with you any day," one of them wisecracked to Satomi. "Just let me know when you get lonely, sugar."

"You've been lucky," Haru says. "Most likely you and Tamura would have had an old woman forced on you. You would have had nothing but complaints. And if it had been an old man you would have ended up doing everything for him. And just think of it, you have a room all to yourselves."

"I guess. Mother is a very private person, so she appreciates the space." She is thinking of Tamura's shame at her cough, her night cries.

"Yes, she is a fine lady," Haru says.

"She's a bit like you, Haru. She looks for the good in things."

"And you look for trouble where there is none. Anyway, I was thinking of asking your mother if she would let me use your room to study. Only when you are out, of course. My grandmother thinks that I can read and talk to her at the same time. I find myself going over the same paragraph again and again."

"Ask her. I guess she won't mind. I'm surprised you were allowed to bring books in, though."

"I only have a few, not enough for what I need. It bothered my mother more than the guards. She thought I should have used the space for more practical things. But if you think about it, books are more practical than dishes and bedding. Dishes and bedding can't promise a future, can't make you forget that you are not free."

"Would I like your books, Haru?"

"You? Well, maybe you would, I don't know. Did you enjoy reading at school? The classroom books, I mean."

"I guess I did."

"Well, it's good to read. We won't always be in this place. We should use the time here to make our future better, not let it slip through our hands like sand."

"Perhaps I'll borrow your books sometime. Okay?"

"Maybe. But are you sure you want to?"

"I do, I really do."

"You would have to be careful with them."

She can tell that he's unwilling, that he doesn't trust her with his precious books.

"It doesn't matter. It's fine with me if you don't want to share them." She can't keep the irritation from her voice. "I hear there's to be a library here soon, anyway. You're not the only one who wants to read, you know?"

"I know that." His voice is full of apology. Look, I've just finished *This Side of Paradise*, you can borrow it if you like.

"Oh, Fitzgerald, I've read it," she lies.

"Really! You've read the whole thing?"

He sounds just like Mr. Beck.

Taking her lead from Eriko, Tamura divides their barrack using the silk butterfly robe that Aaron had loved her to wear. She threads a stick through the arms, balancing each end on a rusty nail so that it hangs suspended, a pink quivering scarecrow.

"Oh, Tamura," Eriko enthuses. "It's beautiful, not real silk, of course, but beautiful just the same."

Tamura looks at the garment with disbelief—it is a design from ancient times, a piece of history that surely belonged to a different woman than the one she is now. What had induced her to pack such a thing? At the sight of its brilliance in dusty Manzanar, her thoughts turn to images of geishas, of obedience, of Aaron. Why had she allowed him to keep her in the last century? Why had she attempted to fix Satomi there with her?

"I would never wear such a thing here!" she exclaims to Satomi. "It would look ridiculous. I will never wear it again. You need some privacy, I can't think of a better use for it."

Fingering the robe, Satomi has to swallow hard to keep the tears at bay. Her saliva seems to have dried to sand. The silly, pretty thing is the very trinity of Aaron, Tamura, and her childhood self.

It isn't much privacy, a roughly hung gown that moves in the drafts as though alive, but she is grateful for it. She rests behind it stretched out on her iron cot, one of Haru's books in hand, imagining him doing the same on the other side of the thin divide between them. Her hand goes to the wall, where she holds it as though she can feel his warmth heating her palm. Sometimes late into the night she hears him turning the pages of his book, sighing.

Behind her pink screen she can deal discreetly with her monthly bleeds, while on the other side of it, Tamura, hawking up the muck from her lungs, indulges the idea of privacy too.

Tamura has quickly let go the expectations she had of Manzanar, and has settled to making the best of it. Satomi, though, along with half of the camp, is on alert, waiting. Waiting for news that their confinement has been a mistake, waiting to hear that the war has ended, waiting perhaps for something more terrible. Wherever people gather at Manzanar, hope and fear are the text of their chatter.

"Have you heard anything?"

"There seem to be more guards, don't you think?"

"Did I imagine a shot in the night?"

The slightest change in routine takes on meaning, unsettles everyone. And the rumors, like the dust storms, appear to arrive out of nowhere.

"We are all to be shot."

"I heard only the men."

"A guard told me we are to be shipped to Japan."

Being sent to Japan, for the Nisei generation, seems almost as bad as being shot. They are native-born Americans, after all, pumped with the notion of sadistic yellow bastards and murdering Japs. Why would they fare better in Japan? Japanese-Americans are a different breed than their ancestors. They are democrats, modern citizens, proud of the American way.

But some of the young men have begun to challenge this view. They call themselves the "Kibei" and welcome the idea of returning to Japan. It's their homeland, they tell each other, the land of their fathers, after all, they would not be imprisoned there. They go around in gangs, not listening to their elders, causing everyone problems. They challenge the guards by hanging around the fencing, and running through the alleys at night, calling out wildly to each other.

"They are nothing but trouble," Haru says. "They make things worse for everyone.

"At least they have spirit," Satomi argues. "You have to give them that."

"Ha, spirit, is that what you call it? Their spirit tars us all with the traitor's brush."

To help counteract their influence and show his loyalty to America, Haru has joined the American Citizens League. League members have asked to join the American forces. Haru, for one, can't wait to fight for his country, to go to war in its name.

But even his loyalty is challenged when a hundred and one orphans are rounded up and brought to Manzanar. The all-to-be-shot rumors gain momentum for a while. Why else would they imprison babies, what harm are they capable of?

Manzanar's director, Mr. Merrit, has been ordered by the Army's evacuation architect, Colonel Bendetsen, to confine the children to the camp.

Bendetsen has ignored the frantic pleas of the adopted families and the Catholic missions who have been caring for them to let the children remain in their care.

"They are our family."

"Only children, after all."

"How can it harm, for them to stay with us?"

Deaf to their pleas, he insists against reason that the children might be a threat to national security.

Some come to Manzanar from the white families who adopted them, grieving a second time at the loss of yet another set of parents. There are babies as young as six months old, the children, it's said, of schoolgirl-mothers from the other camps; there are toddlers taking their first precarious steps, and confused six-year-olds.

The babies, sensing change, cry for attention. The older ones gather together in silence, frightened at the deep pitch of the guards' voices, the dull metal gleam of their guns.

Manzanar's inmates are disturbed by the sight of the children. Seeing such innocence lined up feeds the sense they have that the madness has no limits.

"Why else would they be taken out of white homes, if not to kill us all?" they say.

"This must be the big, the final, roundup."

Racially the children are a mixed bunch, some with as little as one-eighth Japanese ancestry. The blond ones stand out among their fellows, reminders that even the tiniest trace of Japanese blood, no matter how far back in your family, condemns you. Watching those little souls arrive, it's hard for Satomi too not to feel so hated that genocide seems unlikely.

"How can those kids possibly be a threat to anybody?" she fumes, while Haru despairs. He wants to keep faith with his country, but at the sound of the children singing "God Bless America" he has to agree with Satomi that it makes no sense.

As the children settle into the Children's Village, the three large tar-papered barracks hastily erected to house them, fears of mass murder recede and other rumors get a look in. Hope floats around the one that says they are to be allowed home. But after a while hope itself makes them feel foolish. The more you hope for home, the farther away it seems to get.

Resignation is taking over so that even the horror stories of rats in the babies' cots fail to impress. Rats are no strangers in Manzanar, they have outnumbered the human residents from day one. In the company of cockroaches the ubiquitous creatures scuttle under the barracks, run across the beds at night. They have to be chased from the dripping water spigots, pulled each morning from the glue traps set on the many mess hall floors.

"Check my bed for me, pleeease," Satomi begs Haru every evening.

"They won't be there now," he says. "They come when it's dark, when you are sleeping." His voice takes on a ghostly moan. He likes to hear her squeal.

The scraps of good news that come, however small, are welcome and made much of. A post office is to be set up, an occasional movie is to be allowed, and there is an extra sugar ration on its way.

The bad news, though, is always major, always dramatic. Tamura and Eriko fly into a panic when they hear that a congressman, noting the high birth rate in the camps, has proposed that all Japanese women of child-bearing age should be sterilized.

"It would ruin our girls' lives." Tamura can't stop the tears.

"He must be a wicked man," Eriko wails, her arms tight around the squirming Yumi, who has only just started menstruating.

"No one's taking him seriously," John Harper, the popular camp doctor, says to Ralph and Satomi as they sit on the ground outside his office. "Congress is not completely mad."

"They'll have to shoot me before they try, the bastards," Satomi says, and Dr. Harper, not for the first time, is shocked at her language, impressed by her passion. Since they first met when she came to him with a splinter in her hand that had festered, he has felt a connection with her.

"This will hurt," he had warned. "I'm going to have to dig a bit."

He had laughed when she had cursed at the pain.

"Damn!"

"Never heard a Japanese female swear before," he said.

Since that time, she and Dr. Harper have shared what Haru

thinks of as an unsuitable friendship. Along with Ralph, they debate politics, discuss how the war is going, have conversations that sometimes turn argumentative. They agree that America will win the war and wonder together what life will be like when it is over.

Despite that he represents authority, it is hard, Satomi thinks, not to like Dr. Harper. There's no doubt that he is a good man. He may be ungainly, always dropping things, losing his papers, searching for his spectacles, but none of that counts for anything. Dr. Harper is a man filled with goodness and grace.

"There's a glow in him, don't you think?" she says to Ralph.

"Yes, that's it exactly, Satomi. He's the hail-fellow-well-met sort."

Now and then, breaking the camp's rules with pleasure in his heart, Dr. Harper gives Satomi his old newspapers. It staves his guilt for a while, and what harm can it do? He never, before Manzanar, thought of himself as a rule breaker, but stupid rules don't deserve to be followed. Rules that say people must be kept in the dark, no papers, no radio, stay ignorant, beg to be broken.

"If you won't go to school, then it's time you went to work," Haru insists. You should stop bothering the doctor, Satomi."

"We're friends, Haru. We think alike. He agrees that America has betrayed its Japanese citizens. Unlike Dr. Harper, I didn't hear you complaining when they spoke of sterilizing us."

"There are fools in every government," he says, more to console himself than to placate her. "It was never going to happen."

Their neighbor Mr. Sano, with his usual lack of tact, has an unpopular take on the sterilization threat.

"I can see the sense in it. Just look at the Hamadas," he declares, referring to the family of nine from the row behind Sewer Alley. "Mrs. Hamada is pregnant again. The children run wild, disturbing everyone. If they can't control themselves, it should be done for them."

Tamura and Eriko look at him with mouths open.

"He is blind to his own faults," Tamura says.

"A disgrace," says Naomi.

Along with Eriko, Tamura takes a camp job sewing camou-flage for the Army. She is paid six dollars a month, which, added to the prisoners' clothing allowance of three dollars and sixty cents, allows her to order little things from the Sears and Roebuck catalogue.

"You shouldn't be working in that drafty old hangar, Mama. It's not good for you. The dust from the cotton isn't giving your cough a chance."

"But I enjoy it, Satomi. I like the company, and it's fun. And anyway, what would I do all day otherwise? Besides, we need the money. You must have cotton for your dresses, thread and needles for me to sew them with."

At quiet times they go together to the mess hall and pore over the wonderful things the catalogue has to offer. Flower-printed head scarves, the prettiest shoes, silky nylons with straight dark seams, and pink suspender belts with rubber clasps that look like the teats from babies' bottles. The most popular items are the short white socks that are fashionable among the older girls, who think they look neat with their black oxfords. Satomi, though, prefers in summer to wear her oxfords without socks, and she likes simple skirts, the plain white T-shirts from the boys' section.

"No wonder the girls think you're odd," Tamura despairs.

Yumi, sparing no one her sulks, refuses to speak to Eriko until she agrees that she can give up the gray socks of the younger chil-dren and buy two pairs of the white ones.

"What can I do?" Eriko says. "She won't even listen to Haru."

"It's just a phase," Tamura says.

"Did Satomi go through it?"

"Sometimes, Eriko, it seems like she was born going through it. I can't say that she has ever been an easy child."

"She's not a child anymore, Tamura. I'd give up hoping, if I were you."

Eriko is used to hard work and enjoys the company too. She could have taken more pleasure in it if it hadn't been for having to kneel on the cement floor all day, which makes her knees ache.

"You are the only one not working," Tamura complains to Satomi. "All you do is read Haru's books and talk to Dr. Harper. No wonder you are bored. Work would console you."

"I won't do anything here that helps them, Mama. Nobody should. In any case, I am not bored, I love reading."

"You could help Haru with his volunteer work," Tamura persists. "Anyone can see how much pride he takes in it."

Haru has found his vocation and is teaching reading to the third-grade children. He coaches the softball team and helps distribute the care packages that come from the Quakers. Tin toys for the children, comics and pencils, and sometimes soft blanket-stitched scarves and hats.

Yumi was hoping for bobby pins, a watch, perhaps; instead she receives a fan made from cedar wood, which she hangs on the wall by her bed. She pretends that it is a silly thing of no use to anyone, but she keeps it free from dust so that it won't lose its scent, and no one but her is allowed to touch it.

Haru, a little embarrassed at the Quakers' charity, takes pleasure at least in the children's joy at receiving the toys. He could have earned eight dollars a month if he had wanted, laying drainage pipes around the camp, but he has his pride.

"It's insulting. Eight dollars! What other Americans would work for that kind of money? They would be paid ten times more." He may be loyal to America, but like Aaron he is not to be predicted.

"I'd have thought you would be happy to help, since you love America so much," Satomi teases.

"You don't know what you're talking about, Sati. Loving America and working for less than a citizen is not the same thing at all."

Yumi is at the camp school, and old Naomi Okihiro knits when she can get the wool, or sleeps her days away, dreaming of sunlit rooms and the plum tree she sat under as a child in Japan. Her English is not good, her nature suspicious, and, apart from Tamura and Satomi, she rarely speaks to anyone outside of her family.

Satomi won't admit it, but Tamura is right, the days are long and she is bored. They would be longer, though, if it hadn't been for Haru's books, for Dr. Harper's company.

Dr. Harper is taking up more and more of her time. He encourages her to call at his office, is debating with himself whether to take her on his rounds. The thing about Satomi is that she's not hampered by the cultural manners that keep his other patients from challenging him, from having the intimacy with them that he would like. And she must have somewhere useful to place her outrage, after all, some outlet for the kindness she smothers.

He questions her about the minutia of things that go on in the camp that he would otherwise have no way of finding out, listing them in his journal meticulously. *Liver served for five days on the trot,* he writes. *On the whole the Japanese don't eat liver.*

"My little archive," he says. "A gateway to memory for me, when Manzanar is over and you are all allowed to go home."

He is attached to his collection, to the grim photos he has taken of the sparsely furnished, poorly lit barracks, the portraits of the inmates, who smile for the camera and manage to look hopeful. He has blurry pictures of rats on the run in the latrines, bugs in the children's beds. He has drawings that the children at school have drawn in the dust; strange shapes, and trees without leaves, and guards with guns, stick men smaller than their weapons. He treasures the little carvings people give him in gratitude for his skills, naïve ironwood netsuke, hares and rabbits, rats with serpent tails, infants tumbling together with stones for eyes. It's a strange archive, but so potent that sometimes when he goes through it he imagines he can smell the camp, sweat and disease, dust and blood, and the burning reek of carbolic.

In his determination to let nothing of Manzanar be lost, he sees purpose in his job, and is able to keep faith with his country. There will be others like him, he thinks, Americans who witness the unfairness, the damage done. Others who, when the time is right, will work for recompense, for justice. He believes that Satomi will be one of them.

"You never stop writing in that thing," his wife complains. "I think you find that place more interesting than real life."

He doesn't challenge her on the "real life" thing, prefers to keep Manzanar, the revulsion it holds for him, from her. "Someone has to keep a record," he says. "I don't want to forget the truth of it."

MEDICAL ROUNDS

I SUSPECTED THAT SHE wouldn't go full term," Dr. Harper says to Satomi on their way to Mrs. Takei's barrack. "The lining of her womb might as well be paper, it's so thin with childbearing. If it's what I suspect, it won't be a pretty sight, Satomi. You don't have to come in."

"I'll come in," she says nervously.

He's burdening her, he knows, putting her to the test, but then we are all put to the test and he doesn't want to allow her the getout clause of ignorance. It's right that she should see things for what they are, right that she should be good and mad about it, and she's strong enough for the truth.

He's strong enough too, yet still he would like himself to be saved from the horrors that he sees, the ones that rob him of the free will to live a conventional, untroubled life.

Satomi hasn't visited this part of the camp before. It's the outer circle of the site, the periphery line of barracks that are the border between civilization and the rude acres of sagebrush. The barracks here take the full force of the winds, of all the extreme forms of weather their desert-floor home throws at them

"The badlands," Dr. Harper calls them. "Home to the stragglers, latecomers too shocked at the sight of Manzanar to push their way to the front of the lines."

Mrs. Takei's barrack is fourth from the end. Her husband is sitting on the steps with their children, seven boys who look to Satomi to be about the same age, although that can't be so. Their mother must have popped them out with hardly a space in between.

Mr. Takei stands when he sees them, stepping aside to allow them to climb the steps, bowing to them as though they are royalty. Dr. Harper puts his hand on the man's shoulder and sighs. The men look at each other with what Satomi takes to be resignation.

Inside, it takes a second or two for their eyes to adjust in the stygian light. Mrs. Takei is perched on the edge of the bed with her knees drawn up to her chin. Her face, Satomi thinks, as green as Palmolive soap. A dark stain pumps its way up the thin brown fabric of her dress, there's a puddle of blood on the floor, streaks of it across her face where she has pushed her hair back with bloodied hands.

Satomi shuts her mouth and holds her nose, a brief protection against the offal smell that comes hot to her nostrils. An acid sharpness of vomit clots at the back of her throat and she swallows hard and prays not to be sick. The stench and the blood are shocking.

Even though Dr. Harper had been expecting it, he shakes his head at the sight of Mrs. Takei in such a poor state. It has always seemed a little miracle to him that the body's odors are contained inside something as thin, as porous, as skin.

"When did the bleeding start?" he asks, easing Mrs. Takei gently down on the bed, straightening her legs.

"Last night." She lowers her eyes from his.

"*Tshh*, and you've waited this long to send for me," he says, not unkindly.

"The baby came quickly," she says, looking to the corner of the room, where a bloody towel-wrapped bundle lays lifeless. "I thought the bleeding would stop, but it just keeps coming."

"Water, please, Satomi. Lots of it, if you can manage, and the cloths from my bag." His movements are sure, his voice calm, his heart sinking.

Outside at the spigot, Satomi fills a thin tin bucket up to the worn part where holes pepper the sides, and gulps down the fresh air as if it were a long cool drink. She hesitates, not wanting to go back in, only moving when Dr. Harper calls her name urgently as though it is a question.

Inside, as the doctor is examining the dead baby, Satomi takes Mrs. Takei's hand. "I'm sorry, Mrs. Takei," she says. "About the baby, I mean." She meant to sound sympathetic, warm, but her voice comes out small, useless.

Mrs. Takei takes two days to die. The blood transfusions Dr. Harper administers seem to pump in and flow out in equal measure. Mrs. Takei can't hold on, either to the blood or to life.

She's buried with her baby in her arms, leaving her husband and her seven boys to fend for themselves.

Satomi carries the vision of that desperate day, the blood and the brutal sight of the parceled infant, around with her for weeks. Forever after, the smell of blood makes her queasy, sets her heart racing.

On her rounds with Dr. Harper, one crisis runs into another so that faces blur, names are forgotten. There are cases of adult measles, strange fevers, and plenty of the geriatric pneumonia that Dr. Harper calls "the old man's friend."

"Speeds them along the path to meet their maker," he says.

Mrs. Takei, though, stays in her mind with frightening clarity, as does the man with septicemia, who left untreated the cut he received from a broken pan in the latrines. By the time Dr. Harper got to him, you could feel the heat coming off his leg from a foot away. Thick pus oozed from the wound, and a long red line snaked up his skin from thigh to waist. In his spiking fever there was no sense to be had from him. He was hallucinating, thrashing about, shouting warnings to the wall.

Dr. Harper got him into the camp hospital and set up twenty-four-hour nursing, but he couldn't save him. The man's blood was poisoned, his organs failed, and he died in agony.

"Just from a cut," Satomi said to Dr. Harper in amazement.

"An easy route into the body for bacteria, Satomi."

"Yes, but just from a cut."

She wondered if the camp was the cause of the disasters, or whether such things happened in the world outside too. Perhaps she had just been unaware of them.

"It's the same the world over," Dr. Harper says. "It's just that here the lack of facilities, the poor hygiene, turns sickness to tragedy more often."

One case she knew that she could blame on the camp for sure was that of a boy a year or so younger than Haru. He had fallen into a depression and in his lowest moment had drunk industrial-strength chlorine, stolen from the mess hall while his mother was at work.

She had found him in agony, blisters the size of cookies around his mouth, his throat scorched from first swallowing the chlorine and then vomiting it up, so that he could hardly speak.

"He was always a happy boy before we came to this place," his mother said bitterly. "He wanted to be a doctor like you, Dr. Harper. He likes helping people."

"He still can be," Dr. Harper assured her. "You must help him to look on the world as promising. Keep him from attempting anything like this again."

"But he has spoiled his beautiful face. He will be scarred forever."

Dr. Harper, usually good with words, could find none. It

would be more than a bit of scarring the boy would suffer. What was inside, what his mother couldn't see, would be more of a problem.

"It's this place," Satomi hissed to Dr. Harper on their way out of the barrack. "This disgusting, filthy place."

There have been days since that time when she can't bring herself to accompany Dr. Harper on his rounds. Days when she just wants to forget other people's troubles. Sometimes it's more than she can manage to stay mad. She waits for Haru to return from work, losing herself in stories until he does. Books take her away from Manzanar, allow her to live other lives in her head for a while. And books are available to her now since the library has finally opened.

"We have a lot to thank the Quakers for," she tells Dr. Harper in a rare moment of gratitude. "That people who have never met us care for us, well, it's . . ."

He has never heard her so pleased, so fulsome about anything before. It's a good sign, he thinks, there must be balance in life after all.

Tamura, though, is not of the same mind.

"You need more than books, more than the company of an old man to fill your days," she says. She has never met Dr. Harper, and, like Haru but for a mother's reasons, she disapproves of the friendship. It's odd, for a start, and she worries that Dr. Harper is exposing Satomi to things best left to her elders. And there's the nuisance of Satomi pleading with her to let Dr. Harper examine her.

"Please, Mother. Just let him give you something for your cough, examine your chest."

"Soon, maybe," she says reluctantly.

"Keep out of the medics' hands for as long as you can," Aaron used to say. "Once they get their hands on you, it's all downhill."

————

Satomi loves the way Haru flirts with her now, even though he keeps up the pretense that she is still a kid. He plays at being irked that he has to put up with her, the annoying girl from next door, shaking his head when she teases him, letting the smile slip from him, frowning a little. He is on the point of kissing her, she knows, and just the anticipation of it warms her up.

Sometimes in the afternoons, to stop herself thinking of him, to keep her heart from flipping at the thought of them touching, she helps Mrs. Hamada out with her brood, washing the little ones' shining faces, taking their pudgy little hands in her own as she makes up games and tells them stories. She enjoys being with the children and it gives Mrs. Hamada an hour or two of peace, time to take a shower, to catch up with the washing.

"You had better be careful," Eriko says, smothering a smile. "Before you know it you'll be popular."

"Oh, it's just something to do," Satomi says.

"You don't have to apologize for it, Satomi," Naomi says, woken from her afternoon sleep by their chatter. "It's good to fill your days, to help others."

Unlike Naomi, Satomi is filled with restless energy and can't sleep in the day. At night her dreams are of a different sort than the old woman's.

"Mine are always about home, and food," Naomi says. "Sweet fried fish, red beans, rice soup."

In Satomi's, memories work themselves through her mind so that the past becomes whole again. She sees the fox, haughty by the porcelainberry bush, hears Mr. Beck's voice, "Know what 'exotic' means, Satomi?"

Sometimes she dreams of Tamura disappearing from her view like smoke dissolving as she reaches out for her. She wakes from those dreams to the form of the robe hovering over her like some Oriental specter.

"It's the same for me," Haru says. "I dream of losing my family. This place does that to you. It changes everything. Yumi no longer eats with us. She goes to a different mess hall with her friends, as though she is ashamed to be one of us. My grandmother's bones ache and her memory is going, she is losing the present, living more and more in the past. It makes me wonder how I am to take care of them here.

Confessing their fears, they find themselves one evening under a waxing moon, kissing for the first time. She has longed for it, imagined how it would be, but when it comes, when Haru leans in to her, she feels like running. Should she open her mouth and taste him, let him taste her, as she had with Artie? She wants to reach up and put her arms around him, pull him to her, but something stops her, some reserve in him, the uncomfortable idea that she wants it more than he does.

He is unflatteringly measured in his approach, in the small pause he takes as though he is debating it, fighting it.

When he does kiss her, there is nothing of the fumbling boy in him, he isn't carried away as she is. His kiss is an accomplished kiss, not hungry as Artie's had been. Not as wholehearted either, she thinks.

It would have hurt her to know that after, when they had walked in silence back to Sewer Alley, he was already regretting it, wishing that they had never gotten started. She is just a kid, after all, not that much older than Yumi. He doesn't want things to get complicated, messed up, doesn't want his mother and Tamura on his case, having expectations.

As the days pass, though, he can't deny that the scent of her, clean as a bolt of new cotton, the warm spread of her breasts pushed up against his chest, have stirred him up so that he can hardly think of anything else. A girl like her, offering herself, seems at once both shameful and irresistible.

"What's the matter with you these days, Haru?" Eriko asks. "You are off somewhere in your head all the time. Tamura is still waiting for you to fix the split in her floor."

"I'll get to it, Mother, just as soon as . . ."

And he will. He will stop wasting time thinking of Satomi, keep it light with her. He has his plans, has held them too long to let a pretty face hold him back. It makes him uncomfortable that he thinks of her a hundred times a day, that she takes his mind off more important things.

"I know that you like Satomi," Eriko says. "I have seen you looking at her, but I don't think that she is for you. And even if she is, that is more reason for you to treat her with respect."

"I'm not interested," he insists. "We're friends, that's all. We have things in common."

"What things?"

"Well, this place, for a start, and she's intelligent, you know, interested in books and ideas. I can talk to her."

The world as Haru had known it has slipped from his grasp, but he is determined to get it back. If he has to fight to be an American, then so be it. His family has worked hard to build the American dream. He believes in it still. Despite Manzanar, the stupid awful things that go on in the camp, he can't let the beautiful idea of the American dream go.

"I'm going to sign up just as soon as they'll let me. I'm going to sign up and fight for my country," he warns Satomi.

"Some country," she scoffs. "It isn't our country anymore. We're the enemy"

"No, we're not, and that's the point. Why can't you see that?"

"It's not me that's blind, Haru."

"Look, Sati, sometimes the things you love don't live up to your expectations. But you can't just give up on them, can you? Whatever you feel now, this is your country as much as anyone's."

"I don't see how you can think that in this place. You'd have to be mad to think that."

"I think it because all Americans are immigrants of one sort or another. Being white doesn't make you more American than if you're black or any color in between."

"Hard to believe that when you're locked up for it, though."

"No country in the world beats America, Sati. It's our home. We'll get over this."

"Well, I'm going to get out of it just as soon as I can. I'm going to travel the world and never come back here."

"What nationality will you put on your passport?"

"Oh, I don't know. I don't have a choice, do I? It would have to be American, I guess."

"Exactly, you don't have a choice. You are as American as the rest of us."

PIONEERS

HARU SAYS THAT they are pioneers at Manzanar, frontiers-people who must invent ways of coping with the little at hand they have to see them through.

"The Japanese are an ingenious people," he says. "We find answers to problems."

But even he runs for cover when the dust storms come. Everyone does. Ingenious or not, no one has found an answer to them. Sucking up dirt on their way into camp, they rain it back down on Manzanar's inmates on their stampede out. The gales are impervious to whatever Manzanar puts up against them. When they blow, there is nothing to be done but to huddle inside and wait them out, to bear the gritty winds that banshee-howl through the cracks in their walls.

Satomi and Tamura, with their knees up to their chins and their heads down, squat together beside their stove under the cover of a blanket.

"We are so often buried alive in the dirt," Eriko says, "that death, when it comes, won't seem much different."

"It's hell's mouth opening," Tamura says. "Spewing out its rage."

She has learned how to spot when the storms are on the horizon long before the distant moan of them can be heard.

"It's on its way," she warns with resignation. "The clouds are sitting right on top of the mountain, all bunched up and ready to pounce."

"Have you got your cotton strips ready, Mama?"

Tamura saves the camouflage off-cuts from the factory floor to cover her mouth with on her way to and from work.

"There is a use for everything," she says with satisfaction.

But Satomi can't accept as Tamura accepts. The storms might be an act of nature, but she rails against them as though they are man-made, as though they are prescribed punishment from the government.

"It makes me mad," she tells Haru. "Those damn storms are like living things, with a will to spoil. Each one makes Mother a bit worse."

But Haru's commiseration only makes her feel more helpless; his sympathy is passive, when what she wants is action.

"I don't know what you expect me to do about them, Satomi. We all have to bear them, even the guards."

"You could get angry, maybe."

"You are a silly girl. Everything makes you mad. I don't know why I bother with you."

For days after the storms blow out, Tamura and Satomi's eyes burn, it hurts their mouths to eat. The dust creeps into their bedding so that their skin is sore from their grit-beds. No amount of shaking will get rid of it. There are times when Satomi fancies that the dust is stacking up inside her, slowly turning her into the fabric of Manzanar.

Lone Pine, their nearest town, has a sprinkler wagon that settles the dust, and there is talk of the camp sharing it.

"It ain't that effective anyway," the guard called Lawson, who talks with her sometimes, tells her. "It just damps down the side-walk for a bit, that's all."

"Still, it must be better than nothing, Lawson," she says, enjoying how easily he is made to feel guilty.

"You'll get used to it, girl, we all do. Inyo weather is a law unto itself."

"You'd think the mountains would give some protection, but they don't, do they?"

"Nope, where you get mountains, you get extremes. But they're pretty, ain't they? Cigarette?" he always offers. She usually accepts.

"I wouldn't say pretty, exactly."

She can't bring herself to admit it to him, but she is often moved, her heart filled to bursting, by the austere beauty of Manzanar. If she narrows her eyes and dismisses the clutter of the camp, she sees only the vast plains of the sky, the mountain peaks stabbing the clouds, inking them with indigo and purple and the kind of orange that Eriko calls *burnt*. In their jagged summits she conjures up church spires, and the roofscape of a city etched against the sky, a far-off Shangri-la.

But there's no escaping to that Shangri-la, there is no easy place to set her mind in Manzanar, there are no kind seasons to look forward to. It is a habitat of extremes that is always one thing or the other, too cold, too hot, too humid, it is never just right.

"Change is good," Lawson says. "Just when you think you can't bear the cold anymore, it gets hot. Things move fast in earthquake country."

On a day in a hundred-degree summer, when the tar paper on their roof is melting, turning their barrack into a furnace that near enough cooks them, she takes her complaints to Dr. Harper.

"My mother fainted clean away today, Dr. Harper. You could boil hot dogs on those barrack roofs."

"They faint in the mess hall lines too. We have always suffered hot summers here," he says sympathetically.

He thinks guiltily of the fans in his own house that his wife sets near bowls of ice to cool the air. There are no fans, there is no ice to be had in Manzanar.

"It's worse for my mother, she is so ill," Satomi says. "Her chest never gets better and she is too thin. It is very hard on her."

"Why don't you bring her to see me, Satomi? I would be happy to examine her, and I would like to meet her."

"You wouldn't believe how stubborn she is, Dr. Harper. No one would. People love her sweetness; they can't imagine how when she sets her will to something she can't be moved."

"And she doesn't want to come?"

"No, she says she is getting better, but she isn't. She isn't one little bit better."

"Well, if she would allow me, I could visit your barrack. I would like to see what sort of mother grows a daughter like you."

Naomi Okihiro refuses to see Dr. Harper too, even though a strange pain overtakes her heart every now and then and her arthritis aches worse than a toothache as it sets her bones to stone. Sometimes it throbs in her so fiercely that she can't get out of her chair, let alone make it to the spigot at the end of their alley.

"Do you need water?" Satomi checks with her every afternoon.

"No, I have plenty," she lies, wanting only her daughter Eriko, to see to her needs.

It is not uncommon for Eriko to return from work to find her mother so dehydrated that she can hardly speak. She must be wrapped in a wet sheet, made to sip water slowly until she returns to herself.

"Things are getting worse with her," Eriko says. "But she will not see a male doctor. She has her own way of doing things."

"Which is no way at all," Satomi says. "I prefer more modern methods, myself."

She nags at Tamura until, running out of will, her mother agrees to go with her to the camp hospital.

"It's a fuss about nothing," Tamura apologizes to Dr. Harper, making light, in her shyness, of her cough, the pain in her chest. "Satomi worries about me, but there are worse here. I can manage."

Dr. Harper is a little shy himself, taken aback by the feelings that the sight of Tamura has stirred in him. She is ill, that much is obvious, but it is more than a doctor's concern he is feeling. No sound has ever touched him quite as viscerally as Tamura's voice touches him. She is, he thinks, a woman of delightful beauty. Despite her pallor, he sees the rosy girl in her, the sweetness Satomi spoke of. The heat in him rises to match that of the day. It has been a long time since he has felt such a tugging, fluttering thing, such a soft explosion inside. He feels foolish. It is unseemly for a married man who won't see sixty again, a doctor, to feel so arrested by a patient.

"She won't complain, but this place is killing her," Satomi says, breaking into his thoughts.

"I can see you are not well, Mrs. Baker," he says, listening through his stethoscope to the thick thud of Tamura's chest as she responds to his direction to cough. "Perhaps a few days' rest will help."

"I have tried that, Dr. Harper. It only makes me more restless. I like to keep occupied. It is better to work, don't you think?"

He prescribes a tonic to build her strength, knowing it might as well be sugar water. He has no medicine to cure what she has, no magic. He is overcome with a profound sadness.

"I've seen that stuff before," Eriko says. "It's nothing more than treacle laced with cheap alcohol. Hot tea would do more good."

"I'll take it back and ask for something better," Satomi says, knowing that Dr. Harper will indulge her. He is a man with a conscience and likes to find answers to her challenges.

She longs for Tamura to be returned to her old self, wants her Angelina mother back. She has a picture in her head of Tamura sitting on their porch shelling peas, the glossy loop of her hair shining, her profile silhouetted in the soft light; she pictures her straining rice, stirring clothes in the copper boiler at the back of the house. There are no chores that can diminish Tamura's dignity. Her every movement has a refinement about it.

At night just before sleep she summons up a picture of the old Tamura in her head, hoping to dream of her in better times, of Aaron, of the farm.

Sleep, though, is a hard thing to sustain in the camp. Something is always on the boil with one or another of Manzanar's ten thousand inhabitants. Women give birth at all hours, and the ill and the old die, not always quietly, even though some of them welcome death. Crying babies and the moans of nightmares are the order of the confined nights. Worst of all for Satomi, though, are the noises that come from closer to home.

"I can't bear it," she whispers to Tamura through their silk partition, despairing at the embarrassing sounds of lovemaking that nightly beat through the half-inch division wall from Mr. and Mrs. Sano's room. Their enthusiasm seems quite horrible, considering they share their quarters with their daughter-in-law and their two grandchildren. Their son is confined to a citizens' isolation center in Catalina, for making too many complaints of a political nature.

"My son is a fine man," Mrs. Sano says. "He takes after his father."

Hardly a sound emanates from the Okihiros' side, but the Sanos live their life regardless and have no consideration at all.

Mr. Sano at sixty-five is a bent man, his back stooped from years of picking strawberries for a living, his skin like buffalo hide, but he is surprisingly energetic when he wants to be.

"He looks like a wrinkled old turtle." Satomi shudders. "More like eighty-five than sixty-five—ninety, even."

"It gives them comfort," Tamura says, mortified herself at Mr. Sano's grunts, his wife's high-pitched mews. "It's worse for their daughter-in-law, poor girl. She has a lot to put up with."

"But they are so old, Mother. It's disgusting."

"It is better not to whisper," Tamura advises, coughing out her words. "Whispering only makes our neighbors more interested in our conversation. I wouldn't like them to hear us talking about them."

Satomi is surprised at the strength Tamura has found to cope with everything that has been thrown at her since she lost husband and home. Her mother has a knack for friendship. People may still be suspicious of her strange daughter, a girl who thinks herself equal to her superiors, but their hearts are open to Tamura. They like her honest approach, her modesty.

"'Honor' is the word for Tamura," Eriko says. "There's nothing false about her."

"Your mother is the sweetest lady," Ralph teases her. "Guess you must take after your father, huh?"

Tamura, the woman now that she would never have become if Aaron had lived, goes to work cheerfully and sings "God Bless America" every morning alongside the Stars and Stripes with her fellow workers in the breakfast line. When all they get is canned wieners and spinach cooked to slime, her complaints are merely for form. Yet there are times when she longs to hold one perfect just-laid egg in her hand, to touch it to her lips and feel its gentle warmth, times when she remembers the pleasure in being a wife, the joy of a good harvest. Recalling those things, it is a small embarrassment to her that she is happy at Manzanar.

"How can you sing, Mother? What is there to sing about here? And 'God Bless America,' of all songs!"

"You should try it yourself, Satomi. You can't be unhappy while you are singing."

However hard it is for Satomi to understand, the truth is that Tamura isn't afraid of anything anymore. Even the idea of death, close as she suspects it is, has found its place and settled. She has found friendship and laughter at Manzanar, and in the companionship of the Okihiros she has been returned to the camaraderie of family, albeit not one of blood.

Her love of country, of America, is strong in her. She caught that germ from her parents long ago and will never be cured of it. Japan for her is simply a place in her imagination, a legendary land where the fables of her mother's childhood are set. It is not to be confused with the Japan that drops bombs on America, the Japan that killed Aaron. She trusts in an American future.

"You have to let your anger go," she tells Satomi. "The only person it is having an effect on is you."

When Tamura gets food poisoning from a mess hall stew that had been reheated once too often, the residents of Sewer Alley are surprised to see Dr. Harper come calling twice daily until she is recovered.

"White men seem to like her," they gossip without spite.

Few in the camp escape the infections that stalk the place. Dirty water brings dysentery, proximity spreads whooping cough and the pitiless episodes of measles that are rife among the children.

"It seems the orphanage is always quarantined," Satomi observes to Dr. Harper.

"Yes, from fleas to flu," he agrees. "There's no end to it."

"Poor little things, without mothers to comfort them."

"I've noticed you talking to the children, Satomi. I've seen them run to you. They like you. You should help out there. Too many of your fellows speak of being an orphan as something shameful."

"Some do, I know. The Japanese word for it is *burakamin*, it means untouchable. But it's not a common view, Dr. Harper, we are not savages, you know?"

Apart from the diseases, people die of other natural causes too, of heart attacks and old age. Some, it's said, of shame and broken hearts, and there have been suicides. One man was so distressed at being separated from his family that he attempted to bite off his tongue; when that didn't work, he climbed the camp fence and was shot by a guard. Murder or suicide, it was hard to tell.

"Murder, of course," Satomi said.

"Perhaps," Haru dithered.

The hastily cleared ground of the once-tiny cemetery is constantly having its boundaries widened. The dead are quickly laid to rest, their families marking their graves with a simple ring of rocks. A small obelisk fashioned from stone has been placed in the heart of the graveyard as a monument to the dead.

"A consoling tower," Naomi says.

Tamura weeps for the dead whether she knew them or not. "They died wondering what it has all been for," she says. "They never found their way home."

One afternoon in the camouflage shed, suffering from lack of breath and cutting pains in her chest, she is carted off to the hospital barrack, where, serving as a ward, three iron beds are arranged in the open air alongside the hospital's latrines. There are two more beds inside and the part-time nurse tells Tamura to sit on one while she waits for Dr. Harper.

"It's written on your notes that Dr. Harper wishes to deal with you himself," she says, giving Tamura a suspicious look. "You'll have to wait while we find him."

Eriko, fearing for Tamura's life, rushes to find Satomi, who is in the showers, where she goes at quiet times to wash her hair with the scented soap that Lawson gives her. When she can't be found in her usual hangouts it's a fair bet that Satomi will be in the showers, lost in the sweet reward of floral foam.

"Your mother is stable," Dr. Harper says. "She has a weak constitution, of course, and the food poisoning didn't help, but . . ."

"How can she be stable? Look how she fights for breath."

"Don't pester Dr. Harper, Satomi." Tamura pants, struggling for air. "He is doing his best. It is not his fault. There is nothing to be done."

"Is that true, Dr. Harper? There is nothing to be done?"

"There are things you can do to help, Satomi. Keep your mother warm, see that she eats regularly. I would suggest that she gives up work on the camouflage nets, but I guess she'll fight you on that one. The dust there is full of fibers. It's a problem there's no answer to."

"Letting her go home would keep her from the dust, Dr. Harper."

"If it was up to me, Satomi, then . . . of course . . ."

If he had the power to order it, he would free all of Manzanar's inmates. He wishes with all his heart that he could save Tamura. It hurts him that he can't cure her. The thought that, like his wife, she might be disappointed in him too, adds to his feelings of impotence. Without reason he has taken on himself the blame for him and his wife being childless, it is the least he can do for the wife he had long ago lost interest in.

"Isn't there proper medicine for her cough, at least?"

"Well, nothing that will do much good. I'll see that she gets an extra blanket, though, that should help."

How can he tell Satomi what Tamura knows and has chosen not to tell her? The girl is bright enough to see others in the camp with the same condition. She just isn't ready to see it in her mother.

The tuberculosis has advanced beyond medicine. Tamura is already coughing up blood, having to sit upright through the night just to keep breathing. One foot in front of the other is the only way to go now. And Satomi looks scared enough already, no point in telling her there is worse to come.

"Have you thought about helping at the Children's Village, Satomi?" he says, to distract her. "I have spoken to them about you. They can do with all the help they can get, you know."

"If they'll have me, I will. Mother wants me to, and I guess that I do too."

"Good, it will suit you, I think."

"Just the thought of you helping there makes me feel better." Tamura smiles. "You are a good girl at heart."

"And there's other good news," Dr. Harper says. "You'll be pleased to hear that work starts on the new hospital this week. There will be more doctors coming to join us, Japanese ones among them. Things here are looking up."

"We won't be holding our breath," Satomi says under hers, but loud enough to be heard.

"No, no, it's for real. And there are to be more latrines too. We're gonna get on top of these infections for sure. You can count on it." He hopes that he is right. It seems to him that one way or another the whole camp is diseased.

"I'll keep my fingers crossed for new latrines, at least, Dr. Harper. Guess you've never had to wait in line for them yourself?"

"Well—" he manages before she interrupts him.

"We try not to notice the sour air, or see the sewage bubbling up through our feet. We put up with the paper always running out and the flies everywhere."

"I'm sorry they are so bad. It will help when there are more, I'm sure."

"You can't imagine how humiliating it is for the women in those lines, or how vulgar the men can be."

"No, I can't say that . . ."

Tamura joins in to help him out. "They only joke to ease their embarrassment," she says, frowning at Satomi.

"I will mention it to the superintendent in charge," Dr. Harper says. "You are right, something must be done."

Later, as Tamura sits chatting to Eriko, she protests Satomi's behavior. "I felt sorry for Dr. Harper, Eriko. Honestly, Satomi gives him such a hard time. They seem to be friends, yet still I am shocked at her lack of respect."

"She is too outspoken," Eriko agrees. "But there is nothing to be done about it, she is already made. In any case, I think that Dr. Harper likes her enough to forgive her. Did he give you anything for your cough?"

"Yes, a blanket." Tamura giggles. "What else can he do? Oh, and good news. He says that new latrines are to be built soon."

"Really? My mother will be pleased, if that's true. It's the old who suffer most. Mother will only go at the quietest time of day, and even then it's torture for her. It's the same for all the old women. They have to go in pairs, one always on guard for the other."

"Mmm, they were formed in Japan's clay. They are modest. We have become used to it, but they never will."

"Well, neither will I," Satomi's voice comes rudely through their dividing wall, against which she is propped with *Wuthering Heights* in hand. "I can't bear those filthy latrines."

"Oh, Satomi, it's not the same thing at all. And I notice you have no such inhibitions when it comes to the showers."

"It's no wonder people take against you," Eriko joins in crossly. "You never know when to be still, when to stay quiet. You are forever in the line for the showers, keeping people waiting."

If there is one thing that makes Eriko irritable, it's talking through the wall, it seems to her to be the height of bad manners.

But she instantly regrets her irritation, even though she is only speaking the truth.

Sometimes Satomi will finish one shower and straight off join the end of the line to take another. Her reputation suffers and people find relief in grumbling about her.

"Her manners are bad."

"It's to be expected, I suppose."

"But Tamura is so kind, so polite."

"She is a cuckoo in Tamura's nest."

"I hear she takes soap from the guards."

Tamura is gently critical too. "You must learn to manage. I do not like you taking things from Lawson, it will make you unpopular."

"Oh, Mama, I've never been popular here, now, have I?"

"Well, it's your own fault, you never try to please. And what does he want in return for the soap that only you receive?"

She doesn't like the question. It is her business, after all.

"He never asks me for anything. Ralph says that Lawson is kind to everyone, that he's a people person and likes to talk."

"Well, you won't have time to talk when you are working at the orphanage. You'll be too busy with the little ones."

"I'm looking forward to it, Mama. Don't be cross."

"And you are good with children," Tamura says, softening. "People will see that and like you better for it."

REMEDIES

THE ORPHANAGE BARRACKS have their own running water and a small block of toilets for their own use. That in itself is enough to recommend them to Satomi, without the warmth
that opened her heart to the children on her first day there.

"They're sweet and naughty," she tells Haru. "And they smell
like kittens."

The babies, in their ignorance of desertion, cry as babies will,
but they are more easily comforted than the older ones—a clean
diaper, a bottle of warm milk soothes quickly enough. The others, though, suffer the feral instinct of wariness and hold themselves back from consolation.

"Oh, Mama, you should see them. So frightened of everything
that they wet the bed and think they will be beaten for it. Some
are like me, of mixed blood, you know. There's a red-haired
child, and two or three with golden hair. There's a little boy who
says he's Mexican. He speaks Spanish and only knows a word or
two of English."

"Perhaps you will find who you are among them," Tamura says
mysteriously.

Arriving at Manzanar with their tiny carrying cases, the children
have everything taken off them. Clothes are sorted into piles by
age rather than ownership. There are dungarees, little felt jackets,

knitted hats and shoes set in a line by size. It's easier to store their possessions together, to jumble them up, so that no one knows who came with what. Some came with nothing anyway, not even identity papers. Too young to speak their names, not knowing where they came from, no information can be coaxed from them. Satomi gives them names, guesses at their ages.

The few who have toys are made to share them, to watch, heartbroken, as a loved grubby doll, a tin car, is taken off by another child. One little boy has started a collection of empty bean cans, no one but him wants them, they are his alone. Another holds on tight to a small handkerchief, sniffing at it, rubbing it against his cheeks.

"It's not right," Satomi tells Dr. Harper. "They need families, people of their own." She is thinking of Mrs. Hamada's brood, their easy smiles, their confident fights, the love that bolsters them.

There are days in the orphanage when, despite the strict rules, chaos takes over, when it is hard to make yourself heard above the children's howling. The naughtier boys who misbehave have to run the "swat line." They dodge and dive between the legs of the children who need no encouragement to whack their fellows' hides. Whackers and whacked make a game of it, minding more the cross word than any physical punishment.

"They get bored," Satomi tells Haru. "There are hardly any books or toys. They can't think of anything to do but fight."

"You must be firmer, Sati. Bring order."

"They have so little, Haru. I can't bear to punish them."

"They have you, Satomi. They have food and a roof over their head. It's not a family, but nothing in life is equal. They cannot be allowed to run wild."

She hears his words as a reproach, hears his disappointment in her. If only he would stop lecturing and take her side for once. If only he would kiss her more often, hold her, tell her whatever she does is all right with him. She has competition for Haru, she knows. There are plenty of girls trying to catch his eye, girls who play better to his wanting-to-be-in-charge nature. She feels more challenged, though, by his view of the world, the formality in him, the way he thinks a woman should be.

"You have forgotten what it is like to be a child, Haru."

"You are right, I suppose. I think more like a father these days."

Soothed by the act of giving, the guard Lawson begins to bring gifts for the orphanage children, marbles, and crayons, his old baseball and glove, his daughter's discarded dolls. He is a man full of guilt for what he has to guard. His left-the-nest daughter is only a few years older than Satomi and according to him not unlike her in looks.

"She married a no-gooder," he says. "Lives five miles away, but we never see her."

Lawson's wife has Indian blood. "A quarter Shoshone," he says. "Although she is fierce enough for it to be Apache."

"He can hardly be accused of bigotry," Satomi defends him to Haru.

No matter what anyone says, it's fine by her if Lawson finds relief in giving the children presents, in giving her soap.

"You take it, honey, I know you girls like to smell good."

She doesn't like upsetting Tamura, getting on the wrong side of Haru, but where should she take her friends from in this place? The girls of her own age are wary of her, and so much duller than Lily ever was, for all her sneakiness.

"You don't give them a chance, Satomi. You don't give anyone but Dr. Harper and Ralph a chance. If you're unpopular it's your own fault," Tamura says.

If only Tamura knew the truth of it, how it is the other way around. How she is ogled by the men in the camp in a way the full

Japanese girls are not. How the one who is always offering her mother his place in the noontime lunch line had, in the alley that is the shortcut to the mess hall, exposed himself to her daughter. The sight of the sallow thing hanging there hadn't shocked her in the least, but she had kept the information to herself, not wanting Haru to know and feel obliged to do something about it.

"Oh, put it away, you fool," she had said dismissively.

"Sorry," the old man faltered, scrutinizing her face. "It was an accident. Everyone has accidents."

It had struck her as a pointless thing for the old man to do, like showing someone your snot.

And he isn't the only one to pester her. Without the inhibitions they would have been subject to at home, a few of the old men in their humiliation look around with their faded eyes and see her, the girl who is not really one of them, but lush and full of sap, with that American cocksureness about her. It's a mind-easing sport, tormenting the *movie star.*

"Hey baby, hey baby," they call in exaggerated jazz-speak. "You wanna help us out?"

She brushes aside their stares, the sight of their open mouths and their odd, quite terrible smiles. She tells herself they are beneath noticing. Quick to take offense, they feel insulted to be so ignored.

It would have surprised her to know that Haru sees it all and is angry with her for attracting the attention. He despises the old men. If they had been young he could have fought them, but the young men who pursue Satomi seem in better control of themselves, they have their pride, and their pursuit is only natural, after all. As it is, he has to content himself with the fact that his elders are not always his betters. When his world is made whole again, he hopes to forget the many disturbing ways in which Manzanar has altered it.

He should act honorably himself, he thinks, give Satomi up. It's only fair, but the feel of her as she melts into him in the dark places they find together, the scent of her skin, their long kisses, keep him wanting, keep him unsure. He tells himself that if he is certain of one thing, it is that he fears the life he would have with her more than he fears losing her. She will always try to pull him her way, refuse to be led, and she is a stranger to humility. She is too much for him, all heat and desire, lacking the rod of reserve he expects in a woman.

"Are we or are we not going steady, Haru?"

"There's no going steady here, Sati. Things are too unsettled to commit ourselves. We don't have to give our friendship a name, do we?"

"I was going steady with Artie before I was fourteen."

"That was just kids' stuff."

She wants to slap him at the same time as kiss him. "So this is nothing special, then?" she says, as though it hardly matters to her.

"We can't let it be. It isn't going to last."

Consequences hang over him, will trap him if he isn't careful. With luck he will be drafted soon, he can't wait to go, but it gnaws at him that Sati will have no one then to rein her in.

"You're too independent for your own good," he says.

"That's the American in me," she taunts. "Thought you liked everything American."

"Why doesn't she make friends among the girls?" he asks Eriko. "It's not natural, surely, to always be in the company of old men and boys."

"The girls bore her," Eriko says. "She's a swan among ducks, I suppose. Satomi goes her own way, you know that. Don't think that you can change her, Haru, you never will."

"It's unsuitable," he persists. "Dr. Harper is far above her in position, yet she challenges him at every turn. Things are bad enough with Yumi, without Satomi's example of do-as-you-like next door."

He complains, but the pull of her is getting stronger, he can't hold out for much longer, no matter his mother, no matter Tamura. She is at the root of his sudden awakenings in the night, the selfish need in him. His head says no, his stirred-up body doesn't want to hear. Sometimes when he looks at her, at her radiant skin, the waves of her dark hair breaking over her shoulders, he marvels at her interest in him. When she gives him that white smile, he sees her all bright and shell-clean and falters in his resolve. He desires her, but he doesn't love her, not enough to compromise his plans for, anyway. He takes refuge in criticism.

"You are upsetting your mother, you know, taking cigarettes and soap from Lawson. Your ration would last if you didn't spend so long in the showers."

"I'm just washing away Manzanar, Haru. In any case, the soap issue doesn't lather, you know that. It smells of disinfectant. What's wrong with wanting to be clean, to smell nice?"

She is prepared to take his disapproval. It is worth it if only to smell good for him, she so loves to smell good for him. And those few minutes when she stands under the water soaping her hair, rinsing it until it is squeaky clean, are heaven. Water alone doesn't cut it, it's the soap that satisfies.

"I will buy you scented soap," Tamura says. "What do I work for, if not to care for you?"

"Buy yourself things, Mama. Don't fret about me."

In summer the shower block, pleasantly warm for a change, presents her with a new problem. A colony of black horseflies have set up camp in the dank building, hovering over the scummy water that pools in the cracked floor, landing on her as she dries herself. She hates their popping eyes, their swollen blood-filled bellies. Everyone is disgusted by them. The ugly things refuse to be swatted away until they have drunk their fill of blood. Their bites leave great red swellings that take a week to subside.

The throbbing bite that Satomi suffered on her eyelid encouraged Tamura to find a remedy that would soothe it. It occurred to her that an infusion of tea and nettle might calm things down. When it did, she set about making other remedies.

Just as once she had sent Satomi to the woods in Angelina for mushrooms, now she sends her to pick the coarse mountain mint that grows at the west perimeter, to rummage in the mess hall trash for sprouting potatoes that she can plant around her barrack's steps.

People marvel at what Tamura gets out of the dry soil. She grows drills of radish to remedy sluggish circulation, makes onion poultices for flu, and in the summer months lettuce juice to clear the blood of infection. She has even found a use for the hated sagebrush that grows everywhere, poking itself rudely through the holes in the latrine walls, reminding them that they have left civilization behind.

"Mrs. Sano says that she makes a tea from it to cool fever," Tamura tells Eriko.

"Doesn't seem to be doing much for her husband's," Eriko says dryly.

"It would be hard to cure him of his burden, Eriko. It seems to work on others, though."

There is no science to it. Tamura goes on instinct, on childhood memories of her mother's concoctions. Some things work, most don't, but the word spreads, and often in the evening she has a line of patients at her door in Sewer Alley. There is comfort to be had in feeling that at least you are being treated, that you don't have to stand silent in the doctor's line. How can a doctor understand as Mrs. Baker understands? Her smile alone can cure.

Satomi complains that now she has no privacy at all. But it is a good excuse for her to spend more time with Haru, walking and kissing, and dodging the sweeping searchlights that at night hone in on their slightest movement.

Nothing that Tamura makes, though, touches her own cough or stops the hateful night sweats that soak her bedding, chilling her to the bone. Satomi lies feigning sleep, hearing her fighting for breath. It upsets Tamura to disturb her daughter's sleep.

"Go back to sleep," she says, when Satomi pulls aside the robe. "There is nothing you can do. It will be better in the morning."

And it always is a little better when the light comes, although she is fooling no one. Her ashen face mirrors her illness for the world to see, her breath has taken on the peculiar sweet-damp smell of blood and mucus.

"I feel better standing," Tamura says, relieved, when dawn comes. "I breathe better when I'm active."

"It's amazing that she keeps on working," Satomi tells Haru. Let alone that she stays up half the night mashing and blending, thinking up new remedies."

"You should learn from her," he says, unaware of how stern he sounds.

Tamura never fails to tend her little garden, or clean the barrack, even though Satomi has assumed the task to save her the effort.

"You do not even see the dust in front of your eyes," Tamura says. "In any case, I like to do it."

Eriko says that her friend's determination to keep going is something wonderful.

"Your mother is a most remarkable woman, Satomi. How proud of her your father must have been."

With her kind nature and generosity in sharing her concoctions, Tamura, as ever, draws people to her. Her warmth lends forgiveness to Satomi's offhandedness.

"It hardly seems possible the girl is Tamura's daughter," most say.

"She grows on you," a few reply.

There is a softening toward her, but Satomi will never be one of them and they judge her for it, ignorant of the fact that they too have their prejudices.

In return for Tamura's medications, presents come that it would be bad manners to refuse. No one wishes to be in debt, after all. A three-legged stool made from scrap lumber, flowers fashioned from paper, a vase formed from a discarded corn tin, and best of all a saucepan with a well-fitting lid.

"The water won't evaporate when we boil it now," Tamura says, thanking the giver delightedly. Water rarely reaches more than a low simmer on their lukewarm stove.

"Hmm, if you can get the wood for it," he says.

In gratitude for Tamura treating his children's boils with her soot-and-spider's-web paste, Mr. Hamada, who works clearing the land for the new farm project, brings a selection of the little wooden birds he carves in his spare time, for her to choose from.

"He is a true artist," Eriko remarks at the sight of them. "They may not have blood or organs, but there is life in those little creatures."

Tamura takes a long time choosing.

"They are all so beautiful, Mr. Hamada. How can I decide?"

In the end she opts for the smallest unpainted one, it seems to beckon her.

"It's a titmouse," Mr. Hamada says. "In life they are gray, with an eager expression."

The little bird sits in the cup of Tamura's hand, its wings half open, bringing to mind billowing clouds, wind in the grass, memories of birdsong.

"I love it more than anything," she says gratefully.

With these gifts, their room, like many others in the camp, has taken on a character of its own so that the word "home" has regained its meaning.

"Even in Sewer Alley people have pride," Haru says. "Pride in how you live is an ancient Japanese virtue."

The proof of the pride he speaks of is to be seen all around them. There are hobby gardens where flowers grown from seed bloom in splashes of welcome color, furniture made from scraps of wood, jewelry from chicken bones and the newfangled dental floss that sometimes comes free with toothpaste. Brushes hang neatly in line on exterior walls, and small rough-hewn benches are placed by scrubbed steps. Someone has positioned the splayed limb of a dead pear tree as a sculpture by their door.

"It's very pleasing," Naomi says.

"Fine now, maybe," Mr. Sano sneers. "Come winter it'll be better burned for firewood."

Everyone, it seems, is busy with some sort of crafting. Haru has made his mother a set of drawers from discarded cardboard boxes. And Naomi, with her failing sight, her arthritic hands, knits mittens for the orphans. She likes to feel useful.

"When I was young," she boasts, "my needles went so fast the wool crackled."

"Sparks flew," Eriko confirms.

Eriko has fashioned curtains for their one small window from a flowered skirt that the ever-expanding Yumi has grown out of.

"They look so pretty," Tamura says.

"Playing at doll's houses, I see," Mr. Sano remarks on his way past.

Longing to indulge her dressmaker's love of frills and bows, Tamura makes aprons for the orphans out of the factory off-cuts. She wishes she could have afforded better, pink and white gingham, perhaps, plaids with red in them. She would like to treat the girls, indulge herself in lovely things.

With Naomi's mittens, Tamura's aprons, and Lawson's toys, Satomi rarely goes empty-handed to the orphanage, where she spends the best part of her days caring for the babies, reading to the older children, letting them, to the superintendent's disapproval, clamber all over her. She tries to be even-handed with them but can't help favoring the serious little four-year-old, Cora, who is always at her side. The child, who she thinks resembles Tamura a little, has worked her way into her heart so that she can hardly wait to see her each morning, to pick her up, kiss the smooth cheek, the rosebud lips.

"Oh, Mama, you can't help loving Cora. She just melts your heart."

Cora has blue-black hair cut short, with bangs that frame her doll-pretty face. She is quick and bright, a frightened, brave little girl who knows how to please.

Satomi wonders what experiences have given Cora the extraordinary ability to sense what adults require of her. She is quiet when they want her to be, always helpful, and a little mother to the babies, quite capable of changing diapers and warming bottles.

As far as anyone can make out, and judging from the way she crosses herself at prayer, she must have come from a Catholic orphanage. Her papers have been mislaid, and when questioned she says she lived in a big house with other children. They guess her age to be about four, they would have said five, six even, if she hadn't been so small. She is certain, though, that her name is Cora. The superintendent says that it's not a Japanese name, unless Cora herself has mixed it up with *Kora*, the Japanese demand for, *Listen, you.*

"She is a sweet child," she says. "If only they were all like her."

Joining in with the remaking of Manzanar, the orphanage has planted a lawn, and built a wraparound porch to unite its three barracks. They plan flower borders, a swing for the children if they can find someone to make it.

There are no curbs or sidewalks in the camp, no stores, but if the barbed wire and the gun towers were suddenly to disappear, Manzanar these days might look, through forgiving eyes, much the same as any small American town. The American dream of hearth and home, although battered, seems to be recovering. Yet somehow Manzanar looking more like home only serves to high-light the fact that they are not free.

Frustration boils away under the surface. There is always the sense of waiting in the air, humor is more often than not dark, and irony has replaced optimism. The tension between the Citizens League and the Kibei is a constant, and to add to it, gangs of youths loyal to neither strut about the camp, less willing to please than their older siblings. The feeling that Manzanar's internees have that they are being unfairly, even cruelly treated, that they have lost something precious that can never be regained, refuses to fade.

RIOT

IN THE FREEZING air of December when no one is warm enough and everyone is hungry for the food of home, a riot erupts in the camp seemingly out of nowhere.

Settling down for the evening, and far from the heart of it, the residents of Sewer Alley are among the last to open their doors, to listen and try to make out what the distant rumble of feet, the shouting, are all about.

Dr. Harper comes to advise Tamura to stay in their barrack.

"The military police have arrested three men for beating up an informer," he tells her. "They took him from his bed and almost killed him. We have him in the hospital. Everyone is angry at the arrest, and there is a crowd demanding their release. I don't think they are going to settle anytime soon. Please stay home, Tamura, keep out of it. And put your light out, no point in attracting attention."

"It was kind of you to come," Tamura says, blushing at being singled out by him. "We are all grateful, Dr. Harper."

"No need for gratitude, Tamura. I am concerned for you, that's all." He fights the urge he has to stay, to keep by her side, to protect her. "Well, remember the light," he says, hovering at the door. "I'll be in the hospital all night if you need me."

Hearing Dr. Harper's advice through the wall, Naomi asks

Eriko to leave their light on. "The moon's on the wane and I can't
bear to sit in the dark. It makes the cold seem worse somehow."
Her voice is wispy, shaking a little.

Naomi has had enough of the cold. Her hand is still bandaged
from where it stuck to the barrack's frozen doorknob, pulling the
skin from her palm as she tugged her hand free.

"It's stubborn to heal," she complains. "Old age makes the
body stubborn."

She can hardly move these days, and knitting now is out of the
question. The bones in her fingers are stiff, frozen into immobility.

Haru, on his way to Sewer Alley, stops Dr. Harper on his own
way to the hospital. "It's nothing much, is it, Doctor? It'll all blow
over soon, won't it?"

"Hard to say, could go either way, boy." He puts a hand on
Haru's shoulder. "Look after them," he says, thinking in the moment only of Tamura.

Haru paces the alley, not knowing what he is looking for, his
eyes tracking every movement. He guesses that the informer is a
member of his own American Citizens League.

"Japanese Uncle Toms," the Kibei accuse league members.

"Traitors to America," the league members retort to the Kibei.

Haru thinks the Kibei mad, troublemakers, out to spoil.

As he paces, the news spreads. Mothers begin appearing at
doors, calling their children in from play, worrying about where
the older ones might be.

"Have you seen Toru?"

"Where is Yukio? He should be home by now."

Lights go out, people stop calling to each other. Sewer Alley, lit
only by a thin portion of moon, looks dim and ghostly.

Eriko pleads for Haru to come inside, but he doesn't want to
hide indoors like a coward.

"What could this informer have told them that would create all this trouble?" Tamura asks him on her way to Eriko's. "They already know there is gambling and liquor, they have always looked the other way."

"It's more likely to be that he has given them the names of those Kibei who call themselves Japan's underground. You must have heard their talk, Tamura, seen the way they stir up trouble."

"Yes, but they are only boys trying to be men."

"Maybe, but they are not harmless."

Tamura joins the Okihiros in their room, where Satomi finds her on her return from the orphanage. She has been running and is out of breath.

"I was worried about you. You are very late, Satomi."

"I came the long way around to avoid the fights. That show-off boy who works with Haru at the school asked me if I was with them or against them. I didn't know what he was talking about."

"Is the crowd dispersing?" Haru calls through the open door.

"I don't think so. I heard them shouting and chanting. I tried to find Lawson to ask him what was going on, but I couldn't see him anywhere." She is more excited than afraid, thrilled by the drama, the change of pace in the day.

"We must stay together," Eriko says. "There is safety in numbers."

"Yes, and at least only one stove will need feeding," Tamura says, looking on the bright side as usual.

For once Satomi approves of her mother's optimism. It's good to be near Haru, who at his mother's pleading has reluctantly come inside.

"Just for a moment, just to get warm," he says.

As they sit close, she attempts nonchalance, as though the salty scent of him, the warmth of his body against hers, isn't sending a run of pleasure through her. It hurts to love him so much, to be the one who loves more. If only he would lose the desire to re-form her she might in turn try harder to please him.

"I wish I could bring Cora here," she says. "Keep her safe with us. She was so sweet today, clinging to me, not wanting me to leave."

"She is safer where she is," Haru says. "No one is going to bother with the orphanage."

They hear the rioters trawling the camp, seeking out the *inu*, a word that Satomi has never heard before.

"It's a special word," Eriko says. "It means both dog and traitor."

"Oh, yes, I had forgotten it," Tamura says. "I have forgotten so much."

There are bangs and shouts and the sound of running feet, and Mr. Sano comes to tell them that the rioters are smashing up property and beating up those they have named as traitors to their race.

"We are herded here like animals," he says. "Our administrators have been black-marketing our meat and sugar, and still there are informers, traitors. Damn stoolies, no wonder people are mad."

"Are they traitors or just good Americans?" Haru is getting more agitated by the minute. "It's not enough just to say that we are loyal, Mr. Sano. We must prove it."

Mr. Sano stares at him scornfully. "It's the young who will be the death of us," he exclaims, raising his hands in exasperation. "Their blood is always hot, their passions ridiculous."

Eriko and Tamura can't meet each other's eyes for fear they may laugh.

Shortly after Mr. Sano leaves, two wild-eyed young men with baseball bats burst through their door, shouting something about freedom before running off toward the new drainage works by the cemetery.

"We should have listened to Dr. Harper and put the light out," Yumi says reclaiming her child's voice. She is shaking with fright.

The shock of the intrusion, along with the rush of cold air entering their barrack, has brought them to their feet. Eriko puts out their light.

"What's happening now?" Haru shouts after the men. "What's the latest?"

"We're taking control, you bonehead," one of them shouts back. "We're going to smash up the waterworks. Come with us."

"I'm frightened," Eriko tells Haru. "Your sister and grandmother are frightened. You must stay with us, Haru, please don't go out."

She thinks that Mr. Sano is right about the young. They want to be warriors, and Haru is no different. If he leaves their barrack, she fears that she might never see him alive again.

But he has had enough of being among the women, and when a burst of gunfire brings a few seconds' silence in its wake he makes for the door.

"I'm going to find out what is happening. I'll be back soon." He pulls his arm away from Eriko's hold on it. "Let me be a man, Mother," he insists, and she releases him.

"I'm coming with you, Haru."

"No, Satomi, stay with your mother. Your place is with her."

"Don't tell me what to do. I want to see for myself." She is out of the door before Tamura can say anything.

He begins to run, long strides that put a distance between them, making it hard for her to keep up. He wants to be with his friends from the league, he wants to find Ralph and talk it over with him. It's too shameful having a girl tagging along. But when she falls behind he gets worried and stops, looking back to see if she has turned for home.

"You shouldn't have come if you can't keep up," he shouts, catching sight of her. "Why must you insist on acting like a man?"

"Why must you insist on acting like my father?" she screams back.

As they near the mess hall, a gang of youths wearing white headbands scrawled with *toukon*, the Japanese symbol for fighting spirit, come toward them, chanting.

"Long Live His Majesty the Emperor."

They are wielding weapons, kendo fighting sticks, knives, some roughly made hatchets, anything they have been able to lay their hands on.

Satomi stops running, mesmerized by the sight of their brutal arsenal.

"Haru, Haru," she calls breathlessly, but her voice is thin, lost in the air. Without intent, the chanting youths knock her about in their charge.

The searchlights are tracking the boys and a wide cone of light has them in its sights, catching her in its beam too, blinding her so that it's impossible to see anything but the glaring white light.

The youths pass, leaving her in the dark as the quaking sound of the guards' oncoming feet running to catch up with the trouble-makers adds to her confusion. She stumbles down the nearest alley, pressing herself against the side of a barrack wall as they pass, kicking up a flurry of dust with their heavy boots.

Her hand goes to her heart as though to stop it from leaping from her chest, her lungs are burning from the effort of trying to keep up with Haru, she can feel her blood pulsing. Haru has disappeared, deserted her. She is alone and frightened in the moments before she hears his shout, hoarse and panicky.

"Sati, where the hell are you?"

"I'm here, over here," she yells from the shadows, as a man reeking of sweat and potato vodka grabs her arm, ripping the sleeve of her jacket.

"I'll save you," he slurs. "Stay with me."

As she struggles, Haru appears at her side, pulls the man off her, takes her hand roughly, and forces her to run with him.

In front of the jailhouse in the crammed square the searchlights dazzle. Ranks of soldiers have drawn a line three deep in the sand. The thought crosses her mind that next door to the jailhouse Dr. Harper is inside the hospital. He will be soothing his patients, who will be as scared as her, maybe. She would like to join him, but it would take a tank to make a path through the mob.

Corralled in front of the soldiers, who are attempting to hold their ground, the crowd moves like the sea, a huge tide of bodies surging forward. A truck is pushed through the soldiers' ranks into the jailhouse. Glass shatters, there is a crunching sound, a cheer goes up.

Haru is mouthing something to her that she can't hear—she thinks he is telling her to stay close, but in the throng's pitching they are forced apart, so that her hand is torn from his just as a guard takes aim and shoots into the crowd.

In the alarm the gunfire causes she is knocked to the ground, where, among the feet and the dust, things seem to go into slow motion.

In case another round should come and split the air as horribly as the first, she covers her ears with her hands and curls her body tight, knees up, head down.

Through the tangle of legs she can see a boy crouched on the ground like her, but somehow not like her. His body is still, his head twisted unnaturally to the side, his hand open as though it has frozen in the act of waving. As she looks, a spurt of blood wells up through his pale T-shirt, spreading across his chest, a red flower opening its petals. He slumps forward, and drops of blood plop slowly to the ground and mix with the dirt. And suddenly she is screaming, struggling to move, scanning the forest of legs

for a space to crawl through. A booted foot treads on her ankle
and the searing pain draws a yelp from her. She thinks she sees
Ralph's legs through the stirred-up dust, cotton trousers, the
sneakers that have lost their laces. He is too far away to get to.

"I told you not to come," Haru roars above her head, pulling
her to her feet. "Did you really want to see that?"

"No. Did you?" Her body is shuddering, her legs weak, she is
covered in dirt, bruises already blooming on her forehead, a dark
graze on her ankle.

Acrid smoke fills the air as people begin to cough and splutter
and hastily withdraw from the square. Something is happening to
Haru, he can't seem to speak, and just as she begins to choke herself she sees that the whites of his eyes have become bloodshot.

"It's gas," he croaks.

Satomi takes his hand and they stagger away from the crowd,
hoping to find some good air to breathe.

Three hours later they emerge from under the barrack where
they took shelter. Shaken and silent, with each other, they return
home red-eyed with the news that things are finally quieting down.

"There was no order to fire," Haru says angrily. "But they did
anyway. There are two dead, and ten more wounded." He absentmindedly picks up the sleeping Naomi's blanket, which has
slipped to the floor, and covers her lap with it.

"Two boys dead," he repeats, as though he can't take it in himself.

"They used tear gas to calm things down," Satomi adds in a
rush. "It was horrible, it made our eyes burn, and Haru was sick."

Haru looks embarrassed. "Nothing to make a fuss about," he
says irritably, as Eriko forces him to sit. He is ashamed that he was
the one to be sick. Satomi could have kept quiet about it, but she
has no sense about such things. She allows him no pride.

"People were dizzy and stumbling all over the place, but angry too, really angry." She can't seem to stop talking, the words

tumbling out of her as she moves restlessly about. Haru, sitting now, has gone quiet.

The bruises on Satomi's face have deepened to a livid puce, her clothes are torn and filthy. Pictures of the fallen boy, of his bloody T-shirt, flash horribly at intervals in her mind.

At the sight of Satomi bruised but alive, Tamura suffers the flash of anger that comes after child-lost, child-found, is over.

"You shouldn't have gone," she says disapprovingly. "You should have listened to Haru."

Yumi is picking at her skirt, hopping from one foot to the other. She needs to pee but is scared to go to the latrines on her own.

"You're sure it's all over?" she keeps asking Haru.

"Yes, go," he says. "It's all quiet now."

It is past dawn already and none of them, apart from Naomi, has slept.

Tamura goes to their barrack for her toothbrush, for the sliver of soap she is making last.

"I'll wash at the spigot this morning," she calls to Eriko.

When she returns she is in a better mood. She never sleeps much anyway, and what can she do about Satomi? The truth is the girl is a copy of her father, another Aaron. She won't be ruled.

"Should we go to work, do you think?" Eriko asks Haru.

"I think you should. We must help get things back to normal. I will walk my class to school. You come with me, Yumi. I'll see you into yours." He is finding relief in taking charge.

"I'll walk with you and Eriko, Mother," Satomi says. "Give me a moment to change. I guess they won't be opening the mess halls for a while, so breakfast will be late."

She holds Tamura's hand as they walk. It feels thin, more bone than flesh, as though she is holding a tiny newborn mouse. Eriko *tsks* at the mess the camp is in, shaking her head at the madness in the world.

There's a handwritten sign on their mess hall door: BREAKFAST IN ONE HOUR.

"We are fine, you know," Eriko says to Satomi. "You don't have to walk us like children. You're the one who is limping."

"I want to. I won't settle until I see Mother through the door. Then I'll backtrack and take the shortcut to the orphanage."

"Eriko's right, there's no need," Tamura agrees. "Who would want to hurt me? You go back, I know you want to check on Cora."

"No point, we're nearly there, Mama."

Across the way from the factory two white fire officers from Lone Pine stand beside a fire engine, looking around as though on alert for a predator.

Tamura and Eriko's supervisor is at the door ushering the workers in.

"It's on loan from the Forest Service, just in case," he says archly, nodding toward the fire engine. He has a cut above his lip repaired with four catgut stitches. Like a half mustache, Satomi thinks. It gives him a jaunty air, but no one mentions it. They have passed similar on their way here, closed eyes, cuts, swellings. Already it is bad form to ask what side you are on.

"Hey, little darlin'," one of the officers calls, giving a long low whistle. "Are you looking for a fight too?"

Tamura lets go of Satomi's hand and marches up to him. "Do you want to cause more trouble?" she asks as though talking to a child. "Is my daughter never to be left in peace?"

The soldier gives a nasty laugh and turns his back on her. A truck comes toward them slowly, two guards at its side gathering the wood from the smashed-up laundry tubs, throwing it into the back of the pickup as they go.

"Tricky customers, these Nips, go off like fireworks at the slightest thing. Better not to get too familiar," they advise the Lone Pine officers.

"I was going to wash my mother's clothes today," Eriko says placidly to Tamura. "Now what will we do?"

"They can't all be broken, Eriko. We will just have to share."

The mess hall bells are ringing in memory of the two dead boys. A strangely playful sound, betraying the sadness in the air.

"One was seventeen, the other twenty-one," the supervisor says. "Ten more wounded in the hospital."

On hearing who the dead boys are, Eriko says that she had known one of them.

"I can't believe it's him," she says, sighing. "He was a gentle boy, very polite to his elders. A good boy."

On her way to the orphanage, Satomi comes across Lawson overseeing a gang of Japanese who are sweeping the debris of the battle into piles in readiness for the truck to pick up.

"There'll be questions to answer," he says sorrowfully. "You can't just fire without an order, not in America anyway."

"Then why did they, Lawson?"

"The military got nervous, I guess. Things got out of hand, but still we have laws, don't we. You can't go around shooting people."

"Seems you have, though, doesn't it?"

"Not me, Satomi, not me. In any case, you'll get justice, you'll see."

"It's a bit late for that, isn't it?"

"I guess, maybe. Anyway, I'm pleased to see that you are all right, at least. How are you doing for soap?"

"Nothing against you, Lawson, but I won't be taking soap anymore."

The dissent in the camp has been revealed. Bones have been broken, blood spilled, to say the least. She doesn't know on which side to stand, but it would be wrong now to accept gifts from Lawson. Things will never go back to how they were. No doubt the dead will be buried, the wreckage of the battle cleared, but the riot has already left something less tangible than bodies and debris in its wake, a postscript provoked by outrage. The Japanese inmates are no longer sheep to be herded.

By the time she reaches the alleyway that is the cut-through to the orphanage, the bells have stopped ringing. A short tolling for two short lives, she thinks, surprised that death comes so unexpectedly to some.

And then the picture flashes into her mind again, the twisted head, that pathetic hand, the black blood in the dust. She pauses for a moment, looking back, trembling a little. It is very cold, the air quite still, for once. Apart from two old men sitting around a tin-can fire at its far end, the alleyway is empty. People are at work or behind the safety of their closed doors. Better to keep your head down on such a day. They should have known that, since Pearl Harbor, December is a dangerous month.

How can she go to work as though nothing has happened, resume her routine as easily as Tamura and Eriko seem to have done? She is so tired that if it wasn't for Cora she would return to Sewer Alley and sleep the day away. But Cora will be anxious, looking toward the door for her, and she wants to see the little girl, hold her close. Tears come streaming, she is suddenly filled with sympathy for the world, for the dead boys, for the look now in Yumi's once-innocent eyes, for the hurt that is Cora.

The desire for a cigarette comes as it often does, but she has none. She pictures herself setting the match, drawing deep, the familiar catch in her throat as the smoke snakes through her. Why had she let Haru talk her into giving them up?

"You don't have the money for them anyway, Sati."

"I could share yours."

"No, it's horrible to see a girl smoking. I can't bear the smell on you."

Halfway down the alley, as she stops to knot her scarf against the cold, her eyes are drawn to movement at an open doorway. Two boys of around Haru's age are joined together kissing. She stands stock-still, staring, her mouth open, her bottom lip pendulous. In the middle of the kiss one begins to unbuckle the other's belt, laughing as their lips part. They move in a secret primitive language, boy against boy, slim on slim, no curves, equal strengths.

It seems to her a nonsensical scene, like something out of those dreams that you feel shame for when you wake, as though you had conjured them out of the dark bit inside you that nobody knows about. The riot must have created a mad sort of electricity in the air, turned things on their head.

The one whose buckle has been undone catches sight of her staring, but she can't look away, she might as well be rooted in the frozen mud beneath her feet. His body stills for a moment, but then he returns her stare, exaggerating the incline of his head, raising his eyebrows in a sort of challenge that she has no idea how to meet. With a half smile on his face, he shrugs and kicks the door shut.

She doesn't mention what she has seen to Haru. Will never, she thinks, mention it to anyone. She feels sure that she wouldn't be believed.

After that day, whenever she thinks about those boys, their lean embrace, it seems to her that she has witnessed a wonderfully rebellious, entirely independent act. It's all wrong, of course, surely not what nature intended, but it pleases her to know that she isn't the only outsider at Manzanar.

She scans the newspapers that Dr. Harper gives her for reports of the riot and finds none. It's as though America has forgotten their incarcerated fellows. There is news of German U-boats harassing shipping on the East Coast; news of the movie actress Carol Lombard who has died in a plane crash, on her way back from a tour to promote the sale of war bonds. A radio station called the Voice of America has begun broadcasting, and the British have asked their citizens to bathe in five inches of water to help the war effort. There's a new drink called *instant coffee* and Glenn Miller has sold a million copies of "Chattanooga Choo Choo." Gas has gone up to fifteen cents a gallon, and Joe Louis has taken the heavyweight title in one. The world outside of Manzanar is in those pages, the world that interests America.

"What has happened to the American conscience?" Ralph asks Dr. Harper. "It's shaming that under pressure we have forgotten that we are a democracy."

"They may have reasons for censoring it," Dr. Harper suggests.

"Not so much censored as ignored, I bet," Satomi says. "I guess as far as news is concerned we're not worth the print."

The three of them sit in silence for a while musing on it.

The riot's fallout takes its effect. Everyone is on edge, captors and caught alike. The guards aren't so ready anymore with their smiles, and they don't call greetings from the gun towers as they used to. The known leaders of the Kibei are being segregated, ready to be sent off to the Tule Lake camp in northern California, where, droved together, it will be easier to control them. The meaner guards have their fun with them, telling them they are being rounded up for the firing squad.

"You creeps are gonna pay the price now," they taunt.

Haru is ordered to join a line to sign the new loyalty oath that will distinguish loyal Japanese from potential enemies. Signing your name on the *yes* form confirms that you are loyal to America, and if you are a male of the right age, you will be drafted into the Army.

"I'm happy to do it," he boasts to his friends in the line behind him as he signs with a flourish.

Ralph Lazo is not required to sign the loyalty oath, but he walks the eight miles into Lone Pine to register with the local draft board.

"We'll see those Germans off, eh, Ralph?" Haru says when Ralph returns.

"Sure thing." Ralph smiles. "Only hope I can stay with my buddies."

Those who refuse to sign are nicknamed the No No Boys. They are full of bravado, singing "Kimigayo," the Japanese national anthem, at the top of their voices. Not sure if they are to be deported or culled, they stand up straight, waiting.

The elderly Issei, who were born in Japan, have the toughest decision to make in the signings. If they autograph the *yes* paper, they automatically abjure their allegiance to the emperor of Japan.

"What are we meant to do?" Mr. Sano says in despair. "We are not allowed American citizenship. It will render us stateless."

It is the same for Naomi, who is more sanguine about it than Mr. Sano. "What difference does it make?" she says. "They do what they like with us whether we are citizens or not."

JOINING UP

"ARE YOU SAD?" Cora asks Satomi.

"Yes, I am, Cora." It seems that little can be kept from the child. "I will lose a friend soon, you see."

"Not me?"

"No, not you. You're my special girl," she comforts.

She doesn't want to think about losing Cora, it's enough that Haru will be gone soon, that Tamura is fading by the day. Her love for the little girl has grown until it seems to her like a mother's love. She's touched by everything about the child, the feel of her hand in her own, her sweet silvery voice, and her eyes so clear, so honest that it hurts sometimes to look at them.

"You won't ever lose me, will you, Satomi?" Cora asks, subject herself to the fear of yet more loss.

"I will try not to, Cora."

It would be wrong, she thinks, to make promises. Lately Cora's nerves are getting the better of her. She has taken to sleeping under her bed with only her thin Army blanket for cover. Since security has tightened up, she is frightened by the guards patrolling past the windows, by the searchlights sweeping the dormitories at night.

"There are ghosts," she tells Satomi. "They want to take me away."

She keeps her few possessions with her, while she sleeps, in a small string-tied bundle so that in an emergency she can grab it and run.

"It's a responsibility," Tamura says when hearing of it. "You are like a sister to her."

The Bakers and the Okihiros in their evening routine sit bunched together on the wooden steps of their barracks. They drink tea and chat companionably. Not, as Naomi frequently remarks, that it can be called tea, really. Tea tastes quite different than the twice-used dregs that if you are quick enough can be had from the mess hall's kitchen.

"Hardly better than dust," she complains. "Still, it satisfies the habit."

Long after Naomi and Yumi have gone to bed, Tamura and Eriko stay talking in the dark, reminiscing about their child-hoods. They won't admit it, but they can't settle until Haru and Satomi return from their walk. Since the riot it's foolhardy to be out in the dark, but the young won't listen. They worry that their children don't have sense enough to stay out of trouble. They worry that since the riot the guards have become trigger-happy, they worry now about everything.

"Haru is a man now," Eriko says. "Yet I fret about him as though he were still a boy."

"It's hard to let them go," Tamura says. "I expect our mothers felt the same."

"I have never spent a day of my life without my mother in it," Eriko says. "You must miss yours, Tamura."

"I try not to think about her too much. Although I long some-times for the flavor of her food, a spoonful of her plum oil. You should have tasted it, Eriko." Tamura adds to her tea a shot of the potato spirit she brewed with a cure for chest complaints in mind. "Just the scent of it made my mouth water with anticipation."

"My mother is a poor cook," Eriko whispers out of earshot of Naomi. "Her rice is too sticky."

"Still, you are lucky to have her."

"This is your best medicine yet," Eriko compliments her, topping up her cup until it becomes more alcohol than tea. "It never fails to make me feel better."

By choice, Haru and Satomi on their evening strolls would have walked by the stream that tracks the north boundary of the camp, but the searchlights pick them out there as though for the guards' sport. They have been lit up more than once for everyone to see and know their business. Lately, though, they have found a place to be together in one of the Buddhist workshops that is never locked.

The priest, a trusting man, blind to the new order taking place around him, thinks more of the soul than of practical matters. He believes that filial duty is still the order of the day in Manzanar. What point would there be in going to the bother of replacing the lost key? There is little to steal, and not, he believes, even one thief among his congregation.

They dart into the hut separately, dodging the searchlights, bending their bodies low to the ground to cast a short shadow. Other couples use the workshop too, but it's first come, first served. No one wants to share.

If it wasn't for the reserve in Haru's nature that reminds her not to show herself reckless, Satomi would give her all and not care for the consequences. Haru must be the one in charge, it seems. While she might go against him in other things, she finds herself cautious in this. They are inching forward, but stubbornness and pride in his strength of will tortures them both.

"Nobody likes a tease," she mimics Artie, not understanding herself why since the riot she feels the urge to be the pursuer, to break the pattern of stop and start.

"Don't speak like a whore, Sati. You sound like the worst kind of white girl."

The touch of her tongue on his lips, her dress half open in invitation, is causing him problems. He wishes that she had been a whore, that she wasn't Tamura's daughter.

It's odd, he thinks, that she is not the one. He guesses that when the time comes he wants a daisy, not an orchid, for a wife. Satomi has been urging him on since he signed the loyalty paper. Her nature is sensual and he has only to go there, to take without asking. It's getting so that he can't trust himself. He's ready to run.

He longs more than anything now to have the chance to prove himself, to show America that he is made of the right stuff. He's determined to go to war, to be out in the world free of Manzanar and of Satomi's expectations.

For Satomi the thought that she is about to lose him translates into the strangest pains. She feels them in her lungs when he is near, a coiling twisting thing, and in the bowl of her spine, which aches when he touches her, and in her head, which throbs dully in her absent moments when his image lopes across her mind.

"So it's certain you'll be drafted now." She can't look at Haru, doesn't want him to see her pain.

"Looks that way," he says. "They won't take our loyalty for granted, so we have to prove it. I'm glad of the chance."

"Can't wait to go, can you?" The words are out before she can stop herself. They sound so self-pitying she would take them back if she could, swallow them whole.

"I haven't lied," he says defensively. "You knew I was going to join up first chance I got."

"So that's it, then, you're off?"

"Yes, it'll be soon, I think. Don't try to make me feel bad about it, Sati."

He has never promised her anything, after all. Why should he feel guilty?

"Things will be better here for everyone once we men are in uniform," he says.

"Ah, yes, men in uniform," she says sagely. "My father said the same when he went to fight for America."

All their conversations now are unsatisfactory and usually end on a quarrelsome note. It's hard for her to claim a calm moment in her day, one when the thought of losing Haru is not niggling there in the background, sucking the pleasure out of everything.

Tamura has noticed her distraction, the anxiety in her, the way her fingers drum on the covers of the books that Haru has listed for her as required reading.

The titles taunt Satomi. *The Last of the Mohicans. The Touch-stone.* She is fed up with romance, with made-up lives. She is thinking of giving up reading altogether. These days happy endings seem just another thing designed to wound her.

"My heart hurts for her," Tamura tells Eriko. "But she has her pride still, I hope."

Eriko sighs. "We must trust Haru not to be foolish."

"We can't," Haru insists. "You're too young, I'm leaving. You don't know what you would be giving up."

"I'll be eighteen in a month. It's old enough."

"Stop it, Sati. Remember whose daughter you are."

He can't claim to have been a saint himself, but it's different for men, after all. He started young with white girls, real pretty ones who went all the way, girls who would eat you up if you let them. With Japanese girls, though, he has always felt a reserve, the need to respect, to think of their families. It is hard to know where to stand with Satomi. She's neither one thing nor the other. He guesses that if it hadn't been for Tamura, he would have taken her long ago.

"I know exactly what I would be giving, Haru. Don't treat me as a child, I'm not Yumi."

"No, you are more daring than Yumi, more willing to take risks. Your nature is a dangerous one."

It thrills her that he thinks her dangerous, hurts her too.

"Why can't you trust me? I'm not who you think."

"You have no idea who you are, Sati. I know you better than you know yourself."

"I can be who you want me to be, Haru. I can change."

"Then I would have killed who you are."

When it's too painful to kiss, to hold each other, they lie on the floor of the little workshop mute and motionless, a ruler's width between their bodies, each feeling the other's heat, the other's regret.

If ever they talk of the future, it is always about Haru's. In his company she lets go of herself, it is him that matters, he is everything. Only the smallest part of her asks, *But what of me?*

She tells herself that if she could have Haru she would let go of ambition, the desires she once harbored for her own life. She would meld herself to his shape, conform to his manners, and consider being a dutiful wife. She fears the loss of him more than the loss of herself.

Haru stretches out on the workshop floor, eyes closed, listening to the drone of the traffic beyond the wire fences. The fences they had been made to put up to imprison themselves. Eight hundred Japanese volunteers built Manzanar, the barracks, the latrines, the hated mocking fences. Somehow the thought of it adds insult to the injury of the place.

"They're there to protect you," Lawson says.

"Then why do they turn inwards at the top?"

"I don't know, Satomi, just the way they're made, I guess."

It's the same with the guns. It bugs her that they are trained into the camp, since no matter what Lawson says everyone knows they are there to keep internees in, not free men out.

"For me it's not so much the fencing and the guns that make it hard to be here," Haru says. "It's the waste of time. I want to get on with my life, join the Army. I want to go to college, to be a teacher. I want to do something I can feel good about."

His long silences irritate her, but against her nature she has learned when to be still, learned when not to speak. She takes her pleasure in lying next to him, hearing his breathing, imagining the life she might have with him. With surprise she thinks that she must be more like her mother than she had thought. She too is capable of sacrifice for the man she loves.

Sometimes, when the grind of a truck takes the rise of the road, Haru will jump up and pace the room.

"Listen to that, people coming and going as they please, living their lives free as birds just yards away."

He had seen a dog once sauntering by on the outside of the wire, tail up, wandering at will. *Even the dogs*, he had thought, *even the dogs*.

Satomi is impressed by the urgency in him, the barely contained animal energy that at Manzanar he has little outlet for. Despite wanting to hold on to him, she longs sometimes to pull apart the barbed wire, set him free, see him run toward the life that he is so certain waits for him.

Despite that Haru is on alert, the months pass without news of a draft date. She allows herself to relax into the idea that the Japanese boys will never be called to war. Never mind that they had answered *yes*. It's all talk, talk to keep them on hold, talk to keep at bay another riot. It isn't in the government's nature, she thinks, to trust its Japanese countrymen.

But then on an afternoon when the air is tender, the spumy clouds shot through with gold, a rosy day when work is finished and there is nothing to do but sit in the sinking sunlight watching Cora running with the Sewer Alley girls, Haru is summoned to the camp director's office.

"Time you took Cora back," he says, not looking at her, already looking toward the battlefield.

All down their alley the *yes* boys are pouring out of their doors, linking arms, talking excitedly. Haru joins them. His shoulders are back, his body taut and straight, he might already be a soldier. He is almost free.

She is late returning Cora, so that the child is hurried in to eat the meal that has gone cold on her plate.

"You shouldn't take her out if you can't get her back on time," one of the kinder supervisors complains.

"You won't report it, will you?" Satomi pleads. "She was so happy playing, I forgot the time."

"Favoring Cora hasn't gone unnoticed, Satomi. Don't push them to ban you from taking her out at all."

On the way back to Sewer Alley she comes across Haru sitting on the ground with Ralph and some of his Citizens League friends. They are smoking and talking animatedly, so primed up that Haru doesn't notice her at first. When he does, he signals with a brief nod of his head toward Sewer Alley. It's an order for her to move on, a dismissal.

"My papers have come. I'll be drafted in a week or so," he tells her later.

He turns from her as he says it, pushing his hands through his thick hair. He can't look at her, won't be trapped by her hurt.

"It's an all-Nisei combat regiment. Boys are joining from all over. We're getting our chance at last."

The delight in his voice cuts her so that she is too angry to feel sad. "You needn't look so pleased about it. You are leaving your family, after all." *Leaving me*, she wants to sob, *leaving me.*

"Look, I'm sorry about it, Sati. You're not going to cry, are you? It's bad enough for my mother and Yumi; if they see you crying, then . . ." His voice is hard, unkind. Kindness might encourage tears, he might make promises, risk the clean break that if he is strong is only days away.

"I'm not crying. I won't cry, you needn't worry. I guess I'll just go and get your books. You'll want your books back."

"You keep them. I won't have much time for reading for a while."

"I don't want them. I've finished them anyway."

"Okay, I get it that you're angry. Sure, I'm leaving now, but everyone will be out of this place soon. It's all going to work out, Sati, you'll see. Once Manzanar is behind you, you'll find what you want to do in life."

"I know what I want. You know what I want, Haru."

"What you think you want. Look, forget us for a bit, your mother needs you now. She's much worse, isn't she? Give her the best of yourself while you can, you will never regret it."

His words sting her. How can he think that she needs reminding of how much Tamura needs her? Death is loitering outside their barrack now, waiting for her mother to welcome it in. Tamura can hardly stand, these days; she has given up making her medicines, given up going to work.

"Just for the time being," she says. "Just for now."

Every inch of Tamura's body aches, she can hardly raise her arms, and she is subject to swellings in her legs and feet, to strange pains in her organs.

"It will pass," she insists to Satomi. "Don't make a fuss."

On Haru's last night in the camp, their last together, Satomi walks to the Buddhist workshop early, to be sure of it. The air is damp, speckled with squads of clustered flies, and dark is falling fast. In the noises off in the distance she can hear the crackling of an illicit radio, the ubiquitous low hum of conversation that is a constant in the camp.

There are always shadows in Manzanar, quick glimpsed movements, whispering in the alleyways. Rumor has it that the camp is haunted, that the ghosts of old inmates wander around trying to find their way home. It's nonsense, she knows, but still she is pleased when the stars come fast and the moon waxes full.

In the cupboard under the altar she finds a cloth and a small broom, and suddenly she is tidying and dusting like a housewife.

When Haru comes he is sulky with her, fed up with women's sad faces. He has heard Eriko crying in the night, and Naomi looks at him now as if each glance might be her last. He is borne down by the weight of women, the need they have of him.

"Take your clothes off, Satomi," he orders, his words as much a surprise to him as to her. "I want to see you naked, to remember you naked."

She hardly hesitates. First her dress, then her slip spilling down, then the Sears and Roebuck peach bras and panties saved and longed for, flung now to the floor. She can't help feeling pleased she had swept away the dust earlier. Shivering a little, she watches him watching her. If he wants her enough to take her now, she won't be bargaining for their future. She won't deny him, even if he is already lost to her.

He comes close, runs his hands from her breasts to her waist, drawing his breath in sharply when he reaches the soft measure of skin on the inside of her thighs. She is perfect and he yearns to be inside her, to take what he wants.

Dreading a last rejection, she puts her hands around his neck and links her fingers as though to chain him there, keep him close. His hair is damp from the shower, the scent of him sweet and familiar. She buries her face in his neck, the painful rise and fall of hope sinking her.

Something in Haru tightens and then breaks. It comes to him suddenly that he wants to hurt her, to make her see that want isn't the same as love. He has had enough of the struggle, enough of wanting, enough of everything at Manzanar. Shoving his hand between her legs, he lets his fingers enter her, pushing hard.

"Don't, Haru, it hurts," she blurts out, pushing him away so that he stumbles against a chair, knocking it over.

"See, you don't want it, you never did. It's good I didn't take you seriously, Satomi Baker."

"Is it?"

He doesn't answer; what is there to say? She's got the message. He is saved.

"What more could you want, Haru?" she says quietly before he reaches the door. "I'm asking nothing of you. Do you want me to feel ugly for the rest of my life?" Her words sound like blackmail to her; still, she can't help herself. "I know you want to, just as much as I do."

"Put your dress on, Sati. It's time to go home."

"No. You put it on for me."

What he had thought of as honor, so long harbored, falls from him in the putting on of the dress. It slips away unnoticed in the pretense, in the dance of him buttoning while she unbuttons.

Only later, when she looks back on it, can she give it words; hug to herself how it had been, the good and the bad of it, the bloody bit that hurt and the bit that felt like swimming deep, so that when she surfaced, everything shimmered in a beaded light. She had longed for it, thinking it would change everything, knows now that it will not. Haru is the same Haru, unbending as always, while she hurts more than ever.

———

Tamura says her goodbyes to Haru from her bed. She would like to have waved him away outside with the others, but her legs have swollen in the night and are too painful to stand on.

"You are a good son to your mother, Haru," she says. "And a good friend to us too. Don't get yourself killed out there, it is easily done."

She is thinking of Aaron, his last wave, that final faraway smile. Men, it seems, are always longing to be gone.

"Death is not the worst thing, Tamura." He kisses her forehead. "Even so, best not to look towards it, best to live in the day."

Tamura knows that he isn't talking about himself. She is near the end, although no one will speak of it for fear of attracting death a moment before its time.

Outside, Cora is with the others, holding Eriko's hand. She knows all the women are sad, but she is used to sadness, used to seeing people leave, having to leave herself.

"I'm staying," she says, letting go of Eriko's hand, moving to Satomi's side. "I'm staying, aren't I?"

"Yes, you are staying." Satomi picks her up, holds her tight. "You are staying, little one."

Seeing Haru vault onto the truck crowded with his friends, she is the first of the little group in Sewer Alley to turn away. He looks so handsome, so happy to be leaving. She takes a mental snapshot in case she should forget the look of him, his strong square hands, the soft blush of his eyelids, and the grace that Tamura speaks of. He will always be the one to pattern by now, she thinks. It will take that same reserve, the same taking charge, to stir desire in her. She is not pleased about it.

"If you don't count the women, it's just the old and the young left now," Mr. Sano observes.

"I must go to Mother," Satomi calls to Haru, putting Cora down. "Good luck, Haru."

"I'll write, Sati," he calls as the truck's engine starts up.

The words feel like an empty promise to both of them.

Eriko and Naomi are weeping. It's hard to watch their boy leave. He is going to war, after all, and to make matters worse, they know that Tamura won't rise from her bed again.

"It's not a good day," Naomi says, her old face crumpling as she swallows hard.

Yumi looks sullen. She can't bring herself to wave. Who will stick up for her now?

"Be an obedient girl, Yumi," Haru calls as the truck speeds up. "Promise?"

The day is a rare one, cold but bright, so bright and clear that the mountains appear to be hard up against the camp, so that you might reach out and touch them. Sunlight pours through the four tiny windowpanes of the Bakers' barrack, tracing a pattern of squares on Tamura's sheet. From outside, Satomi can hear the crows squawking overhead, she can hear Eriko fussing over Cora. It should be raining, she thinks. It should be as gray and cold outside as she feels inside. She could bear it better if the sun wasn't shining.

"He is not for you." Tamura takes her hand and puts it to her lips. "Give your affection to Cora now. That sweet child deserves someone of her own."

The advice that comes daily from everyone is constant. "Care for your mother." "Care for Cora."

It's good advice, but it's no cure for what she's feeling. And apart from the ache for Haru, so sharp sometimes that it's like the stitch in her side she gets from running, she is scared for Tamura, so scared that she can't deny any longer the truth that her mother will not magically recover.

Her talks with Dr. Harper are no longer about external events, about her complaints, about how the war is going. They are about practicalities, about helping Tamura, who refuses to leave their barrack, despite that the narrow dusty room is quite unsuitable for someone as ill as her.

"I won't finish my days in the camp hospital," she insists. "I don't want to be with sick people. I want to be with you, Satomi, and with Eriko."

Things have become worse faster than Satomi could have imagined, and now there seems little else in life but sleepless nights and days of listening to Tamura chasing her breath.

Eriko comes to sit with her friend while Satomi visits with Cora at the orphanage.

"It is only fair I have Tamura to myself for a bit," she says. "We have to catch up with our gossip."

At the orphanage, Cora, standing alone, twisting her hair in a new habit, runs to her.

"Will your mother die, like mine did?" she asks.

Satomi doesn't answer. She can't say the words that will give truth to her fears. Cora can't remember her own mother but knows that she is dead, knows she has lost what is precious.

"Shall we have a story, Cora? Would you like that?"

Cora devours stories, lives in them long after the telling of them is over. All the children like the stories Satomi tells, especially the ones she makes up, in which she likes to weave their names, their little habits. She is a good storyteller, and how should they know that they have become characters in such classics as *Huckleberry Finn* and *Treasure Island*? There is only so much she can invent, after all.

"You must be proud of who you are," she says, looking at the mix of them. "Your mothers and fathers were beautiful Americans. And you are all brave little Americans because you are like them."

In the telling to them of who they are, she is flooded with

gratitude for who she is herself. It is a wonderful thing to be the daughter of Tamura Baker, to have Aaron Baker's determined blood in her veins. How could she have ever thought otherwise?

"You teach me as much as I do you," she tells the children.

Cora hates sharing Satomi. She sets up camp next to her in the storytelling sessions, and has been known to shove away the children who get too close to Satomi.

"She is mine," she says, as though speaking of her little string-tied bundle of possessions.

"You mustn't mind that I talk to the others, Cora. It doesn't change the fact that you are special to me, you silly girl."

"Can I live with you when your mother dies, Satomi?"

"I will ask, Cora. But don't get your hopes up, they don't say yes to much, do they? But you can still visit, and I am here every day, after all."

She worries that Cora seems agitated these days, more needy than before. The orphanage can be a lonely place despite that it is full of children and loud with the crying of babies. There is too little for the children to do, and they are all suffering from loss of the familiar. Perhaps she shouldn't have allowed herself to get so close, but it is done now, she can't desert Cora, she loves her.

Dr. Harper agrees to ask permission from the orphanage for Cora to live with her, but not, as he puts it delicately, while Tamura is so ill. It wouldn't be fair for any of them.

"I can't imagine they will allow it anyway, Sati. It would hardly be a conventional arrangement."

He longs to get Tamura into his hospital, to see her cocooned in clean white sheets where she will be available to him the whole day long. He wants to care for her in her last days, be on hand to ease her pain.

"She should be in the new hospital," he tells Satomi. "You can't look after her properly in the barracks."

There is a morgue attached to the hospital, but he doesn't say that would be more convenient too. Taking the dead from the barracks is bad for morale, it unsettles the inmates. Since the riot and the No No Boys looking for trouble, tearing down the American flag, being insolent to the guards, they hardly need more to unsettle them.

"She wants to stay at home," Satomi says, quoting Tamura.

The absurdity of Manzanar being spoken of as home by her mother is not lost on her. Yet even in the face of the horror of the place she has come to understand that Tamura has experienced something rather wonderful in the camp, something that has restored her to herself.

Since she insists on staying where she is, there isn't much that Dr. Harper can do for his favorite patient, except to visit her daily, a pleasure, he thinks, more for himself than for her. He shouldn't favor patients, he knows, but who could not love Tamura, after all?

More like a nurse than a doctor, he plumps her pillow, places pans of steaming water nearby, futilely hoping to create a space in her lungs so that she might catch a few easier breaths. The science is not good; the hope, though, is a comfort. He has rigged up a line of oxygen, but Tamura doesn't want it, doesn't want to prolong things. In any case, it's hardly more than a placebo at this stage of her disease. Occasionally he takes the unearned liberty of a lover and strokes her hair, caresses her hand.

"You are pale yourself," she tells him teasingly. "I recommend lettuce juice twice a day."

They laugh together. He wonders if it will be the last time Tamura laughs, he wonders if everything she does will be for the last time. The thought of never seeing her smile again, or push her hair back in the delicate way she does, hurts too much to dwell on.

"It won't be long," she says, as though in apology for putting him to the trouble.

"I'm not listening," he replies. "I'm not listening, Tamura."

It seems to Satomi that Tamura must be shared with everyone, so that only a small part of her mother is hers alone. The days are taken up with Dr. Harper's visits, with Eriko's nursing, and with Naomi, who comes to sit with Tamura, talking to her all the time in Japanese, her shaky old voice full of tenderness.

Cora comes to visit too, eyes wide with curiosity at the sight of Tamura propped on her pillow. She is not sure what death is, except she thinks perhaps an angel might come to take Tamura away, like in the story she heard long ago but can't remember where. She has set up her daytime camp at Eriko's, where she can hear Tamura's labors through the wall. Eriko and Naomi are kind, but it is Satomi she wants, Satomi she waits for, as she takes Yumi's fan from the wall despite the fact that she knows that Yumi has forbidden it. She wafts it in front of her face to smell the sweet clean scent of cedar.

Only at night does Satomi have her mother to herself, lying next to her on the mattress that she has pushed up against Tamura's bed. She talks quietly until Tamura dozes off, hardly sleeping herself, terrified that she will wake to her mother gone.

"I know that you will be surprised to hear it," Tamura says softly, "but I have enjoyed my life here with you."

"You have enjoyed Manzanar, Mama?"

"Well, it is strange, but I have. After your father died, I couldn't imagine making a life of my own, having friends. Now our friends will help you after I have gone. Eriko is like a mother to you already."

"Nobody but you will ever be like a mother to me."

Eriko has stopped going to work. Every morning she boils water and gently washes Tamura's wasted body, she brushes her hair tenderly and brings her sweet pears and miso from their favorite mess hall, which Tamura has no appetite for. Her heart seems to shatter over and over at the sight of Tamura's smile, at the effort her dear neighbor still puts into their friendship.

"Try a little sip, Tamura," she encourages. "Just one little sip, for me."

Over time their neighborliness has turned to friendship, their friendship to love. They have become like loving sisters. Eriko is already grieving for the loss that is to come.

Tamura is not afraid. She thinks of Aaron and hopes that she will see him soon. He would be at odds with her for thinking it, but there is nothing to be done about that, she can't make herself believe in oblivion. And Satomi will rally, what else can the young do? She is strong and full of life. And even though Haru will not come for her, something tells her that her daughter will prosper. She is ready to go, worn out with the fight against the inch-by-inch drowning. She is longing not to come up for air.

"You have the choice of burial or cremation," Dr. Harper says, the words ringing brutally in his ears, sickening as the cracking of bones, so that he shudders and shakes his head as though to dismiss them. He should feel embarrassed for loving Tamura, he thinks, but he can't regret it. He has loved her in a way his wife would have thought of as betrayal, although no word of his had ever communicated that love, which he is certain Tamura did not return.

"It's up to you, Satomi," Eriko says. "It's you who must decide."

"Yes, of course we will do as you want, Satomi. I was her doctor, but we never spoke of it. Of such arrangements, I mean."

"She would have thought it bad manners to burden you, Dr. Harper. You are not an easy man to talk to about such intimate things."

It's not the truth, but in the moment she wants to hurt where she can, to off-load the terrible pain she is feeling.

"I did my best, Satomi, and you know, whatever small things we spoke about, your mother and I found pleasure in those conversations."

"I'm sorry, so sorry, Dr. Harper." She is ashamed. "I know that you did. My mother always said that you do your job honorably."

"Did she? Did she say that?"

He hopes that it's the truth, that he has been honorable with all of his imprisoned patients. His job, which started out as something patriotic he could do for his country, has become a burden to him. He is amazed now that he ever could have thought it would be anything else. Manzanar has knocked that idealism, and much more, out of him. It's a pointless place, a place to feel shame for. Thousands of people incarcerated in a monument to stupidity. And the time, money, and effort spent on things that don't work, that never have from the start. He feels only disgust at the cruelty of crushing people together as though they are livestock, not to mention the ridiculous business of guarding people who don't attempt escape. Food in, trash out, diseased sewers, schools without desks, orphans being guarded at play, lines to be able to eat, to wash, to shit, it is all a horrible, inhuman nonsense.

If there are such things as Japanese spies in his country, then it is the camps that have made them. Dissent has germinated behind the barbed wire and under the guns. And what is it that America is fighting for anyway, if not for liberty, and the freedom of its citizens? Along with that of its inmates, Manzanar has stolen a portion of his life too, robbed him of his pride in being an American.

"Here, Satomi." He sighs. "Your mother's death certificate is ready. You must sign in two places, there and there. Her ashes can be sent home, if that is what you want."

As though to soothe him, to steady his trembling hand, Satomi touches it lightly as she takes the pen from him.

"We will bury my mother here, Dr. Harper, at Manzanar,

close to her friends and neighbors. Angelina is not our home anymore. I have heard that there are strangers in our house, that our
land has been given to them."

"I'm sure that you will get it back. War is tough on everyone,
but every war has its end, and this one will be no different. We are
getting on top of it."

"I don't care anymore. I wanted my mother to live to see it. I
wanted to walk arm in arm with her from Manzanar, although
she would have been sad to leave you all."

"At least you had the good fortune to have Tamura as your
mother. What a stroke of luck, Satomi. What a start in life."

The past tense hurts. She has already overtaken Tamura, left
her behind. She couldn't keep Tamura in the world, although on
the night of her death she had held her in her arms in an attempt
to transfer her own warmth, the life in her, to her mother.

"Don't leave me, Mama. Please don't go."

Tamura had lifted her hand to Satomi's cheek. Satomi, kissing
it, had taken up the other one, kissing that too. Her mother's hands,
rough from sewing the camouflage nets, from pulling sagebrush up
by the roots, were nothing like the ones that she remembered from
her childhood. She liked them better now somehow. The calluses
and torn skin mapped Tamura's more independent existence,
showed even in her failing that she had lived a muscular life.

"Listen to me, Satomi. Obey me this one last time."

She had to bend close to hear Tamura's words.

"Once you leave Manzanar, don't ever come back. Whatever
they do with my body, I will not be here. I will be with your father somewhere, perhaps. And never think of the life you might
have had if we had never come here. Make a better one."

Hearing more the cadence, the familiar rhythm, rather than
the reason the words conveyed, Satomi was all pain. She was lost

to everything except the idea of drawing into herself the sound of Tamura's voice, which had accompanied her her whole life. She feared the time was coming when it would be lost to her, when she might forget it.

"Take my little bird, Satomi," Tamura said. "Keep the little titmouse for luck. It is such a pretty thing, the most precious object I have. And, my sweet daughter, don't feed your anger anymore, you only nourish your own enemy."

The weight of Eriko Okihiro's hefty arm across Satomi's shoulders is causing an ache, but there is comfort to be had in her solidity, in the heat that emanates from her ample body.

So this is what being without Tamura is like. It's being homeless despite having a bed to sleep in, it's not caring if the sun shines, it's feeling nothing when the mountains turn from blue to mauve in the blink of an eye, it's being orphaned.

"You mustn't sleep alone tonight, Satomi. Stay with us, we would be happy to have you."

"I'm not afraid, Eriko, and there are things I must do."

She will clean their barrack, take down the silk robe and wash it with the rose bath crystals that Lawson has brought at her request. Surely Tamura will forgive her that. Rose oil would have been better, but it wasn't to be had.

"No such thing in Lone Pine," Lawson told her, shaking his head. "Nearest thing I could get to it was this."

It takes three washes to reveal the colors of the robe, to bring back to life the butterflies and the dark little moths. Only in the final rinse does the cheap scent of the bath crystals waft up the merest trace of rose. Still, it is the scent of Tamura. It catches at the back of her throat and suddenly she is doubled up on the floor moaning, her head buried deep in the wet folds.

"Oh, Mama, I can't bear it."

Naomi hears her cries and, breaking her daughter's rules, she calls through the wall.

"I am coming, Satomi."

"No, don't, Naomi. I am fine, and I must finish here."

A picture of Tamura wearing the robe comes to her; she is sitting on the floor by Aaron's chair, teaching her the words for the tea ceremony.

"*Wa*, for harmony; *kei*, for respect; *sei*, for purity; *jaku*, for tranquillity.

"It's a good day, Satomi, when you can feel all of these things and know that you have spent the hours well."

Tamura had been torn between the centuries, just as she has been torn between her two races. Satomi Baker, the very name says it all.

"Who am I?" she sobs. "Who am I without you, Mother?"

When the robe is dry she folds it carefully and takes it with her to relieve Eriko, who is sitting by Tamura's coffin in the morgue so that her friend will not be alone in such a place.

In death's stillness Tamura is wearing the dress she had worn on the day that they had left their farm. A modern American dress, as she would have wanted. With the robe folded neatly at her feet, her hands crossed, the paper money that Eriko has placed by her side so that she might pay the toll to cross the River of the Three Hells, she is returned to something of her old beauty. Satomi bends to kiss her, she must take her leave, but she is afraid to feel Tamura's cold lips on her own and can't move.

"We have to close the lid now, honey." says Dr. Harper's nurse with a pitying smile. She pushes Satomi toward Eriko, who is crying.

"Oh, Tamura," Eriko sobs as the lid goes down. "My dear, dear friend."

Dr. Harper wrote to Ralph to tell him of Tamura's death, and a letter comes to Satomi by return from him. It is a sweet letter, full of Ralph's humanity, his optimism for her.

Haru has written too, a formal letter of condolence. He can't get leave to be at Tamura's funeral. He wants her to know that he had admired and loved her mother.

She is grateful that she is not able to differentiate the pain of losing him from her grief for Tamura, which leaves no space to distinguish one ache from another. The loss of Haru, which had cut so deeply, seems such a tiny thing now in comparison to the loss of Tamura.

"Did he say anything else?" Eriko asks.

"I think that he may have, but a page is missing and the censor's pen has been at it."

"The contraband check is getting worse," Eriko says. "I've had pages of other people's letters mixed up with mine more than once lately."

Satomi doesn't tell Eriko that Haru had written that they were lucky to be safe in Manzanar; that the inmates of the camp have no idea of what people on the outside are suffering. Europe is being destroyed and we are lucky to be American, he says.

Well, she doesn't feel lucky. She and Haru will never agree on what being an American means.

"It is very annoying," Naomi says, tutting. "Perhaps what they blacked out was important. It's too bad."

"He sent you all his love, of course, and his good wishes to me."

"Oh, Satomi," Eriko says with a sigh.

"Would he have wanted me if I were entirely Japanese, do you think, Eriko?"

"Perhaps, but it isn't about being Japanese, is it? It's about love, and you can't summon that at will no matter what your race."

"I think it's about not being what people want you to be, Eriko.

I was never the person that Haru wanted me to be. Even the Japanese part of me is not compliant enough for him!"

The wind is getting up as Tamura is put in the ground. Strings of origami brought to honor her blow about like ribbons at a carnival, getting caught in tree limbs and in the mourners' hair.

Tamura's allotted plot is just a few yards from the little consoling tower.

"It's a good spot," Naomi says. "You couldn't ask for better."

"It's very dry," the Buddhist priest remarks. "You must remember to bring water in your offerings."

A rusty blackbird sits on the branch of a dead pear tree, shrugging in the damp air as though it is pulling up the collar of a feathery coat. It looks as miserable as the mourners.

"It's so cold," Naomi complains, and Satomi takes off her scarf and wraps it around Naomi's head, tying it in a knot under her chin.

"Just like Tamura. Just like your mother," Naomi says.

The wind is in wicked flight now, whisking the dirt from the ground, covering their shoes, worming grit into their mouths. It hums through the cluster of stunted apple trees at the margin of the burial ground, creating a lament on the air.

"We must be quick," the priest says. "The storm is almost here."

Satomi looks toward the mountains and gauges by the way clouds have not yet settled on the peaks that it won't hit full force until nightfall.

"At least this is one 'dust devil' that she won't have to suffer," Eriko whispers to Satomi. "She hated them, didn't she?"

"Yes, but I think I hated them more for her. I don't care when they come now. I can't even be bothered to fight them anymore."

Later that day, outside the Buddhist workshop as the storm moves closer, people file past her the grieving daughter, bowing, not smiling.

"So many have come to say goodbye to her," Dr. Harper says. "I'm not surprised, Tamura was easy to love."

Cora is at her side despite Eriko's opinion that it is a bad idea.

"She is too young to understand, Satomi. She will only be confused."

Perhaps it is all too much for Cora, the solemnity of it, the distraction of the grown-ups. But she had wanted to come, would have felt excluded if she had not been allowed to share the day. And, since beginning her work at the orphanage, Satomi has realized that children understand so much more than adults give them credit for. From the age of four she thinks they have a hold on pretty much everything.

It disturbs her that she knows so few in the line. How have so many of the inmates come to know Tamura? They all seem to be claiming her as their own someone special.

"I worked with your mother. Did she never speak of me?"

"She had a fine singing voice."

"She had no enemies."

"Tamura Baker will be missed."

Satomi recognizes the white-haired woman who is crying. She is usually to be seen walking around the camp carrying a shabby cardboard suitcase as though she has just arrived. There had been speculation in the first year or two as to what she might have in the case. Money or medicine, had been a popular guess, until it had split open in the mess hall one day, and was shown to contain nothing more than a child's rattle and a pair of baby shoes.

"She must have lost her child," Tamura had guessed. "That's a grief there's no recovery from. Make sure you give her a greeting when you pass her, Satomi."

At least the old woman could cry for a lost friend, whereas she herself, the beloved child, seems incapable of it. What is wrong with her? Her eyes are as dry as her mouth, her blood is slow, her heart dull and cold.

She calmly acknowledges the mourners one by one, unaware of the trail of blood that is seeping from her clenched hands, tinting her dress brick-red, as her nails bite into her palms.

"Who is the man with the bloated face, Eriko?"

"I'm not sure. I've seen him around, though. Probably someone Tamura was kind to, someone who used her salves. Plenty of that sort here today, I should think."

Mr. and Mrs. Sano come. He's holding his wife's arm firmly in case she should wander off. Lately Mrs. Sano has taken to muttering out loud, flicking her hands around as though she is beset by bees. She goes missing for hours on end, so that strangers bring her home from her wanderings, from her setting up home in their barracks. She doesn't brush her hair anymore, and where once she wouldn't look you in the eye, now she stares at people with a child's unswerving gaze. Her mind may be wandering so that she hardly knows who she is, but Mr. Sano still takes his pleasure of her. These days, though, his is the only moaning to be heard through the wall.

"We have come to sign," he says. "We have no complaints of your mother as a neighbor, at least."

"He is well practiced in rudeness," Naomi says, not bothering to whisper.

A condolence book has been placed on a table at the entrance to the workshop. It has fifty signatures in it by noon and a line of people waiting to sign.

"We are like Pavlov's dogs," the old man who had exposed himself to her says. "Trained by habit to wait in line for everything."

Yumi is playing jacks with a group of girls in the grime at the old man's feet. They are wearing freshly laundered dresses under their jackets, the hems already covered in dirt. Despite a coating of dust, their dark hair gleams, and their olive black eyes shine.

Hearing their chatter, Satomi is reminded of the schoolyard in Angelina, and memories of Lily are stirred. Haru's little sister has grown up while Satomi had been preoccupied with him. Under the stretched fabric of Yumi's dress her breasts are full, her hips rounding. She has already made out with at least two of the boys from the camp's softball team, and with her provocative stance she is the star of the baton-twirling troop. Haru, when he returns, will have his hands full keeping her in check.

"Go and play somewhere else," Eriko scolds, frowning at Yumi. "Have some respect."

"They only know how to live in the moment," Satomi says. "They are lucky; we lose the art of it as we grow."

But she feels herself that she can only live in the moment too. It's too hard to think of the future without Tamura in it. Grief has sapped her energy and she can't be bothered to wonder what she will do when freedom comes, except that she must somehow keep Cora in her future.

Like Aaron, Tamura now will only come to her in memory. There is no one left to share the recollections of her childhood with. Life is changed forever.

She has already been ordered to vacate their barrack, to leave the place that Tamura had made home. It has been allotted to Mr. and Mrs. Hamada. They have added a baby to their family of nine since coming to Manzanar, and are so overcrowded that in summer the older children prefer to sleep in the open underneath their barrack, despite that the rats run there. In winter, their human huddle keeps the warmth in, at least.

Mr. Hamada has turned their present barrack into a little palace with his carvings. Their door has a tree carved in relief on it, and lifelike birds perch on its branches. There is no doubt that he is a true artist.

The Sanos too have been told to move. They are to have the

Hamadas' barrack so that the bigger family can occupy both theirs and Satomi's old homes. Mr. Sano is full of complaints. He goes about with his old tortoise face screwed up with anger, his eyes dark and hooded.

"They have no consideration at all. I will have to move everything myself, my wife is incapable of anything these days. My daughter-in-law might as well not exist, she is so unreliable, always off somewhere."

Mrs. Hamada avoids Mr. Sano, but she apologizes to Satomi. "I am so sorry, but what can we do? And the older children are so excited at having some space to themselves. If it hadn't been us, someone else would have taken it from you."

"Don't worry about it, Mrs. Hamada, you are welcome. It can't be helped. It's only fair, after all."

"It is easy to tell that your mother lives in you, Satomi," Mrs. Hamada says, relieved that there isn't to be a fuss.

"You must stay with us or you'll be housed with strangers," Eriko insists. "You can have Haru's bed."

She can smell him on the blanket: soap and salt and something in the dry down that she couldn't have described but would have recognized anywhere. It's the tormenting essence of him.

She thinks of Aaron, who said that everything had its own peculiar smell, that he could tell what month it was simply by sniffing the air, it was the same for the time of day. He could smell fog before you could see it, smell the rare frosts that iced his fields before they arrived.

"What does fog smell like, Father?"

"It smells like the sea after a storm."

She hugs Haru's blanket to her, runs her fingers down the length of sacking that Eriko has left hanging. His books are piled neatly on the floor, a pencil as a bookmark in his yellowing copy of *The Grapes of Wrath*. She picks it up and starts to read where Haru has left off. He has underlined in pencil, *migratory family, California.*

When the time comes to leave the camp she will abandon Haru, let him go. For now, though, she burrows down with his books, his scent and his family nearby.

Since the superintendent has refused her permission to have Cora live with her, she spends most of her time at the orphanage.

"I can't blame them," she says to Eriko. "It's enough to take care of myself, let alone be responsible for a child. And I am a guest in your home, after all. But I so long to keep Cora with me."

She worries about what will happen to Cora when the war ends. There is talk that the children will be evacuated to places as far away as Alaska, to any orphanage, any family prepared to take them. They are little nomads who must make their homes over and over.

Dr. Harper has spirited away a letter he saw on the superintendent's desk as he was writing a report on a child with diphtheria. It was a request from a farmer in Oregon: *"I'll take any boy strong enough to work on the land."*

"Shameless!" he exclaimed to Satomi. "Well, at least I can save one boy from the horror of that."

The letter will add to his archive, which grows daily. He squirrels away papers, takes his forbidden photographs, lists a daily count of the rats that he sees in broad daylight, in the mess hall kitchens, the latrines, on the roofs of the barracks nibbling away at the peeling tar paper so that the rain gets through. He has a collection of objects that have touched him and will be a better aid to memory than facts and figures, he thinks. There is a necklace made from bark strung with string that an inmate left in the hospital, it's strangely sophisticated, he thinks. He keeps a discarded wooden geta shoe, a split tin plate. He has made sketches of the new hospital, and one of the library. They look impressive, and after all there must in any archive be balance.

As time passes in Manzanar the seasons continue in much the same way they have done since Satomi first arrived. The camp's inmates suffer the same bitter winters, the same heat-logged summers, and the ever-present dust, always the dust. But the weather aside, even Satomi has to agree with Eriko, that over the last couple years conditions in the camp have improved.

Dr. Harper had been right. New latrines have been built, there are Japanese doctors in the hospital, and the inmates' health has stepped up a notch, as drug treatments are easier to come by. And now there's a barber shop, art classes, a camp newspaper; there's tofu and soy sauce to be had in the mess halls.

A shallow sort of settling has taken over from the restlessness that was, in the first year of their confinement, the more usual mindset. There's still talk of freedom, but an end to the war seems a distant prospect, and the question of who will win it, not yet to be predicted.

Satomi and Cora are closer than ever.

"Like you and Tamura," Eriko says sentimentally to Satomi.

Cora has turned out to be a good pupil in her classes, she's quick to pick up on things, and her skill at math calls Lily to Satomi's mind. But she is a fragile child, slow to trust, clinging to Satomi, jealous of sharing with her peers.

Haru has had leave only once, and then only for two days. He came to the camp, handsome in his uniform, bringing little gifts: violet scent for Satomi and Yumi, a sewing box for Eriko, and fleece-lined gloves for Naomi. He didn't walk out with Satomi, and she was never alone with him.

"He treats me like he does Yumi," she said to Eriko. "As though I am his sister."

"It's for the best, Satomi," Eriko said, not wanting to give Satomi false hope.

Haru had slept in his old bed while Satomi lay next to Yumi under her Indian blanket, unable to sleep at all. He is somewhere in Europe now, which distresses Eriko.

"Europe," she says, all concern. "What is there in Europe but war and the killing of our sons?"

"Will you take me to the new cinema?" Cora asks Satomi. "It cost ten cents and I don't even have one."

Since Cora first asked, they have never missed a show. They go together hand in hand, Haru's blanket under Satomi's arm for them to sit on in the damp sagebrush field where the screen is put up once a month. Cora's favorite is Flash Gordon. She loves the all-American boy, his unbelievably golden hair, the light that seems to shine out of him. The Emperor Ming is a popular hate figure. Along with the other children, and brave in their company, Cora shouts at him scornfully. At night, though, curled under her bed, she dreams of him in her restless sleep; dreams of his cruel eyes, his long clawlike nails.

"Is he real?" she asks Satomi.

"No, he is a person made up to frighten us. Just make-believe."

Satomi marvels at how the children lose themselves in make-believe. Their imaginings seem more real to them than their actual lives.

The boys are American heroes, playing capture the flag, fighting to keep the enemy from the Stars and Stripes. The girls play house, feeding pretend meat loaf and ketchup to the cotton stuffed dolls, knitted for them by fine women like Naomi.

In the late afternoons Satomi walks from the orphanage with Cora to Eriko's, where the child spends an hour or so being spoiled. She plays with the girls in Sewer Alley, hopscotch and kick the can. It's favoring her, and against the rules, but the supervisors look the other way. Cora is a special child, after all, a little angel. Who would deny her Satomi's attention, some time of her own?

"You are only making it harder on yourself," Eriko says, fussing around the child, pinching her cheeks, pulling her socks up. "Your heart will break when the parting comes."

"I will write to her, Eriko. And I will visit when I can."

"It won't be as easy as you think, Satomi. They have no idea where the children will end up. And even if they did, I'd bet a dollar that there will be a rule prohibiting you from knowing."

LITTLE BOY. FAT MAN.

S UCH NAMES," ERIKO says, tears streaming down her face as she bites her lips until they bleed. "To give bombs pet names as though they are family members."

Satomi shakes her head in disbelief. "Was America ever what we thought it to be?"

"It is the bully of the world," Naomi says regretfully.

They didn't need to hear the reports of the atomic bombings on Hiroshima and Nagasaki from the guards—the illegal radios in Manzanar spread the news quicker. But those who heard it by word of mouth thought it so exaggerated as to be more rumor than fact.

How could such a weapon exist? A weapon that could kill a hundred thousand in one go. How could a plane named *Enola Gay*, in honor of the pilot's mother, house a bomb so big that it could suck up and digest the earth till nothing remained but cinders? What mother would consider such a namesake an honor?

But when Emperor Hirohito's capitulation speech is put out over the Tannoy, they are convinced. They may never have heard his voice before, but there is no room for doubt.

"It could only be him," they say.

"Yes. It is a samurai's voice. Ancient, from the old world. Like your grandfather's grandfather might sound."

At first, not knowing the difference between atomic and normal destruction, people liken the devastation to that of Pearl Harbor.

"So the debt is paid," they say. "The score settled, honor restored."

Soon, though, the tales of a burning the like of which has never been seen, and of the annihilation of those sad islands where some of Manzanar's inmates have relatives, takes hold, and the reports become the stuff of Greek tragedy.

"They say it has cracked the earth's crust and will get us all in the end."

"There isn't a soul left, I hear."

"Even the children have gone."

"Even the ghosts."

In the privacy of their barracks some of those who have relatives on the burned up islands quietly sing the Japanese national anthem.

"Only out of respect," they assure each other. "In memory of Uncle Toru, of cousin Sakamoto."

Pearl Harbor has been revenged at last. The enemy has been crushed and there is talk of Manzanar closing. Two months pass before the official notice comes—the camp will close in November. Soon they will all be free.

"We need time to work out what it means to us," Naomi says with a quavering voice. "Just when we are settled, everything must change again."

"She is afraid to leave," Eriko says. "We are all a bit afraid, I guess. We don't even know if we will get our homes and businesses back. It's going to be a struggle."

"You are going home, then?" Satomi asks.

"Yes, we are going home." Eriko pauses, the words seem so strange. "Going home!"

"Haru will be pleased," Satomi says.

"Yes, he wrote as soon as he heard. He says that we mustn't let them relocate us away from the West Coast. He's keen on our rights to choose where we settle."

"Haru is right," Naomi says. "Who knows where they will send us this time if we let them? Another Manzanar, perhaps! We have heard the word 'relocate' before, I think."

"You must come with us," Eriko offers. "I don't know if we can get our shop back, we only rented it in the first place, but we must try. We left our furniture, even rice in the cupboard, we left everything. It's possible it's all still there, I suppose, but I hardly dare hope for it."

"Oh, Eriko, thank you, but I have to go to Angelina. We owned our farm outright and we left money in the bank, crops in our fields. My father would expect me to see that his life's work has not been stolen away."

"Then you'll come? After, when you have done what you have to, then you will come?"

"I can't, you know that. It would be wrong for me to live in the same house as Haru. He wouldn't want it, and neither do I."

"But what will you do, Satomi? Who will look after you?"

"I am near nineteen, Eriko, a woman. I will look after myself."

The words sound false even to her. What will she do? How will she live? A job somewhere, she supposes, a room of her own. She has longed for a room of her own, for privacy. The thought of it now, though, seems too strange to contemplate.

Tamura had advised her to go east if she had the chance.

"It will be better in the East," she had said. "The West will never forgive us for the Harbor."

The order has come from the War Department to demolish Manzanar. In its upheaval it begins to look again as dismal as it did when they had first arrived. Those who opt for relocation are already being shipped out to government housing projects, their barracks razed the instant they leave. The rats run for cover, the cockroaches scatter as the empty barracks are reduced to piles of lumber. Before the authorities have a chance to gather it up, the wood is snatched. With such a wealth of fuel, stoves blaze in defense against the bitter November air.

Outside the director's office, piles of papers are stacked high, waiting to be loaded onto trucks and sent off to the War Department.

"So many of them," Satomi says to Dr. Harper as they walk past on their way to the orphanage. "What are they, do you think?"

"Records of you all, I guess," he says, retracing his steps and scooping up a bundle, stuffing them into his bag.

"What will happen to them?"

"If I had to bet, I'd say they were on their way to the furnace."

The hospital wards, save for a bed or two left for emergencies, have closed. Tables and chairs are removed from the mess halls, the new school barracks are dismantled as the children are sent home to help their parents prepare for evacuation.

At the orphanage the children's things are being packed up too. When Satomi asks where the children are to be sent, one of the wardens shrugs her shoulders.

"Who knows?" she says. "We will be lucky to find places for them anywhere. Nobody wants Japanese children these days."

"I'm willing to take Cora with me. She will be happy with me."

"Oh, Satomi, you couldn't look after her. It will be enough to manage yourself."

"If I have my parents' money we could manage, I'm sure."

"I don't think the superintendent will just give Cora to you simply because you ask. It's a foolish idea and probably against the law."

"No harm in asking, though."

"Don't get your hopes up, you're bound to be disappointed."

She must have hope, though. It's too hard to think about letting Cora go without a fight. She conjures up a family who might treat her badly, an orphanage where love has to be shared out so that no child ever gets enough. Just the thought of it sickens her.

Knocking on the superintendent's door, she tells herself that she mustn't lose her temper. If she can just keep calm, smother her desire to insist, things will go better. Nothing much, she knows, works out when she loses her temper.

"Surely Cora would be better off with me than in an orphanage?" she says reasonably.

"It can't be done, Satomi. Simple as that," the superintendent says. "But you needn't worry about Cora. She will be the first to find a family. Such a sweet, obedient child."

"But she already knows me. We are like sisters."

"But not sisters. And there is no guarantee that you will get this money you speak of. How would you manage then?"

"I'll get a job, of course. We all have to work."

"Look, Satomi, it's kind of you, but it is a foolish idea. You will have problems enough of your own. We all will."

"Cora should be with me, we should be together." She can't keep the fury out of her voice.

"Don't blame me, Satomi. I'm Japanese. I have no authority in this place."

"Then I'll go to the director, he won't refuse me."

"If you must. Who knows, you may catch him on a good day."

The director, though, is too busy overseeing the dismantling of the camp to take time to see her. He smiles at her weakly on his way out of the office and directs her to one of his assistants.

"You'll need to write it all down." The assistant, busy with writing something himself, hardly looks at her. "Here are paper and pencil. Bring them back when you've finished."

The words are hard to find. The director doesn't know her, doesn't know Cora; how can she make him understand? She writes of the love they have for each other, of her hope for her parents' inheritance. *We are like sisters,* she assures him. *Surely whatever the circumstances it is better that sisters should be together.*

Her letter is put with others on a desk crowded with papers.

"It's very important," she says, noting the piled-high papers, the ones that have carelessly been allowed to slip to the floor. "Make sure that he gets it."

"Of course. I hardly need you to tell me how to do my job." He feels she has ordered rather than asked. "I can't guarantee that the director will have time to answer you."

But an answer comes a day later in the form of a brief note left for her at the orphanage.

What you request is not possible. It would be against American law for this office to grant you a child that is in the care of the state. You can rest assured that Cora is in good hands. Everything will be done to find all of the children suitable placements.

John Holmes
Assistant to Director Merrit

Eriko says that she shouldn't blame the director. It takes a special kind of person to break the rules, a hero like Ralph Lazo. Courage is needed, she says, to go against the regulations, to take the human decision.

"Don't expect humanity to triumph in Manzanar, Satomi. It never has before."

In Satomi's distress, old dreams of Tamura disappearing return to plague her sleep.

"You call your mother's name out in your sleep," Eriko says. "It is natural, I suppose."

"I think that Mama and Cora have become one in my dreams."

"It's cruel, I know, Satomi, but you must not think of Cora so much. You are an orphan yourself, remember."

But it's impossible not to think of Cora, of the child's dark eyes, her sweet mouth, and her dented innocence. Only she truly understands Cora, no one else will take the time to note her little ways, calm her fears, learn the things that make her laugh. Such a rare little laugh, but so joyful when it spills out of her. Who now will make up stories just for her, tell her that she is pretty, that she is their special girl?

"I will keep in touch with Dr. Harper," she tells the orphanage superintendent. Will you at least let him know where Cora is? I must be able to keep in touch with her."

"I'll do my best, Satomi, but I can't promise anything. We must hope that she stays in California, at least."

"That would be better than Alaska, I suppose."

"Yes, Alaska seems like another country, doesn't it? I know it's hard to hear, but you'll forget her, you know. We all have to think of ourselves in the end."

Cora isn't in the general playroom when Satomi calls at the orphanage the next day. She is sitting on her cot bed swinging her legs, her little black shoes polished, her dress starched, a knitted wool bow in her dark hair.

"I'm coming with you," she tells Satomi, her eyes welling with tears. "When you leave, I'm coming with you."

"I would take you if I could, Cora, but they won't allow it. I will find you, though, wherever you go. We will see each other again."

"You won't come for me. Nobody comes for me."

"I will come. When I am settled, Cora, I will come and visit

you. You may have your own family by then, a mother and father
to love you."

Cora's cries are pitiful, little mewls, muffled sobs.

"We have almost a week left together, Cora. Perhaps they will
show a movie, and school is finished, so you can come to Eriko's
and play with your friends in the alley all day, if you like."

Just a week, she thinks. Seven days left to console Cora, to
calm the little girl's fears, to gather herself.

Only the young are excited. For the rest, the fear of leaving the
known is mixed with apprehension for what lies ahead of them.
Some of the older ones would choose to stay in Manazar if they
could. They have established it out of nothing and want it to live
on. Once the majority have left, space will not be a hard thing to
come by, and they have had enough of the sadness of looking
back, they want the world to forget them now.

"They must go," Lawson says. "The Supreme Court has ruled
the camps illegal. In any case, how would they live? The mess
halls won't be working, or much else, I imagine."

"So now this place is illegal." Satomi can't keep the sneer out of
her voice. "Does it ever occur to you, Lawson, that to be American is to be governed by fools?"

"Well, you can vote them out now. That's progress, ain't it?"

Dr. Harper tells her that he is relieved beyond imagination that
the camp is finally to close.

"You may not believe it, Sati, but you have been my conscience
in Manzanar."

"I think that honor should go to my mother, Doctor, don't
you?"

"No, your mother's sweetness was a gift to me, but it was your
anger that stirred my own."

She visits Tamura's grave for the last time. *She's here beneath my feet*, she thinks, summoning to mind her last view of Tamura in her freshly laundered dress, blocking from it how her mother's body must look now. She thinks of the weather to come at Manzanar, of the sweeping winds and the deep snowdrifts, of the cold moon that will for always now shine down on Tamura's little plot. She won't ever be able to think of the seasons at Manzanar without picturing Tamura's grave suffering them. She hardly knows anymore the little girl in her who whispers with a sob, "Goodbye Mama."

Out of the blue Dr. Harper has offered to drive her to Angelina, to help her with her claim to the farm, and to whatever monies remain in the Baker bank account.

"You will need someone on your side, Satomi. They won't take a girl of your age seriously. When it comes to money, such people don't take justice into account."

His wife is furious with him. She has seen the girl, a pretty enough one for a wife to be suspicious of a husband's motives. But when she thinks about it, Satomi is not pretty, exactly, she is beautiful, and, strangely, beauty is less of a concern to her than pretty.

Still, he is too old for the long drive. She knows it even if he doesn't. And he will be gone for days, and for what? To appease some ache in him, some need to feel he is paying an overdue debt to humankind.

"Don't ask me to go with you," she says. "It's a ridiculous idea."

"It will do me good to see a bit of this country," he says, hoping she isn't playing for an invitation. "And the girl needs help."

"There are plenty of others who need help. Why her?"

"I couldn't save her mother," he says, knowing that it's not a good enough explanation.

"No doctor can save everyone."

"No, but I would like to save her."

———

In the unaccustomed warmth of Eriko's barrack, Satomi takes her leave of the Okihiros. It is hard to believe that Manzanar is over, that she will never sleep in the barrack again. Despite the heat from the stove, roaring now with its belly full of unrationed wood, she can smell the familiar scent of mold, feel the damp. She squints to keep back the tears.

"It's painful to part," Eriko says.

"It's not too late to change your mind and come with us," Naomi offers.

Suddenly the offer is tempting, the idea of merging herself into the Okihiro family a comforting one.

"Thank you, Naomi, but I must go to Angelina. I'm determined to get some justice for my parents. They have to pay me the value of my father's land, allow me the savings he sweated for. They think that giving us twenty-five dollars and a few ration coupons will keep us quiet—it's an insult."

"They would like to wipe out our memories of this place," Eriko says. "Forget that we have been judged, imprisoned without trial."

"It doesn't matter what they would like, only the gods can take away our memories," Naomi reminds them.

Yumi is excited. "We are going home," she sings.

"I don't want to think of home," Eriko says nervously. "Not until we know for sure that we still have one."

Driving with Dr. Harper in his old Plymouth past the lines of people waiting for the same buses that brought them into Manzanar to take them out of it, Satomi turns her head for a last view of the mountains. Their summits are hidden in the mist, rocks in the wheeling clouds. At their foot the rubble of Manzanar is already being swept away by the winds, buried in the dust, their human stain scoured. The camp has been a grubby aberration on the map of the twentieth century, but soon it will be as though it never was.

Nausea stirs in her stomach, rises through her body, fills her mouth with a metallic wash. She is all emotion, frazzled, hurt, outraged. And she is leaving Tamura behind and is afraid now of what is ahead of her.

Reminiscent of that first roundup in Angelina, people mill around, sitting on their cases, looking agitated. Children with their family names now, rather than the old hated numbers pinned to their clothes, cling to their parents; old people wait to be told where to go by the soldiers, who have put their guns aside.

As they head toward the gate, they come across the orphanage children being shepherded onto buses. There's no room for them to pass and Dr. Harper slows the car to a stop and cuts the engine.

Satomi shivers, her skin prickles as she scans the line for Cora, but she is nowhere to be seen. Their leave-taking had been hard on both of them, unsatisfactory. Satomi had expected Cora to sob, but she hadn't been prepared for her own rising panic. She had attempted calm, hadn't wanted to frighten Cora with her own fears, but it hadn't worked.

"I kissed her, hugged her," she told the Okihiros. "But she isn't reassured. She thinks that I will forget her."

She reaches across to the old duffel bag on the backseat of the Plymouth, fumbling around for something.

"I have it," she says, opening the door and leaping out. "I won't be long, Dr. Harper."

The first bus is passing through the gate before she reaches the second already on the move. Cora could be gone, on the road, lost to her. Without hope she bangs on the bus door, holding on to the handle doggedly so that the driver has to stop his vehicle and open up. To her relief, Cora is seated up front behind the driver.

The child's face is expressionless. She is on the edge of her seat, sitting upright as though ready to take flight. The metal buttons on her felt coat are done up to the neck, she is wearing the yellow mittens that Naomi knitted for her, her arms straining tight around her little bundle of possessions.

"Oh, Cora, you're here. I thought I'd missed you."

Cora doesn't smile, doesn't say anything as Satomi bends down in front of her.

"Be quick," the driver says crabbily. "You're holding everyone up."

"Look, Cora, see this little bird?" Satomi opens her hand to show Tamura's carved titmouse sitting in her palm.

Cora nods and touches the little beak.

"He is called a titmouse, Cora. He is sweet, isn't he?"

"Is it for me?"

"Well, I'm giving him to you for a little while. He was my mother's gift to me and it hurts me to part with him, so I will want him back when we next meet. Keep him safe, Cora, and I will come for him. It won't be soon, but I will come."

She imagines for a moment hauling Cora off the bus, the two of them making a run for it. But she knows that they wouldn't get far, and what then?

"You getting off or staying for the ride?" the driver says, putting the bus into gear. "Either way, I'm leaving now."

"Okay. Okay. What difference will a few seconds make?"

She kisses Cora's cheeks, her tiny lips, touches the collar of her coat. Everything about the child is diminutive, fragile. She is filled with shame. She has failed to keep Cora with her.

"Where are you heading to?" she demands of the driver.

"Back to the relocation camp, we hand them over there."

"And then? Where are they taken then?"

"How the hell should I know?"

Waving the bus away, she attempts a smile, but her lips tremble, her eyes spike with the tears that come instead. Cora presses her nose to the window, gives a hesitant half wave as her face crumples in distress.

In a futile effort to comfort herself, Satomi sobs, "She'll be fine. Who could not choose Cora?" Then Dr. Harper is at her side, his arm around her shoulders, guiding her back to the car.

"It's not fair, Satomi," he says. "But you will make it right one day. I truly believe that you will. For the time being, though, you must find a way that allows you to remember what is past without spoiling the present."

He hands her his handkerchief, starts up the engine, and swallows hard. They are all counting what is lost, he thinks.

"It's so odd to just be driving out, no one to stop us," she says, drying her eyes with his handkerchief, which smells, like his shirt, of laundry powder.

"Well, then, we'll play a fanfare to mark the day." Easing the old sedan into a leisurely roll, he hits the horn in three short playful toots. A guard looks up and tips his hat to him. He feels almost festive.

Near the gate, Mrs. Hamada steps out of a bus line and waves them down.

"I am sorry that you had to leave your home for us, Satomi. Good luck with your life."

"You needed the space more than me, Mrs. Hamada. Did the children enjoy it?"

"They did. My little Ava said that she could smell roses there. '*It smells of roses, Mama*,' she would say."

RETURNING

THINGS LOOK PRETTY much the same in Angelina, the same stores, the same church, the same crumbling plaster walls on the post office building. Even Mr. Stedall's dog, gray in the muzzle now, is lying in its usual place by the post office door, waiting for him to finish work.

But it's not her Angelina anymore. It's a weird and disorientating place, at one and the same time both strange and familiar. Like a still from some old movie, where she remembers the scene but has forgotten the plot.

Dr. Harper has parked up by the general store and they are sitting in the car gathering themselves after the long drive.

"So, first thoughts?" he asks.

"It's so much smaller than I remember," she says.

"Well, that's the way it is when you visit old haunts."

"Yes, I've read that. Didn't believe it until now, though."

It isn't only about things being smaller, although the schoolyard, immeasurable to her childhood eye, she sees now is merely a yard or two of asphalt, the main street no longer than Sewer Alley. It's more that she feels herself to be a stranger in the town, a town that she knows fears strangers. Yet the sight of Angelina quiet in the afternoon sun fills her with longing, a longing that she knows it can never satisfy.

"We all experience it at some time," Dr. Harper says sympathetically. "A yearning to go back to how things were. It's not so much the place we miss, I think, but our childhoods."

Out of the car she stands in front of the school, unable for a moment to move. She hasn't thought of Lily for a while, but now, closing her eyes, her old friend appears in absolute clarity, the scattering of freckles on Lily's low cheekbones, the wary look in her eyes. A tingle runs the length of her body, makes the hairs on her arms stand to attention. For a second she wishes those old skipping days back. Oh, Lily, Lily.

The wind, the wind, the wind blows high
Blowing Lily through the sky.
She is handsome, she is pretty,
She is the girl from the golden city.
She has a boyfriend, one, two, three.
Won't you tell me who is he?

"Don't go so fast, Sati, I can't jump in," Lily's voice echoes through her mind.

Mr. Beck is in her head too, staring, ogling her as she skips. He's a thin, insubstantial figure, hovering with bell in hand. Playtime over.

"I feel sick," she says, opening her eyes, swaying a little.

Dr. Harper puts his hand to her forehead. "No fever," he says. "I diagnose time-travel sickness."

"You're so smart." She smiles at him.

He sighs. "Just old."

As though he hasn't moved since she last saw him, Mr. Taylor is in his usual place behind the counter of his drugstore, mixing sodas, bagging up candies. He licks his fingers to open the paper bags one by one, lick—flick—open—fill, never missing a beat.

How Tamura had loved those candies, how they had satisfied the sweet tooth that she had been ashamed to indulge in front of Aaron.

She wonders if while they have been incarcerated Mr. Taylor has given a thought to his old customers. Has anyone in Angelina thought about the Baker women?

Dr. Harper orders them coffee at the counter; it comes in thick white mugs that her lips have trouble getting around. She's used to thin tin, hasn't drunk from china since that last breakfast with Tamura in the farm's kitchen.

Why had she and Tamura never ordered coffee? It was too ordinary, she supposes something that could be had at home. Bubblegum soda had been the thing. She had loved the sweet marshmallow taste of it, but had Tamura really liked the childish drink too? Perhaps she had only ordered it to please her daughter, to share in the fun.

"You're the Baker kid, aren't you?" Mr. Taylor says. "You've grown a bit."

Across the street the bank sits shiny in its glossy slick of brown paint. Housed between the general store and the haberdasher's, it makes its neighboring storefronts look drab. The sidewalk in front of it has been scrubbed, bleached to white, its cleaned-daily windows gleam. If a bank can't show a good front, then things must be on the slide.

Back in the street, she gets an acrid whiff of smoke from Cromer's Cannery, it takes her a while to place it. When she does, she thinks of Lily's cousin Dorothy, of Davey Cromer not wanting to marry beneath him, denying responsibility for the baby. She thinks of Angelina's unforgiving hierarchy.

Dr. Harper pats her back, gives her a smile, and pushes open the bank's door confidently. She can tell that he is nervous too. The clerk is smoking behind the polished grille. He's just like any store clerk, she tells herself, taking a deep breath. Selling a different kind of stock, is all.

"We'd like to see the manager," Dr. Harper says.

"Sure, I'll ask. Want me to tell him what it's about?"

"It's private business," Satomi says.

He looks at her quizzically, puckering up his brow. "You're Sati Baker, aren't you? I'm Greg, Artie's big brother."

"Oh, sure, I recognize you. How have you been?"

"Got shot up in the war, right leg not much use, but I manage."

"How's Artie?"

"Haven't heard from him in six months. Working at a fifty-cent dance hall in San Fran, last time he wrote. Always fancied the big city, didn't he?"

"Couldn't wait to get away." She doesn't ask about Lily.

"Guess you know your farm's been sold? Guess that's why you're here. What name shall I say?"

"Satomi Baker, of course. And this is Dr. Harper."

In his airless office at the rear of the bank the manager stands to greet them. He's a fleshy-looking man with a tobacco-stained mustache, a sham smile, a stranger to her. A sour man, she decides on the spot.

The room is small, stuffy, its faded green blinds drawn against the sun, giving a false impression of coolness. Used to mountain weather, she had forgotten how humid it can get in Angelina in November. A fan rattles the air around and she stands in front of it, closing her eyes for a moment.

"Bill Port. Pleased to meet you, Doctor." He offers his hand from across the desk, ignoring Satomi.

"John Harper. Likewise."

It comes as a surprise to her, his name, John; she hadn't known it before. Why had she never thought to ask? "Dr. Harper" has defined him well enough, she supposes.

"And this"—Dr. Harper turns to Satomi—"is your client, Miss Satomi Baker."

"So, all the way from Manzanar, Doc! I've heard tell of the place." He allows his eyes to settle on Satomi for a moment. "Good of you, very good of you to help the girl." His voice has a gloopy mucus gurgle to it, like the sound stirred-up river mud makes.

"Emphysema," Dr. Harper tells her later. "Strange disease for a bank manager."

"Sit, sit. How can I help?"

"Your clerk told us that you have sold my farm," Satomi says quietly. "I don't recall giving you permission to do that."

He is taken aback by the way she has launched straight into things.

"We didn't need your permission, Miss Baker. Associated Farmers bought up a lot of the land around here with the government's permission. They plan to grow on a big scale. Best thing for Angelina."

"Why didn't you need my permission? I own the farm."

"Well, that's debatable. No papers to show that you or your mother had a legal stake in anything."

He didn't like her tone, she was pretty uppity for a girl, too sure of herself. He guessed that was a fault with lookers, they expected you to dance to their tune. Her father was the same, he hears, chip on the shoulder, looking for trouble, thinking himself better than the whole town put together.

"So you sold my farm from under me. What did I get for it, Mr. Port?"

"Well, offhand without looking at the papers, I seem to recall something near three hundred dollars. Land isn't bringing much these days, less than a quarter of its prewar value, I'd say." His eyes slide from Dr. Harper's. "We've all had to make sacrifices for America, no doubt of that."

"I don't believe you had the right to accept an offer on my mother's behalf, Mr. Port. Mine, either."

"Well, let's get things straight here, young lady. It isn't exactly your farm, now, is it? It was your father's, and he didn't leave a will, so I reckon you should be grateful to be getting anything, considering." He flips open a pack of Chesterfields and offers Dr. Harper one. "I go through three packs of these a day, Doc," he confides as though they are old friends. "You won't find a smoother smoke anywhere."

"Considering what, exactly, Mr. Port?" Dr. Harper asks, declining the cigarette.

"Well, considering the war and what took us into it." He sneaks a look at Satomi, confirming to himself the Jap in her. "It changed everything, Doc, you gotta know that. Angelina isn't as trusting as it used to be, we rely on ourselves these days, don't want foreigners owning our land. And I guess you don't need telling how people in these parts feel about Pearl Harbor? You won't find Japs working the land around here anymore."

He's easy to despise, Satomi thinks, disgusting, full of bigotry. But she holds her anger back, she isn't here about Bill Port. She's here about Aaron and Tamura, she's here about the farm that they had loved and had worked together. They had picked and packed their crop with care, sheltered their little family in the house that Aaron had built. It's about Aaron's pride in his land, the way he had resented every cent spent on living, thinking land the only thing worth shelling out his dollars for. If she doesn't fight for it, it will be like forgetting who her father was. It will be like saying her parents' life counted for nothing.

"Did you take a commission on the sale, Mr. Port?"

"Just the usual."

"Seems like everyone did well out of my father except his family. I could fight you on this, Mr. Port. The law's still the law, isn't it? Our farm wasn't yours to sell, let alone for three hundred dollars."

"Sure, you could go ahead with that, but I'd advise you to take the money, Miss Baker. We can string the process out, if that's what you want. I'm simply showing goodwill on the bank's part." He purses his lips so hard that for a moment they disappear altogether and he seems fishlike.

"Goodwill! You've stolen my father's farm. Is that goodwill?"

"No need for that kind of talk in here, miss." The worm of his mustache hair quivers delicately as though in tune with his shaking voice.

"Nobody's stolen anything. There's been a war, and the government had to take over deserted land. It would have gone to ruin otherwise."

"We didn't desert it voluntarily, Mr. Port. We were shipped out against our will."

"Well, that's nothing to do with me, nothing to do with the bank. Guess if you don't want to take what's on offer you could write to our head office, although I hear they're pretty snowed under, what with all the claims folk are making. Could be years before they clear the backlog. Even then there'd be no guarantees you would get more, no guarantees you'd get anything. As I said, it's all a question of goodwill."

He's sure of himself, has the law on his side, and the mother being dead makes things easier. And everything has been stamped by the government, after all. Not to mention that it's his duty to do right by his employers, by his American customers.

"However you care to describe it," he scoffs. "Twelve acres is hardly a farm."

"Plenty of farms the same around here," Satomi says. "And

there's our house, what about our house?" She is thinking of how her father had transformed the small cabin that he and Tamura had first bought into a home fit for a family. She is thinking of the cool apple light in Tamura's comforting kitchen, the lean-to laundry with its copper boiler and wooden hanging rails, the familiar scent of rice and miso.

"Not much more than a shack now, I'm sorry to say. It's due for demolition any day soon."

"Seems like sharp dealing on the part of the bank to me," Dr. Harper says. "Whatever shape the house is in, surely combined with the land it must be worth more than three hundred dollars."

"Well, you have to take into account that the place had a tenant for a while, Doc. Yugoslavian fellow, turned out he was a drinking man, he let the land run to ruin. They had a fire a couple of years back and half the house burned down. Knocked the value out of it. You're a doctor, a man of the world. I guess you've seen it all in your time. A drinking man can run things into the ground quicker than you or I can blink."

Dr. Harper is disappointed in himself; he's finding out that when it comes to matters of finance he's no match for the likes of Bill Port.

"I guess it would help if you paid interest on the money, and added your commission to it," he says. "You should do that, at least. United Farmers is a big company, they got the land at an unreasonably low price."

"Can't do it, I don't have the authority. I might wish it different, but that's the way it is. What I'm offering is the only deal to be had in Angelina today."

"Well, I guess you know the deal stinks." Dr. Harper shakes his head and turns to Satomi. "A bird-in-the-hand, Sati?"

Bill Port opens the desk drawer and withdraws a checkbook in anticipation.

"You intend on staying around Angelina, Miss Baker?"

"What do you think, Mr. Port?"

"Girl like you, I guess not. I reckon not many of the Japs will come back. Being resettled elsewhere, I hear."

A girl like you, a girl like you. How many times has she heard that? What did he mean by a girl like her? He didn't know her, not like she knew him, anyway. *A man like you, Mr. Port,* she thought, *at home in Angelina, small town big fish, big fish small mind.*

"And my parents' account with you. That had money in it. My mother told me there should be around a hundred dollars in that."

"Maybe there was, I seem to recall more like seventy. We closed a lot of accounts around that time. They were small feed, mostly, cost more to manage than made sense. They weren't being used, you see."

"We could hardly use it while we were interned, now, could we?"

"You'll have to take that up with the head office too."

"I guess there's going to be a long line at the head office."

"I guess."

"I'll have to let it go, then. I've given up waiting in line."

"You make sure you don't go spending it all at once, now." he hands the check to Dr. Harper.

"A young girl with all that cash, eh, John?" He winks at Dr. Harper. "Pretty dresses, makeup, gone in a flash if she's not careful, eh?"

"You've made it out for two hundred and sixty dollars," Dr. Harper says, confused.

"Tax." Bill Port moves toward the door.

Satomi takes the check that Dr. Harper hands her and waves it in the air. "What would you do with the money, Bill?" she says, experiencing a moment of pleasure as his body stiffens at the use of his first name.

"Well, Satomi, I . . . guess . . ."

"Oh, better if you call me Miss Baker, Bill. More professional, don't you think? Me being your valued customer after all."

The color rises in Bill Port's face. His hand trembles as he lights a fresh cigarette from the stub of his old one. *Damn Japs, who the hell does the girl think she is?*

"You'll cash the draft for her here, today?" Dr. Harper makes it sound like a demand.

"Sure, Doc, we're here to help."

"I guess you know the girl's been cheated, Port? But then, that's the business you're in, it seems."

"Look here, Doc, no need for that kinda talk. I've never cheated anyone. It's the way things are, that's all."

"Do you like your job, Bill?"

"I sure do, Doc. I like to help the folks in Angelina get along. How about you?"

"More than I thought before I met you, Bill. I can see now that there are worse things than being a small-town doctor."

Back on the sidewalk, Dr. Harper takes her hand as they cross the road, although there is no traffic in sight.

"Nothing seems respectable anymore," he says as they settle themselves in the car. "The man was shameless. Time was when bank managers could be trusted, when fairness counted."

"I didn't really expect anything different, Dr. Harper. Felt I had to make a stand, though."

"What now?"

"Well, maybe it's not such a good idea, but I guess I'd like to take a last look at the farm."

"You sure that's what you want, Satomi? If there's been a fire, it may, you know . . ."

"I'm not sure, but let's go anyway. I know I'll regret it if I don't."

"And after that?"

"I'm thinking of heading East, New York. My old teacher, Mr. Beck, advised it once, my mother too. I think they were right. I've money now for the fare, and a bit besides. Things around here aren't going to change anytime soon."

"I can help you there, Satomi. My cousin Edward and his wife Betty live in New York. Maybe they could put you up until you find your feet."

"Are you sure, Dr. Harper? You've already done enough for me."

"I'm sure, and why not call me John?"

"I like calling you Dr. Harper. Calling you John would make you seem like a stranger to me. Besides, my mother wouldn't have approved. It's only proper to give you the title you've worked for."

They smile at each other, sharing the memory of Tamura.

"I imagine New York won't be easy, you know?" he says. You're a country girl, after all. It's a pretty hard place to make your way in."

"Well, I'm not expecting easy, and it feels as right as anywhere, I suppose. There's nothing left for me in Angelina. I guess I'd rather be Japanese in New York than in California."

"I envy you," he says. "It's the American way to up sticks, start over."

"Well, I'm going to give it a try."

"And you won't be alone. I'll call my cousin before you get there, so you'll be expected. Maybe he can help find you work, and you'll have a place to stay until you can sort something out for yourself. His wife is kind, and he's a warm person."

"It must run in your family."

"You sound surprised."

"No, not at all. My mother was a good judge of character."

They stop for gas on the way. The JAP TRADE NOT WANTED sign

is still there, but it's a stranger who comes to serve them. He fills
the tank without looking at her.

"Time to take that sign down, don't you think?" Dr. Harper
says, with a flick of his head toward it.

"I'll think about it." The man grins at him.

"It's sickening, makes me ashamed, Sati."

"Oh, Dr. Harper, you have nothing in this world to feel ashamed
about."

Along the road out of town she asks him to stop the car. He
waits with the window down, watching her pace the road, feeling
her panic. It won't be light for much longer, they should hurry.

She squats down and picks up a handful of earth, letting it run
through her fingers, testing its friability in the way that Aaron
used to do.

"It's good earth here," she calls to him. "You can grow anything in it."

"You don't have to go, you know," he says. "Maybe it's better
to remember it as it was."

"It's only a few hundred yards or so down the road," she says.
"We've come this far, how can I not go?"

She half expects to see their old truck still stalled at the roadside, but it is gone.

"You can tell it was a good building once," he says, noticing
the set of her shoulders as the house comes into view. She's pale,
attempting to rally herself. He wants to comfort but can't think of
how—words, he knows, won't help.

The spectacle of the ailing house is hard to look at. Her chest
tightens with the memory of how it used to be. A sudden desperate longing for Tamura overtakes her.

There are cracks like lightning hits in the whitewashed windowpanes. All the frames are rotting away, and Aaron's tough old
enemy bindweed races up the smoke-blackened walls to the roof.

KEEP OUT. PRIVATE PROPERTY is splashed across the padlocked door in red paint.

"I could break the lock easy if you want, Sati."

"Oh, Dr. Harper, I didn't have you down as a housebreaker." She gives him a tense smile. "I can get in through my bedroom window if I want. I've done it often enough before."

"Sure?"

"Sure."

"There's no hurry, Sati." He doesn't care about the dark coming now. "Take your time"

"Okay."

At the back of the house she hunkers down by the kitchen door and smothers a wail. She doesn't want to upset Dr. Harper. She thinks of what she has lost, what she can never get back. Her mother, she knows, would say different, she would say that she had a happy childhood and that can never be taken from her.

The kitchen door is padlocked like the front one, but no KEEP OUT warning. She doesn't want to go inside; just standing in the yard is pain enough.

It's a surprise to find Tamura's henhouse still standing. No hens, the straw swept out, a few molding seeds set in the mud floor. A child's basket stands rotting in one corner with peppercress growing through it, she doesn't recognize it. How Tamura had loved her hens, those homely little things that she had thought beautiful. How she had cared for them.

Their packing sheds have been knocked down and replaced with long aluminum buildings. Neat piles of boxes stand around stamped with the United Farmers logo. A chemical smell hangs in the air; the place feels dead. The years of her father's attention have been swallowed up, gone. Aaron's passage through his land forgotten. There's nothing left of him for her to see or touch or smell. Home is nowhere to be found on the ground here.

On her way back to the car she flips open the mailbox; it's
empty. A moment of disappointment connects her with her younger
self, as though the place isn't dead to her yet. How she had loved
to find things there, seed catalogues, Aaron's paper. She remembers the penciled note from Elena that had brought comfort to
Tamura.

"I need to go back into Angelina. One more thing to do."

"Sure, we should find a place to stay for the night anyway. It's
getting late."

She looks at the white orb of the sun low in the sky, a rising
slice of moon already visible. She remembers how the sun takes its
time here, dunking its way down into the woods before dropping
out of sight. They have twenty minutes at least before dark, she
guesses.

"I doubt anyone would give me a room in Angelina, Doctor."

"Then we'll drive to somewhere that has a better class of people." He is angry on her behalf.

At the side door of the post office, Mr. Stedall, with his dog at
his feet, is oiling the chain on his bike. It's the same old bike, with
its straight handlebars, the big bell that looks like a shiny hamburger. In his post office uniform Mr. Stedall looks the same too,
a handsome man, she notices now, if you like thin. He smiles at
her, anxious, bracing himself against life.

"Hello, Mr. Stedall. Remember me?"

"Satomi, isn't it? How's your mother?"

"She's dead, Mr. Stedall. She died in Manzanar."

"That's too bad." He looks crestfallen. "Nice woman, your
mother."

"Are the Kaplans still at their place? I'd like to send Elena a
note."

"He is. She died around the time you left."

"Elena died?"

"Yep, one of those freak-type accidents. She fell and hit her head against their tractor. Never woke up."

"I can't believe it, Elena dead."

"News to you, maybe; it's an old sore to Hal, though. He grieved something terrible. I reckon he'll never get over the shock of it."

"Do you know, Mr. Stedall, I can't help wondering sometimes if the devil lives in Angelina."

"Can't blame you for thinking it, Satomi."

THE GREAT PORT

Southport Street
New York

Dearest Eriko,

Dr. Harper forwarded your letter and it has found me at last. He's been such a good friend to me in so many ways that I wonder now why I was so hard on him in the camp. His letters come to me as if from home, just as yours did. I guess for me now home is not so much a place as the people I love.

I should have answered sooner but as you can see by the address I have left the West Coast behind me. Honestly, Eriko, it takes so much time to settle in this city, it's a crazy place and it's so big, I could never have imagined how big.

I was sorry to hear that Little Tokyo has changed so much and that the Negroes have taken it over. I know you hoped for familiar faces but I guess most inmates opted for relocation hoping for better things. You'll make friends, though, I'm sure. We learned the lesson of getting along with each other well at Manzanar, didn't we? If you can live alongside Mr. Sano you can live alongside anyone.

I can see you smiling as you read this thinking that most learned that lesson better than me. I guess I'll never walk in my mother's shoes, that's too much to hope for, but I'm trying.

The camps are never spoken of here. As far as New York is concerned they may never have happened. We Japanese are as much to blame for that as the government, there seems to be a conspiracy of silence among us. Why should we be ashamed, though?

It must be good to have your business back, even if as you say people only buy cheap cotton these days.

When I thanked Dr. Harper for helping me, for taking me back to Angelina, he said that it was the least he could do for Tamura's daughter. He had tears in his eyes, Eriko, and his voice trembled. He said that he had been very fond of Tamura. I think that he loved her. I think that Dr. Harper is a romantic. He saw the girl in my mother from the start, the very thing I think my father loved in her too. Perhaps men are more romantic than women altogether.

It seems to me you have to be lucky to do well in New York, lucky to get a job, lucky to make friends, lucky not to be taken in by the "con men" that hover on every street corner. Dr. Harper's cousin Edward warned me about them. He said to be careful or they would empty my purse before I knew it.

People here are infected with the "New York" bug. Everyone wants to get rich. I guess that dream makes New York what it is. People see what it has to offer and are ambitious for it. Edward says that there are more victims of hope here than in any other city in the world.

I don't stand out here at all. Everyone seems to be a refugee of one sort or another. There are Japanese around, and lots of Chinese, and honestly I don't think most people can tell the difference. I'm always being taken for Italian anyway. Still, I cherish my Japanese half, the half that makes me part of you.

I know now, though, that I will never be just right for everyone, none of us will. There's nothing to be done about that.

I'm not sorry that I came here, although I can't get used to
the thin light or the small sky, and there's too much concrete
and not enough green. And you will find it strange that I miss
the mountains. A part of me is forever spinning, not knowing
quite how to settle. The contrast between here and the camp is
extreme. It rocks me sometimes, but I'm not afraid. I know you
can never be free of the past but I'm determined not to live off
it, to make it an excuse for every bad thing that happens.

Today is a good day, but they are not all good. It's odd to
be lonely in a city teeming with people. For all the awful
things about Manzanar, I don't remember ever feeling lonely
there. The other night from the harbor I heard the Queen
Mary blow. It sounded marooned, just like me.

When I first arrived I stayed with Dr. Harper's cousin and
his wife. They have a tiny apartment and I had to sleep on an
"Easy" bed in their sitting room, which was fine for me but
not so nice for them I imagine. Being childless they weren't
used to sharing their small space. They tried not to show it
but I think that they were uneasy with me there. I moved a
couple of weeks ago into a small room of my own—I have a
gas ring and a sink and a bed that drops down from a cupboard. Luxury.

There's no rationing here, you can even get steak if you
have the money. I long sometimes though for miso and, oddly,
for mess-hall rice.

My room has a window looking onto a brick wall. It's dark
but it's better I suppose than peering into someone else's
apartment. My neighbor in the room next door, Mrs. Copeland, is very old, eighty perhaps. She has a sharp tongue but
manages to be charming. She won't take a shower until I

return from work. "Listen out for me, darling," she says. "I'll die in that shower one day."

She has no family here but is well known in the neighborhood. I only see old people in this building. I'm pretty sure I must be its youngest resident.

Dr. Harper's cousin got me a job in their local library unpacking and putting out the new books. The good thing about that job was all the books I got to read without it costing me a cent.

I have taken a job now in the cloakroom of the Clare House Museum. It's known for its collection of Flemish paintings, and it has two galleries full of French porcelain. Are you used to using china again now?

This job pays more than the library one, but I'm not sure that it's a step up. I take in hats and hang up coats all day long. Sometimes it feels like I am hiding in my cubicle, keeping myself from the world. See, I am not as brave as I would like you to believe. But I get to see the art, and the director, a man who goes around straightening pictures and looking for dust, although I guess he has more important things to do, says that he likes my look and my manner, and that he is sure my fluency in Japanese can be put to good use. "But Japanese," he says, screwing up his face. "Are we ready to hear it?"

Are you wondering about Cora? I think of her all the time. I'm still angry that they wouldn't let me have her. It would have been hard but I think we could have managed. What should I do, Eriko? What can I do about that? I don't suppose you have heard anything? Dr. Harper is trying to find out where she is so that I can write to her. You would think that he was asking them to disclose a state secret, but as he says, the likelihood is that they don't know where she is and can't be bothered to find out. I long to know how she is doing, and

I watch for the mail and hope. Please look out for her. You never know, it's possible she could turn up somewhere in Little Tokyo.

It made me smile to hear that Yumi is getting hard to handle. I miss her naughtiness, the way she laughs that cheeky laugh and you have to forgive her everything. Children of the camp are bound to be unruly, I think.

I'm not at all surprised that Haru has become a hero. He always gives the best of himself. I read that his combat unit was among the bravest, the most decorated of them all. And Ralph too, so brave that they gave him the Bronze Star for bravery in combat. Was it Manzanar that made them so strong, do you think?

Please give my love to your mother, and to Yumi, and my best wishes to Haru.

I miss you all, Eriko.

Satomi

The air in her apartment building smells bad, a stale, ever-present, meaty sort of odor. It's the first thing to assail the senses on entering the building, before the crumbling walls and scuffed floors meet the eye.

"It's the stench of poverty," Mrs. Copeland says. "I've lived here for twenty years and I'll never get used to it."

"I know of worse, Mrs Copeland. But it sure is unpleasant."

"Well, be like me, darling, plan to get yourself a rich man and move on." Her laugh is not without bitterness.

Mrs. Copeland calls herself "a woman of independent means." It's her way of describing how she struggles to live off the diminishing capital from the sale of her small dress shop that she retired from seven years before the war.

She is curious about Satomi, about the American internment camps, horrified at the idea of them. She couldn't believe what went on in them at first, but now she is angry on Satomi's behalf, appalled that it's not only Germany to be condemned.

"A black mark against us," she says. "Such a tragedy, for you to have lost your mother there."

She is mourning herself, for her German cousins, the last of her known family, whom she hasn't heard from in years.

"They must be lost, like all those others," she says. "I'll probably never know what happened to them."

As old as she is, Mrs. Copeland volunteers at the local refugee center twice a week, helping in the kitchen, handing out second-hand clothes, pinning up the lists of people looking for their relatives. You never know, someone might turn up there who knows of her cousins, and what else is she to do with her time anyway?

"And your Cora," she says to Satomi. "Your hope is realistic. Keep your spirits up, there's a chance you'll find her."

To counteract the smell in her building, Satomi scents her room with the cheap bleach she buys at the big Woolworth's store a block from her building. She cleans like a demon these days in a way that would amaze and please Tamura. Her room has become her refuge from the city, a place where she doesn't have to be on alert. In its shabby confines she can let go of the confident show she puts on at work and in the subway, when the panic of being underground rattles her.

Like a true city girl, she jostles for space in the coffee shops with the best of them, shouting her order over the counters, where the help hardly ever return a smile. She is learning to be a New Yorker by pretending to be one. Life in the city is tricky, people move fast, have no patience, and she is always running to catch up, to wise up.

"Keep your foot hard down on the gas, it's the only way," Mrs. Copeland advises.

Her wages run out by Friday, so that she lives during the weekends on her last bit of bread, a smear of butter. And she has lost weight, so that she notices that she is skinnier than the better-fed New Yorkers she sees around her.

Apart from her fare to New York, she has twice broken into the money she got for the farm. Once to buy a child's charm bracelet for Cora, which she couldn't resist. It has a little bell hanging on it and a tiny bucket, and space for plenty more. She keeps it in a chocolate box that was left in the trash at the library. The box is well made, a three-layer deep one, shiny brown edged with gold, she can only imagine the kind of chocolates it housed. It's surprising to her the things that New Yorkers throw away. She has put a dollar in the box along with a little peg doll Mrs. Copeland saved for her from the refuge. It helps her to collect things for Cora, to keep the child in mind.

And for herself she needed clothes for work, two dark skirts, two shirts, one white, one striped, and a jacket for colder days. She is reinventing herself, creating a new style. Haru would not approve of the short hemlines, the high-wedged heels of her shoes. Oxfords don't cut it in New York. She tells herself that she must stop judging things by what Haru would think. She can please herself now.

There's plenty more she'd like to buy, a dress or two, ankle-strap shoes in the softest leather like nothing she ever saw in the Sears and Roebuck catalogue. She's tempted but can't bring herself to be so extravagant. The money put aside is her safety net, the last bit of Aaron and Tamura to make her feel cared for. It's hard to be without kin.

She sees families together and feels intensely lonely, aches to be among the Japanese again. But when she speaks to them in Japanese they don't hang around.

"They think I'm a strange white girl," she tells Mrs. Copeland. "Guess I look like trouble to them."

Her neighborhood teems with every sort, Germans, Polish, Chinese, Romanians, Italians, and Jews like Mrs. Copeland. She wonders if there's such thing as a pure New Yorker. It should make her feel included, but she has never felt so alone.

"Don't let New York gobble you up," Mrs. Copeland says. "Take the first bite yourself."

On a Sunday afternoon when her building is hushed with the slumbering old, she takes the advice and walks the streets to the park to sit on the grass and watch the passersby. A Japanese family is doing the same nearby, father, mother, three well-behaved children. Just the sight of them lifts her heart, the familiar dark hair, the lyrical sound of Japanese catching her by her heels.

"It's a lovely day, isn't it?" she says in Japanese. "Such a lovely day."

And there it is, that confused, suspicious look. How is it that a white girl speaks Japanese so well?

"My mother was Japanese," she tries to explain as they gather their things and hurry off. "We were in Manzanar," she calls after them. They half turn, bowing their heads, smiling to be polite.

Since Pearl Harbor, since Hiroshima and Nagasaki, since the camps, they are afraid. They've done nothing wrong, but it's best to stick to your own. They fear being singled out, being noticed.

She remembers Dr. Harper's parting words to her. "Find a way to be that allows you to remember the past without spoiling the present." Well, she's trying.

She's still grieving for Tamura, still longing for Cora, and there's a low fever, a desire in her that it's hard to admit to. She has a longing to make love again, to be lost again in the intimacy she had that one time with Haru. It bothers her that she may be the loose kind, just as Lily had suspected. Are women meant to have such thoughts?

Men approach her and she isn't sure how to judge their natures. They are not of the kind she knew in Angelina or in the camp.

"Everyone's on the make, darling," Mrs. Copeland warns. "Watch yourself."

And she does, although she hadn't been prepared in those early days working in the library for her first date in the city to end so badly.

"Randal Daly, pure Irish," he had introduced himself to her as she was stacking books on the crime section shelves.

A nice enough guy, she thought, a library regular who devoured detective novels. He ran an oyster stall at the Fulton Fish Market and smelled of the lemons he cleaned himself off with at night. He was big and comfortable-looking, not handsome, but a good face, she thought. She hadn't minded his brashness; she was getting used to brashness, it was a New York thing.

She had dressed with care, folding her hair into a soft chignon, smudging her lips with a rose-colored lipstick. She bought fifteen-denier nylons, not caring that they were impractical. She wet her hands and ran them from ankle to thigh, setting the seams straight. It was good to feel pretty.

"My God, is it you?" Mrs. Copeland said appreciatively. "Be careful, now. You're still on the wrong side of green for New York, you know."

He had taken her to Sloppy Louie's restaurant near his work, a favorite with the fishmongers.

"I eat breakfast here every day," he said. "I like to be near the river."

The restaurant was spacious; they were early, but it was already more than half full. Randal thought it a bad idea to eat late.

"Better to give things time to go down," he said.

On their way to the table he greeted people at theirs, exchanging pleasantries, slapping the men on the back, complimenting the women.

"It'll be jam-packed in an hour," he said proudly, as though it were his own place doing so well.

The barnlike eatery was decorated with things of the sea, model sailing ships marooned in rye bottles, giant lobster claws hooking the air, hulking oyster shells glued randomly on the walls. It was hard to hear over the din of people chatting, calling to the waiters, clattering the cutlery—it reminded her of the mess halls in Manzanar. A brothy scent of fish, rich and steamy, made the room feel warm and living. It was good to be out, to be part of the world.

Randal's cheeks had turned red in the heat of the room; she wondered if her own had done the same. He ordered for her.

"I know what's good," he said.

"That's fine." She was glad, nervous at the thought of having to make a choice.

"You'll like the chowder," he said, proffering the pepper. "It's good with pepper."

He had advised against the eels. "Dirty things," he said. "Bottom of the harbor trash, night scavengers. Only fish I never touch."

He did most of the talking, telling her that he liked his job, it gave him a good living, and there was more to oysters than people thought.

"Got to know the good from the bad, the sweet from the sour," he said. "Trade secret how it's done."

He had never dated anyone who worked in a library, he said with a laugh. "Guess you're pretty smart, but nothing wrong with that."

"Oh, not so smart. I'm only the shelf-stacker."

He had an odd way of not responding, as though he hardly

heard her, as though he were working out what he was going to say next himself. Perhaps, though, it was only that he was lonely too, eager to talk.

By the time dessert came she knew his age, the kind of movies he liked, "westerns and detectives." She knew that his mother was dead and that he lived with his father, who worked with him in the fish market.

"This place is the best, isn't it? Louie's Italian like you," he said over coffee, waving to the proprietor. "Married to an Irish-American. It's a good combination, like you and me."

She laughed, used to the mistake. "Oh, I'm not Italian, Randal. I'm half Japanese."

The moment she said it she saw the effect it had on him. He couldn't have been more surprised if she had reached across the table and punched him in the face for no good reason. He stared at her, confused, his eyes screwing up as though he were trying to work out some difficult math problem.

"What?" His face darkened. His voice was suddenly harder, mean.

"You're a Jap? A Jap?"

"Yes, I'm Japanese. I'm Japanese and you're Irish. So?"

He stood up without looking at her, kicked the chair aside, and threw a few dollars on the table.

"Warn a guy next time," he flung at her, heading to the door.

The room went quiet, people began to stare. She watched him clumsily navigating the tables, heard his "Jesus" addressed to no one in particular. She put a napkin to her lips, swallowed hard, fighting nausea.

"You okay, honey?" the woman at the next table asked. "You don't look so good."

Outside the restaurant, she felt disoriented, out of place on the sidewalk in the dark. It was raining, the drops falling like snow, thick and slow. The insistent whisper of the river came to her. She thought of the eels Randal had spoken of curling in the deep dirty depths of the harbor, comfortable down there in the dark, knowing their place.

She wasn't sure where the subway was, hadn't wanted to ask a stranger, so for the first time in her life she took a cab.

Angry at herself for being such a bad judge of character, she couldn't wait to get to her room, to bolt the door and be alone. It was hard to admit to being hurt—that would be giving Randal and his kind the upper hand—but she couldn't sleep that night, something horrible scratched in her.

Next morning as Satomi picked her mail up, Mrs. Copeland called to her over the banister.

"How did it go, honey? Is it love?"

"Let's put it this way, Mrs. Copeland: the man was hardly a prince."

"I told you, darling, it's a hard-hearted city."

The letter in her mail was from Eriko. The news was sad. Naomi had died. Her heart had given out in her sleep.

I'm grateful that she didn't suffer, but I miss her so much, Satomi. My only comfort is that she is with Tamura. Now we are both orphans.

Another link gone. She didn't have to cry about Randal now, she could cry for Naomi, beloved Naomi, contrary but kind Naomi, Naomi who with her arthritic hands had knitted mittens for orphans.

After the incident with Randal, New York didn't seem so scary to her; she had survived her baptism and hadn't drowned. If anything, it had become more like Angelina. Not everyone was on your side.

It went against her nature to take advice from someone like Randal Daly, but she determined in the future to make it clear from the start to anyone who was interested, who she is.

There had been other dates that had gone better, but none of them had stirred her much. She had no idea what she was looking for, someone like Haru, perhaps. None of them, though, fit that bill. Not the guy who was all over her in the first hour, or the one who thought himself funny but wasn't, or the nice one who got on her nerves. Sometimes she thought it would be better just to stay at home, where nothing was required of her.

Now she takes refuge in books, in the conversations that she has with Mrs. Copeland about relatives finding each other, about the joy of being found. Nothing interests her more than those stories of reunion.

"It happens," Mrs. Copeland says. "Not that often, but when it does, it's wonderful. You should see their faces when they discover a brother, a cousin, when a loved one is found alive and longing to hear from them."

Satomi can't help picturing a scene where she and Cora are reunited. She imagines them walking together holding hands, eating in the diner three blocks down that serves ten different flavors of ice cream, sitting in the movies thrilling to Flash Gordon.

"You're haunted by that child," Mrs. Copeland observes. "But you must make a life for yourself before you can make one for her."

It's good advice, not that Mrs Copeland seems interested much in her own life. She is looking toward death with the sort of practicality that Satomi thinks must come with age.

"I thought my time was up the other night, could see myself lying in that shower clear as day. But it was just a dream."

"How horrible for you."

"No, honey, I don't mind those dreams so much. No one lives forever, and they sort of prepare you for what's coming."

AT CLARE HOUSE

Y OU'RE NEW." JOSEPH Rodman takes his time handing
Satomi his coat. The party at the museum is almost over, but
he is not sorry to be late, he is more often late than not for most
things. His expectations of the show, of his fellow guests, are low.

Satomi nods her head slightly, doesn't answer. Her hand is out,
ready to take his coat, but he is fiddling in the pocket searching in
a disinterested way.

"You've lost something?"

"No, not really, just playing for time."

"Playing for time?" she turns from him, takes a hanger from
the rail, wonders why she feels embarrassed.

He can't quite place the accent. She's definitely not a New
Yorker, more West Coast than East, he thinks. The low pitch of her
voice, and her unhurried way of speaking is measured in comparison to the city's gabble. He likes the cool look of her. It's strange
that he should be so instantly charmed, especially as she has nothing
of the boy about her, except maybe a linear sort of elegance.

"I'd rather look at you than what's on show here tonight," he
says. He isn't flirting, it's the truth.

She's used now to New York flattery, but his compliment
doesn't feel like flattery—not the standard kind, at least. She senses
that the usual banter doesn't apply here. She sees sympathy in his

stare and is irritated. Has he worked out that she's hiding in the cloakroom? Does he feel sorry for her? He is making her uncomfortable, and she wishes he would hand over his coat and go away.

"My name's Joseph. Yours?"

"It's Satomi. Satomi Baker."

"Satomi?"

"It's Japanese."

"But you aren't . . ."

"I'm half Japanese."

"Perfect. Quite perfect."

Time is running out for Joseph, and if a woman must be courted, if he must keep his promise, then perhaps she is different enough to be the one.

On her way home that evening Satomi wonders whether she was right to refuse his dinner invitation. She's bad at jumping in these days, less willing than she used to be at taking chances. New York makes you cautious. And Joseph Rodman is like no one she has ever known, although there is something of the museum's director about him. She wouldn't know how to be with a man like him.

Two weeks later and on his third request she agrees to dinner, providing that it's somewhere not too smart.

"I don't have the clothes for anywhere smart."

The moment she accepts the invitation she regrets it. It seems to her that Joseph Rodman is a man who expects perfection. He is so well groomed as to be intimidating, he smells of cologne, and he is obviously rich, coming from a world she can only guess at. Her father would not have approved, would hardly think him the kind of man for his daughter. And Tamura, who judged men by Aaron and found most of them wanting, would she have approved? Satomi's mother would have been kinder than her father, of course, less willing to judge.

"Go," Mrs. Copeland has encouraged, feeling herself *in parentis*. "Plenty of time to lie low when you're old."

"Remember, nowhere fancy," Satomi warns, hoping it might put him off.

But he is stirred by the idea of it, of finding somewhere "not too smart," of being out with the hat-check girl on an ordinary date.

You could start from scratch with a girl like her. He has found a Vermeer languishing in a cupboard, a delight of color and composition. All she needs is the right frame. Relief floods him. Things might work out after all.

It seems to Satomi that Joseph under his smartness has a good character, although he doesn't give much of himself away. A frank smile and impeccable manners are hardly enough to go on. He's conceited, that much is obvious in his head-to-toe neatness, the sleek cut of his hair, the perfect ovals of his nails. But are such things flaws? Perhaps that sort of perfection is natural for the rich, how would she know? She has noticed that in art, though, his eye is taken by the simple—a costly sort of simple, but still a taste she shares.

Joseph, despite his exacting style, has honed his taste to be the opposite of that of his widowed mother, Dulcibele, who revels in what he considers to be a vulgar sort of fondness for the overdone. His infrequent visits to her glittering white mansion on the shores of the Hudson are uncomfortable, the times they come across each other in town unwelcome to them both.

He blames his mother's selfishness for not caring for his father, for the broken thing in himself that he's finding hard to fix. She can't be blamed, though, for the promise his father had extracted from him. A deathbed promise, he thinks dramatically, although it was given months before the old man died.

"You must marry, Joseph. It's the right thing for you."

"I don't think I'm made for marriage, Father."

"But it will make you happy, Joseph. I know it. Promise me. Promise me that you will."

His son must make an heir to the Rodmans' great fortune, just as he had done himself. It's a duty not to be dodged. A man of Joseph's tastes could too easily lose the way. At the very least, a wife on his son's arm would put paid to the gossip. A pretty one might even switch Joseph's taste to the more conventional.

With the promise given, the old man when the time came had let go of life with a deep sigh and a pleasurable sense of relief. Joseph, along with the Rodman fortune, was left with the pledge, and the novel feeling of being committed.

Unused to courtship, he fumbles through his now-regular outings with Satomi, pleased when she finds his jokes funny, flattered when he has her attention. He is already fond of her, charmed by how different she is from those smart uptown girls his mother has her eye on for him. Having a girl on his arm is odd, but not as unpleasant a sensation as he had feared.

Satomi feels more the Angelina girl than ever when she is with Joseph. Before him, she hadn't thought herself to be so ignorant. But she's learning, and she likes it. She knows now that wine is not for her, but she enjoys the bookish flavor of whiskey and the taste of a New York strip steak. It's amazing to discover that she likes opera, amazing that she should even go to the opera. The linking of Satomi Baker with Joseph Rodman is so extraordinary a thing that she is tempted herself sometimes to repeat in her head, *a girl like you*. She loves the plays Joseph takes her to on Broadway, even though he often thinks them poor. It's shocking to her how little impresses Joseph.

"What's he like, darling?" Mrs. Copeland asks Satomi as they stand in their hallway together, looking down through the window at Joseph's waiting cab in the street below.

"Um, he's sort of fine, I guess. He makes me laugh quite a lot, and he's rich, I think, but he's not for me, really."

"Are you sure, darling? The words 'lucky girl' come to mind."

But Satomi doesn't so much feel lucky as false. Despite herself she can't help judging. Joseph is far too extravagant, too wasteful. To see him leave food on his plate, wine in his glass, is painful to her. He buys things just to try them, a new brand of cigarettes that he throws away after one drag, books that he likes the cover of but will never read, and so much cologne that it makes her dizzy.

Yet the sense that Joseph, like her, is dislocated in some way draws her to him. And there is something of Dr. Harper's warmth and wit about him that she likes. She wonders what it's like to be him, to never have to worry if there will be enough money at the end of the week for food, to never question your good fortune or deny yourself anything.

Oh, money, she can hear her mother say. *It isn't a child of your own, or even a fresh-laid egg.*

I wish I could be like you, Mama, she replies in this conversation in her head. *You always knew the path to take.*

In Joseph's efforts to charm Satomi, he tells himself that art is the thing. If he can't seduce with his manliness, he will do it with art. So they stroll the long arcades in the hushed atmosphere of New York's galleries, gazing at the glorious paintings of battles, of lush naked women, and of misty landscapes. She can recognize now the pure light of a Raphael, the sweeping brushstrokes of a Gauguin.

It pleases the teacher in Joseph. He hopes the passion on the canvases will satisfy enough to deflect for a while what he imagines must be Satomi's expectations of him.

He takes her to those restaurants that have an intimate atmosphere, but where he doesn't have to be alone with her. He is saving himself from those moments when a different man would take the opportunity to make his move, those moments that could lose him the game. In its own way it is a romantic sort of wooing, he thinks.

Satomi, though, is confused as to what she and Joseph are, exactly. It seems to her that he is more teacher than boyfriend. There's something about him that she can't get a hold of. Perhaps it's the sense she has that Joseph is in hiding, she wishes she knew from what. Whatever it is, though, it doesn't feel like a regular boy-girl thing. She's relieved that he hasn't made a move, but she can't help thinking it strange, asking herself questions. *Why doesn't he kiss me? Why is taking my arm to cross the road the nearest he gets to touching?*

Aware that he is not pulling off the boyfriend thing, he steps up what he thinks of as treats for her. He takes her on a tour of his New York. They pound the streets, and visit the grand buildings of Lower Manhattan. He points out ornate ceilings and reels off dates.

"This is New York classical," he says, trawling her to the Cunard Building to marvel at its great hall. "Nothing much left of New Amsterdam these days, but the American Renaissance style compares with Paris, with Rome, even. It's marvelous, don't you think?"

It's a step too far, but she can't help laughing.

"Oh, for goodness' sake, Joseph, no more, please. Let's get some coffee. I can't face another museum, another bank, another set of Corinthian columns."

Buildings are not her thing and she is bored, reminded of those times in Mr. Beck's class when her mind had wandered, when she and Lily had caught each other's eyes and raised them to heaven.

"It's the worst thing, to be bored," Joseph says. "Sorry, Sati, I'm a fool. What would you like to do?"

He is glad that she speaks up for herself, that she is not in his thrall. It would feel more like cheating to him if she was.

"I'd really like to visit the Statue of Liberty, and I want to ride the elevator to the top of the Empire State Building."

"Really! You know it's twelve hundred and fifty feet above the ground up there?"

"Are you scared of heights, Joseph?"

"No, only of tourists." They both laugh.

If only they could agree to be nothing more than friends, she would be able to enjoy his company better. Joseph makes the best of friends; he is good at listening when she needs to talk, easy with her silences when she doesn't. But though it seems to her that they are playacting the man woman thing, though nothing of what they are to each other is spoken about, she senses that he is aiming for something different than friendship. So, as though she is cheating, she feels guilty when she goes with someone else on a date without telling him.

"Only to save his feelings," she says to Mrs. Copeland.

"Really?" Mrs. Copeland shrugs her shoulders, raises one eyebrow.

Knowing nothing about Joseph, Dr. Harper's cousin Edward, in a matchmaking move, had set it up.

"Pete Elderkin. A nice guy," he said. "I think you'll hit it off."

And he is a nice guy, sort of. Fresh out of the Army, with a crew-cut bullishness about him, Satomi can tell he is the sort of man who takes life on the run. He had grabbed himself a job in a big cross-state delivery business, in the same week of his demobilize from the Army. Competition doesn't bother him, only standing still bothers him, he says.

"I'll make it up to transport manager in no time," he tells her. "I pretty much run the place on my own now. Wouldn't surprise me if I end up owning the whole damn thing."

It wouldn't surprise her either, since he has that bounce-back thing about him. Nothing is going to keep him down.

They walk in the park and she feels small beside the bulk of him, she was used these days to walking with Joseph, who is slim and only a couple of inches taller than her.

Pete tells her about his time in the Army, about the war, about the German concentration camps he has seen. He believes that America has single-handedly set the world to rights.

"God, those German bastards," he says. "Europe's had it. It's the most decadent place on earth. Thank God for America."

America this, America that, he is in love with his country; nothing bad about that, she supposes, it reminds her of Haru. But he takes it too far, until she wishes he would stop crowing about the US of A, as he calls it. It feels to her like preaching, like one of Haru's lectures.

"We live in the most decent country on earth," he says. "You'd know that if you'd seen what I've seen."

"I was in a camp too. An American one," she ventures. "I wasn't thanking God for America then."

He looks away from her, gives an embarrassed laugh as though she has made an inappropriate joke.

"Sure, Edward told me. But hell, it's not the same thing at all."

"No, maybe not. Still, it was a camp. It was imprisonment."

It wasn't the same thing, she knew that. She had read about those concentration camps, the inhuman things that went on in them. Mrs. Copeland often spoke of it, had periods of depression about it, cried for her lost relatives, and thought herself lucky as a Jew that she was also an American. You couldn't compare Manzanar to those malignant places, yet still she thought it wrong to judge the camps against each other. It occurs to her that there is a ranking of what it was okay to talk about in these postwar times. Germany's treatment of the Jews, fine; America's of the Japanese, not.

"Things happen," he says. "Long as they work out well in the end, I guess."

"You can't just dismiss innocent people losing their homes, being caged, Pete. What if it had been you?"

"Yeah, I kinda see your point, but . . ."

"Really?" she senses that he hasn't seen her point at all. "I don't think you can bear to think about America being in the wrong about anything." She wants him to know that just because things had been worse in Germany, she wouldn't be silenced about the camps in America.

"Well, I'm not sure that's—"

"There were deaths, some would say murders, in Manzanar. Boys shot, an old man killed for refusing to halt at the guards' command. And plenty who didn't survive the conditions. Did you know that orphaned babies were imprisoned there?"

"Look." He is in a conciliatory mood. "I guess I didn't think it out. Let's not talk about it, huh. The war's over, after all. We'll make a proper night of it next time, shall we? Start over."

It was unforgiving of her, she knew, but she couldn't help herself. "No next time," she said lightly. "I don't think we're going to work out."

Pete Elderkin was never going to think it out. His blind love of country, what seemed to her to be his denial of what went on in the American camps, played on her mind for a few days until a letter from Dr. Harper arrived, which put things back in perspective. She hadn't been making too much of it. It was cheating yourself to love in ignorance, to love what you didn't know, and wherever it took place injustice was injustice.

I hadn't realized I had collected quite so much. It's a bigger archive than I had at first thought. When you are ready I want you to have it. I'm not expecting you to do anything with it, but I'm shocked by the silence of our leaders, the lack of an apology. Perhaps the time's not right yet, but someday you might be pleased to have it, if only to show your children.

She isn't sure that she does want it. His reports on sick inmates, the personal things he has collected, the photographs and the journals that will surely include Tamura's life, her death, might be too much for her. He might as well be handing over the earth of Manzanar, her mother's grave, the dead riot boys, the skin and blood of the camp's inmates. She is afraid of Dr. Harper's archive, of the pain it will cause her to go through it.

I'm still trying to trace Cora, he assures her.

I've written to various orphanages. They take their time replying, but none so far know of Cora. I think it means that she must have found a family, which would be the best news if only we could be sure of it.

Her own efforts to find Cora are not nearly enough, she thinks. She feels powerless, hardly up to the task, so far away from wherever Cora might be. And none of the letters she has written to government offices have met with any success. The chocolate box is filling up with trinkets for the child, satin ribbons, a necklace, a child's hairbrush, things she is beginning to fear Cora will never see.

But along with Eriko's less frequent letters, Dr. Harper's serve to anchor her, keep her linked to her past. Manzanar is always with her, Cora too, but New York is an intrusive city and won't be ignored.

With her feelings of home stirred, she writes to Haru care of

Eriko, a short exploratory letter to ask if he thinks of her as she does him. Even if he doesn't, she asks him to make inquiries in his locality about Cora, to visit the orphanages on her behalf.

My feelings haven't changed, and I feel brave enough to ask if yours have. I could return to California, but I would only come if you wanted it.

His answering letter is brief, lecturing in tone:

You must let Cora go, make your own life now, Satomi. It would be a mistake to return here. Stick to what you have chosen.

It hurts to read his disinterest on the page, the truth of his feelings written so bluntly. It's obvious to her now that Haru had only found her beautiful on the outside. The thing between them, so large a part in her life, had after all only played out in a minor key in his. She must shed the hope she harbored that one day they would be reunited. The truth is bleak, but at least she won't miss the preaching.

Joseph has kept her from what he terms *society*, from any introduction that might go wrong, that might offend her. You never know how uptown will react to outsiders, and he doesn't want to see her hurt. He introduces her to his best friend Hunter, though. Not much of a risk, he thinks, as Hunter isn't cursed with snobbery or, amazingly, with bitterness. Wheelchair-bound for life since being wounded at Pearl Harbor, Hunter has a lighthearted take on even the most serious things in life.

"Satomi's father was killed at Pearl Harbor," Joseph tells him straight off, wanting them to have something in common, even something so horrible. "It's extraordinary that you were both there, don't you think?"

"So he and I were colleagues-in-arms, then," Hunter says, taking her hand, smiling at her.

"I guess."

"I was luckier than your father. Just the legs," he says, as though they were the smallest of concerns.

She thinks it ridiculous that this boyish man, dressed like an Ivy League frat boy, still sporting a childlike smile, would have ranked over her father. But she instantly likes him, can see why Joseph is so fond of him, why even in a wheelchair he is, if Joseph is to be believed, able to play the field with one cute girl after another.

"Don't know what you've done to my boy," Hunter says. "I've never seen him so happy. It's a surprise."

On their dates now Joseph greets her with a brief kiss on the cheek. He never kisses her good night, though, suspecting something more will be expected of him if he does. He picks her up from her building in a cab, returns her in a cab. He can't bear the subway, can't bear being crushed up against the masses. It's surprising to Satomi he has never learned to drive.

"I was a chauffeur-driven city boy," he excuses himself. "You're a country girl; I bet you had old trucks and tractors to practice on."

"You guess right." She laughs, thinking with a pang of their old truck, of her mother facing up to mean old Tom Myers.

They eat early and unless he takes her to the theater he has her home by ten, as though he is expecting an anxious parent to confront him. She is beginning to think that he has other places to go. It doesn't bother her, she is forgiving of him. As unlikely as it seems, she believes that Joseph needs her friendship more than she needs his.

———

On a damp evening when the thought of another rich meal in an uptown restaurant fills her with gloom, she suggests that they go to the movies.

"Can't bear being in a crowd in the dark," Joseph says. "You never know who you will be sitting next to in a movie house."

"You mean ordinary people, Joseph?"

"Well, perhaps."

"I'm ordinary."

"Rubbish, dear girl. You are extraordinary."

She likes to believe that her reasons for being with Joseph are because he is entertaining, because they are both lonely, because they have developed an intimacy outside of the physical. There is truth in this, she knows, but she isn't sure these days that she doesn't enjoy the money thing a bit too much, the presents of clothes and jewelry that Joseph has begun buying her. She fights with herself about it, but she is seduced by the beauty that money buys, the fineness of the life it offers. She appreciates the luxury of decent food, the balanced weight of silver cutlery, and the crisp white linen of restaurant tablecloths. It's hard to resist the treat of fresh flowers and the expensive perfumes that Joseph sends on such a regular basis that she is on first-name terms with the delivery boys who bring them to her door.

"You mustn't," she had said at first as the presents began arriving. Even to her the words had sounded hollow, halfhearted. Would Tamura be disappointed in her? Is she disappointed in herself? Is this who *a girl like her* truly is?

Joseph takes no notice of her protests. He enjoys buying her presents, enriching her life, he thinks.

"We'll need to buy you a dress, something wonderful. I've tickets for *Petrushka*." He waves them at her. "You're going to love it."

And she does love it, is reliving it in her head in the cab on the way home, so that she is shocked out of her reverie when they reach her building to see an ambulance parked outside with its doors open, the neighbors gathered on the sidewalk.

"It's Mrs. Copeland," a gray-haired man in his dressing gown calls to her. "They're bringing her body out now."

Her hand flies to her mouth, she shakes her head, begins to tremble.

"Are you sure it's her?"

"Yeah, I'm sure. 'Less she's got a twin. I'm the one who found her."

She hasn't seen her friend for a couple of days and feels guilty now, responsible somehow. Had Mrs. Copeland been feeling ill in those two days, had she called out for help and found none?

"Did she slip in the shower?" she asks.

"No, she had a weak heart, you know?"

She hadn't known, Mrs. Copeland had never mentioned an unreliable heart to her.

"I found her in the hallway," the old man boasts. "She had her key in her hand, couldn't tell if she was on her way in or out."

It's hard news to take. She will never see Mrs. Copeland again. She will never talk with her, or laugh at her jokes, never again buy her little treats. Mrs. Copeland, like Tamura, had loved candy.

She is stunned, the joy of the evening, her delight in *Petrushka* evaporated. She had forgotten how easy it is to lose people, how separation comes so swiftly.

Seeing how upset she is, Joseph touches her shaking shoulder.

"Come home with me, Satomi," he offers. "You don't want to be on your own tonight. It's obviously been a shock."

"No, but will you come inside with me, Joseph? Just for a little while."

He is repelled by the room's dimensions, its shabbiness, and the rooming-house smell of the place. But he sets to making her tea, pained at her empty cupboards, the dime-fed gas fire.

He thinks of his spacious Art Deco duplex on Fifth Avenue, of the stylish straight-limbed furniture, the pale rugs, and the discreet lighting. The walls there are hung with the clean lines of Cocteau drawings and naïve paintings. There's nothing on Satomi's dingy walls, except a small mirror in a chipped frame. While he can walk through his apartment unimpeded by clutter, go from room to room forgetting even how many he has, she hardly has space to breathe in the doll's-house scale of hers. He has glimpsed her poverty, and it's meaner than he'd thought.

"It's very beautiful," Satomi says on her first visit to Joseph's home. "It's the perfect apartment."

She is seeing it at its best, on one of those flushed Manhattan evenings when the zodiacal light lends beauty to the skyline of the metropolis, when the palaces of Ninety-first Street, as Joseph calls them, seem washed with gold.

"It is, isn't it?" he says, satisfied. "It's the most beautiful apartment in New York, I think."

She is good at seeing his melancholia off, a thing he suffers from on and off. He loves that she approves of the understated style of the place, that she matches that style, looks right in it. He has no idea that she doesn't feel right in it, doesn't feel at ease in its lofty space. Her emotions are still informed by Manzanar, her eyes still measure on its scale.

On later visits, though, when she is used to it, comparisons with the camp fade. She looks forward to being there, to being with Joseph, and now that she knows that there's no criticism in it, she even finds his teachy side charming. The contrasts in her life are great between what was and what is, but then, as they are always saying in New York, *Only in America.*

As for Joseph, he marvels that her single company is often

enough for him. It's a first. He is popular among his set, but apart from Hunter, he has never sought particular friendships. They are too intrusive, too exposing.

He likes to watch Satomi reading, her slim legs tucked beneath her on his low sofas, unconsciously graceful as he might have arranged her there himself, just so. If he has to, he could live with a girl like her. And he does have to. What kind of man, after all, would break a promise to a dying father?

On the night he decides to propose, he catches sight of himself in a mirror, eyes gleaming, lips dry, and recognizes the expression. He has glimpsed it before and knows it appears when he gambles against the odds. It's the look that lets him down in poker. Satomi will be astonished, taken off guard, his timing may be wrong, but there's danger too in waiting. How much longer will she continue to cruise along with him before some stranger, some more appealing man, comes along and takes them both by surprise?

"Well, I have to say this place certainly suits you, Sati." The words sound rehearsed, as they have been. "You look at home here."

"Do I?"

"Mmm, just as we are with each other, wouldn't you say?"

"Sure, I would, Joseph."

He pops the cork of what he hopes will be a celebratory bottle of Dom Pérignon. He would prefer his usual evening martini, crushed ice and more vermouth than gin so that it is extra dry, no olive, but a lemon twist, and leave the bitters out. And she might enjoy a whiskey more, but he wants to do things by the book, so champagne it has to be.

"Champagne, dear girl," he says, clinking their glasses.

"Are we celebrating something?"

She senses his excitement, his unaccustomed nervousness, and sits up straight, unsettled now herself. As he hovers with the glasses, she is suddenly filled with affection for him. Joseph is not as cool as he would like her to think. In those times when he spares her his sophistication, he is more like a little boy, sweet and naughty, entirely unpredictable.

"We may be," he says hopefully. "Celebrating something, I mean."

He hates that he can't be honest with her, but he can't risk the truth of it. Learning that he doesn't want to bed her or any other woman might scare her off. He consoles himself with the truth that he cares for her, loves her in his way. And if she accepts him she will benefit from the arrangement too. She is alone in the world, vulnerable. He will take care of her, share his wealth, save her from that squalid little room with its mean gas ring, the sink with the black crack running its length, harboring goodness knows what germs. He was meant to find her, she was meant for better things.

He thinks briefly of the boy he slept with the night before. He had been less than honest with him too. He hardly remembers his name, any of their names. It's a long list, after all. He takes a guess at Chuck. Chuck had it in spades, all right, the look that gets him every time, full lips, snake hips, the walk. The look he likes, the character not so much.

Joseph had long ago given up the battle of fighting his nature, but still he is torn between the sensual and the intellectual, and the boy had been quite stupid, had spoiled the pleasure of the act by talking too much.

"I can come again. Tonight, if you like. Shall I come tonight?" He had made a joke about the coming bit, but it had sounded too much like pleading, for Joseph to agree.

"No, I am going abroad," he lied. "I'll find you when I return."

It's remarkable to him how quickly the joy disappears the moment the coupling is over, a switch flicked. He never hangs around for long. All he wants is to hoof it to the familiar surrounds of Li's hangout, where, since he was eighteen years old, opium dreams have guaranteed oblivion.

"Joseph? Are we celebrating something?" she prompts.

"I hope so."

"You're being mysterious. Come on, tell me what it is."

"It's just this, Sati, and I don't want to make a big deal of it . . . but here goes. I want you to know that I won't ever be careless with you. Whatever happens between us, I'll make sure that nothing like Manzanar ever touches you again. If you let me, I'll be your protector, your best friend."

"Oh, Joseph, there's no need. I—"

"Let me finish, Sati." He runs his hand through his hair, finding himself more nervous than he could have imagined. "More champagne, let me fill your glass."

"Are you trying to get me drunk?" She's on edge now, guesses what's coming, hopes she's wrong.

"I'm trying to ask you to marry me. I want you to marry me, dear girl."

He hadn't planned on blurting it out so bluntly. He can see that she is stunned.

"But why, Joseph?"

"Why does anyone ask a girl to marry them?"

"You tell me."

"Well, it would annoy my mother, and that's never a bad thing." He instantly regrets his flippancy.

"My parents married because they loved each other so much that there was no other option," she says.

It's not that Joseph is unattractive to her, but when she thinks of how it had been with Haru that one time, how it had completed something in her, the idea of accepting Joseph's proposal seems ridiculous.

"I love you in my way Sati," he says. "But if I'm honest about the reason for wanting to marry, well, the truth is that I made a promise to my father to marry. You're the only girl I have ever met that I can imagine sharing my life with."

"Is that the truth?"

"Yes."

"The whole truth?"

"Who ever tells the whole truth?"

"Joseph!" Her face widens in surprise.

"I know, a shocking thing to say."

"In any case, Joseph, I can't say yes. Love is supposed to be the thing, isn't it? The thing that goes with marriage."

"It's not the law, is it, Sati? And it needn't be our rule, we can make our own. And to be blunt, that kind of marriage was never in the cards for me. You have to trust me on that."

"Well, I don't. Love is like luck, it comes when you least expect it." She wishes they weren't having this conversation. She feels put on the spot, unkind. She gulps the last of her champagne and coughs as it goes down the wrong way.

"You're a romantic," Joseph says, patting her back. "I didn't have you down for one."

"Is that so bad?"

"No, a bit unrealistic, though."

"It's a crazy idea, Joseph. Honestly, can you see us together for life in that way? We like each other, but . . . ."

"Well, how many married people can say that?"

"Plenty, I guess. You're such a cynic."

"You can't lose out, you know. You'll never have to worry about money again. Never have to want for anything."

"I don't think money keeps you from wanting."

"Maybe not, but I can give you the sort of life you deserve. I'll never be cruel to you, and I'll be your best friend. You have had enough of struggle, surely?"

"Yes, but my struggles don't have much to do with money."

"Don't tell me you're a secret heiress."

"Not unless you count ninety dollars or so as the definition of heiress."

He can't stop the pity he feels from reaching his eyes. She has ninety dollars to face the rest of her life with, small change to him. It would scare him witless to have so little, yet she seems unafraid.

"In any case, Joseph, what you see, what you think you know, is only the smallest part of who I am."

"Who are you, then? Tell me the worst of it."

"Well, for one thing, I'm not as nice as you think."

"Did I ever say that I thought you were nice?"

"No, but anyway, apart from that you would find me very hard to live with. There are days when I don't want company, when nothing much pleases me, when you would find me horrible to be with."

"I know that already, Sati, I'm the same. We will leave each other to our own devices on those days."

"I'm argumentative, you know? I wouldn't give you an easy ride."

"I know that too."

"Oh, it doesn't stop there." She is irritated by his refusal to let her off the hook. "I take long showers that use up all the hot water and I refuse now to wait in line for anything. And however you might want to change me, in the way that men do, it won't work. If my father couldn't do it no, one can. Would you want to be saddled with such a person for a wife?"

"I would," he says, joining her on the sofa. "There are six

bathrooms in this place and the hot water never runs out. Shower to your heart's content. I'll see to it that you never have to wait in line for anything. And the last thing I want to do is change you."

"I'm not a virgin, you know." She hopes to shock, to stop the marriage talk.

In the pause as he thinks about it, he realizes that he knew that she wasn't. She is too complete to be a virgin. That guy Haru she told him about, he supposes. It hardly makes a difference, except that she is being honest with him, whereas he can't find trust enough to be the same with her.

He puts his arm around her, feeling the womanly slope of her shoulder, the swell of her breast against his chest. Because it is Sati and her body is slim, pared down, it isn't unpleasant, but it is disturbing. It's hard for him not to shy away from the way women are made, from the heat that comes off them. They are designed to drip milk and blood, and there is something animallike at their core, something deep and murky. He has felt a faint disgust at it since infancy, since first being aware of the smothering sensation he suffered as a baby at his mother's fulsome breasts.

He feels himself drawing away and rallies. He must marry, that's that. He wants her, just doesn't *want* her. They are the answer to each other's problems, they are synchronicity.

"Well, I'm not a virgin either." He smiles. "So we are equal, dear girl."

"Stop, Joseph. Please let's stop talking about it."

"Take a chance on me, Sati. Don't be like those dreamers waiting for fortune to shine on them. They always die disappointed, you know."

She moves on the sofa, creating a space between them, wishing she were somewhere else. Joseph isn't giving up.

"Just imagine for a moment all those dull little rooms in New York, filled with people growing old, hoping to win life's lottery.

To be chosen!" he says. You know that *Only in America* thing? It works for one in a million, maybe. You could be the one."

"They may have love, Joseph. You always dismiss love."

"Because that's the biggest con of all, don't you think? Put up with all the dross and wait for the great romance, the one true love that will surely transform everything."

"Perhaps when it comes, it does. Perhaps it's worth waiting for."

"I thought that you had already been burned by that fire."

"Mmm, maybe."

"You have to make things happen yourself, Sati. Take the opportunities when they come."

"And you're my opportunity, Joseph?"

"Why shouldn't I be? Look, it can get pretty cold out there on your own, you know. You have so little to lose just now, so much to gain if you say yes."

On her third glass of champagne, and caught up in the force of Joseph's words, she is relaxing into the idea. Being married to Joseph would be an adventure, would be extraordinary. And what if she waits for true love, what guarantee is there that it will ever come? Maybe it has already left for good, left with Haru. Maybe its very nature is to be one-sided, to wound the one who loves most. She's had enough of being the one who loves most.

Joseph feels the give in her, the leap to the finish line in himself. It would be too hard to lose now; he will never find anyone who fits the bill as well as Satomi Baker. She is offbeat, unexpected, and off the New York society radar. She is his last chance to save himself from those uptown girls with their long teeth and above-reproach credentials.

"There is no reason, Joseph," his mother insists, "why you shouldn't marry a Whitney, or a Cameron. The Rodmans have earned their place in society by now, I should think."

"God forbid it, Mother. The boredom would kill me."

He can't imagine ever being bored with Satomi. She is open to the world, to ideas, and surprisingly sure of herself, given her background. He likes the idea of being a teacher in their relationship even though she is not always in the mood to listen to him. It is something he can offer her that has nothing to do with money. These days the thought of being married to her seems like something he wants rather than something imposed on him.

"Say yes, Satomi. Don't sleepwalk your life away waiting for things to happen to you. Decide that they will."

And in the moment, in the picture he has drawn so vividly of the kind of life that he can offer her, but mostly in the terrible idea that it is possible to sleepwalk your life away, she hears herself asking for time.

"Of course, of course. Take as much time as you need." It's in the bag, he thinks. "Absolutely no hurry."

A memory of the honest intimacies of love, of Aaron lightly touching Tamura's hand as he passed her, of Tamura lighting his cigarette with sweet concentration, comes to her with a pang. She dismisses it. The thought of making things happen, of not waiting around for luck to choose her, is suddenly appealing. Luck hasn't done such a great job for her in the past, after all.

"I should have gone down on one knee, shouldn't I?"

He kisses her lightly on the lips, the lime-sharp cologne scent of him overpowering. She leans into him, returning the kiss, feeling his mouth close against her half-open one, feeling herself a fraud. Could she love him, make love with him? He is almost handsome, certainly glamorous. It's not enough, she knows.

If she turns him down, will she ever get out of her dismal room, with its brick wall view, the memory of Mrs. Copeland an ever-present ghost in the hallway? There are times when that room seems to her to be the loneliest place on earth. How long had

Mrs. Copeland been fading in hers before her death? Perhaps Joseph is right. You have to seize your opportunities.

"Your family, Joseph? Can't imagine they'd be happy about you choosing me, somehow."

"There's only my mother, some odd upstate cousins. They hardly matter. I never see them if I can help it."

"How sad for you."

"Not really. My father's opinion is the only one I ever cared for, and he would have loved you."

UPTOWN

Y OU CAN'T STAY in that awful place. You don't have to decide the marriage thing now, just come and stay as a guest." Joseph's insistence, her own fear of stasis, had driven the decision.

"I can't bear the thought of you in that nasty little room. Look at all the space here. Have your own rooms, as many as you want." A nervous tick had fluttered at the corner of Joseph's right eye. If she turned him down it would probably mean that marriage was off the table too.

"I won't bother you. I'll just be your landlord for the time being. Only a nicer one than you have at present."

"But what will people think?"

"What people?"

"Oh, you know."

"It's nobody's business but ours."

"Still no pressure?"

"I told you, no hurry."

"Well, maybe for a while."

"Or forever, if you like."

She is shaky about it. It feels risky, the choice a loose woman might make, certainly one Tamura would have advised against. Is this the rashness in her that Haru saw when he called her dangerous?

Her regular kind of life has collided with Joseph's extraordinary one and she feels like a child grasping at something too big for tiny hands to hold on to. But since Mrs. Copeland died she can hardly bear to be in her building anymore. Things have changed there, and not for the better.

A woman in her early sixties has moved into Mrs. Copeland's room. She has a tight unfriendly smile, a buttoned-up way of walking, and the smell of cheap rye and perspiration wafts from her as she passes. She hadn't been there a week when she began banging on the wall when Satomi played the radio, although her own plays on high volume all through the night.

Satomi, glad to go, has packed up her things and moved in with Joseph. But strangely, while living with him has dispelled her loneliness, it has only added to her sense of displacement. Questions come to her mind so that she can't settle; is she grabbing at the chance to forget the past, is she excusing herself from the promise she made to Cora? Is she letting Dr. Harper down, failing to live up to Ralph Lazo's example?

Be honest, she tells herself, *you wanted to be saved.* But from what? From the effort of making her own way, perhaps, from collecting dimes to feed the gas meter in her insistently cold room, or from the shower water running cold before she's had time to rinse the soap from her hair. But it's mostly, she thinks, from the dreadful fear she suffers of nothing changing. *I wanted to be saved from real life,* she thinks. Perhaps, after years of want, it is simply greed for a bigger slice of the cake.

Joseph finds himself completely satisfied in the waiting for her answer. He has done his part. He isn't breaking his promise, it's just on hold. For the moment nothing needs to change and he is at peace.

But in his splendid apartment the girl she knew has been replaced with another, less certain one. Who is this person wandering the huge rooms, gazing at paintings worth thousands of dollars, trailing her fingers on sculptures of the kind she would normally only see in museums? Nothing in her past life had hinted at the one she lives now with Joseph. She's in alien territory, attempting to merge. In her daydreaming moments she imagines herself becoming part of the art, alive only when looked at.

Sometimes to steady herself she has to close her eyes, to hold life at bay for a moment or two. She summons pictures of Angelina's woods, wraps herself in its greenery, smells the wild mint that she imagines still grows around the sitting stone, and sees the fox, wild and clean. She breathes deeply, gathering herself like an actress waiting for the camera to roll so that she can play her part. It has all happened too quickly, she has hardly had time to adjust to city living, and life with Joseph may be luxurious, but it's big and scary too.

What more could you possibly want? she asks herself, and knows the answer.

What she wants is Tamura making tea on their little stove, dented metal mugs, a radish or two in the right season. Oh, to sit with Tamura on the barrack steps, the mountains dark as forests in the distance, the sound of Yumi arguing with Eriko, and Cora's little arms around her neck, the sweet child smell of her. That was real life, this one the fantasy.

It's so strange to miss Manzanar, isn't it? Eriko writes in her latest letter.

I can't quite remember how to be out in the world. An alarm triggers in me at noon, shouldn't I be going to the mess hall? My eyes still hold the ground looking for wood for the stove. Three years out of a lifetime is hardly much, yet it seems like the bigger part of it.

Satomi is herself still held by Manzanar, by a horrible longing for it. Dr. Harper says he understands. He thinks she is missing it in the way a soldier might miss the war. You don't want to go back, but nothing in the so-called real world engages you quite as much.

Joseph says he understands too. Perhaps he does. He has offered help with finding Cora, but she can tell that he's not eager to back his offer up with action.

"Perhaps the time is not right yet," he says, thinking this extra dimension of Cora will move them further apart.

Neither of them mentions what they know now, that love is the key, after all; that they are missing that mysterious transformer that turns like to love. They are both pretending.

She finds herself longing for Haru, not so much emotionally, that hunger is fading, but for the physicality of him, for the man scent of him. Joseph smells of soap and cologne, of minty toothpaste and hair cream. There's no balance, it seems to her, between them, they are too compatible.

At night in her lofty room, sleep holds out stubbornly against the ache in her, an ache that she knows Joseph can't cure. She tells herself it's just a primitive urge, the animal part that isn't subject to reason. She's embarrassed by it, but the sensation won't go away. It's like defrosting, she thinks, that painful, burning itch when you hold frozen hands to the fire.

Disturbed by the daily compulsion she feels to run, to scuttle back to a life dictated by her own circumstances, she overrides her fears with a determination to hold on to the Satomi Baker that Tamura would recognize.

"I'm a kept woman," she jokes with Joseph. "It's got to stop."

"You insist on paying rent, so you're not kept in the true sense," he says. He hardly knows what to do with the cash she hands him every week. He tips hotel doormen more for whistling down a cab.

"You're sort of my protégée." He likes the sound of it better than the kept woman thing.

"Well, at least stop buying me presents all the time. You know I can't return the favor."

"You must have the right clothes. How can I take you anywhere without the right clothes?"

He escorts her to Dior, enjoying as much as her the parade of evening gowns cut from fabrics so fine they feel like gossamer.

"You'll need a fur to go with that, shoes for that bag, earrings if your hair is to be swept up."

There are twelve negligees in her dressing room drawers. A glut, she thinks. Their colors blush reproachfully through sheets of thin tissue, peach and primrose, lilac and eau de nil. No such thing as mend and make do in Joseph's world. She can't deny, though, that she loves the feel of silk, the slope of the high-heeled shoes. It's all a sham, she thinks, but the thrill of dressing up is a childlike pleasure. Will she ever be able to settle now for less?

"Who needs twelve nightgowns?" she had groaned at the sight of them.

"Just a start, dear girl," Joseph had said, the bit between his teeth now.

He has found a new and distracting occupation. He hasn't enjoyed himself so much since what he thinks of now in retrospect as his good war. He was playing a part in that too, playing the straight guy, a guy just like the rest of them.

"I wanted to be like them, not the spoiled rich guy."

She feels pity for him, can't imagine that he pulled that one off.

"It's hard to have secrets," she says.

Joseph had turned down his mother's bought offer to work in the White House as some sort of an assistant to an assistant, choosing to spend his war years in the Army instead.

"I don't want to cower at home while the rest of you go to war," he had told Hunter, who was already in uniform.

"What were you doing while I was in Manzanar?" Satomi asks.

"I was in the thick of it in Italy. A bit of a shaky start, I suppose, but I got used to it."

She's surprised. It's hard to picture Joseph in uniform, hard to picture him fighting. When she says as much, he looks hurt.

She couldn't know it, wouldn't guess at it now, but he had been determined not to whine about things; he may have been afraid, but he couldn't bear the idea of being a coward too. Along with his fellows he had experienced the minor and major miseries of war with stoicism and a black sort of humor that his comrades came to rely on; sleeping in wet clothes, the lack of tobacco, stinking mud in their boots were better borne with humor.

The physical difficulties he suffered are forgotten; the memories of dead bodies, bloated silhouettes floating downriver, blood and limbs and the carnal stink, are not so easily let go.

"You're not the only one with unwanted snapshots in your head," he tells Satomi. "Still, I don't regret it. I enjoyed the friendships. It was good being with guys who had your back."

"You still have friends, Joseph."

"Yes, you and Hunter. The rest are hardly what you would call friends."

"Why don't you have a get-together with your Army buddies?"

"Because it could never be the same again. Money distances you in civilian life, sets you apart."

Joseph's fortune is over thirty million dollars. Less than the Woolworth heiress, which irritates his mother, but he's getting there. In addition, he owns a sixteen-story apartment building on Fifth Avenue, a spacious house on Fishers Island above a long white Connecticut beach, and now his father's beloved yacht *Windward*.

All this, and he doesn't even have to run the family business, which rolls on, an unstoppable juggernaut, adding to his wealth by the minute. He's the major shareholder in the Rodman group of companies, but it's a relief to the board that he won't be joining them. He may be a Rodman, but they know what he is, and besides, he has no head for business.

"You hardly need to work, Sati," he says, floating the idea of enrolling her in an art appreciation class. "You deserve to be educated."

"No, I must work." Her tone leaves no room for argument.

The longer she is with Joseph, the stronger her doubts become, the more she questions her reasons for being with him. As much as it feels safe, it doesn't feel right. If it's a means to an end, she doesn't know what that end might be. She doesn't like the feeling that she's being anesthetized or that she's using Joseph.

At Clare House she can tell by the way her fellow workers have begun to treat her that they know about her changed circumstances. Some are overly friendly, others almost hostile.

She hasn't told Edward about Joseph; he would be certain to write to Dr. Harper about it. She can't bear the idea of Dr. Harper being disappointed in her.

So a new address, Dr. Harper writes.

Is your room better than the last? No shared shower, I hope. The address suggests that you have had a promotion at work. It's uptown, isn't it? Let me know how life is treating you.

In her reply she is vague. Her uptown address implies more than a small promotion, but it's true that she's no longer the hat-check girl. The director, on Joseph's insistence, has put her on the front desk, where she gives out information, guides people to the exhibits, looks too exquisitely turned out to be there at all.

Returning each evening to the apartment, to its air of serenity, she is always pleased to find Joseph there. He waits with her whiskey and his martini ready: "First drink of the day," he lies. Joseph, she knows, likes her company in the little ritual, and although she often would have preferred tea, she doesn't want him to be the only one giving.

Her life is more comfortable than it has ever been, but nothing dispels her dark days, those times when she wakes with a snake squirming in her stomach, the sensation of panic that there is still something left to be done for her mother. The pain at the loss of Tamura, the fear that she will never see Cora again, are always there waiting to surface. She feels spoiled, imprisoned by luxury, lost.

In the museum she studies the families who come with more than a little interest. Mothers with their children, little hands held fast, and the secret smiles between them. Once, watching a father clumsily attempting to button his child's coat, she was transported back to the time on the bus that took Cora away, Cora in her little buttoned-up felt coat.

"It's cold outside," the father said, patting the little girl's head as she struggled against his efforts. "Gotta keep you warm, honey."

She's anxious that Cora might not be in such a family. The picture of that happy little group, the father on bended knee, the mother smiling, often returns to alarm her.

"I know that you can never forget Manzanar." Joseph is good at picking up on her mood. "But I'm going to show you a different world, Sati. Take you to wonderful places. We'll travel and I'll teach you to ski and to sail. Wait till you see the yacht. She's a beauty, and there's nothing as great as being out there on the water. You'll love it."

The months roll on, six of them gone before she realizes that she can't go on working at Clare House. Photographs of her and Joseph are appearing in the society pages. People approach her in the museum, smiling, making a fuss.

"It is you, isn't it?"

She and Joseph are caught at the opera, at the white gloved fund-raisers, at the sort of lush parties she had never before suspected existed.

Mr. Joseph Rodman and his companion Miss Baker at the Plaza Hotel Review. Miss Baker is wearing a stunning full-length Balenciaga dress with emerald earrings from Tiffany's.

She blames herself for the hollow feeling that she can't get rid of, the sense she has that she is an impostor. It seems ungrateful not to appreciate what she has been given, but it's all too much and she wants to start again at the beginning. She's swimming in Joseph's slipstream, not making her own life, and this particular American dream, as indulgent as it is, is not her dream. It's more like Lily's or Artie's dream, she thinks. Joseph's life is like cotton candy, tempting at first, then so sickly sweet that your teeth begin to ache.

Dr. Harper's postcard comes as it did the year before on the date of Tamura's death:

Things change, memories fade, but I will always remember Tamura Baker with gratitude.

The same two lines as last year, a tradition now she knows he won't break while he lives. She holds the card close to her heart, picturing her mother's face, hearing again the sound of her voice. It's time to live up to Tamura, to act for herself.

———————

On the morning she hands her notice in at the museum, the city looks shabby, uncared-for. It has rained in the night and the steaming sky suggests there's more to come. A chemical sort of green streaks the clouds, gobbling up the light. The buildings and sidewalks have morphed to gray, litter flaps around in the gutter. She passes two down-and-outs sleeping in the hard bed of a doorway, their heads beneath old newspapers, their feet slippered in paper bags.

Inside Clare House the glow of the overhead lighting lifts her mood. The air is warm, centrally heated, so that people loosen their scarves and take off hats as soon as they are through the door. She loves the place, doesn't want to leave, but her colleagues there have become as ill at ease with her as she is with herself. And it's not fair to the director, who forgives her lateness, forgives the Mondays she can't make it in because Joseph wants to stay on Fishers Island, go sailing with her and Hunter, and lunch at the Yacht Club.

Joseph's generosity to the museum assures indulgence, a looking the other way at lateness, at absence. The director thinks it a small price to pay, a little lateness, a day or two missed. Strange that she should be there at all, but the museum has the best of the deal.

It's not the way it was meant to be, she thinks, as she apologizes to him. Things were meant to be normal, a job, meeting someone, marriage and children. Oddly, those things seem harder now to attain than the lifestyle of the Manhattan rich.

"Of course I understand," the director says. "Your life has changed since you started here. I could tell you were meant for better things. When will you go?"

She hadn't thought of when. She will need time to tell Joseph, for him to get used to it. The director will need time to replace her, and she will need time to find another job, a place to live. She is suddenly nervous about what lies ahead.

The director, noticing her hesitation, feels a stab of sympathy. She seems unsure, a little afraid. He can't help thinking the girl is out of her depth, pitched in the middle, in the tug-of-war between ordinary and extraordinary.

"Take the rest of the day off and think about it," he says kindly. "Weeks, months, if you would prefer. Whatever you decide is fine with me."

She walks around the city at a loss as to what she might do to fill the day. Joseph will be out, but the housekeepers from the service he employs will still be cleaning the apartment. He can't bear being there while they're working.

She had laughed at him when he told her how uneasy he is with them, but she can't face the cleaners herself today.

In a half-smart café she idles time away nursing a coffee that's weak and tastes of chicory. From her window seat she watches a bunch of girls coming out of a bakery, biting into giant pretzels and laughing; there's a woman in a phone booth wearing a red shallow-bowl hat, a match for the velvet collar of her coat. She is shaking her head, gesticulating with her hand as she speaks; a man flags down a cab, but it doesn't stop. She can't hear his shout, but guesses it's a curse, recognizes his crude finger gesture.

Nothing out here is perfect, the weather's bad, people don't smile much, everyone seems in hurry, but it's real life and she wants to join in.

By the time she gets back, the apartment, dim in late afternoon shadow, smells of polish, and the freesias that are Joseph's favorite flower. She turns the lights on and a Charlie Parker record for company, and makes herself a cup of tea to drink while she bathes.

It still feels strange to be in Joseph's apartment without him there. His afternoons are spent at the country club drinking with Hunter or at the Racquet or Union Club being smart with the Madison Avenue tribe. He whiles away his days waiting for the

evening, when he will take her out, show her off in uptown restaurants and the smart functions that have melded into one in her
mind now.

Tonight they are going to a hospital benefit. Just the thought of
it brings on a sigh. She knows she will feel as nothing against Joseph's people, their sureness, their smart show of boredom.

When Joseph has had enough of it he will send her home in a
cab, go on to indulge in the life he keeps secret. She doesn't mind,
she tires long before him and would prefer to read anyway. He is
always there when she wakes, though, making—without vodka,
he says—his morning Bloody Mary, her tea.

"You're a man for the moon hours," she tells him, and he
laughs.

Before he showers she can smell the night on him, kerosene,
she thinks, and something sharp, it's not unpleasant.

"Why kerosene?" she asks.

"You imagine it," he says, not wanting to tell her it's the lamp
oil from Li's place, where he buys his share of bliss.

He wants her approval, can't imagine that he would get it if he
were to tell her the truth of his life. Never mind his need of opium,
what would she make of his lovers, those uptown boys who claim
to be the sons of Russian princes, and the less salubrious breed
who strut between Seventh and Hudson dressed up in boots and
Stetsons?

But she has guessed Joseph's secret. He is living a lie, and the
damage of it is always there between them. It's not so much that
he looks at men when he is out with her, more that he never notices women, unless to observe how badly they are dressed, how
overperfumed.

"Just spray in front of you, dear girl," he advises. "Then walk
into the mist. It's vulgar to overscent."

Whenever she thinks of the time after the riot at Manzanar,

those boys kissing at their barrack door, she knows that Joseph is like them. She had thought that what she had seen was the result of some strange after-riot electricity in the air. But of course it hadn't been that, it's something more, something she can't get a handle on. It makes her feel ignorant, let down by her years of reading. Where had she missed it in those novels that seemed to leave out nothing of life? Had she failed to see a coded message in those lyrical sentences that more worldly people would have been aware of? She is irritated with Joseph. Why didn't he tell her? She didn't have him down for a cheat. She doesn't know if she approves or not, but Joseph is still Joseph, after all, whatever his needs.

Alone in her marbled bathroom, she spies the shockingly expensive bottle of Patou's Joy perfume on the beveled-glass shelf. Its luscious tones call to mind a grown-up sophistication that is not hers. The scent, which she doesn't like, which doesn't suit her, is the real thing—she's the phony.

"You're going to love this perfume," Joseph had said, handing her the exquisite crystal bottle. "It will be your signature fragrance. It's very you."

"Very me?"

"Mmm, smoky and not too sweet. It doesn't smell like makeup as most of them do. You know that powdery Max Factor scent."

She didn't know. Often doesn't know what Joseph is talking about.

She catches a glimpse of herself in the bathroom's mirrored wall and pauses, sponge in midair. With her hair wet, and makeup-free, she might still be the girl from Angelina. She throws the sponge at her reflection and watches a soapy trail sneak down the mirror.

"Where have you been?" she asks quietly, and answers herself: "In a coma, perhaps."

It's hard to hurt a friend, but he must be told that she can't marry him. If she marries at all, she knows now that it must be for love.

And she will tell him that she doesn't mind about that thing he wants to keep from her, the thing she doesn't have a name for. She is glad not to be ignorant about it anymore. And after when she leaves the soft bed of his life they can still be friends. More equal friends. She can't take from him anymore. She must start again, do better.

She will be forgotten soon enough, she imagines, even though she and Joseph have become quite the beautiful couple. Her picture appears so often in *Harper's Bazaar* that she can't anymore walk Fifth Avenue without being recognized.

"You never take a bad photograph," Joseph tells her when they relive their social life through the magazine's society pages.

And there in the pictures is the polished woman who is her but not her, a manicured, gleaming woman with the light capturing her just so. The girl from the camp is lost, the angry girl in her mother's hand-me-down jacket and twice-heeled shoes. Where's the sense in her life now? It's a film, a play, an ongoing dream.

The articles never mention the Japanese in her. Well, who could tell? Who could be sure? Those eyes, the elegantly long neck, the fine skin, all surely good enough indications of breeding. And nobody wants to stir up the bitterness, after all. This is New York, the victorious capital of the world, where nothing shocks, where its *"pulled-up-stakes"* minorities must go on believing in its endless possibilities. There should be no horizons, no barriers to anything in this earthly paradise.

She can't help wondering if Lily, trawling through her hand-me-down magazines, sees and recognizes her. She hopes so, not so much for revenge, more that she doesn't want Lily remembering her as a victim. If Lily is capable of it, she doesn't want her pity.

She has stayed too long in the bath; the water has cooled to the wrong side of comfort, and the skin on her fingers has wrinkled. Shivering a little, she examines herself in the mirror, looking to find in her face, her body, what men might see. All she sees, though, is a girl watching. She looks at her nakedness and it is nothing to her, as it is to Joseph, as it was in the end to Haru.

In her wardrobe, shimmering like jewels, hang the evening dresses from Molyneux and Coco Chanel, lavender silk, gold satin, and her favorite, the Dior midnight-blue velvet that she will wear tonight to the hospital benefit.

There are gloves and little beaded evening bags, lace handkerchiefs, nylons so fine they would seem invisible when held to the light if it hadn't been for their seams. It's odd, but she's looking forward to living without such luxuries; such beautiful things are a responsibility. She can't remember, though, where the clothes she brought with her have gone. It's unsettling.

You will be fine, my girl, Tamura's voice comes to her, as though it is there still in the ether. She will always be able to hear Tamura's voice.

She thinks of Cora's little knitting-wool hair bow and everything in her hurts.

DAUGHTER OF HAPPINESS

There's something very sweet about Joseph when he gets home. He has brought her flowers, a cloud of dark anemones with the white ones taken out so that their garnet colors put her in mind of old tapestries.

"Don't know why they put those white ones in," he says. "White flowers only go with white flowers."

She is amused by him caring about such things, and touched that he takes such care when choosing her something as simple as a bunch of flowers. For a moment she wavers, wondering if she is doing the right thing in leaving Joseph. Being rich doesn't make his need of her any less, and will she ever do better than him, ever be safer than she is with him? Maybe he is right to question whether true love exists. Tamura had despaired of her never taking the sensible path. Perhaps for the first time she should take it now?

Two hours later, as the band at the hospital benefit plays "Rum and Coca-Cola," she is in a different frame of mind. Among Joseph's smart friends, those sure-of-themselves bankers and their urbane wives, the familiar feeling of loneliness has overtaken her. It's not so much that Joseph's friends exclude her, more that they judge her on the superficial level of her Japaneseness. She is

Joseph's exotic girlfriend, not one of them but someone who adds color to their numbers. She will never be an intimate among them, never be at ease with them. She suspects that Joseph has chosen her for the same reason. That exotic thing always in the mix. It comes to her that the so-called safe path is not for her; that it is quite likely a life with Joseph may be neither safe nor sensible.

And Joseph tonight is adding to her disenchantment. There's something wrong with him, she can tell. His movements have speeded up and he seems distracted, not quite connected to what's going on around him. He has left her twice at their table, heading off somewhere with mumbled excuses as if he is late for an urgent appointment. She is used to his mood shifts, but it is uncomfortable being left at the table to charm in his place.

"Come and dance with me," she says, catching sight of him lurking behind a pillar.

"Sure," he says, slurring the word a little. "Sure."

He is clumsy on the floor, not like Joseph at all, who is usually precise in his steps, easy to follow. Exposed out there under the bouncing light of the revolving mirror ball, she wishes she hadn't asked him to dance with her, wishes that she hadn't come this evening, pretending that this is her life, that she is at home here among this other tribe.

And suddenly Joseph is spinning her and she is falling, twisting her ankle, breaking the heel of her shoe, and Joseph is on the floor beside her, smiling a lopsided smile, his eyes looking at but not seeing her. What is the matter with him?

"Let me help." The voice is deep, not quite baritone. "Give me your arm, lean on me. It will hurt to put weight on that foot."

She lets him take her weight as she limps back to their table.

"I'm Abe Robinson, by the way. I'm a doctor."

"I won't be long, dear girl," Joseph mumbles, and rolls his way to the bathroom.

Abe Robinson has her foot in his hands, putting pressure where it hurts, wincing when she does at the pain of it.

"Not broken," he assures her. "But a sprain can hurt worse, I know."

"Thank you." A familiar feeling runs through her, the same one she experienced when she first caught sight of Haru.

"No more dancing for a while." He says with a smile.

"Shame," she says, returning the smile, attempting lightness. "Will you have a drink with us?" It's foolish, but she doesn't want him to go.

"Thank you, but I'm with someone." He points across the room to where a girl, a frowning girl in a shiny dress, is looking toward them.

"Oh, of course, you must go."

"It would be better not to drink anymore, you're going to need a hefty dose of painkillers for a couple of days." He fumbles in his pocket for a pen, picks up a napkin, and hands both to her. "I can call on you tomorrow, if you like. Check your ankle."

She writes the address down, hands it to him, and feels a pang as he walks back toward the waiting girl. Stupid, she tells herself. A few minutes in his presence and she hardly knows herself. It must be the champagne, it always puts her in a silly mood.

Joseph returns just as Abe Robinson turns and says, "Ice, lots of it. And keep the leg up."

"How high?"

"Oh, above your heart if you can."

Four months on, and Joseph is still blaming himself. If he hadn't been so high that night at the hospital benefit, Satomi never would have met Abe Robinson, and she wouldn't be leaving him now. He thinks of it as leaving him, as though he is the lover in this threesome, although she has been dating Abe from the first moment they met.

"So I'm going to lose out to Mr. America," he says.

"Oh, Joseph, you and I, we're better off as friends," she says consolingly.

"Ouch." He slaps his hand to his chest as though she has cracked open his heart.

"It's true, Joseph, you know it is." She's sad for him, but there's nothing to be done about it.

"Damn that dance," Joseph says brightly. "That damn dance."

He can hardly remember the dance that brought Abe Robinson into her life, except that it had a rumba sort of beat about it. But whatever the stupid rhythm had been, he should have caught her. Would have, if it hadn't been for the snort he'd taken discreetly behind a pillar in the moment before Satomi found him and pulled him onto the dance floor.

"All my stupid fault," he says now. "That's the trouble with the good stuff, you never know if it will take you mellow or hard."

"I'm glad of it, Joseph."

She is more than glad, despite the fact that she has wavered over the months, that she still has her doubts about her and Abe. The love between them feels equal and she can't get used to it. Strange, she thinks, that it should be so hard to trust in love. She had imagined when love came it would drown doubt, but perhaps doubt is the ingredient in the mix between men and women that keeps the love alive. Where there is light there must be shadows too.

But doubts aside, she feels blessed, blessed to have slipped, to have broken the heel of her beautiful shoe, to have turned her ankle.

Abe had felt the current between them on that first night too. Such a beautiful patient, flushed cheeks, strands of dark hair escaping from their burnished knot, the grace of her. He took it all in and knew he was setting his sights high.

Earlier that evening he had watched her from across the floor until something in him had faltered so that he had to look away to steady himself. He had been struck by the odd couple that she and Joseph made. The man appeared obsessively neat, hair tamed, his smooth skin so closely shaved as to make you wonder if he had a beard at all. And the tux so perfectly cut it might have been carved on him. Not the sort, he thought with distaste, to have gone for girls.

"She's in all the magazines," his girlfriend Corrine said sharply, following his gaze. "She's got it all, the looks and the money."

"His money?"

"I guess. He's the Rodman heir."

"They're married?"

"Engaged, perhaps. Not sure."

She didn't project socialite, he thought. Rather she looked lost, out of place. He wanted to know her, to save her, he thought, at the same time as telling himself that was a ridiculous idea. He couldn't shake the thought, though. Not for the first time he felt false being with Corrine. Something must be done about that. To think that he nearly hadn't come. That he had dreaded it. Corrine had been stupidly excited at him winning the tickets in the hospital raffle, wouldn't hear of him giving them away.

"It'll be stiff, formal. I hate that kinda thing," he had said, trying to talk her out of it. "We won't know anyone."

"It'll be great," she had insisted. "Just what the doctor ordered."

Her medical jokes had been wearing thin for months, but he gave in, hired the ridiculous suit, and polished his shoes to a patent shine. And now he and Satomi are together and it's how it

should be, or at least it will be when he gets her away from Joseph.
It makes him uneasy that she lives with the man, even though he
believes her explanation as to why.

"We're friends, Abe," she says. "Nothing more."

"But it's odd, Sati. You have to give me that."

"Why not think of us as landlord and tenant, then?"

"It's the 'us' about it that I don't like, honey."

Satomi hates that Abe doesn't want to know Joseph, that he
avoids him whenever possible. She understands it, though, they
are poles apart in everything, and despite the fact that Abe has
chosen her, he is in most ways a conventional man.

At their first meeting Abe's smile had made her want to run
and to draw closer at the same time. Everything about him connected with her at what later she would remember with fondness
as being her heart. At the time, though, it had felt more visceral,
stomach-dropping, throat-constricting.

Nothing about him had jarred, still doesn't. His physicality
touches her more than anything, his brown unwary eyes, his dark
curly hair, and the scent of him that brings the earth to mind. There
is symmetry in his weather-worn face, an open-aired look that sets
him apart from the more usual pale-faced New Yorkers.

She had liked immediately the authoritative pitch of his voice,
the way he had loosened his bow tie, which he was obviously ill at
ease in, the way without being asked people had cleared a space
for him.

But she questions now if there is such a thing as love at first
sight. All that drowning, heart-pounding, mouth-drying thing
that night may simply have been lust, the girlish longing for a man
as masculine as Abe to carry her off. But it's love now, all right,
the sweet and the bitter of it, the open and the guarded heart, the
full-blown flower of it. Being with Abe is like being taken by a

river: there's nothing you can do about it except let the water have you.

A regular caller now, Abe never comes up in the elevator. He gets the doorman to call the apartment while he waits downstairs in the lofty atrium.

It has set a pattern, Joseph thinks. Abe summoning, Sati running.

"He doesn't like me," he tells her flatly.

"He doesn't know you," she says. "He will like you when he gets to know you."

Abe's dislike, which Joseph senses is more like distaste, feels familiar to him. He has experienced it before. Abe's kind of man judges his kind harshly. It's to be expected. He has no doubt that Abe will ride off into the sunset with Satomi. His kind, the tall, tieless kind, always get the girl. Money, he knows, isn't going to get him out of this one.

"He's too conventional for you," he attempts. "He'll always be a doctor, nothing more. You won't have travel, or new people, adventures."

Satomi is living the life now that has always been a mystery to him: walks, and the movies, and meals in diners that he has never heard of. And bike rides in the park. Bikes when there are cabs. It makes no sense. And what's worse, every weekend in Freeport with Abe Robinson's mother, Frances, a woman who Satomi says is reserved with her.

"She has a good heart, though," she assures him. "It's just that Freeport's a pretty tight community, friendly enough but wary of strangers, I guess."

"Just as you told me Angelina was."

"I never said friendly, did I?"

He has shown her the best of New York, given her a cultured life, and she is settling for Freeport.

He can't fake being pleased for her, he is too sorry for himself. But there is time, he thinks, time for them to fall out of love. They have only known each other a few months, after all, less than half a year. Flash fires burn out quickly. In his less optimistic moments, though, he's resigned to her leaving; the pair are hopelessly attracted, it's just a question of when, he knows.

When comes on an evening when a buttery sky, pinkish to the west, leaks its color into the apartment as Joseph is mixing their drinks.

"Abe has asked me to marry him," she ventures, accepting the whiskey he is offering.

"And?"

"And I've said yes, of course."

"Are you sure, really certain? It's all a bit whirlwind, isn't it?"

"Maybe, but it doesn't feel like that. And we both want it."

"Well, marriage, it's a big step. You might live to regret it."

"What else can we do? Abe hates me living here with you. That's natural, isn't it? And we want to be together."

"Have an affair. Get it out of your system."

"I don't want an affair, and neither does Abe. We're sure about each other and we're going to marry. Be happy for me, Joseph."

"So when will it be, this marriage?"

"As soon as we can arrange it. A couple of months or so."

"I'm used to you, Sati. I'll never find anyone like you. You're abandoning me to those uptown mustangs with their long teeth—it's cruel, you know. I'll get eaten."

"Joseph, you shouldn't marry at all." She is firm. "Your father loved you; if he had known how hard the promise would make your life, he would never have let you make it."

"But I did make it, and broken promises breach the dam."

"So do lies, Joseph."

"Yes, I'm sorry about that."

"I don't mind, it's only that you didn't . . ."

"Tell you, I know. I should have been honest. I've always been devious when I want my way."

"Well, I know now."

"I guess you think I'm all out of sync?"

"I can't say I understand it. It seems strange to me, I've never heard or read a word that describes it."

"Oh, there are plenty. 'Homosexual,' 'queer,' 'ponce,' 'nancy boy,' take your pick."

"I don't like any of them. It doesn't matter anyway, we'll always be friends."

"Mmm, if it's to be allowed."

"I'll allow it. Don't worry about that."

"I'm going to miss you."

"I'll still be in New York."

"But not my New York. I mean, a doctor, dear girl! You'll end up spewing out babies, living in Queens or somewhere just as awful. Where do doctors live anyway?"

"Queens, actually! Jackson Heights, to be precise. And I don't think that I'll be spewing babies out, as you so charmingly put it, but I want them. Abe wants them too."

"And what about Cora? You're not going to ditch her too, are you?" It's a cheap shot, he knows.

"Oh, Joseph."

"Sorry, Sati. It's the wound speaking."

She feels guilty, found out. She has hardly given Cora a thought since meeting Abe. Of course she will never give up on finding Cora, but she has finally found something that holds its own against Manzanar. There is a sweet sort of mathematics in the balance now between good and bad luck.

"All's well that ends well, eh?" Joseph says when she tells him as much.

She packs a small suitcase, skirts and tops, a warm jacket, and the chocolate box wrapped against damage in a nightdress. She takes a last look at the jewelry, the evening gowns, the furs that have always made her think of the fox in Angelina's woods. She's sure now that she won't miss any of the fancy dress that never truly belonged to her.

"For God's sake, Sati, it's your jewelry, what would I do with it?"

"Sell it, I suppose."

"You should sell it. It will give you more than enough to see those babies through college."

"Abe doesn't want me to take anything. He says that he wants to be the one to buy me things."

"Very caveman, very masterful, but pretty stupid. Can you really see yourself managing on a doctor's pay?"

"I've managed on less, much less. In any case, why do you imagine that everyone who doesn't have a fortune is poor? Abe isn't poor."

"Let me open an account for you. I want you to have your own money."

"Look, Joseph, I can't take your money. Abe won't stand for it. I can't go against him. Put me in your will, and then live to be a hundred, please."

"Okay, sweet girl, if I must."

They kiss awkwardly, and she feels a stab of guilt for leaving him hurt. Joseph has joined those she thinks of as her family, him and Dr. Harper and Eriko, a small band but true, she believes.

"How will I manage without you, Sati?"

"Just as you did before you met me."

"Oh, yes, that way, I remember now."

The room has darkened as they speak. She puts the suitcase down, and from habit begins switching on the table lamps. Joseph draws the curtains against the dismal evening.

"See what a happy domestic scene we make?" he says.

Outside the window, gray clouds fold in on themselves, a southerly wind pelts rain at the pedestrians. It's the kind of rain Joseph hates, the kind that uses up the cabs, and soaks you through as though your clothes were made of blotting paper.

In the lobby Abe is waiting for her impatiently. Waiting for his girl. He is feeling out of place in the company of the deferential doorman, among the Jackson Pollocks and the huge showy arrangements of silk flowers. He is too outdoorsy to appreciate such man-made displays of wealth. He likes walking, and eating in homely restaurants; he likes the humanity of his patients, his mother's warm house in Freeport, and the little sailing boat that was his father's, his now. He loves his dog, Wilson, loves the friends he would go the whole mile for, and now he loves Satomi, the girl who makes him feel as though luck loves him.

"I have to go, Joseph." She is eager to be with Abe, to have the goodbyes behind her.

"Yes, you must."

"See you soon, then." She settles for the prosaic.

"Yes, on Saturday at your wedding. Ridiculous, isn't it?"

"Not to me."

"It's not too late to change your mind. It's a woman's prerogative, after all."

"Joseph!"

"Sorry, Sati. Go claim your life."

The elevator doors open to Abe's back as he paces the lobby. She pauses, watching his long stride, feeling the heat rising in her. Little beads of rain are quivering on Abe's dark coat like tiny balls of mercury. As he turns toward her, she smiles, imagining a hundred little stars shining in his hair too.

It's not to be a big-deal wedding. No St. James' Church, no big fat reception at the Plaza, as it would have been with Joseph. She's relieved.

"A New York justice of the peace will do us, honey?" Abe had said. "Simple. Our way."

Dr. Harper has sent his best wishes:

I'm relieved to see that I haven't put you off marrying a doctor.

Eriko has splurged on a wire: her words are formal, the usual congratulations. Satomi had hoped for more, but wires are expensive, and formalities on such occasions are the Japanese way, she knows.

Abe's mother, Frances, stands at his side in front of the big mahogany table in City Hall. She's almost as tall as Abe, conscious of it, so that she stoops a little. She is puffy under the same brown eyes as her son's, hoping that no one thinks that she has been crying. The little bags are annoyingly hereditary, what can she do?

She would have preferred a church wedding for Abe in Freeport, the minister she knows, the sea as the backdrop. Her son and this girl have only known each other a few months. Why couldn't they wait a decent amount of time? He had been going out with Corrine for longer, after all. She doesn't know yet whether she likes Satomi or not. The girl is challenging and not at all the sort of daughter-in-law she has pictured for her son. She would have liked the known, not Corrine, if the choice was hers, but still a local girl, someone like herself, she supposes, a more familiar kind of girl. She wants to be happy for him, and Abe, by her side, is grinning at her, brimming over with happiness, so what has she got to complain about? She tells herself it's not so much to do with Satomi, it's just that she's suffering the jealousy of a mother losing her son to another woman.

As Satomi walks the length of the room to stand by Abe's side, she is a little unsteady on her feet. It's the aspirins she took earlier, she supposes. She shouldn't have washed them down with champagne, but the headache had been bad and Joseph had said they would work quicker that way. And they did, accounting now, she suspects, for her dreamlike state.

"It's your wedding day," Joseph said. "You must drink champagne, it's the law."

"Whose law?"

"Mine, of course."

He had booked the suite at the Carlyle for her. Somewhere for her to stay in the few days before the marriage.

"A time of grace, dear girl. A good place to think things over."

"It's lovely, Joseph, but a whole suite . . ."

"My wedding present," he had insisted. "The bone doctor can't object to that, can he?"

Surprisingly, Abe hadn't.

"Enjoy it while you can," he had warned lightheartedly. "Our finances aren't quite up to the Carlyle."

Our finances, us, we—the words fit, not strange at all, she is finally home.

But bathing in the spacious bathroom with the hotel's scented soap, she had experienced a wobble. Would this feeling of euphoria burn out somewhere soon along the line? Does true love really exist? Is Joseph right, has it all happened too quickly? It won't work if, like her father, like Haru, Abe wants to change her. She has looked for signs of that but has found none. All she has seen is his approval.

Wrapping herself in a huge white towel, she returned to the glamorous bedroom to dress. If only Tamura could have been with her, if she could have known Abe, reassured her.

He's the one, isn't he, Mama?

She is struggling to leave the life of Tamura and Cora and Manzanar behind her, to make this new one with Abe.

Hunter had joined them in the suite for the wedding breakfast, eggs and hash browns, and sharp out-of-season strawberries with butter cake. He sat upright in his wheelchair, looking anxiously at Joseph as though his friend might crumble to nothing at any moment.

But Joseph, in full actor's mode, was playing the good loser. Besides, he was considering Satomi's advice about not honoring the promise. If he reneged on it, his life would be restored to the one that suited him best. But to break a promise to a dying father is a sickening thing.

Living with a woman other than Satomi held only terror for him. It was a dilemma. He'd go to Europe after the wedding. Think about it as he walked the streets of Paris, consider the way to go in the beauty of Rome. He needed a break, needed to put the promise on hold for a while.

"You look wonderful," he told her, admiring the simple blue shift, the fresh camellias fixed in the loop of her hair. "It's down to my influence, of course."

After the ceremony she and Abe run through the stinging storm of rice thrown enthusiastically by the small wedding party, Abe's laugh bursting from him, big and genuine. The ache in her has gone, and it's nothing to do with the aspirin, she knows.

Abe's best man Don, his old school friend from Freeport, poses them on the steps of City Hall and clicks away with his camera until his film is used up. The day is cold, bright, and dry, a good day for walking, but they pile into cabs and make their way to Lutèce for lunch, Frances's treat. More champagne, and toasts to their happiness, and Hunter loud in his drunkenness, weeping a little, nobody is sure for what. Joseph leaves before dessert to take him home.

HEAT WAVE

ABE'S LIFE, THE normality of it, she supposes, takes a bit of getting used to, but she isn't the only one acclimatizing. His hometown friends are hesitant with her, suspicious of her past. What is she doing with Abe, a girl like her, the uptown queen of the society pages? Has she really given up a fortune to be with their friend? Is she playing games?

"They'll come around," Abe comforts. "In any case, who cares what they think? You're my girl, not theirs."

They had expected him to marry Corrine, the one Satomi has eclipsed. She is a local girl, after all, known since childhood, highly strung and needy, it's true, but familiar, one of them. Still, Satomi isn't putting on any airs. They'll make the effort for Abe's sake.

Frances, who hadn't cared much for Corrine, is settling to the idea of Satomi, so when Satomi asks her about Corrine she doesn't hold back.

"'Pretty' and 'prissy' are the words I'd choose." She laughs. "I guess she knew she would have a hard job hanging on to him."

"How come?"

"Oh, well, it's just my opinion, of course, but it never seemed right to me. Abe always wanted his friends around when he was with her, never seemed at ease when it was just the two of them. And Corrine couldn't bear being on the water, couldn't swim, was scared of drowning, I think. You couldn't blame her for that, but Abe loves the water, you can't keep him off it. It caused problems. It wasn't like it is with you. He can't wait to get you alone. Even I feel in the way sometimes."

"Oh, Frances, you shouldn't. Abe adores you." She is embarrassed, not yet comfortable enough with Frances to be talking about Abe and the love thing.

"I guess," Frances says. "I understand, though. His father and I were a love match too. No matter how long it lasts, you can't beat that, can you?"

"You can't. Its good luck, isn't it?"

"Mmm, better than winning the lottery. And you deserve some luck, Satomi, after what you've been through, losing your father and mother so young."

Satomi feels protective of Tamura, at a loss as to how to describe to Frances the loveliness that was her mother. Abe understands, though, he speaks of Tamura softly, with a tactfulness that leans toward affection, as though he might have known and loved her too.

"Does Abe ever talk about his father to you?" Frances hurries to fill the silence between them. She thinks that she will never feel entirely at ease with Satomi, silences must be filled, eye contact kept to the minimum. Abe chose not to pattern by his mother when choosing his wife, so they have little other than him in common.

"He says that he has fragments of memory of him, pictures that come to him sometimes. He remembers being picked up and thrown in the air, having his hair stroked as he fell asleep."

"I'm glad he remembers anything at all," Frances says. "He was only three when Ben had his heart attack."

"Oh, my poor Abe," Satomi says. "And you too, Frances."

"I can't tell you what it did to me. Ben had never shown any

signs of being ill at all, you see. Well, nothing that I noticed, anyway. He'd been sailing all that day, and I should have been with
him, only I wanted to stay home and cozy up. I'll never forgive
myself for that."

"You couldn't have known."

"No, but I just wish that I'd been with him. I guess it wouldn't
have changed anything, though. But he was so close to home, to
me, when it happened, you see. I saw his boat come into port from
the kitchen window, saw him on deck, and I waved, but he didn't
wave back. Didn't see me, I guess." She is surprised to find herself
confiding in Satomi, but can't seem to stop. "I was in the middle
of making an egg cream, his favorite. I laid the table and waited,
but he didn't come. I remember being angry that he was puttering
around without a thought for me—that is, until it got dark and he
didn't come, and didn't come. I found him in the cabin lying on
the bunk, peaceful as could be. I knew straight off that he wasn't
sleeping."

"And then it was just you and Abe."

"Yes, but I was hardly a mother to him that year. I did my best,
all the practical things, you know. My heart wasn't with Abe,
though, it was with Ben."

Tears spring to Satomi's eyes at the thought of it. She remembers the time after Aaron had died, the way Tamura in her misery
had forgotten that she was a mother too.

"Did you never consider marrying again, Frances?"

"Only once, much later, but it wouldn't have worked. I was
always measuring the guy against Ben. It sounds crazy, but just
the fact that the socks were different, the choice of newspaper, it
switched me off somehow. You know how it is when you love
someone. You can't stop comparing. And it wasn't just that Ben
was a catch, the handsome local doctor that everyone liked, although I guess all that helped. It was more how he made me feel

about myself, about us as a couple. I wanted to have that feeling again. It just never came with anyone else."

Frances is surprised at how easy it is to confide in Satomi, but she's still anxious. It's her own kind of snobbery, she thinks, but the high-living thing feels dangerous to her. Maybe Satomi will miss it when married life settles down. She can't imagine what it does to you to have such a fortune at your disposal. And the beauty thing is startling, exotic, and she isn't used to startling or exotic. But she can see why Satomi has given up a fortune to be with Abe. It is Abe, after all, and the girl has steel.

"I guess you are finding it quite cramped in Abe's little apartment, huh?"

"It's pretty small, but I have lived in smaller and it's very comfortable, and besides, we are here almost every weekend. And oh, my goodness, Abe's shower is wonderful, so much water, like Niagara Falls."

"Oh, don't tell me you're that easy to please." Frances is genuinely surprised. The girl had lived in a fourteen-room duplex in Manhattan, but she raves about a shower that works in a two-room apartment in Jackson Heights.

"There's nothing as precious as water, Frances. Nothing in the world."

"Well, while we're on the subject of water, you might want to please Abe and learn to sail. Sailing's a big thing around here and Abe has loved it since he was a little boy."

"Oh, I've sailed with Joseph. He always says that it's the best thing . . ." It occurs to her that she is always bringing Joseph into the conversation.

"Do you mind me talking about him?"

"It takes time to let people go. And I guess that you loved him once."

"I still do. Not in a way that is anything like the way I love

Abe. I'll tell you all about it if you want. You won't like it, though."

"Whenever you're ready, honey, I don't need to know."

"I don't want you to think badly of Joseph. Abe doesn't like him, and that's natural, I guess, but he's my best friend in New York. He's a good person."

Frances, with memories of Ben stirred, has trouble imagining what sort of affair Satomi and Joseph had. It was a one-in-a-million chance that Satomi should even have met a man like Joseph, let alone move in with him without being married. But then, who is she to criticize? She couldn't claim to have been the virgin bride when she married Ben. They may not have lived together, but they had the boat with its cozy cabin, and times have changed, after all.

Everything is upside down since the war. People don't trust that they have time anymore. And Satomi must have been lonely in New York, straight out of her years of confinement in the camp. Were there really those places in America? It doesn't bear thinking about.

Abe, usually so considerate of her feelings, doesn't want to hear about Joseph. No matter what Satomi wants, he can't imagine ever having the man as a friend. Joseph's kind unsettles him, he doesn't understand such desires, doesn't want to know about them. If there's anything that disturbs him about Satomi, it's that bit of sophistication that Joseph has exposed her to, the experiences he wishes she'd never had.

And if he's honest, the Cora thing bothers him too. He feels bad about it, but it's hard to understand the connection Satomi feels with the child. He's doing his best, though, fighting off the thought that there's nothing like your own flesh and blood. If Satomi wants Cora, then he can live with it. Whatever happens, whatever compromises they have to make, they're strong enough to weather them.

"We'll want to start a family of our own one day," he says.

"I want that too, Abe. It would be wonderful if Cora is with a family, and happy. That would be fine with me. I just need to see her, to know that she's okay."

But what, he thinks, if she never finds her? Will it come between them, that bit of her that will always be longing, the bit he can do nothing to make better?

New York drips in a heat wave that reminds her of the one in Angelina.

Fresh out of the shower, Abe leaves for work in the mornings, his shirt sticking to his back before he is out the door.

"I've never known it quite this bad," he says. "What I'd give to be on the water."

The temperature is hitting triple digits, blistering the paint on their windowsills, creating asphalt heat islands that bubble up between the trees on the sidewalk. The apartment sweats its way through August with them, no air-conditioning, but the fan going furiously.

"It seems to affect me more than you," Abe says. "How do you manage to look so cool?"

"Years of mountain weather," she says.

The electric feeder cables fail intermittently, so that more often than not their evenings are spent in the dark. In the blackouts they eat dinner by candlelight and read in the greenish glow of a shared flashlight, balanced precariously above their heads in the ironwork of the bedstead. The cold water runs warm, so to save money they switch the water heater off.

"With that and the cuts, we'll halve the energy cost," Abe says.

On investigation Abe discovers the puzzling hum in the bathroom to be a wasp's nest inside the extractor fan. He pours a poisonous powder down through the blades and the wasps go mad, darkening the room as they emerge heading for the light, covering the windowpanes in a thick humming curtain. For days after Satomi comes across dead ones on the floor and the window ledges, two floating in the milk jug.

On his day off, when the sweet cooing of their neighbors' pigeons stops, Abe goes to the roof to investigate and comes back with the news that their drinking water has evaporated in the heat.

"Dead," he says. "Never seen the like. I know for a fact they top that water up every morning before they leave for work."

When they can't sleep, they sit outside on the fire escape and Abe reads the night sky to her, pointing out the stars and the constellations. He loves naming them, as though the words conjure up something magical for him, Ursa Major, and Minor too, Lupus the wolf, and Orion the hunter.

"You get to know the stars at sea," he tells her. "Nothing like a clear night at sea."

It doesn't matter that the butter melts in their ailing icebox, that the milk goes sour in a day—nothing outside of the two of them matters. So what if they can't sleep in the heat? The hot nights are made for love anyway, for talking, for planning their future.

There is nothing like making love with Abe, nothing like the scent of him, fresh and green like ferns. And no feeling compares to the exquisite sense she has that they belong to each other, that they are complete. If the world went away and they were alone, it would be enough.

When Abe covers her, something in her breaks, a break he fills so completely that she forgets the camp, forgets Cora, forgets everything. And after, returned to herself in those quiet moments meant for expressing truths, there is only a small sense of remorse that she hasn't yet told him of Haru. He is hardly resigned to the idea of Joseph in her life, without testing him with a past lover. And he would mind, she believes. He is a predictable man, true to the morals of his time. Abe knowing about Haru wouldn't break them, but she can't bear the thought of hurting him.

While Abe works, she plays housewife, cleaning the apartment, washing and ironing, shopping for their food. The chores are not enough to fill the day, and time stalls in the waiting-for-Abe hours. Long before she needs to, she takes the streetcar across the Queensboro Bridge to meet him from work. She sits on their special bench reading the same page of her book over and over, not able to concentrate on anything but the idea that he is somewhere close, that she will see him soon. Sometimes she changes benches so that he will have to look for her, so that she can watch him looking for her.

They talk of getting a bigger apartment, of how it will be when they have children. "Not yet, but soon," Abe says. They have the names all ready, Aaron for the boy, Iris, after Abe's beloved long-dead grandmother, for the girl. She considers bringing Cora into the conversation but can't seem to get the words out.

"It must be Aaron for the boy," Abe says generously. "He must know he was named for a hero."

Of course they will have a boy and a girl, and in that order. They have found each other and will have everything they want. They are blessed, aren't they?

On Abe's summer break, they go to Freeport. The heat is not so bad on the coast, there is always a breeze and the nights are cooler than in the city. Abe is happy there. So she is happy there.

They sail every day. He's surprised how good she is at it.

"Captain and mate," he says. "Not sure which of us is captain, though."

She watches him raise the sail, admires the muscles in his tanned arms, the creases around his eyes as he squints in the sunlight. Love and lust collide and meld softly in her.

Anchored in port, he takes her on the cabin's impossibly small bunk, still surprised that she is as eager for it as he is for her. They always end up in a heap on the floor, tangled in the cover.

"We'll be black and blue all over if we don't stop this." She laughs. "Then what will Frances think?"

"Let's never stop this, Sati, never, never."

And after, beer straight from the bottle, hauled up from its net in the sea where Abe keeps it cooling. They play cards on deck with Wilson bunched up at their feet, snoring in his doggy sleep. They stay till dark, not wanting to share their time with anyone, not even Frances.

Abe introduces her to *his* Freeport, to the shopkeepers and the people who hunker down in the place after the tourists have gone. They are overly polite with her, cautious.

"Don't let it worry you," Abe says. "They don't matter."

Satomi is reminded of how hard it is to break into the circle. There have been so many circles in her life that she has skimmed around the edge of, never quite making it to the inside. Abe is the only one who sees her for who she is, who loves her because she is Satomi. Artie saw too much Japanese in her, Haru not enough. With Abe, though, she's just right. Even if she never quite fits in with those others he loves, she's inside the circle with him.

"It's a different world in winter," he tells her. "The sailing's not so easy, but I like it better. You'll see, you'll love it in winter."

They walk the canals and on through the fields of pure white salt marshes that open out to the clean Atlantic Ocean.

"It's beautiful, isn't it? Have you ever seen anywhere so beautiful?"

She thinks of Fishers Island, of Joseph's sleek yacht *Windward* cutting through the gray-green ocean. Her first sight of it had taken her breath away.

"No, never, it's just perfect," she says.

He takes her to the Kissing Bridge over the Millburn but refuses to kiss her.

"I've kissed too many girls here," he says seriously. "You're not a bridge-kissing sort of girl, you're for keeps."

"Did you kiss Corrine here?"

"Oh, sure I did, her and a few others besides."

They stroll along the Nautical Mile, where in the Crab Shack Abe's friends, home for the summer, join them. Abe's order is always the same, steamed clams and his favorite light beer, brought to the table in glass pitchers, the liquid trembling gold in the sunlight.

"Nothing like Freeport steamers," he says.

It's a pleasure he savors, dipping each one first into the clam broth, then into the little tin pot of melted butter that comes on the side.

Sitting next to him, with the sound of the gulls bullying, the warmth of his thigh against hers as he helps himself to her fries, Manzanar it seems to her was a time in the life of a different girl. Finding Cora is not so much forgotten as put on hold. It's a honeymoon period for her and Abe. She is slipping into place, no longer defined by her experiences in the camp.

"I can't believe that I have found you," she says. "Just when I wasn't looking."

"It was meant," he says simply.

Back in New York, the heat in mid-July is still fierce. Abe, after having her to himself in Freeport, is reluctant for her to contact Joseph.

"We have our life, honey. It just doesn't fit with his."

"I have to keep in touch with him, Abe. Asking me not to see Joseph is like me asking you not to see your mother. It's cruel."

Their first real argument, though, comes not over Joseph but about Satomi wanting to work.

"You didn't mind living off Joseph's money." He would take the words back if he could. They are unfair and he knows the truth of it.

"I worked for most of the time I was with him," she defends herself, hurt by Abe's tone. "In any case, Abe, it's not the same thing at all. I'm lonely here with you gone all day."

"I don't want you working, Sati," he says flatly. "I can support my wife, I should think."

When she greets him with the news that she's taken a job, as a receptionist at the Bridge Hotel, near his hospital, a frown flits briefly across his brow before he raises his hands to heaven and gives in. She won't be ordered, and he loves that about her. She can't be anyone other than who she is.

"I don't like you working, honey, but if it's what you want . . ."

"You'll hardly notice it, Abe. And it's not forever. Just until we settle, start a family."

The words "settle," "start a family" wrap themselves around her. They're imbued with warmth, with normality. She likes that the language of her world has changed to that of the all-American girl.

Joseph comes to the hotel, winces at the sight of her behind the desk, at the cheap plastic name badge on her dress. His face is a little drawn. He is a few pounds lighter than when she last saw him. He has had trouble finding the hotel, since the cab dropped him on the wrong street. He walked three blocks out of his way before discovering the mistake.

She has no name for the sweet feeling that floods her at the sight of him. Perhaps it's what a sister would feel after not seeing a loved brother for a while.

"God, you look healthy," he says. "But I can't say those clothes do much for you. You look like a schoolteacher."

"I like this dress, its Abe's favorite."

"Now, why doesn't that surprise me?"

Out of the Manhattan village, he's a tree unearthed, too elegant for the sullied midtown territory that she now inhabits. His imported Savile Row suit is fine worsted wool, his soft brogues of obvious quality. He's tanned from his European tour and it gives him a slightly racy look. She remembers the first time that she saw him and had thought him vain. She knows better now: his extreme neatness is his shield, the meniscus he puts between himself and the world.

"I'm getting used to life without you, I suppose." He sighs. "But New York is not the same. I need pastures new, feel the urge to be off again."

Since her wedding he has been working on the Cora thing. No news yet, but he gives her his latest report, all neatly typed up. Families who have adopted Japanese children have been contacted, there are letters from the governor's office with assurances that they will search records but can promise nothing. It's suggested that they should look farther afield, out of the state if need be.

"Anything from Dr. Harper?" he asks.

"Nothing, only that he thinks her name might have been changed, as he can't find a record anywhere of any Cora. It's as though she has disappeared from the world."

"She'll turn up, dear girl." He touches her cheek lightly. "Oh, and believe it or not, Hunter is getting married. A Connecticut family, one of the Harrison girls, Laura. You met her on Fishers Island, remember? She's been sweet on him since they were kids. His family is pleased."

"I'm pleased too. Lucky girl, to have Hunter."

"You'll come to the wedding, of course?"

"Well, it's not Abe's sort of thing, and he doesn't like me going places without him." She can feel herself blushing.

"And what Abe says, goes?"

"Do you really think I've changed that much?"

"Well, I live in hope that you haven't. You look the same, although rather like a rare orchid in a tin can behind that desk. It's quite upsetting. Let me take you to lunch."

"Okay, I'd like that, but nowhere too smart. One of us has to look out of place, so it might as well be you. Somewhere that would suit a schoolteacher would be best, don't you think?"

The offer of a job with the Long Island hospital group comes out of the blue and Abe jumps at the chance.

"We can live in Freeport, buy a house, have our babies. What do you say?"

He hadn't needed to ask, they both knew the answer to that.

He would take up the position in December—time enough to pack up and give notice at the apartment, to honor his contract at the hospital, and for them to find a home of their own in Freeport.

"You can start looking for a house right away," he says. "Give up your job and stay with Frances. She'll love helping us find the right thing. I'll come every spare moment I get." He will miss her, but he will be sending her home, putting her somewhere safe, somewhere away from Joseph. The light of their future is beckoning, and he can't wait to be done with the city.

"It's a wonderful piece of luck, Sati."

"So wonderful," she agrees, even though she doesn't want to leave. Joseph is hardly a threat, and she would rather stay with Abe in Queens until they are ready to move.

There is something confirming, though, in the idea of being in Abe's childhood home, of finding a house of their own, waiting with his mother for him to return to them. Tamura had told her once that women must get used to waiting.

"Work and wars, Satomi," she had said. "It's the women who wait."

In Abe's childhood bed she wakes periodically through the night, gauging the time by the depth of darkness, the quality of the light seeping through the curtains from the sea. Will she ever be able to sleep comfortably on her own again?

In his boyhood room, full of boyish things that Frances can't bear to get rid of, her clothes are squashed up tight against Abe's outgrown ones in the small wardrobe. There are pictures of sailboats on the walls, balsa-wood planes hanging on strings from the ceiling, a baseball nestled in its glove on a shelf, as though waiting for Abe to pick up the game where he left it off.

Among the debris of his childhood there hardly seems room for her. A photograph of Wilson as a puppy, jumping for a ball, ears flying, jostles for space on the small bedside table alongside a picture book on sailing, and two huge pebbles with the faint tracery of fossils inking their surface. She puts the book and the stones in a box under his bed, and the well of her memory is taken to that other bed she put a box under all those years ago. Shoving aside his puzzles, the miniature tool set, and a browning pile of comics, she swallows hard and attempts to banish the memory of that day, of that Angelina girl.

"Move anything you like," Frances had said lightly, but didn't tell her where she might move it to.

When Abe comes on his precious time off, the bed is too narrow for the both of them. They lie knotted together, close and uncomfortable. He pretends not to mind, she does too.

"It's cozy," he says.

"Mmm."

It's nothing against Frances, but she feels stifled being in such close quarters with someone she hardly knows. There is something of camp living in it that unsettles her. And she has noticed how Abe becomes more of a son than a husband in his mother's house. She misses having him to herself, misses the apartment. The need to find a place of their own is urgent in her.

"I'll go with whatever you choose," Abe says. "Long as it doesn't break the bank."

When she finds it on the fifth house viewed, it's obvious to her that it's the one. The day is dazzlingly bright, the noon sun high, the late summer day hot, yet the salt marshes on which the house sits appear to her like fields of pure untrodden snow.

"It looks solid enough," Frances says, seeing Satomi's delight.

It will blow their budget, so they will have to decorate it themselves, make do on the furnishings, but it's perfect.

"Square-built. Nineteen twenties, I guess," Frances says.

Satomi loves the unadorned frontage that belies the charm of its spacious interior. There isn't much of a garden, but you can see the ocean from all sides, and the rooms are filled with light.

"It's beautiful," she says.

"A lot of upkeep," Frances says. "And nothing much will take in the ground here. The salt, you see."

When Abe comes home on the weekends their time is spent decorating, sanding down the woodwork, peeling off the dark wallpaper, painting the rooms in soft grays and blues, the colors of the ocean.

They make love on a blanket on the floor, the smell of paint and ozone mingling in the air. The urge, frequent and overwhelming, can't be resisted.

"We'll move in as soon as the bed comes," Abe says. "What more do we need?"

"So many things." She laughs, picturing them sleeping in a big comfortable bed with cotton covers, a crib by the side of it.

"We'll be in by the end of the month," he says, and kisses her. "Wish we could have Wilson with us here, but it wouldn't be fair to take him."

"A puppy of our own, then?" she suggests.

"I guess."

The windows of the salt marsh house are open in the day to the tang of the marshes. There are drapes now at the windows, a sparse assortment of furniture in the rooms, and Frances has donated two rag rugs. The house has become a home.

There's no picket fence around her salty garden, and she refuses to wear an apron, but she is assuming the identity of the suburban, middle-class American wife, loving it so much that Manzanar has retreated to the less conscious part of her mind. She is hit by the certainty of love, by the contrast of her life with Abe to the unreal time she had spent with Joseph.

She gets a card for the local library, does her marketing at the store that Frances shops in, even has a laundry day. Frances is teaching her to cook Abe's favorite dishes, pickled beets and creamed codfish, broiled chicken and cornbread. People seeing her with Frances include her in their greeting, begin to recognize her when she is on her own. She sees the reserve in them still, but doesn't mind so much. She believes Abe when he tells her it's the same for all newcomers in Freeport. It takes time, that's all.

"Before you know it," Frances says, "you'll be a local."

They have Abe's best friend, Don, and his girlfriend over for dinner, and Abe helps her roast a chicken and she attempts a pear pie. She's a wife like any other. She's happy.

Abe sees and loves the difference in her. She's all his now, apart from those irritating times when she comes to stay overnight with him in the city, and hooks up with Joseph while he's at work. He doesn't mind so much anymore the idea of Cora. That unreachable bit of Satomi, the times when she seems remote from him, has to do with Cora, he thinks. He would like to find Cora too now, to see Satomi at peace.

In their city bed his passion spills over so that he is not always tender. She doesn't know, as Abe himself doesn't know, that it's payback for Joseph. But she's as eager, as demanding as him for it. When he falls asleep across her, she revels in the intimacy of his trust, his sharp after-sex scent. She bears without complaint the weight of him until he chooses to roll away from her.

She is determined not to let the camp impinge on their life, or allow the odd socialite life she had led with Joseph damage them. To make a balance sheet of what is gained, what lost, would be mad. She will be grateful, ignore that contradictory thing that stirs in her heart when memories of Cora are evoked. The girl who was Satomi Baker is lying low under the identity of Mrs. Abe Robinson.

At Abe's request she goes to the city to bring back the last of their things from the apartment. He has to work and the new tenants are eager to take possession. She packs their linen, her books, and the toaster they bought because the grill on the old cooker had stopped working. There's the tin tray illustrated with the New York skyline, and some cream china cups with gold rims that they found together in a bric-a-brac store. There's the silver-framed photograph of their wedding, Abe's binoculars, the alarm clock.

Abe has a week on nights and will sleep in one of the on-call rooms in the hospital.

"It's torture being apart," he says, kissing her.

"Worse than torture," she groans.

They sleep in the apartment for the last time, picnicking on sweet rolls and potato chips, making love in the creaky bed with its cheap mattress.

"We won't miss it," Abe says.

But she can't let go of the ache of leaving. She will never get used to endings.

Abe puts her on the train to Freeport, hauling the packed suitcases onto the rack above her seat in the empty compartment.

"You'll need someone to help you down with those at the other end."

"I'm stronger than you think, Abe."

"I know it, honey. You are strong and I love you. Still, find someone to help you with them anyway. Promise?"

"Promise."

His kiss is firm, without passion, she's disappointed. She can tell he is distracted, wants to be on his way.

"Only a few days before I'll be home for the holiday," he says. "I'll get the earliest Hempstead train I can, and be with you before you know it."

"Time to wish away," she says.

"Frances makes such a big deal of Thanksgiving you're not going to believe it. She'll love having you to show off to."

"I've had enough of missing you, Abe."

"I'll be home before you know it."

She hangs her head out of the window, holding on to the sight of him as he pauses, waving briefly, before striding to the exit. He hates goodbyes, she knows. There's pleasure in knowing what he hates, goodbyes and new shirts, ginger chocolate, milk in his coffee, surprises.

She knows him as he knows her, and everything is as it should be. But as he disappears from her view a feeling of melancholy invades her, and for a moment she debates leaving the train, catching up with him, the pair of them laughing at her silliness. But the train is already moving. It's love, she supposes; with love comes the feeling that every minute apart you are risking something.

"Just till Thanksgiving," she comforts herself. "Just till Thanksgiving."

PENN STATION TO BABYLON

ON THANKSGIVING EVE Frances is in the thick of it. She hasn't been able to keep the smile from her face all day. The oven's heat at full blast is fierce; a fresh-baked chocolate cake is cooling on the table, pumpkins are on the boil, steaming up the windows so that she has to open the door to let the cool air in. It reminds her of last year and all the years before, when she has done the same. Only this year it feels different, nicer, she has to admit. She has Satomi with her, Abe's Satomi, and now she needn't worry about him anymore, he has found his girl.

"Give those cranberries a stir, will you, Sati? I think they're beginning to stick."

The candied smell of the simmering berries, of the sweet pumpkins that she will mash to velvet for her special pie, spice the air.

"I want to get all this out of the way before Abe gets home. We always have hamburgers with my tomato relish on the night before Thanksgiving, and I haven't even started on them yet."

"I can't imagine ever being able to cook like you, Frances."

"Oh, you're learning. And I bet you already have a few of your own traditions."

"I don't know, maybe. We always have a drink on deck after we have put the boat to bed." She flushes at the thought of what else they do, but that is hardly for Frances's ears. "And we never go to sleep on an argument, if you mean that sort of thing. But nothing to do with food, Abe is still a better cook than me. He often cooks for himself in the city."

"Good heavens, does he? I've only ever known him to heat beans."

Both women fall silent as they picture him in their minds. Frances summons her big broad boy waving to her as he comes into harbor, a bitter-sweet reminder of his father. Satomi feels rather than sees his presence, the bulk of him, firm lips, strong hands, that odd contrast of feelings he induces in her, safe and risky at the same time.

"Oh, my God, the turkey." Frances's face is flushed, she is hot, excited. There's nothing like getting ready for Thanksgiving to gin things up.

"We have to cover it with bacon, give it a coat of maple syrup to sit in overnight."

"This Thanksgiving stuff is a real workout, isn't it?"

"Didn't your mother do it?"

"Not really, my father didn't care for turkey. He preferred my mother's Japanese dishes. The mess hall in the camp made an effort, but it was hard to be thankful there, even for the patriotic ones."

"And you didn't feel patriotic?"

"No, not the slightest bit. I spent my whole time at Manzanar angry or afraid. I never felt like celebrating."

"And now?"

"Oh, now everything is different. I want to celebrate with you and Abe, be thankful."

"Where were you last Thanksgiving?"

"We were at the Yacht Club at Fishers Island, Joseph and me, and his best friend, Hunter. He loves it there in the winter and it's smart to be at Fishers for the holiday." She wishes she hadn't said it. The words have a show-off, brittle feel to them.

"Did you enjoy it?"

"Yes, Joseph was in good form, he always is when Hunter is around."

"I guess you miss him, huh?"

"Well, I can still see him in the city when I go."

"You could have asked him here, you know. It would have been a bit odd, but he is your friend, and we will have to get used to that, I guess."

"I thought about it, but honestly, I don't think Abe is ready for that yet, and Joseph wouldn't know what to do with himself in a normal family."

Frances laughs. "I'm glad you think we're normal."

Satomi doesn't want to think about Joseph tonight. Thinking about him induces feelings of guilt, the idea that she is not entitled to her happiness. She has attempted in small ways to make Joseph a part of her and Abe's life, but neither man seems willing to give friendship a try. Inch by inch and without intention it feels as though she is letting Joseph go.

Perhaps, though, her feelings of guilt are really about Cora, about the child she has promised to reclaim. Now that Abe is willing, she must put more effort into finding Cora; she will never be completely happy, she knows, while what happened to that little one remains a mystery. She is due a letter from Dr. Harper anytime soon. Perhaps he has found a trail for them to follow.

Frances, noticing that Satomi has fallen into one of her reveries, puts aside the cooking and suggests they go outside. "We could do with some fresh air," she says, guiding Satomi to the door.

Unhooking Abe's waterproof from the stand on the porch, Satomi hangs it around her shoulders. It flaps against her calves, reminding her of the peacoat issue at Manzanar. She can feel the curve of Wilson's ball in the pocket against her thigh.

The day has been cold, mostly overcast, but as they look up at the night sky the clouds part, allowing a slice of moon to light the sea. It plays on the tips of the waves as they roll into the harbor. All along the coast where sea strikes shore the coves shift in an undulating silver seam.

"Just look at that," Frances marvels. "The moon and the black sea. Now, that sure is a sight."

Satomi slips her arms into the sleeves of Abe's jacket as the moon dusts up behind a cloud. It's Thanksgiving eve and Abe will already be on his way home. It's time to shower, to loosen her hair and put on the blue cardigan and the narrow Capri pants that she brought from home to change into, because Abe says she looks sexy in them.

"You make everything you wear look a million dollars, honey."

"It's an odd time of day," Frances says, turning back toward the house. "Too early for a drink, too late for a nap."

Out on the Richmond Hill track, stalled in the dark, the Hempstead train, with its air brakes jammed, sent its flagman with flag and lamp to slow down the oncoming Babylon train, only four minutes behind it.

Press accounts in the aftermath of the collision made much of the fact that the Babylon train had been barreling down the line close to sixty-five miles an hour when it slammed into the rear of the stationary Penn-to-Hempstead with a boom some likened to the sound of an atomic bomb.

The truth of it was, though, that the motorman of the Babylon, too late to do much about it, had made out in the gloom the stilled train, the panicked flagman at the side of the track frantically waving his flag. In the last seconds of his life he had applied his emergency brakes, slowing his speed to more like thirty than sixty. Still, thirty was speed enough to shunt the Hempstead train seventy-five feet along the track, to toss its last car higher than a house, and send the onrushing train slicing down the middle of the Hempstead, causing "overcoating." Such a word, such an ugly addition to the human vocabulary.

They hear the news of it on the radio as Frances is cutting a lemon for their gin and tonics. It doesn't seem real at first, a story told to frighten, so that you might laugh at it after, might think what a fool you were to have been taken in. It's a Halloween story, not a Thanksgiving one.

"It won't be Abe, not Abe," Satomi cries. But Frances doesn't hear her; her head is full of, *Not again, please, God, not again.* Her knees have buckled under her so that she has to hold on to the sink to keep upright. And Satomi, seeing her distress, can't go to her. If what she sees in Frances is a mother's intuition, then it is a horrible thing. A thing she can't bear the sight of.

The news is coming at them unrelentingly, the voice on the radio almost hysterical. Satomi is shaking, Frances whimpering. On and on it goes, the reporter's voice rising at each new discovery. They listen, sucking the words in, finding it hard to breathe them out.

Neighbors from across the track are the first on the scene. They had been deafened by the sound of the crash, sickened by the sight of it. The train cars are high above the bank, too high for them to reach at first. They had rushed for ladders, blankets, first aid. They are eager now to give witness.

"The ground shuddered. You felt the noise as much as heard it."

"We had to jimmy those doors open to get them out. People were screaming in pain, beating at the windows."

"There were limbs everywhere, arms and legs on the floor, hanging from the windows."

"They were packed like sardines in their own blood."

In Frances's sweet-smelling kitchen they hear on the airwaves fire engines and ambulances ferrying the wounded to the hospital. For some there isn't time even for that, so surgeons have converted the kitchen of a nearby house into a crude operating theater. They work under a bare bulb on the family's kitchen table covered with a sheet.

"People are giving their all," the reporter shrieks.

"Abe will be helping them," Frances says in a moment of hope, her voice hard and emotionless. "He'll be needed there tonight."

"But Abe always goes in the first car," Satomi wails. "He says it makes him feel that he is getting home quicker." She is on the floor now, rocking herself back and forward, banging her head against Frances's leg.

And suddenly Frances too has crumpled to the floor, torrents of hot tears streaming from her eyes, although she doesn't feel as though she is crying. She is merely comforting Satomi, who has gotten everything out of proportion.

Satomi doesn't want to go to the funeral. She doesn't want to see Abe lowered into the wintry ground, see the casket that Frances had chosen on her own, because Satomi is a coward, because she couldn't bear to even look at one.

"Satin-lined oak. Their best line," Frances had reported back in a papery voice.

Satomi had put her hands over her ears. The words were disgusting to her. "Satin-lined," "coffin." What had those things to do with Abe?

If she goes, how will she be able to leave his beautiful broken body there alone in the hard clay? How will she ever be able to say goodbye?

She thinks of Abe's face, the firm set of his mouth, the tiny chip on his third tooth in, the stubble of his beard when he doesn't shave. He can't be dead. In her grief she is more like her mother than ever. Like Tamura, she wants to retreat under the covers of her bed, to never come out.

A magical sort of thinking has taken over her mind. She looks to find him in the stars, in the tiny pearl-eyed bird puffed up with rancor that this morning as she woke in Abe's childhood bed had pecked at the window as though it were trying to get in. Tap, tap, the hammer of its beak shaking the glass.

"Where are you, Abe? Come back to me," she had shouted at the bird, frightening it away.

She had told Frances about it, as if Frances knew about such things, might translate some mysterious Morse code message for her.

"They dig in the putty for insects when the ground's too hard to mine," Frances said pragmatically. "It's the same every year."

Every bone in Abe's body had been crushed, every organ bruised, but it is the tear in his heart leaking blood that is given as the cause of death. A small tear no bigger than a dime, no bigger than a dime. The thought of that little leaking hole breaks her own heart.

"I can't go, Frances," she had sobbed. "Don't make me."

Frances had pleaded with her at first and then insisted.

"You must go. It's Abe's funeral. It's the right thing to do. The only thing left you can do for him. You will regret it always if you don't."

Weak with grief, she had given in.

Frances buttons up Satomi's coat for her, advises gloves, and hugs her briefly. Satomi wonders how Frances can bear to worry about her, how she can think of anyone else but herself. Her mother-in-law's shoulders are hunched, her mouth pinched; she seems smaller somehow, as though she is shriveling by the minute.

"It's cold in that church, even worse in the cemetery," Frances says.

A stony misery creeps through Satomi's body. Time has run out, and she can't remember when she last told Abe that she loved him, and she hadn't yet told him of Haru. She will never, now, be able to tell him anything ever again.

The minister in his church is comfortable in his role. He enjoys the onstage part of his ministry, the sweetness of christenings, the joy of weddings, even the somber air of funerals. He performs well in front of his audience, as he sometimes guiltily thinks of his congregation.

"We think with great sympathy," he says, "of Abe's new bride, widowed after such a brief marriage."

It was to be his only reference to her. He speaks of Abe's history in Freeport, of the town's love of Frances, their love of her boy. It seems to Satomi that he is saying their long knowing of Abe has the bigger claim to grief at his loss.

But she's being unfair, she thinks, small-minded, possessive. Abe had been popular everywhere, always. No one knew better than her how easy he had been to love.

Abe's friends, some holding hands, some with their arms around each other, make a space for her at the graveside. Without the glue of Abe to bind them, they seem already to be separating from her. Their parents, who have known Abe since childhood, stand around the grave too, ashen-faced, their eyes slipping to Abe's father's headstone nearby. They are touched by their children's grief, secretly thankful that it is not one of their own, who might so easily have caught the Penn-to-Babylon that night.

The rain has come on, so that people begin opening umbrellas. Red and blue canopies, a yellow one with blue raindrops dancing on it, carnival colors, she thinks, as Abe's best friend, Don, moves to her side, sheltering her under the shade of his black one.

It takes a while for the exaggerated moan of the fair-haired girl she hadn't noticed before to reach her. Satomi has held herself back from giving vent to the animal part of herself and looks toward her with curiosity. People are embarrassed by the awful sound, they shuffle their feet, cough politely as though to cover it.

It's Corrine, clutching a spray of snowberries to her chest, swaying uncontrollably. Nothing to be done, she has always been a bit of a drama queen.

"Shush, Corrine. Be brave for Frances's sake." A man Satomi doesn't know puts his arm around Corrine's shoulders, a bit too firmly for it to be thought comfort.

Abe's colleagues from the hospital cluster together uncomfortably, their medical skills of no use here. The neighbors from Jackson Heights who had hardly spoken to her, but had thought him a fine neighbor, have come. They have all known and liked Abe. It is odd how she feels an outsider.

Joseph had phoned in distress, concerned for her.

"Oh, my dear girl, I'm coming. You will need me."

"No, don't come. It wouldn't be right. I don't want you to come."

He had been hurt at her dismissal, but she couldn't picture Joseph among Abe's people. He would have been a distraction, would have highlighted the fact that she is cut from a different cloth too.

At the sight of Abe's coffin she is reminded of Tamura's. Were they together now, Abe and Tamura, forever linked by their love for her? She shakes the thought away. She is already feeling the burden of ghosts.

On the walk back, Frances takes her hand as though she is a child. People arrive at the house. Women fuss in Frances's kitchen, food appears as if from nowhere. It is as though a party has broken out. She goes upstairs, and Frances follows.

"You need sleep," Frances says, undressing her.

"I'll come down soon, Frances. I just need a little time."

Sleep is the only thing that holds attraction for either of them. Satomi would sleep forever if she could, but as though an alarm is set in her she can only manage an hour or two at a time. She lies on the bed and buries her head in Abe's pillow. Even the scent of him is fading, she thinks.

"I'm sorry, Frances, it should be me helping you."

"We'll help each other, Satomi. Abe would want that."

"I can't say his name, Frances. It feels like my heart is ripping too when I try."

"Day by day, inch by inch," Frances says, without belief herself.

"Yes, day by day," Satomi repeats mechanically.

"You will stay with me here for a while, won't you, Sati, just for a while? I want to be with someone who loved Abe, someone he loved," Frances says.

"Come back to the apartment," Joseph says. "Let me take care of you, just until you put the pieces back together."

She considers briefly living on her own in their house by the salt marshes. But the thought of occupying their bed without Abe, of taking down a book from the shelves that he had made for their living room, is too painful. She will never live there now, not without Abe. Hope has been eaten up there, sent packing.

She stays with Frances, holed up in Abe's room, breathing him in as her mother had breathed her father in all those years ago. She will look after Frances, make her eat, make her go for walks, act like a daughter-in-law is meant to.

She finds herself either full of a terrible nervous energy or so tired that she can't lift herself from the bed. Sometimes she shuts her eyes and prays that when she opens them she will find herself ten years into the future, ten years away from the misery that runs through her blood, contaminating everything. She can't pray, as some do, for it all to have been no more than a horrible dream. To close her eyes and imagine Abe returned to her wouldn't save her from the pain of opening them to the knowledge that he never would be.

Frances's friends come to comfort.

"Be grateful for the wonderful summer you had here together, for the precious time you shared," they say. "It will get better."

Like Frances, they are the best of women, the best of American mothers. Unlike Frances, though, they rarely say the right thing.

Her days are filled with what is needed next, as though Abe is directing her in some way. Sleep when you must, eat when you remember, sit with Frances, look at the photographs with her, cry with her, make her laugh, and lie with her so that she can sleep a little. And Frances does the same for her in return.

She dreads the nightmares that come in her troubled sleep, black featureless landscapes where she can't find who she's looking for. She doesn't dream in color anymore.

Frances lets her fuss, acquiesces in the game while looking herself for a reference point back to the routine of her old life, which seems to have escaped her.

They find comfort in focusing on Abe's dog, it is the only thing they can do for him now. Wilson won't eat, not even the delicious stews of marrow bone that Frances cooks for him. He lies across the door to Abe's room, head on paws, his body curled around one of Abe's old shoes that he found on the porch, as though he is made for misery.

"Come on, old fella," they imitate Abe. "You can't go on like this, now, can you?"

They go through Christmas in a daze, no decorations, no tree, but "merry Christmas" slips from Frances's lips as Satomi appears at breakfast. Some atavistic memory has triggered the words without her consent.

"I don't think that I will ever be able to cook a turkey again."

"It doesn't matter, Frances, I couldn't eat it anyway."

They walk the two-mile strip alongside a distant canal without seeing anyone, returning home to soup and cornbread. In bed by nine, they have survived their first Christmas without Abe. They are both glad to see the back of it.

Frances rallies first. Perhaps because she knows what her life will be like now, knows what to expect from it. There are no decisions for her to make, the cycles of grief are familiar to her, there will be bad and better times, times so completely terrible that she will look back on them and wonder how she has not been made mad. And even when she thinks that she is better, she knows that the pain will come slicing out of nowhere, catching her off guard. The thought of it exhausts her, but she must start the living of those times, or walk into the sea and be done with it. She tells herself that she doesn't have the courage for that. She isn't made for Greek tragedy.

And Wilson has perked up, pleading for walks, dropping his ball at their feet, hanging around the kitchen before his mealtimes, his big begging eyes full of expectation. He has a better sense of timing than them, knows instinctively when to let go.

Letters have come from Dr. Harper and Eriko. They are worried about her, shocked at what has happened.

It is too cruel, Dr. Harper writes. *A terrible thing.*

It must be borne, Satomi. You don't deserve it, Eriko says.

Her answering letters are brief. *I'm fine, getting better*, she lies. *Don't worry about me.*

She has refused to see Joseph. It's ridiculous, she tells herself, but seeing him would feel like she was betraying Abe.

"Not yet," she says when he phones, his voice all hurt. "I'm not ready to see anyone yet."

By spring she has taken to spending her days on the boat. She doesn't sail, never releases it from its moorings, but in its narrow confines her grief feels contained. She lies on the bunk and reads all day, books from the Freeport library, novels and biographies, books about fishing and the care of dogs, anything that her eyes settle on. She knows now a little about fly fishing, about trees and plants, and Emma Bovary, and Tiny Tim.

She hides in the boat's cabin, unseen, but hearing, outside, the lapping of the water, the voices of Freeport's sailing community.

"Shh," she hears, when someone remarks on the permanently anchored boat. Freeport knows she is there.

When Satomi's tears are no longer a release, when sleep overtakes reading as her choice of escape, Cora inches her way into her grief. She goes through the box of trinkets, touches the little hairbrush, the charm bracelet, the ribbons. And suddenly self-pity is replaced by shame. She is ashamed of herself. It's obvious to her now that if anything good is to come out of Abe's death, she must find Cora. She must give her all to the search, go to California herself. She can't hide from it or begin again until she does. But she's so horribly tired, and how can she leave Frances? It's hardly fair.

Frances, noticing the change in Satomi, the worrying way the girl has now of watching her, takes it to be a turn for the worse in her daughter-in-law.

"Satomi, honey, you can't go on like this," she appeals to her. "Asking me all the time if I am better, when it's obvious to me that you are not. You are too young to let your life just drift. You have to think about what you want to do with it."

"I'm fine. Don't worry about me."

But she does worry. It is time for Satomi to go, but she will have to be the one to move her on, Satomi isn't able.

"This isn't what Abe would have wanted for you. It isn't respecting his memory to just fade away, you know?"

"Well, Abe isn't here, is he? He left us, didn't he?" Her voice is shaking, she is furious. It surprises her, she had no idea she was so angry.

In the silence that follows her outburst, they realize they are both angry with Abe, that they have been simmering for months.

"How could he leave us, Frances? How could he do this to us?"

"He didn't do this, honey, it was an accident, we can't help accidents." Frances tries to regain some equilibrium, it's horrible to find herself angry with Abe.

"I know. It was a stupid thing to say. I'm sorry, Frances. I'm going to bed now. I didn't mean that about Abe, of course I didn't."

"Honey, this is what I mean. It's six o'clock. You're sleeping your life away."

Next morning, with her decision made, Frances watches Satomi make a poor breakfast of coffee and a single slice of toast. She watches her absentmindedly push her toast around the plate, leave the coffee to go cold. The look of the girl never fails to surprise her, she is gloriously striking even though she has lost weight and isn't taking care of herself. It's a waste.

She would like to keep Satomi with her, a companion in grief. It would be wicked, though. Satomi has years ahead of her to find someone else to love, to love her. She has held herself back from saying as much for too long. And if she's honest, between them they keep the pot of grief for Abe constantly on the boil, neither willing for the other to heal.

Dear Mr. Rodman,

I believe that Satomi has asked you not to come to Freeport, but I think that she needs you now and I would like you to come.

I don't seem to be able to help her and I don't think that we are good for each other at present. Grief is always stronger in one or the other of us at any given time, so that there are few lighthearted times in this house anymore.

She is sadly lacking family and as far as I can make out you are her only friend in New York. Can you think of what to do for her?

I should warn you that it won't be easy trying to talk her into anything. She can be very stubborn, but I guess you know that.

I feel strongly that you are the one to help her now. I hope that you will understand that I am not trying to get rid of her. I want to do my best for her. I'm convinced that the best is not to be found here in Freeport.

She will be angry that I have contacted you and I feel bad not taking her into my confidence about it, she is not a child, after all. But she would only arrange to be off somewhere if she knew that you were coming, so I must risk her wrath.

I hope that you will come soon.

With warmest wishes,
Frances Robinson

GATHERING

BEING BACK IN Joseph's apartment doesn't bother her. It's nothing more than a staging post to her now. And it's not for long, just time enough to find a home to bring Cora to if that's what's needed.

Frances has offered to deal with the sale of the salt marsh house. There's no point in hanging on to it, and if she is to make a home elsewhere she will need the money.

"It's temporary," Satomi tells Joseph. "So, ground rules: no presents, no outings, no talk of marriage, just friendship."

"Agreed. What's better for us two than friendship?"

"Oh, other fish to fry, Joseph?"

"Possibly."

Joseph has never known her so full of determination, so sure of her agenda. She has made herself known to the Japanese community in her old New York neighborhood, and won't be ignored this time. She has persisted, and some of them on her behalf are looking for Cora too now, writing to their relatives on the West Coast requesting information. And she has joined the Japanese American Citizens League, who are fighting to put right the injustices the Japanese internees have suffered. It's amazing to her that she didn't know they existed outside of the camp before. They had fought for the right of Japanese-Americans to join the military then, and given Haru back his pride. She hopes with their help she can do the same for herself now.

She is entitled to a fairer settlement of her farm, they say. They will help her fight for it. It will be her purpose now to find Cora and be part of that fight.

Frances phones. The salt marsh house has sold.

"So soon, Frances."

"Well, it's a good enough house, Satomi."

She thinks of the airy rooms, the unsullied light, the way it sits so solidly on its patch of earth. She wonders if the washy colors that she and Abe loved are to the new owners' taste. Perhaps it is already returned to the more conventional browns and creams that she and Abe had thought dull. Who, though, could not love the view of those bleach-white marshes, the way the streams braid through them on their way to the ocean? She would have stayed there if she could, if Abe hadn't lingered in every room. One Robinson widow will have to do for Freeport.

"They look like a happy family," Frances says. "Four children, little sweethearts. Oh, and a puppy. That house needs a dog, don't you think?"

"Yes, it's a house meant for joy." She breathes deeply.

"Oh, Sati, I'm sorry. Damn my practicality. I didn't think."

CAPE COD

THERE HAS BEEN a letter from Dr. Harper. His search has come up with news of a child called Mary who might be their Cora.

Only the tiniest clue, Satomi, so I'm warning about having high hopes. I wait for months for replies to my inquiries, and when I get one there is hardly any information at all. The child is in a Catholic orphanage in Los Angeles, she is of the right age and came to them without papers, and that's about it. It's by no means confirmed to be Cora. I've twice followed this kind of information up without success. It's unlikely, but I'm hoping for third-time lucky. And how many Japanese Marys do you know? It's likely her name was changed to Mary. It's that Catholic thing, claiming people for the Church, naming them after saints. Still, Mary, hardly the most original, is it? No one can verify anything because the child came via another orphanage and no one thought to ask how she ended up there in the first place. I'm waiting for them to send a photograph. I'll be in touch if and when they do.

The news, brief as it is, has astonished her, as though finding Cora had been a fantasy, something she longed for but couldn't quite believe in. She has to agree with Dr. Harper, the chance that it could be Cora is slim, but the thought of it has made her anxious to find a home, to make it ready.

"You can bring her here if you want," Frances had offered.

Satomi knows that she won't. If the child is Cora, she wants to take her to somewhere permanent, somewhere that is forever.

Joseph is unsettled by the news. He thinks of Satomi caring for the child, making a life out of it, giving up her own. Her hopes are up, though, and he can't bear the thought of her being disappointed.

"What are the chances this Mary could be Cora? It's a long shot at best," he warns. "It might not be her, dear girl. You do know that, don't you? We have no idea whether this Mary was even in Manzanar."

"She's an orphan, a Californian Japanese, so she must have been there." She doesn't want Joseph's doubt, she has enough of her own.

"It's possible she's a recent orphan, don't you think?"

"Possible, but if she's not, then she must have been in Manzanar. It was the only camp with an orphanage. Every orphaned West Coast baby, toddler, and child ended up there."

"Extraordinary." Joseph scowls.

"Well, just the threat of those babies," she says. "Who knew what they were capable of?" She had meant to sound sarcastic, but her voice shook as a surge of the old anger surfaced.

She thinks of the children, their dear faces, their names fresh on her tongue. She remembers their characters, the half-feral little boy who was always in trouble for fighting, and the two-year-old slow to speak, whose first word when it came was, *Wait*.

"God, that whole thing, the camps, Cora, it's awful, Sati," Joseph says. "Unfair."

Suddenly she is weeping, haunted by the images in her head. She sees Cora's questioning eyes, Tamura's eyes, she has always thought. She pictures her shy smile, hears her sweet voice. She has let Cora down, not worked hard enough to find her. All through her time with Abe she had let Cora slip. She had indulged herself in happiness, thought it her time, her due. She had played at being an all-American wife, reinventing herself as someone who hardly remembered the suffering in the camp, the people who had meant so much to her. Why had it taken Abe's death to show her how badly she had lost her way?

"I'm going as soon as I hear back from Dr. Harper, Joseph. I'll find us a home, Cora and me, and then I'm going to California."

"What can I do to help?"

"You could send a car to bring Dr. Harper from Lone Pine to Los Angeles."

"I thought a plane, dear girl. A small plane, you know."

"I think he'd like that."

"If it must be by the sea, must be out of the city," Joseph says as they set out from uptown, "Martha's Vineyard is the place." He has a house in mind. A house perfect for Satomi, he thinks, fingering the details in his pocket.

"Why there in particular?"

"Well, you'll like it, that's for sure. And I know people there who will look out for you."

"I don't need people to look out for me."

"Everyone needs people looking out for them, Sati. I don't know why you have to go at all. What's so bad about the city anyway?"

"Oh, apartment buildings, sirens in the night." She is thinking more, though, of where she wants to be rather than where she does not. It's still the East for her, but not the city, not farmland either, somewhere new to make her own.

"I hardly know you these days," Joseph says.

She isn't hiding anymore, doesn't need him to save her from

anything. There is an air of impatience about her, she is on the move. He is the one running to keep up.

He hopes she'll settle for Martha's Vineyard, it's familiar territory, and he can visit her there whenever he wants. He hasn't told her, but he has found a new love, a Russian who claims to be a count, although he hardly believes that. Suddenly he is ready for monogamy, ready to let go of the promise to his father. *I'm like a boy again*, he thinks, *all mouthwatering desire, viewing the world as though it has just been made, thinking everything in life good enough to bottle. Satomi was right. Love is the thing.*

On the Vineyard, Satomi's expectations of it and the house are not met. "I thought this house was made for you." Joseph can't hide his disappointment.

"Well, for one thing, Joseph, I can't afford it."

"Don't let that be a problem, Sati. I can help, you know that."

"You do enough already."

She wants it to be the money from the Freeport house that buys her new home. A gift to her and Cora from Abe.

"It's not for me, far too big," she says, thinking of the atrium that mimics a hotel lobby. The house is full of such pretensions, the atrium, the Cinderella staircase, the high ceilings decorated with overblown plasterwork. And the air in it is stale, sour, lifeless somehow.

"Who lived here before, Joseph?"

"Oh, some old aunt, I expect. It's always some old aunt. These houses don't come up too often. Dead aunt's shoes, you might say."

Outside, the dark waters of Nantucket Sound seem to isolate the island, imprisoning its inhabitants. She had hoped for color, reflection, but the sea looks cinereous, black in parts, as though pools of oil swim just below its surface.

"Might as well be barbed wire," she says as they board the ferry back to the Cape. "Sorry, Joseph, but I can't live here."

"But the Vineyard is charming, everyone says so."

"It's not for me."

A half a mile or so from the small town of Eastham, with a relaxed realtor and details in hand, they view a cedar-shingled cottage that sits on the bay, looking east toward the Atlantic Ocean.

"It's ready to move into," the realtor says. "The owners have moved on."

Satomi smiles. "I can breathe here," she says.

"It's too small," Joseph insists. "A doll's house."

"It's perfect, Joseph. Just the right size for Cora and me, and a spare bedroom for you when you come."

He imagines himself with Leo, his Russian, in the attic bedroom, and smothers a smile. The details promised three spacious bedrooms.

"If you don't mind the ceiling touching your head," he says. "And you would have to shoehorn wardrobes into them."

The cottage is a child's drawing of a house, a broad-framed building with end gables and a chimney right in the center of the steeply pitched roof. It has been built low to withstand the Cape's storms in winter, and to be cool in summer.

There are chalky blue shutters on all but the attic windows, and there's a wooden porch with steps down to the shore. Clumps of beach rose not yet in bloom streak across the sand for as far as the eye can see.

"*Rosa rugosa*," the realtor says. "Grows like a weed around here. Miles of red, in its season."

"Miles of red," Satomi repeats dreamily.

Long ribbons of memory are stirred in her. The plant had grown in Angelina at the roadsides, on bits of scrubland, anywhere that the earth was dry. Tamura had thought it pretty. Aaron had dismissed it as a weed.

She had conjured up a place like this in her imagination moons ago, so that now it feels like coming home. She and the house suit each other.

"Everything could do with a coat of paint," Joseph says, trying not to let his exasperation show.

She nods, although she finds the shabbiness of it rather charming. The house is more than a shelter. You can feel the life in it. Hardy people have lived here, fishing folk, perhaps.

"Whalers, at one time," the realtor says, as if reading her thoughts. "Trawling for right whales."

"How do you spell that?" Joseph's interest is roused.

"Just as it sounds. They were called that because they were right in every way. Big creatures full of baleen, their blubber so thick you could float them in dead. Easier to bring ashore, you see."

Satomi wanders off, leaving Joseph and the realtor talking.

"Leviathans," she hears him say. "Enormous heads. You occasionally see their tail flukes from here. Getting to be a rare sight, though."

Over the sound of the sea, the gulls can be heard impudent in the air. The soft *phut* of an outboard motor churns in the distance. Behind her and farther along the beach, other cottages are scattered about, and behind them an acre or so of woodland, where stringy stands of pitch pine are set among bayberry and beach plum. It's a bare-boned landscape, a monochrome wash. Japanese calligraphy comes to mind, and she adds an imaginary skein of geese, a dark arrow of them in the pale sky.

Promise, she thinks, is thick in the air here, in the vinegar-sharp trace of bramble, the vibrant tang of ozone. Even with the dipping sun hot on her face she can imagine winter here, snow and the spindly trees with their roots gripping the earth as they bend in the wind toward the ocean. It's the edge of the land, the tipping point, where everything holds on tight to its bit of America. The late afternoon light is too pure to be called dusk, it's a moment in time that no one has bothered to name.

Something taut in her is unwinding itself, settling. If home is to be found anywhere, she feels that it is here. Cora, she thinks, will have the bedroom with the faded wallpaper, shells on a flowing seaweed tracery. The light in the room comes from the sea, soft slate with touches of violet. An old paddle fan fixed to the ceiling has a string pull hanging from it, low enough, she thinks, for a child to reach. She will take the room opposite for herself, which, like Cora's, looks out over First Encounter Beach.

"The Indians named it," the realtor says in answer to Joseph's question. "They had their first sighting of the pilgrims on this beach, apparently. Nothing much has changed here since then." He laughs. "Only joking, we're pretty much up to scratch and you hardly see Indians around here anymore." He is thinking movie Indians, the bow-and-arrow kind.

"Well, Cora and I will be like the pilgrims. We will make our home here from scratch. The natives will get used to us."

This perfect house has decided her, she won't wait for a photograph of the child now. She will write to Eriko and Dr. Harper to let them know she is coming. She is counting on Mary being Cora. She must be Cora.

Shivering with the weariness of the insomniac she has become since hearing that Cora might be found, she yields for a moment to a feeling of panic. If it is Cora, how will the child feel about being claimed by her? Chances are she feels let down, double-crossed, even. Maybe Satomi is keeping her promise too late to do either of them any good. If they had guessed Cora's age right in the camp, she will be eight, nearly nine now. She will be different, just as Satomi herself is different. They have made separate journeys, after all.

"Fascinating," she hears Joseph say to the realtor. "Don't you think so, Sati?"

"Mmm." She has no idea what they have been talking about.

"One last look," she says, and turns from them.

Inside the house a more settled feeling overtakes her. It's as though she has already taken possession of it, and it of her. She sits on the box seat in the hall below a row of wooden coat pegs, and listens to the dull crush of the ocean as it runs through the eelgrass and stirs up the shingle at the shore break. Framed by the open door, her view of the water is contained, so that the ocean seems barely wider than a lake. She hadn't known there were so many shades of gray. In the distance the horizon shimmers, a pearly line of pewter tinged with mauve. Such tender colors that her heart begins to ache.

Joseph calls that it's time to go. He is hungry, and wants to try the Nellie's Inn oysters that are famous in these parts. And then they must get back to the city. He will introduce her to Leo, tell her she was right about the promise.

"No need to fret, dear girl," he says. "You have found your home."

PROVIDENCE

In Eriko's small but immaculate apartment above her shop, Satomi wonders how it is possible for them to have become so shy with each other. Manzanar had been their territory, of course, the familiar ground they had stood on, yet she had lived seminal years with Eriko, shared Tamura with her, shared too much to ever feel unknown by Eriko.

"I had forgotten how beautiful you are," Eriko says.

Satomi looks out of place in Eriko's family room, a polished not-of-her-world sort of woman. The kind of glamorous woman, Eriko thinks, that you read about rather than know. She even smells expensive. There is nothing visible of the camp girl left in her, not even that look that marks out inmates, the wariness that says it could happen again. The look she notices in her own mirrored reflection each morning.

"You don't sell fabric anymore, Eriko?"

"There's no call for it. People don't dress-make much around here these days."

She is in the work-clothes business now; cheap checkered shirts, thick cotton overalls, and her special line, the felt fedoras ubiquitous among men from the worker up.

"And Naomi's gone." Satomi hardly dares say it. "It's hard to believe. I'm so sorry, Eriko. Dear Naomi, it hurt not to be with you when I heard. I know how hard it is to lose a mother." She puts her arms around Eriko and can't let go. In Eriko's familiar scent, her comforting bulk, she is a child of the camp again.

"It's just me, Eriko. Whatever you see, it's just me," she sobs.

"I know, Satomi. Of course it's you." Eriko is relieved. She touches her hair affectionately. "It was just in the moment, you know. I had you in my mind as you were in Manzanar."

"And Yumi, and Haru?" she asks, finding it hard to swallow.

"Yumi is married. Can you believe it? She is far too young, but she is happy, even though they have no money and there's a baby on the way. Haru teaches in a Japanese school near San Diego. He wants me to join him there, but I can't leave Yumi."

"And he's married?"

"Yes, he is married, Sati."

"Happy?"

"I think so. He works too much for the future, though, to enjoy the present."

"I'm glad for him, Eriko."

"Really, Sati?"

"Yes, really. I can see now that it would never have worked for us. We were children then."

"Well, it seems to me that there's no boy left in him now. He is all duty."

Eriko makes tea, "real tea," she says, and they share a look. They are waiting for Dr. Harper to arrive from the airport, and the thought of seeing him again excites them.

"What will you do if it isn't Cora?" Eriko asks.

"Keep looking until I find her."

"Good girl."

Satomi feels sixteen again, happy to have Eriko's approval.

"And your home, Sati? What is your home like?"

"It's simple, clean, not enough furniture yet. The breeze from the ocean blows through it, front door to back, just like the house I shared with Abe. You would like it, I think. It won't be a home, though, until I have Cora. I need to see her grow up, see her happy to be an American."

"And are you happy with being an American now?"

"You know, I guess I am. But then, it's easier on the East Coast, so many nationalities that I hardly stand out at all. And they seem to have won a different war than the one we fought. People there hardly know about the camps."

"How is that possible?"

"It's unbelievable, isn't it? Quite wrong that they are never spoken of."

"I'm as much to blame as anyone for that, I suppose," Eriko says. "None of the Japanese left around here speak of them much. We are ashamed, I think. Yumi says that she won't tell her children, that there's no point in making them afraid. She wants them to grow up fearless, like Haru."

"But the shame is not ours, Eriko. We must never let it be ours. You should tell Yumi as much."

They pause for a moment in their talk, both thinking of Yumi as the child she was in the camp, plump and naughty, one of the new breed of disobedient daughters.

"I miss your mother still," Eriko says. "She is the one I miss most in life."

She leads Satomi downstairs to the shop, which has a CLOSED sign on its door. The air there smells of felt and disinfectant.

"Roaches everywhere," Eriko says. "Just like Manzanar."

"We should keep a lookout for Dr. Harper." Satomi goes to the window. "He is a stranger to this district."

"It was brave of you to come alone," Eriko says. "And flying too"

She hadn't wanted Joseph to come with her. Cora doesn't

know him, after all, it will be enough that Satomi is there with Eriko and Dr. Harper.

In any case, Joseph is caught up with Leo, and hates, these days, to be parted from him for long. It turns out that Leo is a count after all, the genuine article. He is new to the city but has found old friends among his fellow émigrés in New York, and has been embraced by the Russian Nobility Association. According to Joseph, new blue blood is rare, and is to be feted among his fellow exiles.

"We are a novelty," he says. "The latest distraction."

She has never seen him less cynical, or so openly happy.

"We are always at some ball or other," he says. "There are at least a hundred dates that must be celebrated with the most extravagant parties that you can imagine. Anything and everything demands a celebration, Peter the Great's victory at Poltava, Gogol's birth, Romanovs visiting from Spain, things I never knew about before Leo. It's quite extraordinary."

Russian nobility, it seems, has the good manners not to pry into their friendship, their particular arrangement.

"We dance with the girls for form's sake," Joseph says. "But the truth is that I'm the nearest thing that Leo is going to get to an heiress.

She is relieved not to feel responsible for Joseph's happiness anymore. Leo is a good match for him, an artist at heart, and the most perfect of traveling companions. Maybe among the disposed Russians Joseph will at last find a place where he can settle.

"And you, Sati," Eriko breaks into her thoughts. "You have been married and widowed since I last saw you. It seems astonishing to me."

"Oh, Eriko, I wish you could have known Abe."

"So many gone." Eriko sighs. "To lose your man so young." She reaches out and pulls Satomi to her.

The tears that come are nothing like those she had shed in the months after Abe's death. They fall warm and soft, without the accompanying urge to howl.

"I took a strange journey after Manzanar, Eriko. My mother would have loved Abe, but she wouldn't have approved of my choices before he came along."

"Maybe, but I never heard her judge anyone. Tamura understood how life can overtake you."

Dr. Harper has been counting the days since the letter from Satomi came. And now the time is here, he is on his way and will see for himself the circle completed. He is hopeful now that the child is Cora. The photo that came is grainy, blurred at the edges, showing a shy-looking girl, older than the Cora he remembers, of course, but something in her stance seems familiar to him. He is ashamed to discover that in their dark-eyed, soft-featured prettiness, all Japanese children's faces look alike to him. He imagines that all white, gray-haired old men look the same to them too. It's no comfort.

His records of Manzanar are packed in boxes, piled up in his garage, ready to send to Satomi when she is finally settled. His heart has been rocking a bit lately, giving him a warning or two. He suspects that if he hoards his little archive for much longer, it will end up as kindling for his wife's fire when he is gone.

It's an unconventional documentation, he knows, a strange collection, but telling all the same. The time is surely coming when the Japanese will fight for compensation, when they will insist on the longed-for apology. He is convinced that Satomi's spirit, her strong open heart, will make her part of that fight.

He asks the cabdriver to stop across the street from Eriko's shop. He needs a minute or two to compose himself. The journey from Lone Pine in the single-engine plane had been something he had looked forward to as eagerly as a boy, but the excitement of it has stirred old ambitions, present regrets. Looking down on the landscape as the little craft battled the wind, seeing woods and rivers, a tiny dot of a boat on the ocean, he was filled with self-reproach. He should have done more with his life, had adventures, been braver.

He watches the women behind the window talking animatedly, waiting for him to come, two where there should be three. It's strangely hurtful. He feels like sitting down on the sidewalk and weeping. Oh, why couldn't Tamura be there waiting too? He shakes his head, takes out a handkerchief to dab at his moist eyes. His recently acquired varicose veins thump uncomfortably in his legs. He hates the look of the raised blue tracks that run along his white liver-spotted skin. He can't remember when he last looked at himself with any satisfaction. His wife is right, he is vain for his age.

To his old man's eyes Satomi looks the same. Eriko is only a little fuller, her dark hair streaked with gray now, that's to be expected, after all. It's good to see them in the real world, good to have Manzanar behind them. Since they left, the place has reverted to wasteland, a picked-over plot he averts his eyes from when driving past.

It had been awful seeing off the last of Manzanar's inhabitants, the old ones who had to be forced out. Painful to observe the women watching their homes demolished, and the old men wondering how they were meant to provide now, how they could feel proud of anything. He thinks that there are too many kinds of impotency to wound men.

And to add insult, those awful lectures, compulsory, so that it was hard to feel like the free men they were told they were now. Inmates, it was insisted, must learn how to behave in the outside world, how to get along with their fellow Americans. The sermons had done little to ease their bewilderment. Having suffered the loss of everything that had been theirs before incarceration, they had wept at their separation from the known. Those old boys were a lost tribe he couldn't feel optimistic for, no matter how much he tried.

It was astounding to him to read that some in the House of Representatives were still angling for their repatriation to Japan. It made him sick with shame. He wrote as much to them, but they never replied.

It's a joyful reunion, a hug for Satomi, a clasping of hands with Eriko.

"It's been too long," Dr. Harper says. "And so much has happened, especially to you, Satomi."

She smiles at him, registering the tremble in his hands, noting that his eyes are a little paler than she remembers, his step slower. She wonders how many times she will see him again, and it comes to her that she loves John Harper. That he means too much to her to let his work be forgotten. She puts her arms around him, lays her head on his shoulder for a moment.

"I'm ready for it now. Send me your archive," she says softly. "I won't let it go to waste. I promise."

Of course, she and Tamura and their kind were not the only victims of the war. There are victims of all kinds all over the world, she knows. Yet still she feels there is a need for justice, for someone to admit that at worst the incarceration had been a wicked betrayal, at best senseless. She doesn't want to see the Japanese inmates' story cleaned up, rewritten, as she and Tamura had rewritten Aaron's story. She wants to be part of the reconciliation, to be around for the longed-for apology. She may never escape her ghosts, but her memories are lighter now and she is healing, she knows.

"We should go," Dr. Harper says. "Put an end to Cora's waiting."

The Sisters of Charity are housed in a three-story red-brick building. There are bars at the windows, no curtains, smudges on the
glass. The place looks shabby, halfhearted, uninviting.

The three of them pause in front of the rusty playground gates
as if by order, and Satomi pushes the bell, which immediately cre-
ates a hissing of white noise.

"Yes?"

"It's Dr. Harper and Mrs. Robinson," Dr. Harper says in the
strongest voice he can muster. Since his school days he has felt
uneasy around the religious. When he was young it had to do
with guilt for his boyhood sins, he supposes. Now he thinks it's
most likely the fear of a day of reckoning.

"Come through the yard and ring the visitors' bell on the front
door. Someone will come for you."

Satomi is the first to enter the bitumen quadrangle. She takes a
deep breath and sends Eriko an anxious smile. In place of flowers,
litter is caught up in the tufts of needlegrass that grow at the base
of the high wire fencing enclosing the playground.

"To keep the children from the road," Eriko says quickly, as if
to reassure Satomi. "At least it doesn't turn in at the top."

They are all thinking of the fencing at Manzanar, and look
around nervously as though seeking gun towers, guards. A
chalked map of hopscotch on the ground is fading under the sun.
Garbage cans are lined up against the building, spilling over with
refuse.

"It's horrible, horrible," Satomi says, feeling the sweat pooling
under her arms and in the palms of her hands. The awful realization that Cora may be here feeling, herself forgotten, panics her.

"It's not so bad, is it, Eriko?" Dr. Harper says. "The street is
nice enough."

"No, it's not bad at all," Eriko says. "Not bad at all."

"She's as fenced in here as she was at Manzanar," Satomi says, not willing to be comforted.

Whenever she had thought of finding Cora, her imaginings had been kinder than the sight of this place. They had included lawns and flowers, trees to shade the child from the sun. She realizes now with shame that they were nothing but pretty pictures, good only for soothing herself.

There is a choice of bells on the black-painted door, a foot-high polished brass crucifix nailed to it. Satomi pushes the VISITORS bell and hears a faint ringing from deep in the house's interior. It reminds her of the one in Mr. Beck's lodgings.

Inside, on the checkered linoleum that runs the length of a narrow hall, so narrow that they have to walk in a line one behind the other, they file behind a nun, who has not spoken, only indicated that they should follow her. Something soapy sticks to the soles of their shoes as they walk, making them squeak. There's a sickly scent of cheap beeswax, the trace of past meals in the air.

"It smells like the mess halls," Eriko whispers.

"Institutional," Dr. Harper says. "Mess halls, hospitals, they all smell the same."

In the Mother Superior's large and comfortable office, Sister Amata, a fluttery sort of woman in a brown habit, who coos somewhat like a pigeon, is sent to find Mary.

"She doesn't know you are coming," she says excitedly as she leaves the room.

The Reverend Mother too is a pale bird of a woman, hawk-nosed, with small brown eyes that Satomi fancies are seeking out quarry. But when she speaks, her voice is soft, her stance kind.

"She has no idea that you have been in touch," she tells them. "She may not be the right one, your one. She came without papers from an orphanage that was being demolished. They called her Coral there, but she could have been Cora, I suppose. Coral did not seem to us a suitable name, and we wished to spare her teasing, so we named her Mary. On the whole she is a helpful child, but she doesn't speak much, and is subject to temper tantrums at times."

Satomi wants to yell, *Of course she is. How could she not be?* The cost to Cora of being left, unloved, she is sure has been a terrible one. But a sudden dread stops her from speaking. Her chest feels heavy, her mouth dry as ash.

"Was she originally at Manzanar?" Dr. Harper asks, anxious now that he has projected Cora into the blurry photo, glad that he had decided against showing it to Satomi.

"I have no idea. I've never heard her speak of it."

"So you have never asked her about the camp? Never wanted to know about her life before she came here?" Satomi, finding her voice, can't keep the criticism out of it.

"No, we have been advised not to talk to the children about the camps. The Japanese children here are in the minority, it would set them apart from their fellows. In any case, all that's better forgotten, don't you think? The important thing here is that we are all Catholics, children of God."

The Reverend Mother finds herself hoping that her Mary is not their Cora. If she is, she will not, she thinks, be brought up in the faith. And after all, it's not as if they have a blood claim on the child. But the promise of Joseph Rodman's astonishingly generous check if she is the child they are looking for is surely a gift from God, a benediction. They could expand, take more children, build a schoolhouse, the possibilities are endless.

And the Mother House, their spiritual home is expecting to receive a good portion of the money. It is only through donations, after all, that the order survives, that it can fulfill its calling in the world, where there is so much human misery to alleviate. One small child in exchange for so much, how can she say no? Mary's soul is not in the balance, after all. Their bishop, on hearing that the child may have found a home, had hurried to confirm her in the faith so that her soul is already saved. And the Blessed Virgin Mary, the child's namesake, has her in her sights.

"We have given the children extra playtime in honor of your visit," Sister Amata trills on her return. You will be able to see Mary at play, make your decision without the child knowing."

In the yard the children dart about. Their cries are distracting and it takes time for Satomi to start singling out the girls one from another. Some of them are at hopscotch, some skipping, but Satomi hardly looks at them. She thinks that Cora will be standing alone, indulging in the lonely child's habit of watching, but she is nowhere to be seen.

"She's there, right there." Eriko grasps Satomi's hand and points out Cora, who is next up to play hopscotch.

Dr. Harper and Eriko are smiling, there's no mistaking that it's Cora. She hasn't grown that much, legs a little longer, and her hair too, but she is still a narrow child, small for her age, pretty as ever.

At the sight of her, Satomi draws in her breath, her hand flies to her mouth, tears stab in her eyes. There's no mistaking that it's Cora, and she can't quite believe it. She finds herself yearning for Tamura. That blue-black hair, the girlishness, the bow perched as precariously on her head as one of Tamura's hats.

"Oh, Cora, little Cora."

After all her imaginings of running to the child, their joyful reunion, she is suddenly afraid, can't seem to move. Sister Amata puts her hand on Satomi's shoulder and propels her forward.

"It's her, isn't it?" she says, and Satomi nods.

Slowly, as one by one the children stop to watch the visitors, Satomi moves toward Cora.

"It's Satomi, Cora. Do you remember me?" She is trembling, her voice not her own.

Cora takes a step backward, hangs her head, and looks at the ground.

"No," she says quietly.

"From Manzanar, Cora. I'm Tamura's daughter. Your friend. You know me, Cora."

Cora has pictures in her head of the camp, of Tamura and Eriko, and especially of Satomi. They are, she thinks, the people of her dreams, the people she suspects she has made up. It's scary to see them now in the flesh, not knowing what they have come for.

"You will have to forgive me for taking so long to come," Satomi says. "I'm sorry, Cora, so very sorry."

She longs to kiss the child's sweet tilting lips, hug her to herself, but she doesn't want to frighten her.

"I want to take you home with me, Cora. We have a lovely house to share. We will be like sisters. Will you come with me?"

Cora doesn't answer; she just stands staring at Satomi, her body swaying a little, her hands clasped tightly together.

"Speak up, Mary," Sister Amata says. "You must answer the lady."

"Don't hurry her," Satomi snaps. "Give her time."

Cora narrows her eyes, she is thinking, figuring things out. She recalls now her time on a bus, the way she had watched Satomi standing in the dust, waving and crying. And now Satomi is crying again, it's strange to see a grown-up crying. Satomi's not her mother, but she knows now she belongs to her in some way, some good way.

"Do you remember me?" Eriko can't resist.

Cora looks at her and nods. Splashes of memory are filling her head. She does know Eriko somehow. Even the man with the white hair is familiar. She remembers rooms made from wood, she remembers playing in the dust and the glimmer of kindling burning in a stove. It's all connected with the things that she keeps in a bundle under her bed. She gives a faint smile, then turns suddenly and runs back into the house.

"I'll go," Sister Amata says, raising her hand in a gesture for them to stay where they are. "She is frightened, I think."

But before she reaches the house, Cora comes flying out the door, rushing past her. Her face is flushed, she is excited.

"I have it," she says to Satomi. "I have it here."

The little wooden titmouse sits in the middle of her open palm, rocking as though it is breathing. Silence gathers as they all stare down at it. Dr. Harper is the first to move; he reaches out, gently touching its wing, connecting himself for a moment to Tamura.

"You have it, Cora," Satomi whispers. "You have our sweet bird."

Cora puts her hand into Satomi's. "You're real," she says. "I thought that you were from a story."

Satomi takes Cora's hand and turns toward the gate. She is thinking of their white-shingled home, where there is fresh linen on the beds and there are puzzles and dolls waiting for Cora, cookies in big glass jars, and the shiny brown chocolate box with its trinkets of hope.

Tamura would have approved of the dresses hung behind the door in Cora's bedroom. Against her own taste, she has bought the prettiest she could find. And best of all there are books, *Gulliver's Travels*, *Anne of Green Gables*, *Heidi*, stories to nourish the child's soul.

Cora will play at the edge of the ocean in the clean air, with the water licking her feet. She will collect shells and ammonite pebbles, make sand castles. And she will run shrieking from the scuttling crabs, hear the whales sounding out in the bay. There is still enough of childhood left to turn the tide.

And for herself, whiskey in the kitchen cupboard, fresh-ground coffee, the big-bellied stove that works like a dream, and no shortage of wood. If happiness can be willed, she will set herself to the task, make it hers and Cora's.

She will open Dr. Harper's archive boxes and go through them with Cora. They will relive their life at Manzanar together, so that Cora will know her own life's journey.

She will make an index of the archive, write her own story of the camp, and, when the time is right, show it to the world. And surely the time will be right soon. So much depends on good timing.

She thinks of the sea at the Cape, the way it laces itself around the caterpillar of land at Eastham, turning at its end in the shape of a question mark. And the East, she thinks, is the place, the place where Pilgrims landed, where seasons have their time, where the sun rises.

ACKNOWLEDGMENTS

It is such a pleasure to thank all the friends and colleagues who have helped me with the writing of *A Girl Like You*.

My heartfelt thanks go to my editor, Alexander Pringle, for thinking me worth the risk, and for sticking with me through the difficult times. And thank you to Erica Jarnes at Bloomsbury UK, for her insightful suggestions and calming presence. I am grateful to Nikki Baldauf, Lea Beresford, and Dave Cole from Bloomsbury USA for a great job in overseeing the American production of the book.

So many thanks to the talented Gillian Stern for her outstanding guidance. Gillian gives 100 percent at all times, as well as a master class in "less is more." I'm grateful to my agent, Robert Caskie, who saw the potential of the story in the brief outline I presented him with, and enthusiastically took it to Bloomsbury. May he always be so successful. As always my thanks go to Clive Lindley, for his invaluable advice, his knowledge, and his generous help. I would like to thank Roy Kakuda from the Japanese American National Museum in Los Angeles, a child of the camps, who shared his time and memories with me. I am indebted to Richard Gregson for his invaluable help with the first draft. Thank you to Jenny Clifford for Oahu cemetery. Those others who helped with read-throughs, with research and in so many helpful ways, were Lucy Dundas, Isabel Evans, and the ever encouraging "shedettes." I would also like to thank Trina Middlecote for keeping the technology working.

A NOTE ON THE AUTHOR

MAUREEN LINDLEY was born in Berkshire and grew up in Scotland. Having worked as a photographer, antique dealer, and dress designer, she eventually trained as a psychotherapist. Her first novel, *The Private Papers of Eastern Jewel*, was published in 2009. She lives in the Wye Valley on the Welsh borders with her husband.